# DRUID'S MOOR

A DCI EVAN WARLOW NOVEL

DCI EVAN WARLOW CRIME THRILLER #18

## RHYS DYLAN

WYRMWOOD
BOOKS

## COPYRIGHT

Print ISBN 978-1-915185-53-2
eBook ISBN 978-1-915185-52-5

Published by Wyrmwood Books.
An imprint of Wyrmwood Media.

# EXCLUSIVE OFFER

**OTHER DCI WARLOW NOVELS**

THE ENGINE HOUSE
CAUTION DEATH AT WORK
ICE COLD MALICE
SUFFER THE DEAD
GRAVELY CONCERNED
A MARK OF IMPERFECTION
BURNT ECHO
A BODY OF WATER
LINES OF INQUIRY
NO ONE NEAR
THE LIGHT REMAINS

A MATTER OF EVIDENCE
THE LAST THROW
DRAGON'S BREATH
THE BOWMAN
ONE LESS SNAKE
A WORD WITH THE DEAD

# CHAPTER ONE

SUNDAY:

As it so often did at this time of year in Mid Wales, a damp, grey, candyfloss mist clung to the hillsides. It would slowly retreat once the weak morning sun asserted itself. But now it cloaked the land. A trap for the unwary.

Rhod Bowen gunned the engine of his quad bike, its drone a familiar rumble in the otherwise silent landscape. Behind him, on a shelf Rhod had mocked up, sat Peg, his sheepdog, alert to every noise and shift on the vast moorlands. They'd made this journey countless times before. In the pitch dark of winter and the glorious sunrises of summer. A daily pilgrimage to check on or feed his scattered flock. One etched into their very being.

'Bloody damp,' he muttered. To himself or to the dog, it mattered not. Out here on the mountain, he'd get the same answer either way. The chill seeped through the many layers of vest, padded shirt, waistcoat, and wax jacket he hadn't bothered to zip up tight. Zipped up protection was reserved for minus temperatures or gales. Today was mild by comparison.

Visibility was poor, and the ATV's headlamps cut a feeble swathe through the mist as it navigated the rutted track, memory guiding him more than sight. The vehicle bumped up over a small rise, taking them out of the mist for a moment, and something caught his eye. A shape where there should have been none.

Rhod, face creased with concentration, stopped the bike, took off his rain-spattered specs, and wiped them with a dry section of shirt teased out from under his jacket. Sliding the glasses back on, he looked again, his gut clenching.

There, just forty yards away, someone was standing motionless against the dark-grey trees.

Rhod had told his wife about the strange things he'd seen on these solitary trips. Shapes at the forest's edge that vanished before he could make sense of them. Sometimes lights that danced away. She'd dismissed them, blaming one too many late-night IPAs. Other farmers shared similar stories. Rumours of big cats surviving out here cropped up every few years. Rhod had seen nothing of those. And his father, after a stout or three, used to tell him about the *Gwrach-y-Rhibyn*. The hag of the mist, with tangled hair, and green eyes and a curse for those who crossed her path.

But this was… different.

'*Beth uffern?*' he said, startled.

He glanced back at Peg, whose ears perked up.

This wasn't a figment of his imagination. Unease and a trace of fear tightened his chest.

A thick silence settled.

This was no place to be alone, and the figure was small.

A child? Surely not.

He stepped off the bike, feet squelching in the damp earth, and took a cautious step forward.

The figure didn't budge.

'Hello,' he called out. 'You all right there?'

No response.

He walked forward with measured steps, Peg slinking low behind him. Details emerged from the mist, and as they did, Rhod's unease deepened.

The figure was a child. A girl. Standing stock-still, arms hanging limply at her sides.

She was a mess, skirt and anorak torn and caked with

mud. She didn't acknowledge him, simply stood shivering. Red scratches criss-crossed her legs beneath the skirt she inexplicably wore for this climate and time of year. She looked like she'd been dragged through a hedge backwards, then forwards again, or spent the night in the wilderness.

Rhod, in his late fifties, had fathered two daughters and a son and knew how to talk to kids.

'Hello.' He stopped and crouched a few yards away. 'Are you lost?'

But the girl's gaze clung to Peg, unwavering. When at last she lifted it to him, Rhod flinched and took a step back. Her eyes would not settle—skittering, twitching, sliding away only to jerk back again—and the sight made his stomach lurch, as though he were staring into something not quite human.

'What's your name?' he asked. 'Where are your mam and dad?'

He took another step, brushing away the fear that she might dissolve into the mist.

Closer now, he saw she was maybe eleven or twelve. Waiflike in a soaked and sagging puffer jacket.

Her lips parted. She whispered something barely audible. He risked a step closer.

'What?'

'We went to see the old ones...' she murmured.

A chill danced down Rhod's spine. Not the words he'd been expecting to hear. 'The old ones? What do you mean, love?'

But she fell silent, her gaze fixed on something unseen.

Rhod straightened, knees protesting.

*Bugger this*, he thought, fumbling for his phone. He dialled 999, eyes never leaving the girl.

She stood as still as one of the ancient stones dotting the landscape, but there was something unnatural about the way she held herself. She appeared... empty.

'Emergency services, what service do you require?' The operator's voice crackled, loud in the morning quiet.

'Police and ambulance,' Rhod said. 'I've found a young girl on the mountainside. Looks like she's been out all night.

She's cold. I'm taking her back to the farm. There's no road up here.'

While the dispatcher took his details, Rhod kept watching the girl, half afraid she'd vanish if he turned away. When the call ended he spoke again. 'Help's coming. We'll get you sorted. But first we need to get you off this hill.'

She gave no sign she'd heard, gaze still on Peg who hadn't shifted from Rhod's side.

He turned to her. 'Say hello, Peg.'

The dog crept forward, low to the ground, tail wagging cautiously.

The girl extended her hand. Peg lifted her nose, pressing it against the girl's palm.

'*Beth yw dy enw?*' he asked in Welsh, then repeated, 'What's your name?'

'Mia,' she whispered.

'Well, Mia, let's get you off this cold mountain. You can have a spin on the quad bike with me. How does that sound?'

Her gaze lifted to meet his. Once again he saw her eyes dance. Rhod's scalp contracted. She was still shivering.

'Come on.' Rhod smiled. 'Those old sheep can wait. Let's you and me get a cup of tea.'

———

SERGEANT TOMO THOMAS OF DYFED-POWYS' Rural Crime Team leaned on the counter in the farmhouse kitchen, hands wrapped around a steaming mug of tea. The warmth of the cup and the room was a welcome change from the damp chill outside.

Janet Bowen bustled about, arranging biscuits on a plate for the third time.

'She hasn't said a word since we got her inside.' Rhod grimaced, his focus on the closed door where paramedics were examining Mia in the Bowens' parlour. 'Just stares at nothing, like she isn't really there.'

Tomo nodded. 'Kids can go into shock after something like this. Let's see what Gerwyn and Bethan say.'

As if on cue, tyres crunched on gravel outside.

Rhod peered out, straightened and frowned. 'Land Rover,' he said, 'Don't recognise it.'

Everyone stepped outside as the car drew up.

The vehicle pulled up next to an ambulance and Tomo's marked SUV, and two figures emerged. A tall, thin woman with wild hair and flowing clothes hurried from the passenger seat, followed by a man with long, dark hair tied back in a ponytail.

'Oh, my God, oh, my God.' The woman stared around. 'Is she here? Is Mia here?' She spoke with a lilting accent.

Janet raised her hands. 'Are you Mia's mother?'

The woman nodded. A frantic gesture full of desperation. 'Noor Marston. This is my husband, Taran. Where's our daughter?'

Tomo straightened. 'Mr and Mrs Marston, I'm Sergeant Thomas. Can you tell us what happened?'

Taran placed a steadying hand on his wife's shoulder. 'We took the kids to see the standing stones at dawn. On Druid's Moor. It's a family tradition. Mia wandered off. We searched everywhere. A neighbour called to say someone had found a girl—'

Noor's eyes darted. 'Please, can we see her?'

Before anyone could answer, the door opened. Gerwyn, the paramedic, stepped out.

'She's fine,' he said. 'A bit dehydrated, some scratches. Nothing serious.'

'Oh, thank the goddess.' Noor pushed past him.

Tomo and Rhod caught the word, sharing a quick, questioning glance.

Taran hung back and met Rhod's eyes. 'Was it you who found her?'

Rhod nodded. '*Rhos Y Derwydd?*' He used the Welsh name for Druid's Moor, where the standing stones were located. 'That's three miles from where I saw her.'

Taran sighed. 'Mia, she's neurodiverse. She does odd things. Thank you for finding her. We were out of our minds.'

Before Rhod could respond, Mia appeared in the doorway, Noor hovering protectively behind her.

'There's our girl.' Taran smiled. 'Ready to go home?'

Mia nodded, eyes still distant.

'You've had quite the adventure,' Tomo said.

Mia looked up at him, and Tomo's brows bunched. He picked up on those butterfly eyes, just as Rhod had earlier, but said nothing. She was a kid and you didn't draw attention to things like that. And neurodiverse could mean all sorts of things.

After more effusive thanks, Tomo, satisfied that they, and Mia, were who they said they were, posed one final question. 'Just for the record, if you don't mind. You said you were at the standing stones? Can I ask why?'

Noor nodded. 'We are very connected to the old ways. We homeschool the children, teach them about the land and its history. Its connection to those who lived here before us.'

Taran cleared his throat. 'We have a smallholding on the forest edge. We like to be self-sufficient, mostly. The stones are part of our spiritual practice.'

Tomo's face remained neutral. 'And you didn't notice Mia was missing straight away?'

A flicker – guilt? fear? – crossed Noor's face. 'It was still dark. We were waiting for dawn, as people have for millennia. We thought she was with her brother and sister.'

'Right.' Tomo jotted something in his notebook. 'And where are your other children now?'

'With our housekeeper,' Taran said.

Another jotted note. Few had housekeepers around here.

Mia was led to the Land Rover in a sleepwalk, her steps hesitant and unsteady.

'Thank you again.' Noor shook Rhod's hand.

'No problem.' Neurodiverse, Taran had said. What did that mean though, really?

Rhod still read the Sunday papers, but most of his news came in Welsh on Radio Cymru. Neurodiversity had become a catch-all term, as far as he understood.

At the vehicle, Mia suddenly burst into tears. The first real emotion she'd shown. Noor quickly scooped her up, murmuring something soothing as she buckled her in.

The Land Rover pulled away. 'All the best,' Tomo called out.

Later, with the paramedics gone, the kitchen felt empty after they'd gone and the ambulance left.

Janet sank into a chair. 'Well, that was… something. I'm still not sure what to make of it.'

Rhod turned to Tomo. 'What about you?'

The sergeant's face was unreadable. 'Hard to say. Could simply be a family outing gone wrong.'

'A family outing? In the dark on a filthy morning?' Rhod said.

Tomo wrinkled his nose. 'Tradition, they said. I've heard worse. But I'll check them out.'

'You didn't see her out there, Tomo. The way she stood, the way she looked at me… like she wasn't really there. And her eyes were dancing…'

Janet crossed her arms. 'Oh, God, Rhod. We both know you have a thing about eyes. You were terrible when your mother had her cataracts done.'

Rhod shivered. 'Can't stand the thought of anyone touching my eyes.'

Tomo snorted. 'Right. Anyway, I'll report the incident. But for now let's be grateful she's safe. Could have been a damned sight worse. At least she's safe.'

Rhod walked him to the door.

The mist had lifted, revealing the moorland stretching to the horizon. His familiarity with the landscape should have brought Rhod some reassurance. Instead, the incident with Mia left him wondering what other unpleasant surprise lurked in the mist. Instead of relief, Rhod felt a pang of unease.

'Keep an eye out,' Tomo said. 'If you hear or see anything else odd, call me.'

Rhod nodded, grateful for Tomo's support. Though he hadn't said as much, he sensed the officer shared his discomfort over the situation. The farmer watched the Land Cruiser disappear down the winding road. But he couldn't shake the image of Mia's eyes constantly shifting, as if afraid to settle on something she didn't want to see.

He turned back to the warmth of the farmhouse, but a disquiet he couldn't shake off accompanied him in. What if he'd taken a different track that morning? She might still be out there, waiting for the cold to claim her.

But the sheep still needed seeing to.

He called Peg and fetched his coat. 'Let's try again, eh, girl?'

The dog wagged its tail, eager as ever.

# CHAPTER TWO

MONDAY

DCI Evan Warlow leaned over the kitchen counter, peering suspiciously at the tepid brown liquid swirling in his mug. Another cup of tea almost gone cold. And instead of bringing any comfort, what he'd drunk sloshed around undigested in his gut.

He had no appetite and could taste bugger all. His dressing gown clung to him like a moulting wolf's pelt, the worn fabric not quite providing the warmth he longed for. He sniffed, sensing the all-too-familiar burn starting in his sinuses.

Brilliant.

And as for his throat… that was pure sandpaper rubbing over an open wound.

Totally bloody brilliant.

Across the room, Jess Allanby bustled about, smart as always, dressed in tailored trousers and boots, a dark-green jumper accentuating grey eyes crinkling in mild amusement. She paused to lean against the doorframe, arms folded, watching him with that raised brow she often deployed when she was trying not to laugh at him.

'It's a cold. Or maybe a touch of flu,' Warlow grumbled, as if repeating it might make the solid headache wedged behind his eyes disappear.

'You look like death warmed up, albeit on very low heat,' Jess eyed him critically. 'Are you sure you should be up? Because most people would assume you've got something more serious… like the plague.'

Warlow shot her a sidelong glance, unimpressed. 'It's definitely more than a cold.'

'Should I call the paramedics now, or give you a chance to collapse dramatically first?' Jess smirked, shifted to the edge of the counter, far enough out of the plague zone, and crossed one leg over the other. 'I hadn't mentioned "man flu" at all, had I?'

'Didn't have to,' he managed between wheezes. 'I anticipated it would be next on the list of possible diagnoses.'

He took a tentative sip of tea before grimacing again. 'Bloody thing tastes of dishwater. I used to shrug these things off. Work through them. I suppose this comes from being old and decrepit.'

'Who said anything about old?' Jess feigned innocence and folded her arms. 'But you are in that dressing gown and drinking weak tea, so it's hard to imagine otherwise.'

'I tried Lemsip, and it made me feel sick.' Warlow raised the mug.

'And that's the mug Molly uses to clean her toothbrush in. Get it from the bathroom, did you?'

Warlow grunted. 'Wasn't thinking.'

Jess's expression softened. 'You're not planning to go in like this, are you? You'll infect half of HQ.'

'I'll wear a mask,' he countered, then sneezed violently into his elbow. 'See? Precautions.'

'Don't come crying to me when your chest is rattling like a bag of marbles because you dragged yourself out in this condition.'

Warlow snorted – or tried to – but the result ended in a wet, unceremonious rattle and cough that left him swaying slightly.

Jess reached out but then withdrew once she remembered his infectivity.

'I can still go in.' He straightened his back more out of

pride than anything. 'I've got meetings. Buchannan's going to lose his rag if I bail.'

'Buchannan,' Jess adjusted an earring, 'is a grown-up. Is this about Lane's book?'

Warlow nodded and stifled another cough.

'It's not like anyone's even seen the damn thing yet.'

Warlow conceded the point. 'January publication. Clever of them. Avoid the Christmas rush of celebrity memoirs. Cash in on the book vouchers.'

'Yes, because what the world needs is another true-crime sensation.' Jess rolled her eyes. 'I'm sure it'll be a riveting account of how Hunt eluded capture for so long.'

'While conveniently glossing over the incompetence that allowed it to happen in the first place,' Warlow added, his voice rough with both irritation and congestion. 'But, unlike the buggers upstairs, Sion Buchannan and I are more worried about what he's going to say about Catrin.'

He didn't need to elaborate further.

Catrin had been abducted by Hunt at a meeting set up by Geraint Lane. He'd paid the price of being beaten and locked in his own car's boot. You could not have made it up, in all honesty.

'Well, Sion Buchannan can reschedule. And, if push comes to shove, there is the internet. Ever heard of Zoom calls? Lockdown taught us all that much. And that's possible from the warmth of this kitchen.'

'There's ventilation in the garden—'

'Ventilation?' Jess shot him a look of disbelief as she stood and gathered her bag from the table. 'Evan, going out to the garden isn't ventilation. It's practically pneumonia-grade exposure.'

He considered objecting but recognised she was right. Bloody hell, Tom, his doctor son, would say the same thing. But stubbornness was second nature. He'd had to be stubborn to survive in this line of work for the last thirty years.

Jess threw him a glance over her shoulder, amused by his general air of martyrdom.

'Staying here is common sense. Something you seem to

have lost with age.' She moved back towards him, reconsidered, and then took two steps back before she spoke. 'Accept it, Evan, you're not invincible anymore.'

That last bit was softened with a smile.

Warlow grunted under the attention, unwilling to capitulate fully but equally unwilling to throw more fuel into that particular conversational fire. 'You're all bloody comedians this morning. You and Gil, who offered no sympathy at all. Meanwhile, I'm heading towards an active recovery. Besides,' he waved vaguely towards the window, 'I need to pick up a Christmas tree later. Can't have Molly complaining we've become Grinches.'

Jess nodded. 'We should probably think about getting some decorations up. Molly will have a fit if there's none when she comes home.'

'I still don't quite understand how an ice cream parlour in Mumbles gets busy over the Christmas holidays and needs extra staff. I can see Mol wouldn't turn down the money, but still. Not exactly Knickerbocker Glory weather, is it?'

Jess laughed. 'Well, a New Year's Eve in Italy does not come cheap, and she needs the money. What would you do?'

'Ah, to be young and fickle,' Warlow mused. 'You reconsidered going with her?'

'No. We've got our Australia trip sorted for April – visiting your family, I might add. Italy can wait until I've... processed it all.'

Jess's inter-family relationship with her diaspora in the country of her mother's birth was a complicated one that she had, as yet, not quite reconciled, despite her daughter's best efforts at mediation.

But mention of Australia and of his son sent a pang through Warlow's chest that had nothing to do with his cold. 'Ah, yes. The great Down Under adventure.'

'Exactly.' Jess zipped up her coat. 'One international trip is enough for now. Anyway, I've got to run. Try not to infect the dog.'

As if on cue, Cadi padded into the kitchen, tail wagging hopefully at the prospect of a walk.

Warlow reached down to scratch her ears. 'No promises. You might be my only company today.'

Jess glanced at her watch, then back at him, her face softening. 'I hate seeing you unwell.'

'Like I said, someone must have brought in red kryptonite,' he muttered.

'You'd better be horizontal with a blanket in thirty minutes. No playing Superman for you today.'

Warlow grunted, acknowledging her concern, but still not entirely ready to relinquish his day. His sore muscles tugged as he straightened up. In truth, his chest troubled him more. Each cough landed a punch below his ribcage, leaving him winded.

He gave her a smile, though. One meant to reassure. 'I'll try to take it easy.'

'Good.'

Then she was off, sweeping out to her car, the echoing sound of the front door shutting behind her a grim reminder that the house was… annoyingly quiet.

Left alone, Warlow moved to the window, glaring at the misting countryside beyond. His chest harboured a tightness, a shortness of breath that seemed… different. Bugger that. All the coddling. No need for it. He turned, and a sudden, sharp cough forced him to sit. Hunched over the kitchen table, he cursed, holding his side.

It had been a while since such weakness had overcome him. Damn chest infection from rainy days out at the building site at Rosebush the weekend before, no doubt. That, or his bloody luck had finally caught up to him.

With a sigh, he rose unsteadily to his feet, heading towards the small annexe Jess jokingly called his "sanctuary", where he usually retreated to get some peace during particularly thorny cases. In the narrow hallway leading to it, his gaze flicked to the medicine cabinet tucked inside the bathroom ceiling's eave. Time for some paracetamol, at least. But there could be no denying that this damned cough had poleaxed him.

He hadn't shared these concerns with Jess. How could he?

The spectre of his HIV diagnosis, though well-managed for years, always lurked in the background.

Was this a bad cold or something more sinister?

Warlow shook his head, trying to dispel the dark thoughts. Pure paranoia. A hot shower and some paracetamol would set him right. He stepped into the bathroom, catching sight of his haggard reflection. An image that brought back all his nagging doubts.

Perhaps Jess was right. His invincibility had limits. God, if Tom spotted him now… his son would probably manifest that ridiculously cocky smile of his, dusting off some medical text-book to explain what his father should already have grasped: don't be daft, it's flu.

But what if it wasn't?

Warlow chastised himself.

*Let it go. You're not dead yet.*

And he sure as hell hadn't come this far by giving in to a bug.

He took the paracetamol, brushed his teeth, and went back into the kitchen. He flicked open the laptop and sent Buchannan an invite to the Zoom party, sinking into his chair by the window. Cadi paced over impatiently.

The dog laid her head against his lap, tail wagging with an unspoken demand for attention.

He gave her a half-hearted scratch behind the ears.

She peered at him in a way that implied she sensed more than he credited her with.

But Jess was wrong about Lane's book. It did require attention. They, the senior staff, needed to strategise.

Five minutes later, after he'd made a new, much stronger cup of tea, Buchannan's bass notes filtered through Warlow's headphones, and his enormous face filled the laptop screen.

'Morning. Still under the weather, Evan?'

Warlow cleared his throat, muffling a cough. His own voice had dropped an octave overnight. Still, he despised the fact that his health was a topic of conversation. 'I've been better.'

'I'd cancel the photo shoot for sure. And you sound bloody awful.'

'Thank you, Matron,' Warlow said.

'Any time.' Despite the banter, Buchannan sounded restless.

Warlow put him out of his misery. 'What did you want to discuss?'

'I'm meeting the ACC and the chief super later. It appears Lane dug his claws in deeper than we anticipated. There are some photos in the book.'

'Of what?'

'Of Hunt… and of Catrin.'

Warlow's already furrowed brow deepened. 'Lane is a sick sod.'

'I need to talk to Catrin. Warn her about that.'

'How did you discover this?'

'Teasers on his Facebook page. He's playing silly buggers. I was going to suggest you coming in and chatting with the higher-ups. What do you reckon?'

He didn't answer. At that precise moment, the thought of physically meeting anyone seemed overwhelming. Still, things could only get better. Colds did that, didn't they?

Buchannan took his silence as a tentative agreement and answered his own question. 'How about I sort something out over a Zoom call?'

'We could do that,' Warlow agreed.

'Right, let's you and I consider this thing dispassionately.'

That was another big ask. Hunt had been a bane in their lives. Now, even dead, he was still twisting the knife. But that was not through any fault of his own. That was all Geraint Lane's doing, bottom-feeding journalist that he was.

Warlow had another coughing fit. It took a minute before he spoke again.

'You okay?' Buchannan asked.

'Yes. That one was all down to thoughts of Geraint Lane.'

'Yeah, the sod has that effect.'

# CHAPTER THREE

MONDAY

The boy on the screen played with some toys on the bed's counterpane. He couldn't have been more than four or five, six at a push, his sandy hair tousled from sleep.

Innocent.

Oblivious.

Sergeant Gil Jones leaned closer to his computer screen, squinting at the grainy footage from *Cân-y-Barcud* – the name of a now infamous rental cottage where a man was murdered and various nefarious activities had taken place.

Gil's stomach churned.

Royston Moyles and his twisted hobby of covert filming demanded no less of an insult.

The fact that this particular folder was labelled "Chicken" made Gil's skin crawl even more. He'd seen enough in his years on Operation Alice to know that seemingly innocuous labels often hid the darkest content when it came to crimes against children.

The boy on screen darted out of view and Gil paused the footage. He leaned back in his chair, the familiar ache in his lower back from sitting too long in a less than ergonomic posture twinging, and stared at the frozen image.

The case had been gnawing at him for months – no,

years, if he were honest. Ever since Freddie Sillitoe had disappeared from that beach on Barry Island where he and his family had been playing cricket. Disappeared in a desperate moment as those he'd loved, and who loved him, glanced the wrong way, caught up in an innocent game.

The boy's face haunted Gil. Freddie's face, or someone who looked just like him, caught on an illicit video file.

*And there's the rub*, he thought to himself. Sillitoe... or his doppelgänger.

There was still a lingering doubt that this was merely wishful thinking on his part.

'Gil, you awake over there?' Rhys Harries's question cut through Gil's thoughts to pull him back to the present.

The younger officer sat at his own desk, a monitor in front of him. Strictly speaking, addressing Gil by his first name was not protocol in the office. But Rhys had passed his sergeant's exams and had acted up temporarily more than once at the higher rank. Though he had not yet been promoted, when they were alone, first names ruled the day.

Gil waved a hand dismissively. 'Just wondering how many showers it'll take to feel clean after watching this lot.'

'I hear you. At least, there's nothing... you know.' Rhys wrinkled his nose. 'Not like the adult stuff.'

'Small mercies.' Gil rubbed his eyes.

Moyles got his kicks from posting videos of innocent adults he'd filmed surreptitiously, doing what came naturally, in a place where they had every right to be doing just that without risk of surveillance.

Gil let out a quiet sigh. He'd been staring at screens for hours, rechecking the thumb drives they'd got from Royston Moyles's hidden stash to see if there were any more images of this kid. Combing through years of his 'partner', John Napier's handwritten diaries alongside the footage from Moyles's secret cameras.

Not for the first time, Gil wondered how he'd got himself embroiled in this bloody case. But, of course, that question was entirely rhetorical. The answer had grown from his work on a separate case involving the murder, first of Moyles, then of Napier by Roger Hunt, a killer whom Moyles had made the mistake of targeting in his sick games.

Napier's death opened up an array of new investigations, including allegations of fraud against the solicitor, but what interested Gil was a potential connection between Napier's activities, Moyles, and the Sillitoe case.

The task was herculean but, somewhere in this mountain of data, Gil hoped, if he was right, there was a thread that would lead him to Freddie Sillitoe. Or details of what might have happened to him.

'Any luck with those "PP" entries?' Gil gestured towards the stack of diaries on Rhys's desk.

Moyles had rented an office above Napier's solicitor's office, from which he'd run the rental business. It was there they'd uncovered the hidden thumb drives containing illegally filmed video footage. But from Moyles's assistant, Charlie Brewer, Gil learnt that Moyles sometimes did off-the-books arrangements and that sometimes, these were fed through from Napier as PPs – Privileged People. Moyles explained them away as guests who needed not to be on anyone's radar. Especially, the paparazzi.

Gil wondered how many minor celebrities had wanted to stay at a property like *Cân-y-Barcud*. One that advertised itself as NON. No One Near. In his experience, minor celebrities were, by definition, so narcissistic, all they ever wanted was to be recognised.

It smelled of fish. And so, Rhys, having volunteered to help Gil, was hunting for PPs.

'Like dogs sniffing lampposts' had been Gil's flowery expression on explaining the task.

Rhys shook his head. 'Nothing concrete yet. But I've got a system going now, cross-referencing dates with known bookings at the cottage. Charlie Brewer's been a big help decoding some of Napier's shorthand, too.'

'Yep, he's a good lad. Speaking of which, I've got another sit-down with Charlie scheduled for tonight to look over our curated lists.'

'But this stuff is hard to decipher and pretty cryptic,' Rhys muttered. 'Like here – this entry mentions another acronym. "BN". No idea who that is, but it might give us something to go on.'

'BN,' Gil tapped his pen against the desk. 'Could be anyone, or anything. But if Napier was involved, and Moyles was helping him… we need to work out who these "privileged people" were.'

Rhys smirked. 'You're like my mate Ed's K9, Moley, when you get your teeth into something.'

'More like a terrier sniffing a lamppost,' Gil said. 'Which brings us back around to PPs.'

They returned to their respective tasks in silence.

The monotony of scanning footage allowed Gil's thoughts to drift towards his friend and team leader, Evan Warlow, laid up at home with what sounded like a nasty bout of flu.

'You hear from the boss today?' Rhys asked, in an almost spooky moment of synchronicity.

'He sounded rough. DI Allanby reckons man flu.'

'The worst kind of flu, then.' Rhys shook his head. 'Has he seen the doctor?'

'Doubt it. Self-medicating with hot whisky and lemon, I reckon. Touch of the Penderyns.' Gil referenced a local tipple. 'Though, it's a recognised crime to adulterate that with water and citrus fruits. Talking of cures and doctors, did I tell you I bumped into an old friend of mine… a doctor who retired and turned crime writer? His books aren't half bad, actually. Though they could do with a bit more sex.'

Gil, realising what he'd just said, cast a jaundiced eye at Rhys, who was about to reply. 'Don't even go there.'

Rhys, though, had a mischievous glint in his eye. 'A doctor turned writer. What kind of titles are we talking about here? *Groin with the Wind*?'

Gil barked out a laugh. 'Hah, like that, is it? Umm… *Liver in a Cold Climate*?'

'*Bridget Jones's Diarrhoea*?' Rhys countered.

'*Brave Pneumonia World*,' Gil shot back.

'*Don Key-hole Surgery*.'

'*Back Passage to India*.'

'*Catshit in the Rye.*'

Both men paused at that one, so awful a pun on Salinger's masterpiece, and having no links at all to medicine, that they both burst out laughing. It took a minute to recover. When Gil did, some of the tension he'd been carrying dissipated.

Moments like these, silly and puerile though they might be, made the job bearable. Finding humour even in the darkest corners of human depravity was a survival skill in their line of work.

'How's Gina settling back into her FLO role?' Gil steered the conversation to more personal territory.

'She's doing all right. Misses us… this…' Rhys smiled a wistful smile. 'Fewer laughs in homes that need Family Liaison Officers by definition. But you know Gina. She's a born empath. Has a proper gift for that sort of stuff.'

Gil nodded.

Gina oozed sensitivity and composure.

'She'll make a cracking DC one day, mark my words.'

'She will,' Rhys agreed with a hint of pride. 'Actually, I've got something planned to cheer her up a bit. Make up for the disappointment of going back to uniform.'

Gil raised an eyebrow. 'All ears.'

Rhys shook his head. 'Nah, not for public consumption yet. But it'll be worth it.'

Gil studied his younger colleague, noting the mix of excitement and nervousness. He had a sneaking idea of what Rhys might be planning. He was, after all, a detective. But he'd let the man keep his secret for now.

'Ah, Rhys, the murky equine. Well, whatever it is, I'm sure she'll love it. You two are good together. Me and DCI Warlow reckon she's a keeper.'

Rhys beamed. 'How about you? The granddaughters keeping you on your toes?'

Gil's face adopted a hangdog expression, but his eyes lit up at the mention of the girls, all three under eight years of age. 'Don't get me started. *Diawled bach*, the lot of them. You know what Eleri did the other day? Decided to ink her sisters and the cat. Trouble is, she mistook a Sharpie for a temporary marker. Now the cat has a Poirot-esque moustache, and her cousin has two stick figures "dancin'" on her forearms. Unfortunately, said dancing looks like a page from a sex manual, so we're keeping her in long sleeves for the foreseeable.'

Rhys laughed. 'Never a dull moment, eh?'

'Never,' Gil agreed. 'Wouldn't have it any other way, though.'

Still the image of the boy playing in the cottage seemed to taunt him. Freddie Sillitoe's face burned in his mind, the missing child's story intertwining with the countless other cases of exploitation he'd encountered over the years.

Rhys, noticing the shift in Gil's mood, cleared his throat. 'Fancy a brew? I reckon we've earned it.'

Gil nodded. 'Go on, then. And while you're at it, some crèmes de custard would not go amiss.'

Rhys grinned. 'Human Tissue for Transplant box it is.' It was a running joke in the office to keep biscuits in a box labelled for medical use, a minor act of rebellion against the grimness of their work.

Gil leaned back in his chair, pondering.

Meeting with Charlie Brewer could be another step towards unravelling this whole mess. They needed something. But he was nothing if not patient – a lesson long learned in the field.

One step at a time, it had to be.

'Here you go.' Rhys set a steaming mug on Gil's desk a few minutes later. One with the logo "That's Sergeant Total Waste of Bloody Space, if You Please" before asking, 'One or two custard creams?'

'Surprise me.' Gil reached for his tea. He took a long sip, savouring the warmth and familiar comfort. '*Arbennig*,' he purred out the word.

He glanced down at the black diaries on the desk. 'There must be something in this lot. PP, BN, SFT.'

'SFT?' Rhys asked.

'Some Foxtrotting Thing.'

Rhys dunked a biscuit into his own tea, paying extra

attention as it was a custard cream, which had a very rapid dissolution dunking time. 'I hope so. For Freddie's sake.'

'If it is him,' Gil muttered.

They withdrew into custard cream self-absorption. Whatever secrets lay hidden in Napier's cryptic entries, whatever horrors Moyles had captured on his cameras, it was all here, waiting to be peeled apart.

Rhys had put only one biscuit on the desk. Gil got up and fetched another one from the Transplant box.

This most definitely was a two-biscuit problem.

# CHAPTER FOUR

MONDAY

Later, in the Stairwell of Secrets – christened by Gil when he'd first started sneaking off there for a quiet moment – Rhys leant his back against the cool concrete wall. It was a tucked-away spot in HQ, a place where the noise of the office faded into a muffled hum, and Rhys could gather his thoughts.

Today, though, he wasn't here for reflection. He was here to speak to Gina.

She sounded slightly breathless. 'Hey, you. What's up?'

'Never mind me, how's your day going?'

'Another day in paradise,' she replied with her usual blend of weariness and humour. 'I'm with the parents of the girl who OD'd in that squat in Ammanford. God, Rhys, it's rough. They're just trying to make sense of it. Trying and failing. There's nothing I can say that'll make it any less... ugly.'

Rhys winced, his free hand clenching involuntarily. 'That sounds pretty tough. You holding up okay?'

'I'm managing. It's just... she was two years younger than me. Two kids who the grandparents are looking after.' She sighed. 'Anyway, what about you? How are things on your end?'

'My end is fine, thanks.' Flippancy. His go-to distraction.

'You know what I mean,' Gina muttered.

'I do. And it's not too bad. I'm still helping Gil with that Napier case thingy. Can't say too much about it, but it's keeping us busy.'

'Ooh, mysterious. Not,' Gina teased. 'It's those video files, right?'

'Yep. Though speaking of mysterious, you are keeping that weekend in January free, right?'

'I have cancelled the Vegas trip.'

'Were you thinking of going to Vegas?'

'Oh, my God, Rhys. Of course not. Why can't you say what it is you're planning?'

'It's a surprise.'

'Not a rugby club do, please.'

'Nope,' Rhys replied, popping the "p" with exaggerated emphasis. 'You'll have to wait and see.'

Their conversation drifted to more mundane topics: what to have for dinner, whether the washing machine was still making that odd noise, Gina's latest attempt at baking that resulted in what she described as "scones that would do as hockey pucks." It was the kind of everyday chatter that anchored them, a reminder of the life they shared beyond the often-grim realities of their work.

'I do miss the team. Give everyone my love, yeah?'

'Will do,' Rhys promised. 'All except the Wolf, who is off sick at the moment.'

'Serious?'

'Man flu, so DI Allanby says.'

'Life-threatening, then,' Gina quipped.

They said their goodbyes, and Rhys pocketed his phone, taking a moment to collect himself before heading back to work.

The conversation left him both buoyed and melancholic – grateful for the connection with Gina, but acutely aware of the weight she carried. He should have told her what Gil had said, that she'd make a great Detective Constable, but somehow that only added salt to the wound for now.

They'd both known that her secondment to the team was

always going to be a temporary appointment covering Catrin's maternity leave. But Gina rose to the task. And now she had a taste for it, despite the pressure.

Ah, well. There'd be more opportunities. He'd make it up to her, too.

———

MEANWHILE, DS Catrin Richards, as per her lanyard, was back at her desk, clicking through yet another online training module with furrowed brow.

Why, though, did they choose someone with the delivery of a droning bee to talk through the material? At this rate, she'd be asleep in ten minutes – especially since her daughter had been up at four a.m., wide awake.

Her phone buzzed, and she glanced down to see a text from Geraint Lane.

> Catrin, hope this finds you well. A red top wants to do a piece on the book. Any chance you'd be up for a quick photo at your desk? Nothing fancy. They want to add some local colour and highlight the real heroes. Let me know! GL.

Catrin stared at the screen, her lips pressing into a thin line.

Real heroes, was it?

Lane had a way of twisting everything, making it seem like he was doing you a favour while really only serving himself. She imagined his smug grin as he typed out the message, soft-soaping, thinking he was being clever.

She didn't reply. She wasn't going to give him the satisfaction. Besides, she could just imagine the newspaper's insistence on pimping photographs with some cringe-worthy element. Handcuffs on the desk, perhaps. Or Hunt's mugshot on the monitor behind her.

The title of his book – *Strangled and Shattered: The Twisted Killings of a Madman* – still churned her stomach. It was all fuel for his own self-promotion, a way to capitalise on the horror she'd lived through, the terror of being kidnapped by Roger Hunt and locked in that godforsaken ROC bunker.

Even now, the memory still haunted her.

She closed her eyes for a moment, her mind drifting to that dark, suffocating underground room.

The smell of damp concrete, the claustrophobic oppression of the surrounding silence, the fear that gnawed at her insides like a living thing. She'd been pregnant at the time, and imagining what might have happened if Warlow, Gil, and Cadi hadn't found her in time… it was sometimes too much to bear.

Her attention drifted to a framed photo on her desk – Betsi, her little girl, now nearly a year old. A reminder of everything she had to be grateful for.

She wouldn't let Lane drag her back into that darkness. Not again.

'Git.' She did not text back.

Out and about, she often started at the noise of machinery. Any grind of metal on concrete could throw her back to that moment when her colleagues finally found her. When they opened up the ventilation louvres and threw in some bottles of water, the relief that washed over her in that moment was indescribable.

And now Lane wanted to dredge it all up again, to splash her trauma across the pages of a book.

Catrin's hand drifted to her abdomen, a habit she developed during those terrifying hours underground. Now, instead of the swell of pregnancy, she put her hand on firm flatness that came from chasing after a precocious almost-one-year-old. And some work in the gym.

Betsi's face flashed in her mind. All chubby cheeks and mischievous eyes. With it came the usual surge of fierce love and gratitude.

'Not now,' she told herself firmly, pushing the memories and emotions back down. 'Focus.'

Her phone buzzed again, but this time it was a call. Catrin answered promptly, 'DS Richards.'

'Hello, DS Richards. This is DI Anna Gwynne from Avon and Somerset Police. I hope I'm not catching you at a bad time?'

'Not at all. What can I do for you?'

The explanation unfolded. Two sisters found dead in a caravan on a site in Weston-super-Mare from likely carbon monoxide poisoning. The other officer's no-nonsense yet friendly manner impressed her. There was something in her accent, too. A lilt that hinted at Welsh roots.

'One victim has an address on your patch,' Anna concluded. 'I was hoping you might do a bit of background for us. No relatives over here as such; hence the request. Nothing too in-depth, crossing the t's. Looks straightforward, but…'

'Of course,' Catrin agreed readily. 'Happy to help. I can put you in touch with DI Allanby. She's in the office today.'

'No need. This may all lead nowhere, but we ought to check.'

'Fine. Can you send over the details?'

'I'll email them right over.' There was a pause, then Anna added, 'I appreciate this, DS Richards – '

'Please call me Catrin. And it's no trouble at all. We had a father and son carbon monoxide death this summer. Primus stove left on for heat in the tent. Hard to believe.'

They chatted for a few more minutes, ironing out the details of what Anna needed, and Catrin found herself oddly reluctant to end the call.

'By the way,' she said, 'is that a bit of an accent I detect?'

The DI laughed. A pleasant sound. 'Caught me out. I'm a Valleys girl. Half an hour north of Cardiff was my stomping ground. Moved to England for uni and never quite made it back. But I always holiday in the west, in your neck of the woods.'

'Good to know, ma'am,' Catrin said.

'*Diolch yn fawr*,' Anna said. 'It's nice to speak to someone who knows the area – makes things easier when we're dealing with cross-border stuff.'

After they hung up, Catrin sat back, feeling oddly energised. The anxiety that had been gnawing at her earlier had receded, thanks to the distraction and a friendly voice.

She glanced at the clock, noting that she still had this and another module to plough through before she could even think about looking into the background of the carbon monoxide victim. And Superintendent Buchannan and the chief super wanted a meeting about Lane's bloody book this afternoon. But later, she promised herself to do some background research on Detective Inspector Anna Gwynne, too.

For now, though, duty called. With a sigh, Catrin turned back to her computer, determined to power through the rest of her online training. The sooner she finished, the sooner she could get to something a bit more interesting.

People came and went in the open-plan office. Catrin barely noticed, engrossed in her work.

She was just finishing up the last of the modules and an MCQ designed to be tricky enough to be fudge-proof when her phone buzzed again.

For a moment, she tensed, thinking it might be another message from Lane. But when she checked, it was a text from her mother, asking if she wanted her to pick up some nappies as she was going to do a big shop that evening. Catrin smiled, quickly tapping out a reply, once again thanking some deity or other for having an extended family to support her. Not everyone was as lucky.

She allowed herself to anticipate the evening ahead. A quiet night in with Craig, who'd be off at five and fetch Betsi. Maybe a glass of wine after the little one was in bed, and then... well, then maybe she'd do a bit of research on DI Anna Gwynne.

Just out of professional curiosity, of course.

# CHAPTER FIVE

MONDAY

In the living room at *Ffau'r Blaidd*, Warlow stifled another cough. He glared at the images populating his laptop screen with a hand hovering over the mute button. Superintendent Sion Buchannan's face filled one square of the Zoom grid, looking far too cheerful for a Monday morning. Beside him, Chief Superintendent Bleddyn Drinkwater was already shifting in his chair, no doubt preparing to launch into one of his tedious soliloquies.

Today, there was also Assistant Chief Constable Steven Reid, mustachioed in a style someone had unkindly compared to having a dead ferret stapled on his upper lip.

The Zoom call from hell, Evan thought bitterly, wishing he could crawl back into bed instead of dealing with this bureaucratic nightmare.

The tickle in his throat threatened to expand into another cough. His head throbbed, his chest felt like it had been filled with gravel, and his patience was wearing thinner than the tissue currently crumpled in his hand. He muted himself in time to avoid coughing directly into the microphone, but the sound still echoed around his study like a dying engine backfiring.

'As I was saying,' Drinkwater droned on, grating on

Warlow's already frayed nerves, 'we need to get ahead of this situation, as it were.'

Warlow's eye twitched. If Drinkwater said "as it were" one more time, he might hurl his laptop out of the window.

Reid nodded sagely, coiffed hair barely moving. 'We can't afford another PR disaster.'

*Another.*

Warlow caught on to that word's leg. He might even have offered a guffaw, but he knew it would trigger another bout of coughing. He kept shtum. Or tried to and failed. He unmuted and rasped, 'If we'd done our jobs properly in the first place, we wouldn't be in this mess.'

Buchannan's eyes widened, while Drinkwater's face turned an interesting shade of puce.

'I beg your pardon, DCI Warlow?' Reid sounded dangerously calm.

Before Warlow dug himself a deeper hole, Rita Clissold, the department's new Media Relations Manager, jumped in. 'If I may,' she said, her tone measured and professional, 'I think what DCI Warlow is trying to say is that we should take the initiative rather than wait for events to unfold.'

Warlow raised an eyebrow, impressed despite himself.

The woman had a knack for diplomacy. He'd give her that.

Rita's fingers flew across her keyboard. 'I've been working on some social media strategies that might help us control the narrative. Start with a series of Instagram posts highlighting the department's successes—'

'Instagram?' Drinkwater adopted a bewildered expression. 'Isn't that for teenagers sharing selfies?'

Warlow bit back a groan, irritated both by Drinkwater's ignorance and by the man himself.

Rita, to her credit, didn't miss a beat. 'Actually, sir, Instagram has a broad demographic reach. It's an excellent platform for visual storytelling and building public trust.'

Warlow sat up a little straighter. Not that it helped. His back ached, and his ribs had been steamrolled. Or so it seemed. He stifled another cough, but the noise still rattled out like stones being shaken in a tin can. It earned him a glance from Buchannan, who raised a brow but said nothing.

Rita launched into a detailed explanation of hashtags and engagement metrics. Warlow sensed his attention drifting. His head throbbed, and that damned tickle kept building in the back of his throat. He reached for his mug of tea only to find it empty.

'DCI Warlow?' Buchannan's question snapped him back to attention. 'Do you have any thoughts on Rita's proposal?'

Warlow cleared his throat, grimacing in discomfort. 'It sounds… comprehensive.' He kept it brief in the hope that his non-answer would suffice. 'Maybe we could do a TikTok?'

Reid leaned forward, his eyes narrowing. He knew enough to detect a sardonic arrow when it was fired.

'You don't sound well, Warlow. Perhaps you should rest instead of attending this meeting. After all, we wouldn't want you to overexert yourself, especially given your… unique working arrangements.'

The jab was clear, and Warlow's temper flared. 'I assure you, sir, I'm more than capable of—'

'Has anyone got an advance copy yet?' Buchannan asked, intercepting Warlow's next missile. Though everyone already knew the answer.

Lane had been tighter than a duck's sphincter with the details, enjoying every moment of the police's discomfort.

Rita shook her head, pursing her lips. 'I've tried, believe me. I've been in contact with the publisher – some second-rate outfit, nothing like Penguin or HarperCollins. They're… well, let's just say they're not exactly cooperative.'

A violent coughing fit cut her off, leaving Warlow gasping for air. Buchannan made the apologies on his behalf.

'I think what Evan means to say is that he's committed to seeing this through, regardless of his current state of health.'

Rita stepped into the breach. 'But we can't just sit back and let this happen. We most certainly need to be proactive – get ahead of the media storm. If we handle this properly, we can control the message. I've got a few ideas for some pre-emptive social media posts—'

'Agreed,' Warlow ignored the tightness building in his chest again. A surefire precursor to another cough. 'But let's be honest. The public are not stupid. They'll see through any sugar-coating. We need to own our mistakes, not bury them under a pile of Instagram filters.'

There was a pause. Rita blinked, clearly unsure whether to be offended or agree. Drinkwater, however, was more predictable.

'That's… well, that's harsh, Evan,' Drinkwater said, in that condescending tone that spiked Warlow's blood pressure. 'We've got reputations to protect, as it were.'

Warlow opened his mouth to retort.

Buchannan, sensing the impending explosion, jumped in once more. 'I agree with Evan. We need a balanced approach. Proactive, yes, but we also need transparency. This must not blow up in our faces.'

'Exactly,' Warlow muttered, though he winced at the explosion analogy. He grasped a tumbler of water and took a sip, grimacing at the pain in his throat.

'Transparency's all well and good. But we can't have this turning into a free-for-all. Lane's going to drag us through the mud if we're not careful. And you should take it easy, Evan.' Reid's moustache twitched. He kept his tone overly casual. A hunter setting a trap.

Warlow stifled another cough.

'You're clearly under the weather. Perhaps it's not the best time for you to get involved. Even if everything that happened took place on your team's watch, didn't it?'

'I think we're all aware of the complexities of the situation, Steven.' Buchannan said. 'No need to go over old ground.'

Warlow could only nod, still trying to catch his breath. He glanced at the corner of his screen, where his hollow-eyed face stared back at him.

Christ, he looked awful. Maybe Reid had a point. But so did he, and he needed to make it now. 'Has someone got hold of Catrin? She's the one with the most to lose in all this.'

There was a brief, awkward silence.

'That's… being handled,' Buchannan said. Was that a flicker of discomfort in his face? 'We'll make sure she's fully briefed.'

'She'd better be,' Warlow muttered. 'Last thing we need is her being portrayed as naïve in Lane's bloody book. She was set up.'

'We are expecting to chat with her, too.' Reid made a small noise in his throat, eager now to wrap things up. 'All right, we'll reconvene once we've got more information. Evan, take some time off. You're clearly not well.'

He was, damn him, right.

Finally, mercifully, the call ended. The others signed off. Buchannan lingered.

'Evan,' he spoke with uncharacteristic gentleness, 'go see a doctor. And that is an order. Last time I saw someone like you , the certificate had already been issued by the coroner.'

Warlow managed a weak chuckle. 'Cheers, Sion. None taken.'

But, as soon as the super's face flicked off the screen, Warlow slumped back in his chair, exhausted. He fumbled for his phone, scrolling through his contacts until he found the number for his HIV nurse at Singleton Hospital. Still something held him back

Should he bother her for just a severe case of the flu? He should see the GP. Or at least chat to one. Wasn't that what you were supposed to do?

He found the surgery's number. Warlow rang and waited, his patience wearing thin with each electronic trill.

Finally, a clipped voice answered, '*Meddygfa'r Afon*, how can I help you?'

Warlow grunted. 'I'd like to see the doctor, please. I've been ill for five days, and it's not getting any better.'

'What are your symptoms?' The receptionist's tone was almost robotic. She must have missed the empathy lecture at induction. Too busy oiling her joints, probably.

'Sore throat, persistent cough, and it's like I've been hit by a lorry,' Warlow croaked. 'And before you ask, it's not Covid. I've checked.'

'Any chest pain?'

'Only when I cough, which I'm not doing at the moment.'
He toyed with adding, "*Or laugh, which is bloody unlikely chatting with you.*"

A pause, then, 'The earliest we can offer is a phone consultation in two days. After that, the doctor will decide if you need an in-person appointment.'

Warlow's frustration bubbled over. 'Two days? What if it gets worse—'

'I understand, Mr, uh…'

'Evan Warlow.' He reeled off his address.

The clack of keys provided a soundtrack as she called up his records. 'There is a very nasty virus going around. Mostly, we're advising people to stay home, hydrated and warm. It's been lasting about a week. We are not recommending people attend surgery because of the transmission risk to vulnerable patients. We're extremely busy. Try your local pharmacist for advice and for some medication to help with the symptoms. But if it's an emergency, I'd suggest going to A and E.'

'So, no possibility of even a quick check?'

'Sorry, we don't have the capacity. Everyone's in the same boat, I'm afraid.'

*That's all bloody right, then. We can all drown on the sinking ship, singing "We'll Meet Again" with a hot Bovril.*

He bit back the retort. She might sound like she had a heart of stone, but she didn't deserve two barrels of curmudgeonly DCI, which were already locked and loaded in his head. Instead, Warlow grunted something that vaguely sounded like a thanks and hung up. He glanced again at his reflection on the darkened laptop screen. Rough was the adjective that sprang to mind.

Rough with a capital "R".

What if this wasn't just the flu? What if it was something worse, something his weakened immune system couldn't fight off? Some bloody weird thing he'd picked up near the quarry in Rosebush, at Jess's unfinished property, when he was helping the builders?

Another coughing fit seized him, leaving him gasping for air. At his feet, Cadi shifted and whined.

'Don't tell me you're telepathic as well as the best ball catcher in Pembrokeshire?' Warlow gave up a weak smile and sighed. 'What I heard from nurse Rachet there was that something is going around and it might get better, right?'

Cadi made no noise.

'More tea and some paracetamol, then?'

The dog wagged her tail.

'Thank you, Doctor Cadi.' Warlow reached down to ruffle the fur on her black head, reflecting on the irony of the situation. Here he was, a detective chief inspector, reduced to relying on his dog for comfort because a simple doctor's appointment was like gold dust.

He thought of Tom. As a junior doctor, albeit one on the cusp of becoming a senior one, he'd been overjoyed at the recent pay rise for NHS staff, but even he admitted the system was buckling under the strain.

And that was a mantra Warlow had been hearing for years.

It was all too easy to turn a blind eye when you weren't the one in need, Warlow realised. Now, faced with his own problems, the failings of the system were all too real. He wasn't a political animal. But the pandemic had politicised public health and turned it into even more of a distasteful weapon.

Tom had a lot to say on the matter from the inside.

But discussion and debate were not what he needed now.

Warlow reached for his phone again, his finger hovering over Nurse Batson's number in Singleton.

Should he call her? Play the HIV card? Or should he just tough it out for a few more days and hope for the best?

With a heavy sigh, he put the phone down. He wasn't ready to admit defeat just yet. Instead, he pushed himself up from the sofa, Cadi at his heels, and shuffled towards the kitchen.

Tea and paracetamol it was, then. For now.

# CHAPTER SIX

MONDAY

Jess's fingers danced across the keyboard; her brow furrowed as she worked on a case that was going to court. Her coffee sat untouched at the corner of her desk, a forgotten casualty of her concentration.

The evidence file had grown bloated with documents – statements, forensic reports, timelines, witness accounts – each one a piece that would hopefully add up to getting McDermott in prison for what he'd done.

The information she was processing: details of human trafficking, arson at an abandoned hospital, and the brutal murders of two NHS administrators, brought back the case in her mind. The kind of case that lingered, that seeped into your bones and made you question humanity.

What she typed appeared on the screen, but there was still a lot of actual paperwork, too. She clicked to the next file in the digital folder, scanning the contents with the practised efficiency of someone who'd done this a hundred times, cross-referencing with ink on paper at her elbow.

There was something both methodical and cathartic about this part of her job. The filing, the organising, the gathering of information into a coherent whole for the CPS.

She paused, rubbed her eyes, and leant back.

The office had descended into relative quiet, save for the distant hum of conversation and the occasional ring of a phone. With Warlow out sick, the bulk of this task had fallen to her, but Jess was nothing if not thorough.

Her phone buzzed briefly. Probably Rhys or Gil, but she ignored it and kept typing.

The National File Standard was strict, and Jess prided herself on getting everything just right. No room for errors. Not when so much was at stake. No big deal. This was her bread and butter, after all.

A knock at the door pulled her from her thoughts. 'Hang on a sec.' She saved her progress before glancing up. 'Come in.'

The door swung open to reveal Sergeant Tomo Thomas's broad frame filling the doorway. He stepped inside, and his seamed face broke into a smile, deepening the creases around his eyes. 'Thought I'd pop in and say hello while I'm in the Big Smoke.'

Jess snorted. She gestured for him to take a seat. 'Carmarthen is hardly the Big Smoke, Tomo, but I guess everything is relative. What brings you down from the hills?'

Tomo's purview was rural crime. And in a patch as big as the Dyfed-Powys Service, the biggest in the country, he covered some ground. They'd worked together on several cases over the past few years.

Jess had always found him straightforward and honest. And underneath the bluff exterior, she knew he harboured a well-honed dislike for anyone who mistreated animals and wildlife, as well as innocent humans. And for that, he'd earned a spot in the Allanby Hall of Friendship.

Tomo eased himself into the chair, his movements deliberate and measured. 'Rural crime meeting. Poaching, fly-tipping, rustling – the usual suspects.' He glanced around the office. 'No sign of the old Wolf today?'

'Evan is off sick,' Jess replied, a hint of concern creeping into her tone. 'Nasty chest infection. How are things up your way?'

Tomo leaned back. 'Same old, though we had an odd one

yesterday. Young girl went missing, turned up miles from home after wandering over the hills. Family's a bit... different.'

'Different how?' Jess asked, her interest piqued.

'The Marstons are homeschoolers, for one thing,' Tomo said. 'Living on this smallholding they call *Dôl y Derwyddon* – Meadow of the Druids, if you can believe it. Thirty acres of New-Age nonsense, if you ask me.'

Jess raised an eyebrow. 'Homeschooling's becoming a lot more common, especially since Covid. Not necessarily a red flag.'

'What's your take on it?'

'Not for me or mine. But it's a safer environment than some schools if the child is vulnerable. Nurtures family bonds, and it guarantees a tailored curriculum, I suppose.'

Tomo appeared unconvinced. 'But what about social interaction? You can't go through life not messing with other kids. How the hell does that prepare you for the real world?'

'I'm not arguing. And however good the home setup, there won't be science labs. And you have to question how qualified someone's mother and father are to actually teach anything.'

'Exactly. But this family... they're definitely alternative. At least, they appear to be, from what I can find out.'

'How?'

Tomo arched his back. 'It's more a cut-down farm they live on, but they do all the New-Age malarky. Eco-friendly glamping in the summer. Petting zoo and animal therapy. Shamanic healing retreat. An organic farm shop with a spiritual twist.'

'You visited, then?'

'Only via the internet. It's all on there. Selling veg that has been planted according to the lunar calendar. I ask you.' Tomo shook his head.

'Just because they're different...' Jess let the sentence hover in the air.

'Yes, I know. I'm way too long in the tooth for all that. But there's something off about the whole setup. I also asked the locals, and...' He made a noise with his lips like a tiny horse. 'They think the mother leans the Wiccan way.'

'Witchcraft?' A laugh followed, bursting from her lips.

'It's the sort of thing rumours grow into, right? Though they were visiting some ancient monoliths at sunrise. That's the explanation they gave for being out and about before it got light. And then there's the girl, Mia – there was something not right about her either. Poor thing. She seems bewildered. Neurodiverse, according to the mother, which as far as I can tell is a bit of a catch-all. And something wrong with her eyes, too. The farmer who found her called it a stigma, whatever that means.'

'Stigma?' Jess frowned. 'Did he mean a squint?'

The door burst open, ending the conversation. Rhys bounded in, his tall frame nearly colliding with the door-frame. 'Tomo! Didn't know you were in town. Where'd you stop for brekkie on the way down?'

Tomo grinned. 'That little garage just outside Newtown. It's opening up around there, and guess what's reared its head next door?'

'Ah,' Rhys said, his face lighting up. 'A Greggfast. Can't beat it.'

Jess rolled her eyes but couldn't suppress a smile. Nothing got these two more energised than a discussion about the best places to stop on long journeys.

Gil followed through the door and stopped to take in the scene. '*Arglwydd*, is this a bring-a-bottle party or can anyone join in?'

'Tomo's been telling me all about his *Hills Have Eyes* encounter,' Jess explained.

'Backcountry stories?' Gil sucked in air. 'Cabin in the Woods' stuff, is it? I'm not surprised, mind. Almost everyone has a chainsaw and a shotgun north of Peniel.'

Tomo obliged the two officers new to the conversation with a retelling.

'But the kid was okay, wasn't she?' Gil asked when Tomo finished.

'Fine. Tired and cold, but fine. Wandered off and got lost,

so the dad said. The family had called it in an hour before, and we were on the point of mobilising when the call came in that she'd been found.'

'But?' Gil asked, clearly sensing his colleague's disquiet.

'Standing stones at dawn in December? The old ones? What does that mean?'

'Ah, but not just December, Sarge. It's the twenty-first. Shortest day. Winter solstice. Yule,' Rhys said.

'Very good, Rhys. Now put those words altogether into a meaningful sentence,' Gil said.

Rhys got into his stride. 'It's the beginning of the pagan year. The solstice means the year has turned. Days get longer, so it's celebrated. I think Yule is Old Norse. So, as the Sun God is reborn at Yule, having died at Samhain at the end of October, the poor sunlight during the short days is showing a God in his infancy. Like, growing before he can come back into his full power.'

The other three officers stared at Rhys.

Gil spoke. 'And you know all of this, how exactly? Don't tell me you're a closet wizard?'

'No, but I've been playing this online game called *Dustin the Warlock*—'

'That's not a real thing, is it?' Jess asked.

'It's a bit tongue in cheek, ma'am,' Rhys explained swiftly. 'But it's full of this kind of stuff.'

'But it's not illegal,' Gil said. 'Visiting standing stones at Yule.'

'I am aware,' Tomo said. 'We often get shenanigans up Machynlleth way. And I don't even know why I brought it up. I mean, I see enough weirdness every day. But she was just a kid.'

'Unconscious bias, Sarge,' Rhys said.

'Who?' Tomo frowned.

'The family are a bit different, and so you're projecting.'

'Am I now,' Tomo bristled.

'Understandable,' Rhys said quickly. 'I mean, you're right, it's hardly normal to find a little kid on a mountain on her own first thing in the morning. But there is an explanation, even if it is weird.'

'Hmmm,' Tomo murmured, a noise oozing disapproval.

'Do you want me to put some feelers out?' Jess asked. 'Find out a bit more about these Marstons?'

'I don't want to waste your time, ma'am. It isn't why I called.'

'I realise that,' Jess said. 'But you have good instincts, Sergeant. Sometimes, they are all you have.'

'That's what a Greggfast will do for you,' Rhys said.

Gil tilted his head. '*Mynuffernu*. Is that what it's called now? Greggfast? A Gregg's breakfast.'

'Common knowledge,' Rhys answered.

'Is it, though?' Gil scrunched his eyes up with a clown smile on his face.

Jess did trust Tomo's instincts. She could see why it nagged at him. No harm in asking Catrin to look into it. Peel away some layers to see what might be lurking beneath. When it came to kids, it did not do to brush things under the carpet. Gil was a perfect example of that. As far as Freddie Sillitoe went, he simply could not let it lie.

For now, though, she allowed herself to enjoy the moment of levity as Rhys came out with another non sequitur that had the older men chortling. Eventually, the conversation wound down, and Tomo stood to leave.

'I should get back. Those poachers won't catch themselves. Mind you, the lot I'm after can barely catch anything.'

Jess nodded. 'Send through some details on the Marstons when you get a chance?'

Tomo's eyebrows rose slightly, but he nodded. 'Will do.'

The big sergeant left with a last grin.

Jess smiled and turned away.

# CHAPTER SEVEN

MONDAY

Warlow squinted at the glowing screen of his phone, his eyes heavy from the fever that had settled behind them, and the fitful sleep he'd been dragged out of. His head felt stuffed with wet kitchen paper, full of his sluggish and disjointed thoughts.

The ringing of the phone drove a spike into his skull, but he forced himself to sit up and answer. He fumbled for the swipe to accept the call, his hand feeling twice its usual size, clumsy with fatigue.

The screen swam into focus, Gil's name flashing accusingly.

'Yeah?' It came over rough and barely more than a rasp.

'Evan, *Iesu*, you sound terrible. How are you holding up?'

Warlow coughed violently into his elbow, the sound wet and grating. He winced at the tightness in his chest.

'Right. Got the message,' Gil said. 'Should I ring for an ambulance?'

'Bugger off,' Warlow replied.

Gil let out a wheezy laugh on the other end of the phone. 'Ah, there he is.'

'This is nothing a drop of hot whisky and lemon wouldn't fix.' Warlow blew his nose. 'What's going on with you?'

'I'll keep this quick. You asked to be kept abreast of things, though I'm sure Jess will fill you in.'

'I like more than one perspective.'

'Tidy. Then an update on the Sillitoe case. If you can call it a case. Not much progress, I'm afraid. We've been through the bookings from *Cân-y-Barcud* a dozen times but ... I'm nailing jelly to a wall.'

Warlow leaned back against the chair, eyes closed, trying to pull his mind out of the fog clouding his brain. 'Remind me how long it's been.'

The Sillitoe case's details... they were there, just on the edges of his memory, but it would do no harm to be reminded.

'Not quite four, vanished from Barry Island beach back in August 2019. Case went cold very fast. There were no real leads, no suspects. Just a child gone without a trace.'

Warlow didn't need to hear Gil's link into this. He could visualise the image he'd seen on the hard drive that had triggered the idea that this could be Sillitoe. Gil had shown it to him a dozen times.

'Nothing useful in Napier's papers?' Warlow breathed heavily.

'I'm not saying that. Rhys and I are going through ledgers. We already know that there were some unofficial bookings there, some of which involved Napier. I'm meeting Charlie Brewer for a quick drink this evening. He handled all the official bookings for Moyles's rentals. To be fair, it was he who mentioned this under-the-radar stuff a while back.'

Warlow grunted, though the effort made his chest ache. 'Good. Get Brewer talking. Anything else?'

'Oh, and Tomo popped by HQ earlier. He's got a weird missing girl case on his plate, but nothing I think we need to worry about. He came in to let off a bit of steam and get some input.' Gil hesitated for a moment, then added, 'But honestly, I was ringing to ask how you're doing. You sound like a broken accordion.'

Warlow managed a scratchy chuckle. 'Well, though I'm

sure it'll be a huge disappointment for some, I'm still here, beating off death with a stick. You know how it is.'

'Yeah, well, take it easy. I don't want to be the only over-fifty-plus in the village.'

'Wow, hang on there. Are you insinuating that we, you and I, are grouped in the same age bracket?' Warlow pulled a throw tighter around his shoulders, a move more in keeping with some shivery old crone than... a shivery old DCI. And one that he was very glad Gil could not see.

'I'd check my sell-by date when you're next able to, if I were you. In the meantime, I'll keep you in the loop about Brewer. And Rhys sends his regards. Next time you see him, ask him about *Dustin the Warlock.*'

Warlow wheezed and bit back on the laugh that threatened. 'Is that some kind of disgusting euphemism? I can see standards have slipped the minute I turn my back.'

'I'll let him explain, and you'll know more about pagan calendars than you'll ever want to within, oh, forty minutes.'

'I can't wait,' Warlow muttered. His hand felt like lead as he ended the call and put the phone down.

He closed his eyes, the pounding in his skull intensifying as the conversation replayed in his foggy mind.

Freddie Sillitoe. The boy had been missing for years. A boy who had been on Gil's radar for almost that long. And perhaps they were miaowing up the wrong shrub, as Rhys was wont to say. But with Napier's fraudulent behaviour exposed, this was the first time Gil had gained access to papers that might hold a clue.

Warlow exhaled slowly through his nose. It made a disgusting bubbly noise, and he turned it into a full-on blow into an already soggy tissue, much to the annoyance of his long-suffering sinuses.

He consoled himself with one thought. If there was anything to be found, Gil would find it. He always did.

AT A LITTLE AFTER TWO P.M., Jess caught sight of Catrin returning from her meeting, with her face a tight mask of barely contained emotion.

'Dare I ask?' she called softly.

Catrin sank into a chair she'd pulled over. 'About as well as you'd expect. Superintendent Drinkwater is projecting what Lane might put in that bloody book of his. And then asking me what I thought might be in it.'

'Why are they asking you?'

'No idea. It's all the chief super's hangups as far as I can see. Not the most enjoyable twenty minutes I've ever had. For some reason, he thought I may have been given some sneak peeks by Lane. I did tell him I had a text asking if it would be okay for a photographer to come here and take some photos.'

'What did you say to that?'

'I did not reply.'

Jess grinned. 'What pearls did Chief Superintendent Drinkwater have?'

'None. Superintendent Buchannan didn't say much either. He looked like he didn't want to be there. I think he was only there for me.'

'Nothing specific to say? And they haven't seen the book either?'

Catrin shook her head, a bitter laugh escaping her. 'No, they asked me some very vague questions about my "experiences" and how I felt about them being "shared with the public". As if I have any idea what Lane's planning to include.'

Jess nodded. She could only imagine the stress Catrin was under, having to revisit those harrowing memories of *Cân-y-Barcud*, of Hunt's attack, of her abduction. But it was clear in the way she held her shoulders rigid and the shadows under her eyes. Some of that would have been down to having a twelve-month-old child. But not all of it.

'The worst part,' Catrin continued in a whisper, 'was that Superintendent Goodey was there.'

Jess's blood ran cold. 'Two Shoes?'

'Mr Drinkwater said that she had skin in the game.'

'Is that what he said?' Jess cringed.

'No, he said she had skin in the game, *as it were.*'

Jess suppressed a giggle.

Catrin shrugged, unable to hide the mix of despondency and anger in her expression. 'She didn't say much, just sat there with that look she has. Like she was enjoying watching me squirm.'

Jess clenched her fists under the desk. 'Evan is going to hit the roof when he hears about this.'

'Perhaps it's best we say nothing, ma'am,' Catrin muttered.

'It will be the first thing he asks me when I get back to the cottage.'

Catrin's smile was downturned.

Jess couldn't help but think back to Goodey's role in all of this.

The woman had practically pushed Catrin into Lane's orbit, touting it as some progressive step for women in policing. But the reality had been far darker, a manipulation that had put Catrin in danger and left lasting scars.

'You know none of this is your fault,' Jess said. 'What Goodey did, what Lane's doing now… it's not on you.'

Catrin nodded, but doubt lingered in her eyes. 'I know. It's the thought of it all being dredged up again, of everyone reading about it.'

Jess reached across the desk, squeezing Catrin's hand. 'You'll get through this. We'll all get through this. And if Lane or Goodey or anyone else tries to twist things, they'll have to go through me and Evan first.'

A ghost of a smile flickered across Catrin's face. 'Thanks. That's… it's good to know.'

Jess returned the smile, then leaned back. 'Actually, there's something else I wanted to talk to you about. Tomo was in earlier. He mentioned a case he was caught up in. Might be nothing, but…'

Catrin straightened, antenna twitching, intrigued despite her exhaustion.

Jess explained about the Marstons, their walkabout daughter, and Tomo's gut feeling.

'Doesn't sound too unusual,' Catrin mused. 'Kids do wander off sometimes.'

Jess nodded. 'True, but there's something hinky about it. The way Tomo described the girl, the family's setup. Home-schooling. I said we'd do some background checking.'

'I can do that,' Catrin said.

'Quietly, of course. Just see if there's anything that might raise flags.'

Catrin nodded. 'Might be good to focus on something else besides online diversity training for a while, to be honest.'

Jess smiled, relieved to see some of the tension leaving Catrin's face. 'Perfect. And if you need to talk about the book or anything else, I'm here. Anytime.'

Catrin nodded. 'Since you mentioned callers, I should tell you about one I received from Avon and Somerset. From a DI Anna Gwynne. She's investigating two women who died in a camping accident. Sisters.'

'What sort of accidents happen when you're camping?' Jess frowned.

'Carbon monoxide poisoning. Left a barbecue lit in an awning outside a caravan. One of the victims is from our patch, lived alone up Llanwrda way. DI Gwynne rang a bell with me. I did a quick go-ogle, and she was involved in those Black Squid killings a few years back. Nasty case. The one she's contacted us about is unrelated, thankfully.'

Jess leaned forward, interest piqued. 'I remember. Llanwrda, you say? Has anyone checked the address?'

'No one's answering the phone. Gwynne's concerned about pets, securing the property, et cetera.'

'Unusual to ring us about checking an address, though?' Jess mused.

'Apparently, the caravan had a broken window hinge opening into the awning. I think DI Gwynne is a stickler.'

Jess perked up at that. 'Hmm. Then I'll go. I'll take Rhys with me. Give me a chance to get away from this evidence file for a bit.'

Jess turned to her computer and called up the information Catrin immediately sent over on Kerry Ford, the dead woman from Gwynne's case. She did have a record — minor shoplifting, possession, and some affray. Not local. From Keynsham, originally. Why she'd chosen to move to Llanwrda was anyone's guess.

But Jess had seen it before. Sometimes, people were "moved" by the local authorities from places where their history haunted them. Sometimes, people left to escape either an environment or a person.

But what that had to do with leaving a barbecue still smouldering outside your caravan was anyone's guess. According to the records, Kerry Ford had been unemployed.

Rhys was away from his desk, and so she texted him the Llanwrda address and suggested they set off at 2:30 p.m. He'd want to drive, and so she said they'd take a job car.

It would be good to escape from paperwork for a while, if only to distract herself from the constant worry over Warlow's health.

Molly was always pulling Jess's leg about the glamour of the job — laughing about how, on TV, detectives somehow looked immaculate, even when they'd been dragged out of bed for a midnight call. Full makeup, no less.

But this was the real deal.

*Just another day in the life of DI Jess Allanby*, she mused, as she ploughed back into her work with the echoing thoughts of ancient stones, missing children, and poisoned corpses in caravans only faintly tugging at the edges of her mind.

# CHAPTER EIGHT

MONDAY

Geraint Lane eyed the half-drunk cup of coffee on the countertop beside him. His partner had already headed off for another long shift at the hospital, leaving the two-bedroom flat they shared silent but for the monotony of Jasper Goldstein's eager voice filtering through from the other side of the call.

'—and, Geraint, you'll be pleased to hear that we've locked in serialisation with *The Indy*. First three chapters. Prime slot. Honestly, mate, it could be huge! I've spoken to an editor there – he's thrilled with it. Couldn't stop going on about how you've really captured the essence of the TV-personality-gone-rogue angle, you know? The cult of personality. And of course, that woman detective, Richards. Alone with Hunt, the madman. What he might have done to her! The nitty-gritty! That's what they want. It turns heads.'

Lane smiled to himself, allowing the flattering warmth of Jasper's praise to run like velvet over him. Everyone needs a pat on the head and a belly rub now and again. Some more than others. He may have never liked Jasper's fake, clipped English accent or the sycophantic tone, but he wasn't immune to flattery. Especially when it came to *Strangled and Shattered*.

The title alone was a hook, and Jasper's promises only fed

his growing sense of triumph. But Lane, pragmatic as ever, knew better than to believe his own hype.

He cut Jasper off, his tone level, though polite. 'I'm glad they're excited, Jasper, but tell me, what else do we have lined up? *The Indy* is all well and good, but if we're going for mass appeal, I'll need something a bit more substantial.'

Jasper's excitement barely faltered. 'Ah, yes, absolutely. We're finalising a string of interviews. Some local radio to start with. Get the groundwork done first, appeal to the locals. One of their own and all that. But – and here's the big bit – if that does well, we're looking at some possible TV coverage.' Jasper dropped his voice. 'Possibly even a slot on *Good Morning UK*. Imagine that, Ger. National coverage before it even hits paperback! Now, obviously, we have to wait for the response to *The Indy's* serialisation, but numbers don't lie. People love a tasty true-crime angle, especially one that sticks it to the police.'

Lane could imagine Jasper's toothy grin, all enthusiasm, all "mate, we've hit gold." What the public – and someone like Jasper – would never understand was how close Lane came to having his career, his entire life, buried. It could have gone wrong in so many ways.

Meeting Roger Hunt had proved more than unpredictable – it was a minefield of suspicion, threats, and whispered promises of violence. What Lane had omitted from his upcoming bestseller, what he'd never even hinted at, was how Hunt had leveraged Lane's dark secrets against him. More than once, he'd suspected Hunt of contemplating his murder. Nearly succeeded, too. That moment in the cottage, tied up while Hunt staged his death, Lane had feared, genuinely feared, for one terrifying instant that he might.

'*Good Morning UK*?' Lane gave a low, appreciative whistle. 'That'd be great. That would do wonders for the numbers.'

Jasper laughed loudly, sounding almost too keen. 'Exactly, exactly. But in all seriousness, we've got momentum here. Radio first, *Indy* second, then TV. And...' Jasper paused, the sound of papers shuffling on the other end crunching through the phone. 'We're aiming to capitalise on that angle you worked in about the systemic failures of the police, the incompetence, the – ah, here it is – "racist, misogynistic colonialist mentality embedded in Dyfed-Powys and other forces." You'll really ruffle some feathers there. People love that angle right now.'

'That's because people are finally waking up to the truth about what really goes on behind these fascist institutions. But that won't sell on its own. It needs someone to bring it into focus. Me, mate. I'm the one threading it all together.'

'You've nailed it, mate. Totally nailed it.'

Lane cradled the phone closer, leaning back in his chair with a self-satisfied smile tugging at his lips. It was pleasing to hear someone else crowing about his success for once. For so long, Lane had been the groomsman and not the rhetorical groom; the investigative journalist who no one seemed to want to touch with a ten-foot pole. Now, though, it might finally pay off.

He'd turned what might have been a complete disaster – a potential bloody death sentence, frankly – into something bigger. Into a book, a career move, and public validation of everything he stood for. And he'd done that himself. Through stealth and cunning. Doing what needed to be done to keep Hunt and the police at arm's length.

'Anyway, Geraint,' Jasper continued, undeterred by his client's quiet, 'we'll get you all the media training you need. You know, managing difficult questions, handling the sensitive stuff, especially on Detective Richards. Make her as sympathetic as possible, but not too much. The BBC eat that stuff up.'

There it was again. Richards and her trauma, plastered all over page one. Maybe it was necessary to sell, to dig deep into Hunt's twisted little playhouse, but Christ, the book wasn't just about her. He'd been careful not to paint her as too self-sufficient. Though a lesser officer might have caved at the thought of never being found, especially while pregnant.

From what he'd learnt – from others, of course, since DS Richards had politely declined any request he'd made for a follow-up "chat" – she'd been a tough cookie. So, he'd crafted the narrative so that his sacrifice to let Hunt use him as a punch bag had saved her in the cottage. Not the way she saw it, by any means. And obviously, not the truth, since he and Hunt had choreographed the whole thing, but then he was the one writing the book, so tough shit. After all, it was his byline that was going to be remembered.

Not that he gave a toss about Richards, or whatever she went by these days. She was a bloody copper. It was in her job description to get deep into the mire and risk her neck. And she would have suffered, if not physically, then mentally. Why not profit from that a little? After all, weren't the police essentially a colonialist relic? A "fascist organisation" clinging to authority through harassment and keeping their boots on the necks of the people? He'd written about that, too.

'I hear you,' Geraint said, his eyes narrowing slightly as he shifted in his seat. 'But remember, this book isn't just shock value. It's an exposé. People need to see the depths of the failures – the incompetence that makes the police's bleating about underfunding and depleted numbers sound like what they really are. Nothing but empty excuses.'

'Of course, mate! Absolutely!' Jasper gushed. 'We've got the *Express* interested in looking into a few more news bites after the release, too, so we can keep this momentum going for a solid month after it hits shelves. But that's why I've sent over those chapters – no biggie! We're shoring up the structure of the earlier section, is all. We want to make the gruesome stuff about Hunt front and centre. Keep them hooked, you know?'

Lane bit his lip.

Front and centre? Get the people all hot and bothered over the most salacious bits. That was one way to push it.

Goldstein's whine elbowed its way into his consciousness: 'The public want all the gory details, Geraint. They need Hunt's insanity painted in loving detail.' Working with Goldstein as an editor had been a challenge. The twat couldn't even say his name properly, placing emphasis on the first syllable, Ger, instead of giving both equal emphases. To begin with, he'd even pronounced the G like Gerry instead of hard like a G in garage.

'All right, Jasper,' Lane said, more out of habit than intent.

Redact Books, a gloves-off offshoot of one of the big six, though far enough removed from the names to appear independent, had given Jasper the hand-holding brief. And he had been relentless in moving this forward.

Lane, bending unusually at the knee, did not put up a fuss. He only wanted to take the money and run. 'I'll look into it all later. Send me over what you need.'

The conversation ended with more niceties, but Lane was pleased when he thumbed the red "end call" button on his phone. Even after he'd hung up, his hand lingered over the device, paralysed as memories from those intense weeks flooded back.

The clandestine meetings with Hunt via their cycles. Never meeting in the same place twice. Having to wear Lycra for the first time and hating it. Knowing all the while that Hunt held every ugly secret about him on that damn phone he'd taken at their first encounter. Or robbed at gunpoint, if truth be told.

A surge of nausea went through him just thinking about it.

He got up and poured himself a fresh cup of coffee while his mind turned over every piece – Hunt's death, the recordings, the night Napier's cottage in faraway Angle became Hunt's final reckoning.

It wasn't just Napier or Hunt who haunted him; it was the implications of everything he'd had to bury to survive.

Hunt had stuck to his word, which seemed incredible now that he thought about it.

The bargain had been Lane delivered Richards at a certain time and place and in return, he got his phone back. Once he had it, he'd tossed it into the river, having avoided cloud backups like the plague to negate the chance of anyone finding anything remotely incriminating. But the ghosts of all that anxiety still haunted him.

Lane lounged back into his chair with some hotter coffee. He had nothing to worry about. The book was a triumph. Lane had done the unthinkable: transforming something near cataclysmic, something that bordered on the end of his career, into something that would push him into the upper echelons of true-crime celebrity.

God, the possibilities.

But, for all the highs, he couldn't quite shake the remaining nagging doubt that gnawed at him.

Napier's death had been deliciously convenient. The solicitor had known things. Details about exchanges of services which had nothing to do with Hunt, but which, God forbid, the idiot might have kept some kind of record of, though he'd been a bloody fool if he had.

And now, the police were knee-deep in Napier's files.

If there was a single fly in the ointment, it was this. All of Napier's dodgy dealings unsorted and ready for them to comb through at their leisure. And while Napier and Lane had never worked together – not officially; there was no paperwork – it would end him if they had even the remotest suspicion of Lane's connection.

He wasn't an idiot. He'd been desperate for money and had risked a great deal under the radar. That little error of judgement should have ended with Napier's demise. But the greedy bastard had embezzled lots of people, and the cops had their hooks into his business.

'Jesus H Christ.' A flush of anxiety flowed through him, and he ran both hands over his face. 'How the hell am I still here?'

You didn't get out of the grime by keeping your hands clean. Everyone knew that. But the problem with climbing mountains was that there were always more cliffs up ahead, waiting to knock you right back down.

Maybe he ought to strategise.

Strategise. Lane shook his head.

Truthfully, though, there was only one person who understood the stakes. But it wasn't his partner. No. Better to keep Amol in the dark, just like always.

He opened his laptop and found the emails from Jasper and the junior editor tasked with supervising the rewrites. One glance told Lane that it wasn't much at all. Still, disquiet rippled through him, stealing some of the warmth that should have come from Jasper's relentless positivity.

He needed to talk to someone close to the case. Find out if the police were interested in anything Napier had done other than swindle some farmers' widows out of their money. But first, he'd post something on social media about the upcoming release. Modify his prologue a bit.

Jasper encouraged all that. And telling his followers about *The Indy* would float their boat.

And give the willies to the sanctimonious cops.

With a smile full of schadenfreude, Lane set to work.

# CHAPTER NINE

MONDAY PM

Rhys guided the Audi along the winding lanes between Llanwrda and Crugybar. They'd left the main roads long ago. These were the sort of lanes where you had to take your time, with too few passing places. Twice already, Rhys had reversed to let a farmer trundle by on a tractor, slow and steady. That was how things worked out here.

Fields rolled by, patchwork green, hedges still hanging on to the last vestiges of foliage. Come February, the whole place would be stripped bare, waiting for spring to drag it back to life, but winter was yet to truly bite here.

Jess sat next to him, scrolling through her phone, the screen reflecting the dull light of the short day. They were heading for Kerry Ford's rented cottage, tucked away somewhere in the rural backside of Crugybar.

'Any word from Mr Warlow?' Rhys broke the silence that had settled between them, comfortable though it was.

Jess sighed, her eyes flicking across to Rhys. 'I hope he's in bed, but something tells me he won't be. When I left this morning, he was doing a fine impression of a grizzly with a sore head.'

Rhys chuckled. 'Still not over it, then?'

'Not even close.' Jess's comment had an edge of exasperation. 'You know what he's like. Thinks he's invincible. Tried convincing me he could go out and get a Christmas tree. How's Gina?'

Rhys's face softened. 'She's fine. But I can tell it's getting to her. Tries to hide it, but it's there.'

Jess nodded, glancing at him.

'She's supporting that family in Ammanford. The girl who OD'd. She puts on a brave face, but she misses the team more than she's letting on.'

Jess thought it over. 'I get it. Going from the thick of things to family cases… it's a shift. But she'll manage. She always does.'

'I just wish she didn't feel like she's doing it alone, you know?'

She sent him a knowing smile. 'She's a keeper, Rhys. Don't let her forget that.'

'Yeah, you, Gil, Catrin, and DCI Warlow have all mentioned it once or twice.'

The landscape shifted as they approached their destination. The road narrowed further, following a stream before dipping into a shallow valley. They rounded a bend, and the mill, set down on the valley floor, came fully into view, its stone walls old and darkly weathered.

'There it is,' Jess announced. 'I presume these things were used for wool production. We have our own fair share up north.'

'But aren't the ones up north all satanic?'

'Very funny, Rhys. Gil would be proud. Even though Milton's reference wasn't literally about mills at all.'

Rhys's chin dropped. 'Wasn't it?'

'No. And do not ask how I know that, but Molly's GCSE English teacher was a Milton fan. I loved that poem, too.'

Rhys kept his eyes on the road, but Jess saw it. The slight shift in his expression, like a switch had been flipped. That look he got before deep diving into one of his historical bubbles.

'Mills were massive in Wales back in the day. Especially with the wool trade. Spinning, carding, fulling. That one is probably a fulling mill where they washed and thickened wool fabrics. You see them all over mid Wales up near Dolgellau, Machynlleth, places like that.'

Jess raised an eyebrow. 'Didn't have you down as a wool expert, Rhys.'

He flashed a grin, clearly enjoying himself. 'Well, you'd think it would be a dull subject, but the Welsh wool industry's got a pretty dark side. I saw a documentary called *Dark Wool*. Ever heard of "Welsh plains"? Coarse fabric, real rough stuff, but they used it to clothe enslaved people in the colonies. Big exporters. It was shipped to America, the West Indies – even Russia. Market for it was massive.'

Jess blinked, not expecting that turn and knowing exactly what Warlow would have said, but she was far too well brought up to say it herself. 'God, there's no escaping that horror, is there? I mean, slavery. Here? I thought Wales was all sheep and rain.'

'It gets worse.' Rhys kept his tone light, but the words were heavy. 'In the late 1700s, places like Dolgellau were obsessed with what was going on in America. They had to be. Those mills? The ones spinning wool, fulling cloth? They all had links to the worst of what people can do to other people. When you see an old mill like this, there's a dark history there. A lot darker than some pretty ivy-covered stones. These mills were just as satanic as yours were, ma'am.'

'Bloody hell, Rhys.' Jess grimaced. 'I was expecting something like, "Mills made wool thicker", not… all that. I am so glad I asked.'

Rhys chuckled, still focused on the road. 'Sorry…' he paused, 'Gina loves her *Melin Tregwynt* blankets, though. No trafficking involved these days. Soft, warm – keeps her happy.'

Jess nodded. She too had a soft spot for the intricate reverse geometric patterns rooted in Welsh tradition. 'And Molly. She likes the colour palettes. I got her one last Christmas.'

'Every blanket's got a story,' Rhys said, throwing her a grin. 'Some are just… more twisted than others.'

*Felingwm*, or Mill Valley as named at the gated entrance, was big. Ford's cottage formed a part of the overall spread, which Jess knew had been a wedding venue before Covid took its toll. Now it was mostly forgotten, rented out only a handful of times a year, with smaller outbuildings like Ford's being rented out long term as a source of more regular income, according to Catrin's research.

Rustic charm oozed from every window, with ivy creeping up the stone wall. Everything oozed solid and dependable. But it also had that quiet feeling of something left behind. Or perhaps that was simply what Rhys's history lesson had instilled in Jess.

They pulled up. Weed-choked gravel crunched beneath the tyres.

The owner, Sarah Pritchard, appeared from the main house, in jeans, wellies, and a face tight with worry.

'DI Allanby?' She extended her hand. 'I still can't believe it about Kerry. Such a tragedy.'

Jess shook her hand but registered the genuine distress in her voice. 'Thanks for meeting us, Mrs Pritchard. We just need to briefly look around, if that's all right.'

Pritchard fished out a key and nodded.

The cottage had that same rustic charm, its stone walls weathered by countless Welsh winters. A stream gurgled nearby, lending a sense of isolation. Inside, it was cosy. Exposed beams, stonework, a wood-burning stove. The room smelt faintly of old ash and furniture polish. It had a genuine feel of well-kept solidity.

'Ooh, she's left it tidy,' Pritchard exclaimed.

'From your surprise, I take it that Kerry didn't always leave it like this?'

'No. I'm not in here often, but... no. Even though she earns a bit of money by cleaning for some people, she never seems to be too fussed when it comes to her own place... oh, what am I saying? She's not going to be here ever again.' Pritchard's eyes shone wet, sudden and unguarded.

'It's okay, Mrs Pritchard,' Rhys said. 'This has come as a shock.'

'How long were you expecting her to be away for?' Jess asked.

Pritchard blew her nose in a crumpled tissue before answering. 'A fortnight. Until between Christmas and New Year,' she said. 'No specific dates. I ought to light a fire.' She glanced at the empty grate. 'The place gets cold quickly. Bathroom's through there, and the bedrooms are upstairs.'

Jess's trained eye took it all in. Nothing seemed out of place. No signs of disturbance, no hints that anything was amiss.

'How long had she been living here?' Jess asked.

'Coming up on six years,' Pritchard replied. 'No trouble at all. Kept to herself.' She faltered slightly. 'Well… I hardly saw her, to be honest.'

They moved through the cottage.

There were few personal touches. No photos, no mementos. It was as if Kerry Ford had been trying to erase herself.

'You say she did some work?' Rhys asked.

'She did cleaning jobs for cash – holiday lets, houses, that sort of thing, but nothing regular,' Pritchard continued. 'Always paid rent on time, though.'

'No problems with payment?' Rhys flipped open his notebook.

Pritchard shook her head. 'None at all. She was reliable. Preferred cash.' She shrugged. 'It's still a thing in the farming community.'

Pritchard had come to a standstill on the threshold. 'I'll go back to the house, shall I?'

Rhys thanked her and promised to let her know when they'd finished.

Jess moved around the ground floor. In a loose binder on a shelf below a coffee table was a folder full of bills, statements, and vouchers hinting at an eye for a supermarket bargain. All functional. Nothing personal. Same in the bedroom. Same everywhere.

'She certainly kept a low profile,' Rhys remarked once they were back in the car. 'Was she putting down roots or hiding away?'

Jess dialled DI Anna Gwynne, putting the call on speaker.

'DI Gwynne? It's DI Jess Allanby. Catrin Richards filled us in re your request. We've just finished at Ford's rental property.'

'Find anything?' Anna asked.

'Nothing obvious,' Jess replied. 'But something's not adding up. What aren't you telling us?'

A pause, then a sigh from Anna. 'We're waiting on full tox reports, but so far only alcohol other than the carbon monoxide.'

'Right,' Jess said.

'But we found no evidence of any cooked food. Nor anything in the caravan's fridge that needed cooking.'

Jess exchanged a glance with Rhys.

'So, why light a barbecue if you had no intention of cooking any food?' Anna asked.

Rhys's eyebrows were halfway to his hairline now.

'What about Ford's history in Keynsham?' Jess pressed.

Anna's voice came back, tight-sounding. 'Let's FaceTime, shall we?'

Rhys pulled in. They had a reasonable signal.

A moment later, a video call came through, and Anna Gwynne's face appeared on Jess's phone screen. And it came as a pleasant surprise. She was fair-haired with large, serious eyes – attractive in a no-nonsense sort of way.

'Nice to put a face to the voice,' Jess said.

'Likewise.'

'And this is Rhys Harries, our DC.'

'Ma'am,' Rhys said.

Anna cleared her throat, bringing them back to the matter at hand. 'About Ford's past. She got involved with a late-twenties waste of space called Darren Lister, small-time drug dealer. He coerced her into running deliveries. It got abusive. She gave him up and then left sunny Keynsham to start over.'

Gave him up meant that she may have set him up for a fall and bargained her way out of prison. No wonder she was out here in the sticks.

'Lister?' Jess asked.

'Recently released from jail.'

The implications required no elaboration. Jess voiced what they were both thinking. 'Are you implying the carbon monoxide wasn't an accident?'

'We – and by we, I mean only me, as my DCI thinks this is a straightforward case of two pissed-up caravaners forgetting to douse the coals – are not ruling anything out,' Anna confirmed. 'You think your team could take a quick forensic once-over at Ford's place? We'd be looking for anything Lister-related.'

'We'll make it happen,' Jess said. 'You'll be talking to Lister?'

'First thing,' Anna replied. 'If we can find him.'

The call ended. Rhys pulled the car back onto the road.

Out of nowhere, Rhys said, 'DI Gwynne resembles that woman from *The Last of Us*.'

'Doesn't everyone get killed in that show?'

'No, not everyone. Well… she did, yeah. But she was the main guy's partner. And the same actor was in *Mindhunter*. The one about the early days of FBI profiling. I loved that show. It'll come to me.'

Jess only half listened. What had started as a simple cross-border case of box-ticking was shaping into something far more complicated.

Rhys, still thinking, suddenly exclaimed, 'Anna Torv! That's who she reminds me of!'

Jess smiled, shaking her head. 'I'll be sure to tell her she epitomises a zombie next time.'

Rhys grinned. 'No, she wasn't a zombie in *The Last of Us*. She was hunting them. Not glamorous, though. Far from it.'

'Zombie hunting rarely is,' Jess quipped.

But the odd emptiness of Kerry Ford's life – and death – lingered in her mind.

The flat had looked neat and tidy, and for some reason, that bothered Jess the most.

# CHAPTER TEN

MONDAY PM

Catrin stood at the kitchen counter in the little alcove that housed the kettle, tea canisters, and fridge. The kettle clicked off, and she cast a quick glance at her phone. The screen glowed with the last article she'd been reading.

Jess and Rhys had just returned from their visit to Kerry Ford's cottage. Conversation about the property had been brief, but now that they were back in the office, Catrin was eager to share what she'd uncovered about DI Anna Gwynne.

She carried three mugs back to the office on a tray, each with a spoon clinking against the porcelain. Only three mugs; Gil had gone across to a colleague in Financial Crimes to check something in the Moyles's case notes.

'Tea's ready.'

Jess looked up from where he sat. He cocked his head in suspicion and glanced at the mug. 'Thanks, Sarge. This isn't anything herbal, is it?'

Catrin's eyeroll was perfunctory. 'Regular builder's tea. God forbid anything without caffeine gets past those lips.'

Jess took a sip and sighed. 'Perfect timing, Catrin. Thank you.'

'Anything interesting at the cottage?'

'It's on the grounds of a huge, defunct mill. Do you want

the Rhys lecture on its dubious ties to colonialism and human trafficking first?'

Catrin opened her mouth to say something but bit it back. 'He is a master of light entertainment, is our Rhys. Perhaps later for that, ma'am.'

'Good call.' Jess exchanged a glance with Rhys, 'Nothing obvious. The place was well kept, almost too well kept. As if she didn't really live there – no personal touches, no photos, nothing. It felt more like a temporary hiding spot than a home.'

Rhys nodded along. 'It was weird. You'd think someone would have a few keepsakes, but there was barely anything. The landlady wasn't much help either. She seemed genuinely shocked, but I'm not sure how much she really knew.'

Catrin stirred her tea slowly, a hypnotic motion at odds with her next words. 'I dug into DI Anna Gwynne. She's undoubtedly got skeletons.'

'Of the *Mindhunter* variety?' Rhys asked. 'FBI, serial killer profiling, that sort of thing?'

Jess shot him a glare, but it lacked proper heat. They were all grasping at normalcy in their own ways. And Rhys spent a lot of time with Gil. You had to take that into consideration.

Catrin set down her spoon and reached for the notes on her phone. 'You're not a million miles off the mark there, Rhys. Gwynne was involved in the Black Squid cases. Ring any bells?'

Rhys tilted his head. 'Black Squid? Sounds like a dodgy nightclub.'

Catrin blinked over at him. 'Not quite. Bottom line, she's definitely got the T-shirt in terms of closing cases. But what really put her in the spotlight was her connection to Hector Shaw.'

Jess nodded. 'Of course. Hector Shaw. He was already in prison for murder. Revenge killing for what someone had done to his daughter.'

'That's the one,' Catrin confirmed. 'She interviewed him while she was working on another case. Shaw always denied any involvement, but he knew things – details about other people involved. Some said Gwynne got too close to him, and it slowed her down. Others argue it's what helped catch the actual killers in the end.'

Rhys, half listening, perked up. 'So, she is a profiler, then? Just like *Mindhunter*?'

'Where is this *Mindhunter* stuff coming from?' Catrin asked.

'We had a video call with her,' Jess explained. 'Rhys thinks she's the spitting image of an actress from the series. Ignore him.'

'As I say,' Catrin continued, 'she's not afraid to get her hands dirty, that's clear. Her career could have taken off faster if it wasn't for Shaw. But she's good, no denying that.'

Jess nodded slowly, processing it all. 'Interesting. She's definitely bugged by something in this Ford case. She wants some forensic input. She's thrown a person of interest named Lister into the mix. Can you speak to Alison Povey? I said I'd get a CSI team up there to give it the once-over. Gwynne wants to know if there's any sign of anyone else having been there besides Ford.'

'I can do that,' Catrin said. 'Will we need a warrant?'

Before Jess could respond, her phone buzzed – *Warlow*. She stepped away to take the call, leaving Catrin and Rhys exchanging curious glances.

'Hey, how're you feeling?' she asked, braced for the inevitable gruff response.

Warlow came through, raspy and punctuated by a fit of coughing. 'Like absolute shite. Worse, if anything. I can barely stop coughing long enough to string a sentence together.'

Jess's brow furrowed, concern warring with frustration. 'You should be in bed. I'll grab the Christmas provisions. We'll survive without mince pies, and Molly's not due back until Christmas Eve—'

Warlow let out a weak chuckle, though it quickly devolved into another cough. 'I promised I'd do Christmas lunch, but at this rate, I'll be lucky if I can manage toast. Maybe I should just hole up in a cave until this damn thing passes. But then, there's no Tesco in a cave—'

'Don't be ridiculous. You'd be like Typhoid Mary in the shops. Even with a mask.'

'All right, all right. You win. But for the record, I'll still help with Christmas dinner, coughs be damned.'

'Molly will help,' Jess said.

'That's what worries me,' Warlow growled.

'Your biting wit has not been affected, I see.'

'Don't make me laugh.'

'Then, just take it easy.'

'Catrin, okay? How did her meeting with the big nobs go?'

'Fine.' Jess glanced across at the woman in question, but Warlow's incessant coughing meant he was in no state to chat.

They said their goodbyes, and Jess slipped her phone back into her pocket. She returned to the table, but before she could sit, a phone buzzed again – this time, an internal call on a landline from the desk sergeant. According to him, one Taran Marston had arrived, asking to speak with Sergeant Thomas, rural crime.

The sergeant knew Tomo had been in to see her. He'd put two and two together and come up with Jess as an answer to his problem of whom to direct Marston to.

'Taran Marston?' Jess repeated in a whisper to herself, glancing at both Catrin and Rhys. 'All right, I'll be down in a minute.'

She ended the call and grabbed her coat again. 'It's Mia Marston's father.'

'What does he want?' Catrin asked.

Jess shrugged, already on her way out the door. 'One way to find out.'

———

MARSTON WAS WAITING in one of the small courtesy rooms downstairs when Jess arrived. He stood as she entered, extending a hand with an overly polite smile. He was tall, with long dark hair tied back, and his eyes held hers with an unsettling intensity.

'Mr Marston.' She shook his hand briefly and sat across from him. 'I understand you wanted to speak with someone about your daughter?'

Marston nodded, sitting slowly. 'Yes, I felt like we didn't really get a chance to explain everything when Mia was found. I realise it wasn't you I spoke to but my wife and I… we wanted to make sure there were no misunderstandings.'

Jess sat, hands folded on her lap. 'Go on.'

Marston's voice took on a measured, almost rehearsed tone. 'Our daughter Mia… she's special. She has behavioural problems that makes traditional schooling a poor fit for her. That's why we homeschooled her and her siblings. Moving to the farm, being around the animals and nature – it's been an enormous help for her neurodiversity. She's improved so much since we left Antwerp.'

'You're Dutch?'

'My wife is half Dutch. I'm from the Marches.'

'I see,' Jess said. 'And how long have you been living on the farm?'

'We moved in a few months before the pandemic hit. Ironically, lockdown gave us the chance to really settle in and adjust to a simpler lifestyle. We're very self-sufficient now, growing our own food, raising animals. Pivoting to the holistic healing side of things, though, that's all my wife's doing. It's been liberating for all of us.'

Jess's gaze didn't waver. 'And what do you do for work, Mr Marston?'

Marston hesitated for the briefest of moments. 'I trade, foreign exchange. It's all online, so I can work from home. My wife is the brains of the partnership. Living on the farm has allowed her to explore her own… spiritual horizons, you could say.'

'And homeschooling Mia has been part of that?' Jess kept her tone neutral.

'Exactly.' He nodded. 'She's thriving. The routine, the closeness to nature – it's what she needs.'

Jess studied him for a moment, sensing there was more beneath the surface of his words, but he'd said his piece. 'I appreciate you taking the time to explain this, Mr Marston. I'll ensure Sergeant Thomas knows you came in.'

Marston stood, offering another polite smile. 'Thank you, DI Allanby.'

But Jess wasn't ready to end things just yet. 'Sergeant Thomas was slightly confused about the visit you made to the standing stones, though. At dawn? In December?'

'We try to teach the children about all forms of spirituality,' he began, his voice adopting a grating, sanctimonious tone. 'Where we are' – he gestured vaguely, as if encompassing some grand, mystical realm – 'has such a rich cultural heritage.'

His response came without hesitation and with the practised ease of a well-rehearsed speech. It was its fluidity that triggered Jess's unease. Suddenly, she understood Tomo's disquiet. This was like watching an actor perform a scene they'd done countless times.

Marston's eyes gleamed with fervour.

Jess's skin crawled.

'Pre-Christian heritage, I might add.' His words dripped with a smug superiority.

Jess catalogued every word, every inflection.

'And we'll celebrate Christmas, of course we will,' he added hastily, as if sensing Jess's scepticism. 'But Yule is just as important, or was, to some people, long before the imposition of the Judeo-Christian faith.'

Jess locked on to the word "imposition" in Marston's carefully constructed narrative of New-Age spirituality and historical revisionism – ideas he stitched together with sickly threads of self-righteousness.

'You're interested in pagan traditions, then?'

She watched the slight tightening around Marston's eyes, the almost imperceptible straightening of his posture.

'Interested is perhaps too mild a word,' Marston replied. 'We're rediscovering our roots, Detective Inspector. The old ways, the traditions that were buried beneath centuries of Christian dogma.'

Jess nodded again. Marston's zealousness smacked of

conviction, but there was something else there, too – a need to convince, to justify.

'And how does Mia feel about these… traditions?' Jess asked, steering the conversation back to the root of why he was there.

Marston's smile faltered for a fraction of a second, so brief Jess might have missed it if she hadn't been watching so closely before he refashioned it.

'Mia loves it,' he said, regaining its earlier smoothness. 'As do her brother and sister. They are all thriving in this environment. As I say, the connection to nature, to the old ways – it's been transformative for her, indeed for us all.'

───

HE LEFT SOON AFTER, his polished veneer never cracking. Jess returned upstairs to join Rhys and Catrin, aware that she was empathising with Tomo after the encounter.

Something seemed off. But you had to be careful in cases like this.

Being weird didn't automatically imply criminality. But spiritual fervour of any kind rankled like nails on a blackboard with Jess. She had her own reasons for that. Reasons that stretched back to a zealous grandfather who'd banished her mother for daring to marry outside his tribe.

But she had insight and always tried to compensate for her own bias.

Rhys looked up, curiosity all over his face. 'What did he want?'

Jess sat, her mind still turning over the conversation. 'He came to explain about his children's homeschooling and their lifestyle, which includes visits to the standing stones to pay tribute to cultures past. It's reasonable, kind of. But the more he talked, the stranger he sounded.' She sighed, once again reining in her judgement. 'But being different is not against the law.'

Catrin frowned. 'When did they move there again?'

'Just before Covid,' Jess replied. 'Which makes sense,

but… I don't know. Instead of putting my mind at ease, I'm with Tomo. Marston's put me on edge.'

Rhys lifted his chin. 'Like you say, ma'am. No crime has been committed. I mean, even if the mother is a witch, that's not illegal either. Witches were sometimes called cunning folk. Countryside healers at one time.'

'Not witches again,' Jess said.

'It's the sort of thing they do, ma'am. Pagan rituals. Druid's Moor at Yule.'

Jess took a deep breath, glancing between the two younger officers. 'I suggest we keep an open mind about the whole thing. But I'm with Tomo. Due diligence. Rhys, get on to the local council. See if anyone oversees homeschooling. Find out if there have been any red flags regarding the family. I don't think that's unreasonable. And it'll put Tomo's mind at rest.'

*Even if it won't mine.*

Wisely, she kept that as an unvoiced thought.

# CHAPTER ELEVEN

MONDAY evening

Having no children of his own, Rhys had so far been spared the trauma of trying to maintain some kind of educational continuity during the enforced lockdown in 2020. As a result, he was relatively unaware of the social and emotional delays that pupils had suffered, which became obvious only when these children returned to normal schooling. But Catrin was of an age where many of her friends had endured the period. She also had friends who were teachers in their own right. She gave Rhys a couple of names of people who might help with understanding homeschooling and what it entailed.

Rhys, God bless him, relished the prospect of a fresh investigation. And it quickly became clear that the Marston family's aim of an off-grid existence was working very well. He marvelled at how, in the digital age where every sneeze seemed catalogued, a family of five could just stay off the radar.

He began with a call to the Family Liaison Officer over at the council's Parent Partner Services. The name alone – so painfully upbeat – made him certain it belonged to a department whose sole mission was to ruin his day.

The FLO, Linda, was the standard overworked public servant: equal parts worn out and vaguely suspicious of

anyone asking too many questions. After the usual pleas-
antries, Rhys cut to the chase.

'I'm looking into homeschooling. How does it work?'

There was a pause that sounded like Linda flipping
through some papers. Or trying to work out if she might pass
him off to someone else. 'Is this for your children?'

'No. We're making enquiries into a case. I'm trying to get
a handle on it.'

'I see. It's every parent's right to homeschool. Since 1996.'
It sounded like she didn't have to think about that statement
much.

'Doesn't there have to be a good reason?'

'Wanting to do it is reason enough.'

'So, do the local authority have people go out and see
what the parents are doing?'

'There's no compulsory inspection for homeschooling.'

Rhys paused. 'What? No inspections at all?'

'Nope,' Linda replied. 'Parents aren't required to tell us if
they're homeschooling either. And unless someone alerts us,
well, we often don't even know they are.'

'You're joking?' Rhys said, disbelief colouring his tone.
'No assessments or tests?'

'We often find out by default. If a child doesn't show up at
school, someone will usually make informal enquiries. That's
most often how we find out.'

Rhys leaned back in his chair. 'Let me get this straight. No
mandatory inspections, no obligation to inform the authorities, so how do you know?'

Linda sighed. 'I realise it sounds a bit mad, but that's the
system we're working with. Of course, we have safeguarding
officers... but there are over six hundred families in the
county homeschooling, and no more than eight officers at one
time. Visiting homeschooled families is not their only job—'

'What about socialisation? I mean, I went to school, we all
did. It wasn't just about learning, was it? It was about... life
skills, making friends, dealing with different people. Pains in
the arse, all the usual stuff.'

Linda's voice softened a notch. 'That's often a concern

with homeschooling, yes. Some families do a great job of getting their kids involved in community activities, sports teams, that sort of thing. Others… well, it varies.'

'Right. Have you come into contact with a family called Marston? They're up near *Cwrt-y-Cadno*.'

There was a rustling of papers on Linda's end. 'The name isn't coming up. Send me the address, and if you can give me a couple of hours… I'm right in the middle of preparing a report at this moment.'

'Sure,' Rhys said. 'One last thing. In your experience, does homeschooling actually prepare kids for the real world?'

Linda's hesitation was telling. 'Depends. If it's done properly, homeschooled kids can be incredibly well-rounded and prepared. But it takes effort, planning, and usually a good support network. Without those… well, it can most definitely be a challenge for the kids later on.'

Rhys thanked Linda and hung up, more unsettled than when he'd started. He stared at the files he'd made on the Marstons. Well, "files" was stretching it a bit. It was more like a single sheet of paper with a few lines: names, ages, and the vague details of their homeschooling arrangement. Nothing else.

He couldn't shake off his confusion.

Three kids, potentially isolated from the world, with no one checking in on their education or well-being. It went against everything he'd experienced growing up.

'This can't be right,' he muttered to himself, reaching for his phone again.

He dialled the number Catrin had given him at the local education authority. After some checks to make sure he was who he said he was, the voice on the other end of the phone – Joyce – sounded a little more on the ball.

'Let me pull up the file… ah, yes. They deregistered their children from formal education from the outset. Standard procedure for homeschooling families. Some homeschooled families anyway. The ones who want to keep it official. And the Marstons did, in fact, fill in a form.'

Rhys' frustration mounted. 'And has anyone checked on

them since? Made sure the kids are actually getting an education?'

Joyce never faltered. 'We don't have the authority to conduct regular checks on curriculums for homeschooling families. That isn't how it works. Unless there's a specific concern raised—'

'So, nobody's laid eyes on these kids in years?' Rhys sounded surprised. 'Nobody's made sure they're learning, or socialising, or… just being kids?'

Joyce wasn't put out. 'Homeschooling is a legal and valid choice for parents. We can't assume there's a problem just because a family chooses this path.'

'I get that. I do. But surely someone should be making sure these kids are okay? That they're learning what they need to.'

After a beat of silence, Joyce's reply sounded a little frostier. 'If you have specific concerns about the welfare of the Marston children, I'd be happy to note them in the file.'

But Rhys had no such thing. Instead, he thanked her and ended the call, feeling no closer to understanding the Marstons' situation.

He studied the sparse information on his desk; the post-code staring back at him like a challenge.

Gil, munching an apple, strolled into the office, took one look at Rhys, and said, 'The last time I saw an expression like that was on that programme about someone desperately wanting to make hats.'

Rhys, distracted still, muttered, 'I must have missed that one, Sarge.'

'No, you've seen it. You know the one. Where you can phone your friend if you can't come up with the answer. I want to be a milliner.'

'It's millionaire.'

Gil paused with his apple about to be bitten into again an inch from his lips to peer at Rhys. 'I know it is. I was attempting to lighten your dark and miserable mood. Obviously, I failed.'

Rhys thought for a bit and then smiled. 'No, you're all right, Sarge. I want to be a milliner is quite good.'

'Can I help in any way? A problem shared is a problem… passed on to another individual for them to go through hell as well.'

'It's Tomo's case. DI Allanby chatted to the girl they found's father.'

'She didn't like what she saw?'

Rhys shook his head.

'Ah, well, DIs and DCIs have Spidey-sense. Best to listen.'

Rhys shrugged. 'You can choose to homeschool your children just like that. You don't have to apply or anything. Just file a form. It's mad. I mean, who knows what some of these people might be teaching these kids?'

'I like the affronted tone, Rhys. Obviously, you are a traditionalist.'

'My mother is a teacher, Sarge.'

'Of course she is. And I am with you on the homeschooling. Getting my three granddaughters to do anything they do not want to do is no easy task.'

'How do you manage then?'

'Persuasion and chocolate buttons. The currency of obedience. However, there are not enough of those in the world to get them to sit down and do multiplication. Is that even a thing these days, or has some postmodern quango decided that all maths is privileged? But then, who needs multiplication when you have a phone glued to your palm, eh? Siri, what is two divided by one, and can you find me a cat video while you're at it?'

Rhys had his phone in his hand. 'Sorry?'

'I rest my case, m'lud.'

'How about you? Any further along with Sillitoe?'

As if the sour expression gurning Gil's face was not enough, he muttered, 'Not a sausage.' But tempered the negativity by pronouncing sausage the French way. 'Napier's PPs are getting me nowhere. No pattern. No links. I was even on the point of ringing DCI Warlow again. See how he is and if he has anything by way of inspiration.'

'I'm game.' Rhys grinned.

'So the rumour goes,' Gil replied.

'Video or sound only, Sarge?'

'Good God, we don't need eye contact.'

They used Rhys's phone and placed it on his desk in front of his monitor.

Warlow's voice rasped through the speaker like death on a bad day.

'Just checking in?' he croaked, which in Warlow-speak meant: "Why aren't you lot doing my job while I'm dying in bed?"

'Right.' Gil grinned at Rhys. 'Well, Napier's still dead, Sillitoe's still vanished, and I've still got no link between the two.'

'Brilliant.' Warlow sniffed, clearly unimpressed. 'Any chance you can get it out of your system before I return?'

'More like *if* you return, from the sound of it. And preferably not as one of the walking dead. But unlikely is the answer to your question,' Gil picked at something on his sleeve.

Warlow sneezed, the sound more of a wheeze combined with a screeching owl. 'What about you, Rhys?'

Rhys clenched his jaw. 'Did anyone tell you about the Marstons, sir?'

'Jess mentioned something. Tomo's got a bee in his bonnet.'

'DI Allanby asked me to do some research into home-schooling, sir.'

'Homeschooling,' Warlow said, his disdain for the word trickling down the line. 'And what have you found out?'

Rhys explained briefly.

Warlow snorted. 'Wonderful. No oversight, no accountability, just blind faith in people who probably can't spell "curriculum".'

'Sounds like some people's dream job. You could lie in bed all day and claim you're teaching the kids quadratic equations,' Gil said. 'No one would be any the wiser. Certainly not the kids.'

Rhys shot him a glance. 'Still, it's hard to believe you can just pull kids out of school and make them vanish. They need friends and interaction.'

'And instead, they get to wander off into the wilderness,' Warlow added drily. 'Isn't that what she did, the daughter?'

'Exactly that, sir,' Rhys stated.

Warlow coughed, a sound that might've been a laugh if he weren't on his deathbed. 'IMHO, if in doubt, get out there. Get in the car and visit the places. Get a feel for it. Perambulate and cogitate.'

'That's your advice?' Rhys raised an eyebrow. Not that Warlow could see. 'Cogitate?'

'Works for me,' Warlow rasped. 'Now excuse me while I check if there are any more iron lungs on eBay. I lost my bid on the last one.' He hung up with a wet-sounding cough.

'Cogitate,' Rhys glanced up. 'Will that solve anything?'

Gil shrugged. 'Who knows? Only one way to find out. I feel a road trip coming on first thing in the morning. But, this evening, I have an appointment with young Mr Brewer. After supper, of course.'

# CHAPTER TWELVE

**MONDAY NIGHT**

Gil pushed open the door of The Salutation. The pub's light and warmth washed over him immediately, accompanied by the usual murmur of conversation and the low clatter of pool balls.

It wasn't packed, but it had a pleasant enough buzz. The TV in the corner showed some European football match, volume low enough to let conversation take place. Not a riot, then. But not dead either. It'd do. At least there was no one standing on tables or preaching from soapboxes, though that could change if the night got busier.

Gil scanned the room, clocking a quieter corner by the fire. Perfect. He bought a half and slid into a cracked leather seat, the creak of it as familiar as his own bones.

He liked this pub. Always had. And to its credit, it hadn't gone the way of so many after the pandemic. Still did live music, had a sizeable garden out the back, function rooms that made it a summer hub. More so at Christmas, when the town's diaspora returned home. Then it could resemble a sardine tin.

With singing.

Charlie Brewer appeared in the doorway. Clean-shaven and neat as ever, with hair carefully combed, and a work tie still on under a jacket and shirt with chinos. A bit naïve in the past, maybe, about Moyles and his dark dealings, but you couldn't fault him for trying.

Gil waved him over.

'Looking sharp as ever, young man,' Gil greeted him.

Charlie's grin flashed quickly. He slipped into the seat opposite. 'Thanks, Sergeant.'

Gil waved off the formalities. 'It's just Gil. What'll you have?'

'A Moretti, thanks.' Charlie shrugged off his jacket and folded it over the back of his chair with careful precision.

Gil nodded and made his way to the bar. No queue, so within three minutes he was back with two drinks – lager for Charlie, the other half of a Gower ale for himself. He took a long, satisfying swig, setting the glass down with a contented smack of his lips.

'Not a bad turnout, tonight,' Gil scanned the room. 'I was half expecting the place to be dead. I used to go to a pub in Cardigan where the landlord kept a parrot. Most foul-mouthed bird you've ever heard. Used to sit on the bar and swear at the customers.'

'You're having me on?' Charlie laughed.

'God's honest truth. Old Tom – that was the parrot – knew more swear words than Chubby Brown.'

'Who's Chubby Brown?'

Gil arched an eyebrow. 'I forgot you were educated in a convent.'

'I wasn't.'

'No, well, look him up. But don't blame me. Anyway, it caused no end of trouble when the vicar came in for his Sunday pint. Foxtrot Oscar, you Canute, if you know what I mean.'

Charlie appeared a little nonplussed. Police call sign jokes were clearly beyond him. 'Nice to see this place surviving.' He took a sip. 'I've seen so many rural pubs shut in the last year.'

Gil leaned back, considering. Charlie Brewer worked for a land agent these days.

'Makes me wonder what's going to happen if the bypass ever comes,' Brewer added.

The bypass was a sore point. Half the town wanted it to stop traffic from choking the streets; the other half feared it'd choke off the tourists instead.

'I reckon it'll help more than hurt,' Gil said after a moment. 'If they play their cards right. Llandeilo's already a popular destination. I mean, you can never have too many galleries and gift shops, right?'

Charlie smiled. If they pedestrianised the centre, injected a bit more of a café society it would pull more people in. As it is, it's a nightmare.'

The conversation wandered for a bit – the slow uptake at the refurbished town market, new housing, the new cycle path – but eventually, Gil steered them back on course.

'Anyway.' He fixed Charlie with a steady gaze. 'I asked you here to talk Napier. Again.'

Charlie's easy smile slipped. 'Sorry I didn't get back to you sooner. Work's been busy. Some farmers want to sell up after the inheritance tax debacle.'

'No need to apologise.' Gil brushed it off. 'I've been going through Napier's papers. I've got back-door access via Financial Crimes. Diaries, mostly. There are references to those "PP" bookings you mentioned, but nothing solid. No names. No leads.'

Charlie took a thoughtful sip. 'The PPs were Napier's gig. He and Moyles handled those off the books. I just made sure the beds were changed and the place was clean.'

Gil tapped his fingers against his glass. 'Still trying to figure out why they'd keep these clients so hush-hush. Privacy, sure, but something more?'

Charlie's eyes darkened with hesitation. 'Napier was… complicated. On the surface, he was the typical country solicitor who talked the talk, walked the walk, involved in everything. But something felt off. I mean, if he knew what Moyles was up to with those cameras, why send clients there?'

'That's the question,' Gil said, pleased that Charlie's thoughts were aligning with his own. 'Did Napier know? And if he did, was he using it as leverage? These "PPs" might have been clients, or were they targets?'

Charlie let out a long breath. 'That's… dark.'

'Stygian,' Gil agreed. 'But then, Moyles and Napier weren't winning Citizen of the Year anytime soon, were they?'

'Honestly, I thought I knew Royston. I feel such an idiot. Is it true what they're saying about Napier cheating people out of their inheritances?'

Gil gave a grim nod. 'Apparently.'

The reason Financial Crimes had wormed their way into Napier's history was simple; people who'd trusted him for years were just now realising he'd forged wills, sneaking himself into legacies he had no business touching. The kindly solicitor left a token in a client's will, a gesture of thanks. Small at first – barely a blip. But it grew. Every time, a little more, the amounts creeping upwards as greed and the illusion of invincibility took over.

Napier wasn't just the man who'd protect his interests. He was the kind of man who'd do anything to make sure no one else touched them.

Charlie shifted in his seat, his gaze darting around the pub. 'Royston Moyles and Napier were thick as thieves.'

Gil waited.

'Napier was the one with connections, though. There's a clutch of media people in the area who've moved out of Cardiff for the good life. They'd meet up in the pubs and bars. Royston liked to hang on to their coattails. Given what we've found out, could there be others out there who've been filmed?'

'That makes a nasty kind of sense.'

'Yeah.' Charlie shifted in his seat. 'Is that why you're asking all these questions, Gil?'

But Gil wasn't ready to broadcast his concerns just yet. Freddie Sillitoe was not for discussion.

Charlie's face clouded, disappointment creeping in. 'I wish I could give you more. Something solid, you know? But I didn't have that kind of access. My job was just keeping things ticking over, getting the properties ready for the next guest. I rarely dealt with the clients directly. Especially not the PPs.'

Gil offered a tired smile. 'You've already helped more than you think.'

Charlie nodded, though the slump in his shoulders stayed. 'I really hope you find something that makes sense of all this.'

Gil took another swallow of beer. Brewer had been useful so far, and there was a chance he could dig deeper. Maybe push a little more.

'Listen,' Gil set his bottle down on a beer mat. 'I've got a stack of Napier's diaries back at the office. Some of it's coded. Or at least written in a way that's… off. Think you could take a peek at some of the things I've curated? You worked near to the guy. You might spot something I've missed.'

Charlie's eyes widened a fraction. 'I worked with Royston Moyles, never with Napier directly. But yes, I can have a look. I'd be happy to.'

'Good man.' Gil kept things businesslike. 'Can't do any harm, right?'

Charlie's earlier frown melted into a faint smile.

'Cheers, Charlie.' Gil raised his beer in a mock toast. 'Much appreciated.'

'Delighted to be of service. How is Mr Warlow?'

'Ah, the old Wolf's not been great. Chest infection, by the sound of it.' He grimaced. 'Probably caught it walking that dog of his in the rain. Stubborn as ever.'

'Sorry to hear that.'

'Yeah, well. He's not getting any younger, is he?' Gil sighed. 'These things hit harder now.'

Charlie grinned. 'I'd say "experienced" is a better word for it.'

'Experienced,' Gil echoed, laughing lightly. 'Better than "over the hill", I suppose.'

They shared a chuckle. The conversation drifted off again into safer waters: local gossip, best takeaways in the area. But Gil's mind was elsewhere.

Napier, Moyles, those bloody PPs. There was something

there. Something hidden in plain sight, ready to come apart with the right tug.

On the TV, the noise from the football match swelled. A bad foul had the crowd up in arms. A red card in the offing. But Gil wasn't interested in the game.

His eyes flicked back to Charlie, who was now engrossed in the match, wincing at the replay of the foul.

'Bloody hell,' Charlie muttered. 'That's a career-ender, that tackle.'

Gil grunted.

*Career-enders.* Wasn't that what they were dealing with here? Not just for Napier and Moyles, but for their clients, too. The PPs. Important people who couldn't afford to have their secrets spilt.

On the screen, the referee was brandishing the red card, the player trudging off the pitch with his head bowed. Game over for him. But not for Gil. Not yet.

He drained the last of his pint and stood. 'Thanks for coming,' he said. 'I hope I haven't kept you from your supper.'

'I eat late anyway.'

'Unlike me, then. But I was too late to eat earlier, so my supper will be ready in a matter of minutes once I give the signal. And the chef is not a person one keeps waiting. The Lady Anwen makes that Ramsay bloke look like Mother Teresa.'

Outside, the clouds had cleared and the temperature had dropped. Gil pulled his collar up and zipped his jacket against the freezing air. Christmas lights blazed. Trees in windows. Santas climbing up walls. He'd probably have to dress up in red for his granddaughters soon. He wondered what kind of Christmas Freddie Sillitoe had to look forward to.

But that way of thinking would do no one any good.

———

In Nevern, Warlow wallowed. Not that he wanted to stay

away from Jess, but apart from the odd word, he kept his distance, declining all offers of help or succour.

'The last thing we want is for you to come down with this bloody thing,' he kept saying.

And so, again, he slept, or tried to, in the second bedroom. The one normally occupied by Molly when she was home. But if it wasn't his throat and the crackly pain it gave him when he tried to swallow, it was the cough that brought him awake. He'd snatch a couple of hours' sleep and then would be awake for an hour, trying and failing to read before exhaustion won the battle against his irritated mucous membranes.

He didn't even get up when Jess got off early, at around seven the next morning. At eight, he dragged himself out to feed the dog, but a bout of dizziness as he stood by the sink forced him to sit with a tasteless cup of tea and tell himself to get a grip.

Maybe hot coffee would help.

It didn't.

# CHAPTER THIRTEEN

TUESDAY

The early morning journey from Dyfed-Powys HQ to *Cân-y-Barcud* wasn't far. A quick trip up the Tywi Valley towards Gil's hometown of Llandeilo and out the other side towards the Abbey at Tally. Both Gil and Rhys had made the journey at least twenty times, the route etched into their memory like a bitter scar. Initially, it was part of the investigation into Royston Moyles's unpleasant death − strung up and left to throttle himself under his own weight. More recently, it had been the focal point of their frantic search for Catrin Richards, abducted by the killer, Hunt.

Geraint Lane, the journalist, had suggested he and Catrin meet at Moyles's cottage for the sake of "atmosphere" as part of his police-service-sanctioned piece about Hunt. But the killer had lain in wait for them. All part of his sick quest for revenge against the men who'd secretly filmed him and ruined his life.

The irony wasn't lost on either of the detectives.

Rhys pulled up in the only space available on the one-way track ending at the cottage. Neither man got out. The silence in the car brooded, thick with unspoken unease.

'Can't say I'm glad to be back here,' Rhys said in a low voice.

'No,' Gil agreed, equally unenthusiastic.

Rhys went to open his door, ready to "perambulate", as Warlow liked to put it. But Gil didn't move.

'Cogitate first.' He lifted a laptop out of the rucksack between his knees.

Rhys stayed quiet while Gil found an MP4 file and played it. A minute of footage appeared on the screen.

A young boy, around four or five years old, sat on a bed with two toys – a green dinosaur with a toothsome smile and a Buzz Lightyear figure. He moved them across the bedspread, making Buzz fly while the dinosaur walked below. Though the boy wore typical children's clothes – jeans and a T-shirt – his face remained expressionless throughout the video, never showing a hint of joy in his play.

At the edge of the screen, a hand appeared and snatched at the toys. The boy made no move to stop what was happening. His eyes became large ovals, his mouth a downturned crescent of despondency.

Whatever happened had happened before, and the boy knew better than to try to stop it.

Rhys turned his eyes to Gil. 'Why are we watching that, Gil? I've seen it before.'

'Not as many times as I have.' Gil's reply emerged as a growl.

'You think it's Freddie Sillitoe. I get that.'

'What else did you get?'

Rhys's eyes flickered to the screen again. A matchboard wall, the top of a stairwell. Familiar. Too familiar.

Gil read his thoughts. 'The same bed, the same matchboard wall, and the same stairwell as in that Crogloft cottage in front of us.'

Rhys's eyes narrowed. 'But we know that because Moyles shot the video. Right?'

'Right,' Gil said, his tone suggesting there was more. 'What else?'

Rhys looked down and then back up again.

Despite Gil's flippancy regarding most things, here he was

being straight. Sometimes, Warlow did the same. Teachable moments, he called these.

'Not alone. There were other kids. The snatching hand was a kid's. And from the way the boy reacts, it suggests older kids. He knew better than to object.'

Gil's lips tightened in approval.

'Then maybe it's a family,' Rhys suggested. 'Doesn't that argue for it not being Freddie Sillitoe?'

'Perhaps.' Gil switched to a different file. A file with a different image of Freddie provided by his family. A family pulverised by what they'd been through, still going through, after years of hope and despair. That knowledge seemed to seep through the screen.

Gil played the video again.

'There's an age discrepancy. Hair colour is different, too. But it could be the same kid,' Rhys said.

'Agreed.' Gil nodded. 'And I also agree we can't be one hundred percent certain. The 2-D photo is not the same as the 3-D video. You can't compare expressions. And the smile from the static is not repeated at any point in the video.'

'No. But I see where you're going with this, Sarge.'

'I think it's him. I think Freddie was in this cottage at some point.' Gil closed the laptop, his movements deliberate, like handling evidence of a crime – which, in a way, he was.

'But you've said nothing to the parents?'

'How can we without being sure?'

'Okay,' Rhys said after a moment. 'Shall we?'

Gil didn't respond. He stared out at the cottage, its innocuous exterior belying the horrors it had witnessed.

'Sometimes, I wonder why the hell we do this job,' he whispered.

Rhys understood all too well. 'Mr Warlow says it's because someone has to.'

Gil opened the door. 'Come on, let's perambulate.'

They revisited the open loft, its sloping sides forcing them to hunch. Only where the roof peaked in the middle could they stand somewhat upright. At least Gil could. Rhys had to do his impression of Igor, Frankenstein's assistant, instead.

Gil pointed to the central ceiling light. 'Remember that Moyles had the cameras here.'

He moved his finger to a spot on the bed. 'I reckon the boy sat here.' Then to the side. 'Which meant the arm came from this side.'

Rhys shook his head. 'You're right.' He shuddered. 'Gives me the creeps being here. I keep having visions of a strung-up Moyles. But I think I'm more freaked out by that video you showed me.'

Gil gave him a half-smile without an iota of mirth. 'That's because you're a normal human being with a good heart, Rhys. And you're standing on the edge of a dark place, staring in.' He turned towards the stairs. 'Come on, let's go outside.'

They strolled the perimeter, crossed the boundary wall, and headed along a path over the moor to stand and peruse the property. No access visible other than that single narrow lane they'd driven up. They crossed fields to a copse, walked through it and back around. They met no one, saw no sign of life. Or paths or roads.

'It's well named, *Cân-y-Barcud*,' Rhys said as a red kite swirled overhead, its forked tail a giveaway, its whistling call eerie and lamenting.

*Barcud* was the Welsh word for kite. *Cân* the word for song.

'I don't think whoever brought this child here was motivated by birdwatching,' Gil muttered. 'I think he was here exactly because this place is isolated and not overlooked. There's only one way in, one way out.'

Rhys focussed on the bird. 'What was the name of the site this place was listed on again?'

'NON,' Gil answered without hesitation. 'No One Near.'

'They got that right,' Rhys muttered.

'They certainly did,' Gil agreed, his voice barely above a whisper.

The red kite circled, keening out its cry once more.

Although they'd found nothing new in terms of evidence on paying a visit to this place, they left it with something changed. A new sense of purpose.

A resolve.

'Next stop?' Gil asked.

'Lead on, Mac—'

'Donald's. Yes, I know. It's coffee time.'

———

In the town of Whitland on the borders of Pembrokeshire and Carmarthenshire, Geraint Lane studied the modified prologue of his book. He'd spent the morning reworking it for the serialisation and was now satisfied.

*I still remember the chill that ran down my spine when I first saw Roger Hunt's face – the hollow, dark eyes that seemed to seethe with quiet rage above the beard, the features distorted with a bitterness that bordered on madness.*

*Within moments, I would be bound and staring down the barrel of his gun, just as the three men he brutally murdered must have done before me.*

*The story began with whispers. Whispers of Roger Hunt's down-fall, a man once on the cusp of fame. He believed that Royston Moyles, John Napier, and Daniel Hughes had conspired against him, secretly filming an intimate moment between him and his lover, a scandalous video they'd leaked which had ruined his career.*

*Whether true or imagined, the betrayal festered in Hunt's psyche until it became an obsession, then a murderous rampage.*

*Daniel Hughes – a possible but unproven cog in the sordid machine that had led to Hunt's fury – was another victim. Tossed like a doll over a railway bridge. Hughes had been left with life-changing injuries, in a coma from which he never recovered. Hughes had lived in the shadows, operating behind layers of anonymity in the underbelly of the black market.*

*John Napier's fate was even more horrifying. A man respected in his community. A man of law, known for his slick charisma and connections. Napier's life had almost ended in a cemetery at a hidden church on the outskirts of the town in which he lived. Almost roasted alive by Hunt's crazed need for vengeance. Napier was lucky to survive that attempt. Not so lucky when the pipe bomb Hunt constructed tore the flesh from Napier's bones several months later.*

The third victim, and the instigator of Hunt's shame, had died horribly after being tortured and strangled in a remote Welsh cottage, a scene that would forever be burned into my memory. And in that cottage is where my life finally intersected with the madman.

Royston Moyles was a man whose perversions led to his downfall. Pity those innocents who found his bound and bloodied body strung up in the infamous property he advertised as a haven of peace and tranquillity. A property he'd rigged to satisfy his addictive urges.

Hunt had left no note, no warning – only the broken body of a man who had played a part in his humiliation.

What haunted the investigators, and me, as I followed the case, was Hunt's grim precision and meticulous planning.

Hunt wasn't sloppy. He left no trace, no fingerprints, only devastation.

And yet, with Hunt forced to dabble with explosives in order to finish his work, his deal with the devil led ultimately to his demise and an end no one could have predicted. Certainly not yours truly.

But to understand, we need to go back. To a point when I was deep in my investigation, piecing together the thread of Hunt's movements. That was when I found myself at Cân-y-Barcud, a secluded cottage. Accompanying me was Sergeant Catrin Richards, a woman who had spent years fighting her way through the misogyny of the police service, only to find herself now at the mercy of Hunt's gun.

The moment we stepped through that door, Hunt was waiting. A predator lying in ambush.

The gunshot that rang out when Hunt fired into the ceiling was deafening. The shock sent both of us cowering on the floor.

Richards tried to reason with him, but there was no reasoning with a man who had descended so deep into his own delusions.

He made me tie her hands – his eyes never leaving Richards – as if he was more afraid of her than of me, the journalist who had spent months tracking him down.

What followed was a true living nightmare.

Hunt forced Richards into her own car at gunpoint, leaving me tethered to the staircase and beaten almost senseless. As I heard the car engine roar to life and watched them disappear into the distance, my mind swirled with a mix of terror and guilt.

*Hunt's words echoed in my head. Words uttered to the police sergeant he was abducting and referring to me: "You don't need to worry about a piece of filth like him."*

*Was I next on his list, or was I simply collateral damage in a deadly game of revenge?*

*But what Hunt didn't realise was that Richards, for all her vulnerability, had already lost the fight. An officer who had struggled against the unfair treatment of women and the problems within the police force.*

*Her scars ran deep. She had spent her career proving herself against a tide of bigotry that sought to undermine her at every turn. And now, she was in the hands of a monster.*

*Though Hunt's reign of terror eventually ended, the wounds left behind remain wide open. The scars Sergeant Richards bears are not only from the hands of a man who saw her as a pawn in his demented quest for "closure" but from the very institution meant to protect her.*

*She had endured years of systemic sexism, fighting not only criminals but also the chauvinistic attitudes deeply ingrained in the UK police service.*

*And what of the investigation that allowed this man to slip through the cracks for so long? What of the forces at play that failed to protect Moyles, Napier, and Hughes before Hunt reached them?*

*The truth is simple – this was no mere case of a man lost in his personal tragedy. It was a damning indictment of a broken system, a police service riddled with incompetence, and a government more interested in covering its own tracks than in protecting its citizens.*

*In the pages that follow, I delve deeper into the institutional failures that enabled Hunt to roam free, a predator stalking his prey, knowing that the system was too inept to stop him.*

*From top-ranking officers to the very heart of the Home Office, the rot runs deep. Policies enabled by the incompetent governments of recent years have bled the police forces dry, forcing budget cuts and eroding trust in our public services.*

*Sergeant Catrin Richards is one of many victims – not just of Roger Hunt, but of the systemic negligence that permeates every level of those entrusted with our safety.*

*How many more women, how many more citizens, will be sacrificed on the altar of political ineptitude before we see real change?*

*The blood of Moyles, Napier, and Hughes is not confined to Roger Hunt's hands. It stains the hands of every official who allowed the system to fail, and it will continue to do so unless we demand accountability.*

'Right, Jasper, you tart,' Lane muttered. He slid the file over to an email. 'Take a look at that and weep.'

# CHAPTER FOURTEEN

TUESDAY

Olwen Napier lived in a substantial property north of the bypass. Not modern, but one of those whitewashed solid houses set in several acres. Though only a couple of miles from the town centre, the land around gave way to rolling pasture and hedgerow.

The turning Gil took was marked by thick, black iron gates. Beyond the bars, the original two-storey farmhouse had been added to and improved over the years.

'Nice gaff,' Rhys observed.

And it was. Though Napier was no longer around to enjoy the spoils. Of course, it was one reason Financial Crimes remained highly interested in the case. If they proved embezzlement, the property would likely be classified as ill-gotten gains, in which case Olwen Napier might have to find somewhere else, probably significantly smaller, to live.

Gil parked across from Napier's old Jag – once the solicitor's pride and joy.

'When was the last time you saw Mrs Napier, Gil?'

'At the funeral,' Gil said.

Rhys had the sense not to pursue this. He didn't need to because Gil had his teeth on the bit.

'And before that, I held her as we watched what was left

of her husband bleed into the ground after Hunt's pipe bomb blew him to smithereens. Oh, yes. Olwen Napier and I have shared some special moments.'

Rhys put his hand on the door handle, ready to get out. 'So, how are we going to play this?'

'Brutal honesty,' Gil replied.

The sound of Tonks, the Napiers' dog, told Gil someone was home when he rang the bell positioned on the frame of a shiny black varnished door. No UPVC here.

Shushing noises filtered through, then the door opened.

Olwen had aged since Gil had last seen her. She'd lost a couple of stone. In some women in their mid-sixties, that sort of thing helped. But in Olwen's case, it had resulted in a shrunken, almost gaunt appearance. An appearance which tailored slacks and pearls hanging over an expensive cashmere turtleneck could not dispel.

'Olwen,' Gil said.

'Oh, my God. It's you.'

The sentiment behind the words was hard to gauge. There was no question about the surprise, but was it coloured by horror or relief?

'Olwen,' Gil began again.

But she put a hand over her mouth in shock. The dog, tail wagging now, circled Gil and Rhys's feet. After a couple of seconds, Olwen took the hand from her mouth and fluttered it into an unspoken invitation to enter.

The place was an old building well cared for. Inside, more of the same. Tasteful furnishings, some antique.

Gil counted at least three grandfather clocks on his way through the big hall to a light-filled room at the rear that looked out onto a sloping lawn ending in trees.

The Napiers had money.

Whether it was all their own was a totally different matter.

'Good to see you, Gil,' Olwen said, a tremor in her voice. 'It's nice to see a friendly face.'

She stepped forward and hugged Gil. Then she stood back and held a hand out.

'Olwen, this is Rhys Harries, one of our DCs,' Gil said.

Rhys took the hand that was offered.

'Tea?' Olwen asked.

'Wouldn't say no,' Gil said.

She disappeared into a kitchen. From there came the noises of a kettle being filled and a chink of cups.

'How are you holding up, Olwen?' Gil called out.

'Just about,' she said. 'The kids are great but… you know how it is.'

'I do.'

'Tell me you're not here to ask questions about John?'

'I'd be lying if I said I wasn't,' Gil said. 'But this is nothing to do with the books.'

Olwen answered from the other room.

'This is to do with Royston Moyles.'

'Then that'll be bad enough,' Olwen said.

'I've been examining Moyles's papers, and now that we've had access to your husband's notes, I wanted to ask you something.'

Olwen came back in with a tray, a teapot, and three cups. But her expression was now one of frowning concern.

'We've got some entries in diaries and calendars that we can't reconcile. Do the initials PP mean anything to you?'

She frowned.

Gil took out his phone. He had some images there of a wall calendar that hung in Moyles's office and some images of entries in the office diaries he now had access to in Napier's office. 'See this? Sometimes where there's PP, there is a BN written as well. Any idea what that might mean?'

Olwen reached for some glasses that were on the table next to an open magazine and slid them on. She peered at Gil's phone. 'BN? Let me think about that. Doesn't bring much to mind immediately.'

'Take your time.'

Gil asked about the children. Olwen was a grandmother.

She told him that things had been difficult. Children were finding the case against their father hard to accept. Many of her friends had stopped coming to see her, although there were one or two who had remained loyal.

There wasn't much more to add. The explosion at the Napiers' cottage in Angle wasn't discussed. They didn't talk about what had happened to her husband there. They didn't talk about the investigation into her husband's fraudulent activities.

Rhys played with the dog.

Halfway through, something happened to Olwen's face. It lit up.

'Show me again.' She pointed to his phone.

Gil obliged.

She scrolled through two entries. 'Yes, there. BN, third in the month? Means boys' night. They played cards together. Him, Royston, and Daniel Hughes.'

A faint smile finally crossed Gil's face.

They finished their tea in companionable silence, said their thanks, and took their leave, knowing there was nothing more to be said.

In the car, Rhys spoke. 'She was glad to see you.'

'She's having a rough time of it.'

'There's always a chance she knew what was going on.'

'Spoken like a true copper,' Gil said.

'But that stuff, BN, that wasn't what you wanted to hear, was it?'

'No. And boys' night sounds all wrong, but they were a close bunch. She may be making it up, but somehow, I don't think so.'

'So, where does that leave us?'

'Not much further forward.'

Rhys headed out through the black gates. 'Got to say, as days out go, I've had better ones.'

'Next time, I'll let you go on the swings and the slide, I promise.' Gil glanced at his wrist. 'I suppose it would be greedy to pop into Llandeilo for another cuppa. We've just had one.'

'Ah,' Rhys said. 'But that one did not have a custard slice to go with it. Mr Warlow always stops for a CS if we're in Llandeilo.'

'Okay. Tea at mine it is. I'll get the Lady Anwen to put the kettle on. I need to call in and fetch something anyway.'

Rhys grinned. 'And I'll call in for a couple of CSs on the way.'

'Not for me.'

'No? You off your food, Gil?'

'If I'm forced to watch you eat a CS, I will be. For the rest of the day, most likely. Besides, it'll show Anwen that I'm trying.'

Rhys, in a terrible American accent, said, 'So, I'm going to be your patsy, huh?'

Gil settled back in his seat. 'What you get up to in your spare time is your business, Rhys. No judgement.'

Rhys flailed, impaled on the horns of unintended meaning. 'No, patsy's American slang. It doesn't mean… I wasn't… '

Gil cut him off with a lazy wave. 'Take a right here. Shortcut. And yes, I know what a patsy is. Now focus on the road and, for clarity's sake, I will be happy to use any pronoun you like when addressing you in the office. I am as broad-minded as the next… officer, as you well know.'

———

JESS WAS at her desk when Catrin hurried over, phone in hand.

'It's Tannard. She's up at Ford's property.'

Catrin had the crime scene investigator on a video call, suited up in fetching white Tyvek but with her hood down.

Jess and Tannard smiled at one another as Catrin leaned the phone against the monitor.

'Anything?' Jess asked.

'First impressions are that it's clean. And I don't mean that in forensic speak. What I mean is someone has done a great job in actually cleansing this place from a forensic stand-point. Didn't you say Ford did some cleaning?'

'I did,' Jess agreed.

Tannard walked through to the kitchen. 'Good. Then she

knows what she is doing. But I'm talking about another level here. There's hardly any dust. And we've tested for bleach on every touchable surface. Someone has been scrupulous.'

'Maybe she had a thing about germs?' Catrin suggested, more as a question than anything else.

'No fingerprints?' Jess asked.

'Yes, fingerprints on the fridge, toilet flush. Where you'd expect to find them. But I'll put money on them being Ford's.'

It was a curious thing to say, and Jess asked her why.

'To make it appear less of a dry-cleaning job.'

'Right. You're saying someone might have been there and cleaned up after themselves?'

Tannard looked straight back at Catrin. 'I am. But we found a few things of note.'

She went back to the lounge and to a double socket on a dividing wall separating the living room from the kitchen. 'There is a bit of dust on the floor under this socket. Easily missed in a cursory sweep.'

She angled the phone so that the officers could see.

And indeed, there was a fine sprinkling of whitish powder on the carpet just under the plastic socket housing.

'So, we unscrewed it.' Tannard's gloved hand reached for the housing above and below. She pulled it free to reveal the white facing and a black box behind. 'It's a wall safe. Key fits into the hole for the plugs, and the front slides out. Your very own safe deposit box.'

'Empty?' Jess asked.

'Just like the rest of this place. Clean as a whistle. We'll swab it, of course.'

'Why would a cleaner have a hidden safe?' Catrin asked.

Tannard turned the phone around so that they could see her face. 'The same question I was asking myself. We looked again.'

The image shifted drunkenly as Tannard moved back through the kitchen to a tiny laundry-cum-mudroom. From there, she picked up a swivel bin.

'This was how we found it. Not empty, but with some food packaging inside. Some of it dated, which might help you know where she shopped.' Tannard took the top off the bin and then removed the plastic liner and tipped the whole thing upside down. 'Very easy to miss this, too.'

She walked into the well-lit kitchen and set the camera down at floor level before laying the now-empty bin on its side. Using a screwdriver jammed into a groove not visible to the officers, she prised open the black plastic base of the bin. It yielded with a pop and out tumbled a blue plastic bag.

Tannard, obviously enjoying the theatrics and having already done all of this once, unwrapped the plastic food bag to reveal the contents.

Jess was slightly disappointed by the absence of a "Ta-da".

The money was in neat bundles held together by elastic bands.

'How much?' Catrin asked.

'Just over three thousand.'

'And are you suggesting someone searched the property, found the socket lockbox, and missed this?'

Tannard stood and retrieved her phone, setting it down on the kitchen worktop, propped up to allow her to speak to camera. 'Classic misdirection. My guess is there might have been some money in the lockbox. Someone finding that might not search any further. Probably why they missed the bin.'

'Are we looking at her savings here?'

'It's a thought. But let me finish the full sweep, and I'll have a report for you by tomorrow.'

'Great job,' Jess said.

'Thanks.' Tannard grinned. 'I quite enjoyed it. Makes a big change from decomposing bodies.'

# CHAPTER FIFTEEN

TUESDAY

Warlow had found over the years that cold and flu – man flu especially – got worse towards the end of the day. Whether that was a confabulation dreamt up by his aching brain or not, it was certainly true today.

Buchannan's anodyne, the one that suggested he might be better in twenty-four hours, had not come to fruition.

Bottom line, by late morning, he felt worse. A lot worse. His chest hurt when he breathed. Doing anything much took a lot of aching effort. He tried taking Cadi out and got as far as the top of the lane. Once he got there, a bout of shivering made him turn around, much to the dog's disgust.

Warlow gritted his teeth, frustrated by his own weakness. He was a man who prided himself on resilience, on pushing through discomfort. He turned back towards the house, each step a battle against the shudders wracking his body, and voiced a note of self-recrimination.

'Come on,' he grumbled. 'It's just a bit of flu.'

But even as the words left his lips, a nagging voice in the back of his mind whispered that this was different and he should stop pretending it wasn't.

He'd tried sleeping, but his skin felt oddly warm, despite a core coldness that two blankets could not dispel. He recognised this as a fever and knew he should have checked his temperature. But he was of an age and generation where keeping a thermometer handy for health never registered as important. In his mind, that was a step towards admitting vulnerability, something he'd spent a lifetime avoiding.

He'd always been the one others leant on, the steady rock in turbulent waters. The idea of being the one in need of care was foreign, almost disturbing.

Another wave of chills washed over him, and he pushed away the creeping thought that maybe it was time to let someone else take the helm for a while.

At 2:25 that afternoon, Warlow made an executive decision. Having secured sod all help from his local GP practice, and after finding a few red flecks on the tissue he held up in front of his face following a violent bout of coughing, he decided it might be time to call the cavalry.

Jenny Batson didn't wear a uniform, and she didn't ride a horse. Parallels with mounted troopers stopped with the colour blue, which, like Custer's men, was the shade of scrubs she wore. She answered his call with a message that asked him to leave a number and she would phone him back.

This she did, forty minutes later. Jenny, the HIV clinic liaison nurse, took no prisoners. She listened to Warlow's apologetic greeting, kept quiet when it broke down in a fit of coughing, then quizzed him about his symptoms.

'I take it you've seen your GP?' she asked.

'Tried. I have a phone call booked tomorrow.'

'Then you need to get down here, ASAP.'

'By here, you mean where you are? Swansea?'

'Yes, to Dr Emerson's clinic.'

'But surely—'

'Don't call me Shirley,' Jenny said.

An ancient joke, but one that made Warlow smile.

He trod on the laugh that threatened for fear of triggering another convulsive coughing bout.

'Is that strictly necessary?' he said.

'You're asking for my advice. That's my advice. This could be nothing. It may be something we need to pay attention to.

If your immune system has taken a holiday, who knows? Best we check. And we offer a VIP service for our favourite patients.'

'So, how come I get to be seen?' Warlow's stab at humour did not elicit a laugh, but at least it got some recognition.

'Lovely to hear you haven't lost your sense of humour, Evan.'

'It's doing an excellent job of playing hard to find.'

'Can someone bring you?' Jenny asked.

'I'll find a way.'

Jenny Batson took that at face value. If she had realised what he'd really meant by that statement – that he would drive himself – she would probably have screamed blue murder.

With good reason.

One part of him, the part that had always been fiercely independent, rebelled against the idea of worrying Jess.

'She's got enough on her plate,' he reasoned, ignoring the way the room seemed to tilt when he stood.

Another part, a quieter part he usually suppressed, whispered that it might be nice to have someone else to lean on, just this once. But old habits die hard, and Warlow, ever the protector, decided he'd handle this on his own, as he always had. And, he reasoned, if he called her, she would probably have dropped everything and come home to Nevern to play taxi.

No need for that.

And so, Warlow fed Cadi, apologised to her with some extra hugs, and got into the Jeep.

The winter solstice had just passed. Warlow needed no reminder that this was the darkest time of the year.

Light clung to a grey afternoon when he left, but by the time he got to Singleton Hospital, darkness had fallen. Oncoming headlights hurt his eyes. He had to force himself to concentrate. His bouts of coughing made negotiating traffic dangerous.

If he'd been stopped, they would have arrested him for being ill in charge of a motor vehicle. And even though no such charge existed, Warlow thought they probably should've made one up.

But he made it.

When Jenny saw him, she expressed genuine surprise. When Emerson saw him, she called him an idiot.

Warlow liked both of them for their honesty.

And despite the fog of fever clouding his mind, he couldn't help but notice the concern etched on Jenny's face and the exasperation in Emerson's.

He straightened his back, summoning what little energy he had left to project an air of nonchalance.

'It's not as bad as it looks. Which is a strong contender for an epitaph.' His words were punctuated by a cough that left him hot and gasping. Even as he fought to maintain his composure, a small part of him felt touched by their obvious worry.

Or was that pure bravado on his part?

Either way, they told him they needed to do some "tests" and to be prepared to stay.

When he did text Jess that evening, as she was on the point of leaving work, it was via a message that he took some time to compose. Partly because the oxygen mask he was wearing kept oozing O2 and drying out his eyes, and partly because he didn't want to scare her. But when he finally finished the paragraph, it was, he had to admit, a masterpiece of understatement – crafted to reassure and not to alarm, he believed.

> Jess. Felt worse. Called Nurse Jenny at
> Singleton. She suggested I popped down.
> They're keeping me in to do some tests. X-rays
> and bloods. Cadi's been fed. Christmas tree
> will have to wait :)

It reached its intended recipient at 6:10, sent from the Medical Assessment Unit, which was where Emerson had admitted Warlow until they did the needful tests. Unsurprisingly, this message achieved almost the complete opposite of its intent.

Fifteen seconds after sending it, Jess phoned.

'What is going on, Evan?'

'Man flu turns out to be pneumonia, they say. Single, not double. You know me, everything in moderation, so I lucked out there.' He wheezed out the words.

'Pneumonia? But… how?'

'One of the great mysteries of the universe,' he said.

'I doubt I'll be home tonight. They're paving the way…' He stopped to cough for a minute. 'Seducing me with words like IV antibiotics and oxygen. I mean, how can I turn that down?'

'Shit, Evan.' Jess's words contained a smidgen of exasperation. 'Why didn't you ring me earlier?'

'No need.'

'Yes, need. Bloody hell, need. I meant it when I said you're not Superman. Right, I'm heading down. What can I bring?'

'Nothing. I need nothing.'

'Of course you do. A toothbrush, at least.'

'Okay. A toothbrush, maybe. Change of underwear, too. But there's no need to—' Another hacking cough cut him off.

Jess waited. 'What were you going to say? No need to what? Be concerned? To look after you?'

Warlow shut up at that.

'You're very kind,' he said finally.

'I'm the very worried kind. I need to see you for reassurance. And I'll bring reinforcements.'

'Molly doesn't need to know, does she?' The sentence was split by a splutter.

'Of course she does. She'd be livid if I didn't tell her.'

More silence.

'I know you're allergic to fuss,' Jess said. 'This is not fuss. My God, Evan. You're not made of Teflon.'

'More carbon… carbon steel, I thought.'

'Not funny.'

'I thought it was pretty…' Another splutter. 'Solid…' Splutter. 'Under the…' Splutter. 'Circumstances.'

'Want me to bring food?'

'I'm not hungry. Honestly.'

'Okay. You're in the MAU?'

They'd both visited Medical Assessment Units enough times, following victims and perpetrators, to not need the acronym spelt out.

'I did say that… only once…' Another cough. 'Must be the detective in you.'

'Shut up. I'll see you soon.'

'Thanks, Jess. How's work?'

'Guess what? We think someone's been murdered. Listening to your shenanigans, I'm minded to add to the total.'

'Wow. It's wrong to mock the afflicted.'

'Just watch me.'

Warlow ended the call and leaned back against the pillows, a mix of emotions washing over him. There was gratitude, warm and unfamiliar, at Jess's unwavering support. But it was tinged with embarrassment and a touch of frustration at his own helplessness.

This was unfamiliar territory, needing help. He'd always been the pillar for the boys, his sons, as their mother descended into her vodka underworld.

And yet, as another coughing fit gripped him, he found comfort in the thought that someone was on their way. Perhaps, he reflected, as exhaustion closed in, there was truth in letting others be strong on your behalf.

It was a novel thought, one that Warlow, in his weakened state, found himself too tired to push away. But there was another text he needed to send. To Tom, the sensible son. The doctor.

He'd probably want to talk to Emerson, too.

He still had his phone in his hand and tried to recompose the text but instead dialled the number.

'Tom, it's Dad,' Warlow said, the effort of speaking clearly taxing.

There was a pause on the other end of the line before Tom replied, concern clear in his voice. 'You okay? You sound a bit… rough.'

Warlow attempted a chuckle, which turned into a suppressed cough. 'A good enough description, since I'm lying in a bed in MAU in Singleton with a touch of pneumonia.'

Somehow, he managed that whole sentence without coughing but then gave in to a fresh salvo, his body shaking with the effort.

'How the hell did that happen?'

*What was it with these people seeking to make him accountable?* Warlow thought.

Between laboured breaths, Warlow quipped, 'You're the doctor. You tell me.'

'Is Dr Emerson looking after you?'

'And a chest guy.' Warlow paused, gathering strength. 'They're doing tests. I think I'll be staying in.'

'I'll come down.'

'No. No need.' Warlow's tone softened, a mix of stubbornness and parental concern. 'I'll get Emerson to ring you once they've got whatever it is they need to do. She's offered.'

'Are you sure, Dad?'

'Yeah.' Warlow's gaze drifted to someone twitching the curtains around his bed. 'Look, someone's approaching me with a trolley. I have to go. Will you let your brother know? And do not worry. I am in good hands.'

'Okay.' Tom hesitated. 'I have Emerson's number. She gave it to me a while back.'

Warlow should not have been surprised; doctors had their own creed. But good to know his son had connections here.

'Right. I'll keep in touch,' Warlow said, his voice fading as fatigue set in.

'Take it easy, Dad. And try to be a good patient.'

'Message received.'

A nurse appeared with a trolley and a drip stand. 'Stay where you are, I'll be back in a sec.'

A quip threatened. But instead, he nodded again and closed his eyes.

*Try to be a good patient.*

He'd give it a shot.

# CHAPTER SIXTEEN

TUESDAY NIGHT

It was Rhys's turn to make supper in the house he shared with Gina in Tabernacle Terrace in Carmarthen Town. This evening, he'd kept things simple with a recipe from his favourite book, *The Bung It in a Tin* book. Tonight would be a hearty one-pan chicken and chorizo bake. He'd called in to a supermarket for chicken thighs and got them on special offer. The chorizo, vegetables, and beans were already in the larder. He'd roast them together with some spices for a simple, flavourful meal that both he and Gina liked.

He'd got home well before her. She was still supporting the parents of that OD over in Ammanford.

When she did get home, she changed into a sweatshirt and yoga pants. Because Gina liked to have the house toasty, Rhys, even in December, often ended up wearing a T-shirt and shorts. This evening was no exception, with the added protection of an apron sporting the face of a dog.

'Smells delish,' Gina said, sidling up to him as he stood near the sink.

'Ready in two—' Rhys's phone chimed with a message. He glanced at it.

'Do we need any sauces on the table?' Gina asked.

'No, I don't think it'll—'

Gina had her back to him. Intrigued, she turned around. 'What's wrong?'

Rhys didn't answer immediately.

'Rhys?' she repeated.

'It's from Jess Allanby. On the team chat. It's about the Wolf.'

Gina froze. She knew Warlow had been ill. When Rhys finally let his eyes drift up to engage hers, he blinked and said, 'He's in hospital. Pneumonia.'

'Oh, my God. I thought… The way your face changed…'

'How do you get pneumonia?' Rhys asked numbly.

'Why don't you ask Jess?'

Rhys's eyebrows twitched almost imperceptibly, a flicker of emotion crossing his face.

Gina had spent some time with both Catrin and Jess Allanby outside of work, forging connections that Rhys hadn't. He felt a touch of discomfort with the casual use of their Christian names, a subtle reminder of the boundaries between personal and professional life that were now blurring.

'I suppose I should.'

'You have to.'

Rhys didn't move.

Gina observed his hesitation and pressed on. 'If you don't, I will.'

Rhys glanced at the table, the carefully laid-out settings now seeming absurdly trivial.

'Should we eat first?' he asked.

Gina shook her head emphatically. 'Of course not. Neither of us are going to eat anything until you find out what's happening.'

Rhys nodded with a mixture of relief and dread. 'You're right.'

Steeling himself for what he might hear, he dialled Jess Allanby's number.

———

GIL WAS at home on grandfather duty. Both of his daughters were at their Pilates class, which they attended together, and the Lady Anwen was at a book club. Gil had been entertaining his granddaughters by reading from a book of Welsh folk tales.

The girls were all on the sofa listening to him read, but really listening to him do all the voices, much to their giggly delight.

Gil got the same group text as Rhys. Immediately, he ceased all grandfather interactions.

'Sorry, girls. Work.'

'Aw, *Tadcu*, why are you always working?' The question came from Eleri, almost eight years old, shop steward of the granddaughters' union and self-appointed spokesperson.

'Because if I didn't work, my three granddaughters would starve. Plus, Santa has started charging for hay for the reindeer. And hay doesn't grow on trees, you know?'

Eleri considered this for all of four seconds. 'No, it grows in fields, silly. Before it's cut and put in big bales. We played hide and seek behind the bales in a field at Lisa Dion's birthday party. Lisa's daddy has a farm.'

'Ee-I-ee-I-oh.'

'No, that's Old Macdonald.'

'I always get that wrong. Like the donkey. Ee-aw, ee-aw, ee-always gets it wrong, too. How about you watch some *Bluey* until I finish my work call?'

A chorus of approving "Yays" followed from all on the shop floor.

Gil rang Jess and got an engaged signal, but she rang back five minutes later and told him exactly what she'd told Rhys a few moments before.

'Pneumonia?' Gil said. 'He can't have a simple chest infection like everybody else?'

'They're keeping him in.'

'Should have happened years ago. That place where you can have fun with ECT. Safe to ring him?'

'Probably not. I think they're doing a CT or an MRI now.'

'Such an attention-seeker, that man. Looks like we'll have to do Secret Santa without him this year, then.'

'It looks that way.'

But Gil registered Jess's concern and reined in the bluff insults. 'How are you holding up?'

'I'll find out when Molly gets here. She'll be the first to tell me.'

'Then I'll leave you to it. Tell him I'll be down in the morning.'

'I will.'

Gil, who'd stepped out of the living room to take the call, stepped back in to see his spot on the sofa occupied by three of the most important people in his life. And all he could do was shake his head.

The news about Warlow had shocked him. Not only because it meant that the old bugger wasn't invincible, but because it underlined something Gil had realised watching the three people in his charge grow.

Time, always precious, was becoming a priceless commodity. Wisdom was knowing how best to spend it.

The kids would be here in front of the TV for a while. He could happily have read the paper or even found something to watch on a TV in a different room.

He did none of those things.

Instead, he made the girls scooch over and sat with them, while a blue dog with ADHD navigated her charming way through the universe.

'*Ti'n licio Bluey, Tadcu?*' Eleri asked, wanting to know if he liked Bluey.

'*Ydw. Y ci glas gore' yn y byd.*'

'*Odi.*' Eleri grinned and, being the closest to him, snuggled into his arm.

No need to lie here. Bluey was indeed his and Eleri's favourite blue dog in the whole wide world.

———

THE HOSPITAL'S sterile fluorescent lights showed no mercy, bleaching Warlow's pale, sick face. He lay propped in bed, an IV drip snaking into his arm, an oxygen mask obscuring his features. Monitors beeped on low volume, tracking two other patients in the room under similar circumstances.

Molly hesitated at the doorway. She'd come straight from her shift at the Mumbles ice cream parlour, a padded coat over her jeans. The scent of sugar and waffle cones clung to her, stronger even than the eau de chlorhexidine aroma of the hospital.

'Hiya,' she said as she stepped into the room. 'Mum's getting us tea. You look like hell.'

Warlow's eyes crinkled at the corners, a smile hidden beneath the mask. She was her mother's daughter, this one.

He lifted a hand weakly in greeting.

Molly pulled up a chair and sat close to the bed. 'Jess said you've got pneumonia. Bit dramatic, isn't it? Couldn't you just catch a cold like a normal person?'

Warlow dragged his mask aside briefly. 'Got to keep things interesting,' he rasped, his voice barely above a whisper. 'Besides, thought it would make Christmas a bit more entertaining.'

Molly rolled her eyes, but there was genuine concern beneath her bravado. 'Well, mission accomplished there, so, well done. You've got Jess in a right state.'

'Have I? Jess doesn't get into states from what I've seen.'

'Well, I was in Manchester when Ricky left. I have the "seeing Jess in a state" T-shirt, and it's one I dislike wearing. So, I can recognise it when it appears.'

'And you?' Warlow asked, eyebrow raised.

'Me? I'm fine,' Molly said, though perhaps a bit too quickly. 'Takes more than a stubborn old DCI with dodgy lungs to worry me, Evan.'

Warlow almost chuckled but clamped down, knowing how it might trigger a cough. 'Good to know. I'll have to try harder next time.'

'Don't you dare,' Molly said.

'Too soon?'

Molly dropped her chin to look up at him with disdain, and they sat in silence for a moment before he cleared his throat; a rattling sound that made Molly wince.

'At least,' he said eventually, 'I've worked out what to put on my epitaph. "Here lies Evan Warlow who finally shut up."'

The words had barely left his mouth when Molly's composure crumbled. Tears welled up, and before Warlow could react, she'd thrown her arms around him, burying her face in his shoulder.

'Don't even joke about leaving. Not you, too,' she cried, her voice muffled and thick with emotion.

Warlow's heart clenched. God, he could be an insensitive idiot. He stretched out his IV-free arm and grabbed her hand.

'Hey, I'm not going anywhere. Take no notice of me. I never could read the room. This is only pneumonia. I'll be back walking Cadi in no time.'

Molly turned away to wipe her eyes. 'Promise?'

'Totes,' Warlow said. He tried a sentence, punctuated by coughs. 'Doctor says I should respond to the antibiotics within twenty-four hours. They know it's strep... streptococcal. Nothing... exotic. I might be stuck here over Christmas, but I'll be back to my miserable self before you know it.'

Molly sniffed. 'Good. Because I was going to cancel my trip to Italy for New Year's if—'

'Absolutely not! You've been looking forward to that... for months. I won't have you... missing out on winter in Italy on my account.'

'But—'

'No buts,' Warlow said firmly. 'You're going, and that's... final. Besides, who else is going to bring me back some proper... Primitivo?'

Molly managed a watery smile. 'Fine. But I'm bringing you a drumstick on Christmas Day. I doubt lunch here will be cordon bleu.'

'Probably not even... cordon yellow.'

Jess appeared in the doorway. She took in the scene before her, registering Molly's red-rimmed eyes and Warlow's concerned expression.

'Everything all right?' she asked.

'Fine, Mum,' Molly gave Warlow a quick peck on the cheek. 'Just sorting out Christmas lunch for the chief inspector. I have one shift left tomorrow. Now I need a shower to wash off the smell of bubble-gum ice cream. I'll see you at home in a couple of days.'

'Don't you want your tea?'

'Of course I do.' Molly took the offered cup.

Once she'd left, Jess turned to Warlow, one eyebrow raised. 'What was that about?'

Warlow sighed, settling back against his pillows. 'Seems I might have underestimated the effect I have on impressionable young minds. Your daughter included.'

Jess shook her head, a fond smile playing at her lips. 'Really? I've told you before, you are in a unique group of one. A male role model she actually likes. Add to that the fact that sometimes you're more aware of other people's feelings than your own. An explosive combo if ever there was one. Now, explain again what they said about the X-ray.'

Later, when Jess had left, Warlow was left alone with his thoughts.

Molly's tears, and the fear in her voice when he'd joked about checking out, had unsettled him. Her father's departure had left deeper scars than any of them had realised.

Warlow closed his eyes, listening to the low beep of the monitors.

He'd never set out to be anything to Molly, but somehow, without even realising it, he'd become an important part of her life. The responsibility of that knowledge was both daunting and oddly comforting.

When he finally drifted off to sleep, he did so replaying the moment she'd spoken into his shoulder. Making him promise to get over this. Reason enough for him to stop messing around and get better.

Family wasn't always about blood. Sometimes, it was about choice, about the people who stuck around even when things got tough. And Warlow had no intention of going anywhere.

# CHAPTER SEVENTEEN

WEDNESDAY

The following morning, the team drifted into the office with only one topic of conversation on the agenda. Jess had been summoned by Buchannan, or rather ordered by Buchannan, to spare a few moments to update him on Warlow's situation.

'He already knows, of course,' Gil muttered when Jess had gone. 'It's probably Drinkwater and above who want clarification.'

The three remaining team members in the office fell silent, pretending it was just another day. Details of Warlow's status had been passed on by Jess. Further discussion would be speculation. But sometimes, a sharing of concerns was a requirement, more so for some people than for others.

Sergeant Catrin Richards had yet to say anything at all that morning. This did not go unnoticed by Rhys.

'You're quiet, Sarge.'

'What's there to say?' She did not lift her gaze from her screen.

'I don't know.' Rhys tried to inject a bit of levity into the cut-with-a-knife atmosphere. 'I was thinking, should we get him a card or something? There are some crackers out there. I saw one in Smith's the other day. We needed one because one of Gina's pals had her appendix out. It said something like, "No wonder the NHS is buggered with time-wasting chancers like you sucking it dry."' He grinned.

Catrin's eyes were dangerously bright when she finally turned in her chair to face him. 'Great idea,' she spat, her voice dripping with sarcasm. 'A card. He can giggle while they adjust the ventilator.'

Rhys, genuinely horrified, asked, 'He's not on a ventilator, is he?'

'Not yet,' Catrin said through gritted teeth. 'But my Uncle Ianto went in with a cough right at the beginning of Covid. Three days later, he was on a ventilator. A week after that, he was in a coma, and when they turned it off, he stopped breathing altogether.'

'It's not Covid, though,' Rhys protested weakly, doubt creeping into his intonation. 'Is it?'

'No, it isn't.' Gil attempted to pour oil on troubled waters. 'And he's had more vaccines than any of us.'

'Mrs Williams, my mother's neighbour, has had no boosters since her son told her the vaccine was made from bits of dead volunteers and placentas,' Rhys said, and immediately regretted it when Catrin's eyes flashed with anger. 'Mind you, he also thinks King Charles is a vampire and the world is being run by lizard people.'

'Thank you, Professor Harries,' Gil said. 'I think tea would be a good idea at this juncture. DI Allanby will be in need to wash down all the platitudes she's had to swallow.'

Rhys got out of his chair. 'Too early for baked goods, I suppose?'

'You suppose correctly,' Gil agreed.

When Rhys left the room, Gil noticed Catrin pretending to be interested in her screen again. After two silent minutes of waiting for her to acknowledge his stare, he spoke gently.

'A card isn't a bad idea, you know?'

Catrin shook her head without turning around. 'It's obvious neither of you have any idea—'

'We lost people to Covid, too, Catrin. Anwen's mother

died in a nursing home. She never got to see her in the month before she passed.'

Catrin didn't turn around, but her shoulders tensed visibly.

'You're right to be worried,' Gil continued. 'And if that means getting shirty with Rhys and me, that's fine. Okay, we don't know how bad this is. But there's nothing wrong with a comedy card. We both know Evan would love it.'

For a few brief seconds, rage seemed ready to swallow Catrin when she snapped her head towards Gil. But he'd read her correctly, and no words emerged. Instead, her face crumpled, and tears flooded her eyes before she reached for a tissue. When she spoke, what she said emerged stilted and muffled.

'It's so bloody unfair. All of it.' Staccato words choked out, her mouth quivering with suppressed sobs.

Gil had suspected from the moment he'd seen her this morning that she'd been battling with demons overnight. Motherhood and the job were taxing enough, but Catrin Richards was up for that challenge. Today's snapping anger, with Rhys the unfortunate target, came simply from a bubbling fountain of guilt.

Warlow's HIV status had been gifted to him by a charming junkie called McLean on the day he'd stepped in to keep a fresh-faced, first-day-on-the-job Catrin Richards from harm. The needle McLean had hidden in her hair had punctured Warlow and delivered to him a gift that kept on giving. Now, if his pneumonia was linked to his possibly compromised immune system, here was another layer of steaming guilt for Catrin to steep in.

'None of this is your fault, Catrin—' Gil objected.

'Isn't it?' she snapped.

Gil winced, recognising the self-blame in her eyes.

He came back at her with a challenge. 'Did you cough germs into his face?'

'Of course not.'

'Exactly,' he said softly. 'A comedy card is exactly what we would normally do, and doing the normal is precisely what

Evan Warlow would want us to do. We both know that. When your waters broke that night at your reception, it was Warlow who suggested we get a card with a photo of the Titanic on it.'

Something like a faint shadow of a smile flickered over Catrin's face. 'Was it?'

'Okay, no, it wasn't. That was all me. But you get my drift.'

Catrin half turned, chin up, her lips quivering again. 'I hope he'll be okay.'

'Hang on. This is Warlow we're talking about,' Gil said. 'He doesn't do wailing and gnashing of teeth. He'd want us to carry on as per. I'm taking Rhys to see him this morning once we've had our tea. If anyone asks, I'm going to discuss ongoing operations.'

'I'd come, but DI Gwynne wants to talk to me and Jess this morning,' Catrin dabbed at her eyes.

'I'll tell the Wolf you're fighting the good fight. That will cheer him up.'

And for once, Gil delivered that completely sarcasm-free, conveying with his eyes the genuine emotion that words alone couldn't express.

————

HAVING EXPLAINED Warlow's health status, Jess used the request from Avon and Somerset Force as a distraction at the meeting. The arranged video call with Anna Gwynne this morning meant Jess could curtail the interview in Buchannan's office for a genuine reason.

Chief Superintendent Drinkwater summed up. 'Keep us informed of Evan's progress, won't you? So we can plan. For cover, et cetera, as it were. We're short-staffed enough as it is.'

His words left her cold. The gist of what Drinkwater said seemed to be full of artifice. But the subtext was clear enough. "How bloody inconvenient this was of Warlow to fall ill. What was he thinking?"

But she also received a text message from the chief constable that came across as genuine and warm:

> Jess, just heard the news. Please keep me posted, and if there's any help you need... if you need time away... speak to me directly.

That was the sort of thing you wanted to hear. Not hand-wringing and expressions of concern over Human Resources implications.

Jess half expected Goodey to turn up like a carrion feeder on a corpse. To step in and be a 'steady hand on the tiller'. A phrase Drinkwater had used in the past and regretted it.

*Well, Evan's not dead yet*, she thought, then immediately chided herself for such a morbid analogy.

He'd been very unwell when she'd left him the night before, but perhaps less ashen than he'd been lately at home. Thanks probably to the oxygen. They'd exchanged texts that morning, and he'd told her that his appetite was better. She therefore promised some M&S sandwiches when she'd visit and got a thumbs-up in response.

By the time she got to the office after her meeting, she had her game face back on. Catrin appeared a lot chirpier than when she'd left an hour before, too.

'How was it?' Catrin asked.

'Like they were planning a wake already,' Jess said and immediately regretted it when Catrin's eyes flared with shock.

'Okay, not quite that bad, and Sion Buchannan had obvi-ously been strong-armed into setting up the thing. But I had a nice message from the chief constable.'

'She's great, isn't she?'

'I like her,' Jess noted. 'So, where are we with DI Gwynne?'

'She's waiting for our call.'

'Let's do it.'

Jess settled in front of a monitor. The office was quiet now. A good time to connect.

A minute later, Anna Gwynne's pleasant face filled the screen. 'How did your meeting go?'

Jess sent Catrin a questioning glance.

Catrin returned it with mock innocence.

'You know how it is,' Jess said.

'I do.'

'Catrin filled you in on what we found out at Kerry Ford's house and what our CSIs think?' Jess asked.

'She did. I have two questions. Where did she get the money from? And do you genuinely think the place was searched?'

'I trust our techs. So, yes to search and sterilisation. That's a new one on me. Normally, burglarised properties are ransacked, but they've seen this before, and they're convinced.'

'This case… it's frustrating to say the least. Some new wrinkle at every turn.' Anna sighed.

'What would you like us to do?'

'The money?'

'Follow the money,' Catrin said. 'Always a good policy.'

'Any ideas?' Anna asked.

Catrin had an answer ready. 'The techs found a receipt in the refuse bin. Ford did some cleaning jobs. This receipt comes from a place up past Dolaucothi. A New Cross garage. I thought we could start there?'

'And I'm meeting with the sister's partner today,' Anna said with a cursory sigh. 'Hard to believe it's almost Christmas.'

'I'm yet to find much Christmas spirit,' Jess agreed.

'I'll get on to the garage,' Catrin said.

Anna smiled. 'I'd say leave it till after Christmas, but…'

'No time like the present,' Jess said.

The call ended. Catrin turned to her computer to get to work and reached for the landline. But she checked herself.

'Almost forgot, follow-up on the Marston case. It's much as the father had explained. They moved here from the Netherlands in 2019. An interesting story. It seems they met when he was on an exchange at university. Three children, all have dual citizenship. Mrs Marston is the surprise. She is the daughter of Nils van Oppen, something to do with shipping in Antwerp. She has no criminal history, but I found something from an online blog about her being a wild child. There's a lot of money there, but the article was one of those frothy pieces. Eligible Danes and their money. She came across as a bit of a maverick. Cut herself off from her family. Became a bit of an eco-warrior. Not sure if that's the husband's influence or not, but stranger things happen.'

Jess didn't argue.

*Stranger things indeed.* Like an Italian woman from an ultra-religious Milanese family marrying a bloke from up north in the UK and being ostracised by her family. At least by the patriarchal head of the family for daring to stray outside the Catholic faith in marriage.

That was her mother's story. Jess was very well aware of how these things – beliefs, money – could be the poison that caused family rifts.

Catrin continued, 'They moved here to get away. And obviously, even though there'd been some kind of unpleasantness, there was clearly enough money to buy the property they live in now. Could explain their desire to shelter the kids from the dangers that too much money can bring.'

'Have you passed all that on to Tomo?'

'I will, ma'am. Though I can't find much information on the children.'

'Well, you don't want anyone to know anything about your kids, so that's not too weird. Especially if the mother was a target for the press,' Jess remarked, understanding the desire for privacy all too well.

She moved to her own desk. 'Let's chase up Ford's grocery trip. Give me half an hour to sort through some emails. It'll be good to get out of the office for a while.'

# CHAPTER EIGHTEEN

WEDNESDAY

This wasn't the first time Gil had visited Warlow in hospital. The job came with a certain risk. Police officers were more likely, by a big factor, to encounter violent, disturbed, and outright malicious members of society. And Warlow had seen his fair share. Notably, a very unstable man who had killed his colleague with an axe and tasered Warlow to prepare for doing the same to him.

Being tasered rarely resulted in life-changing injuries. However, recovering from being tasered more than once in quick succession while attempting to evade the deranged killer had required hospitalisation.

And Warlow had visited Gil whilst he had been hospitalised because of job-related injuries, too.

Yep, the job could be fun-filled.

Gil and Rhys were given strict instructions by the ward manager to stay only fifteen minutes. Judging from Rhys's horrified expression as they entered the room, Gil considered fifteen minutes more than enough.

Warlow had lost weight. He looked gaunt. Though his responses to the two men's questions were sharp enough, there was an underlying frailty that he could not hide.

'What can I say?' Warlow sounded strained. 'I wouldn't

recommend pneumonia. But it is definitely responding to antibiotics.'

'You're better, then, sir?' Rhys asked.

Warlow's lips curled into a sardonic smile. 'Better, yes,' he admitted. Then, after a pause: 'But the bar is set low.'

'Anyone can see you're not well, sir,' Rhys agreed with disarming candour. That earned him a reproachful glance from Gil.

'Ship isn't sinking without me, then?' Warlow asked. Every third or fourth word, he sucked in oxygen through the mask.

'Jess is the captain,' Gil assured him. 'No one has jumped overboard yet.'

'What about Sillitoe? Found him yet?'

A sore point, but it was typical of Warlow's direct approach.

'No.' Gil highlighted his frustration. 'And the fact is that my chat with Olwen Napier has yielded no real intelligence. I'm not sure where to go next. I could go back to Charlie Brewer again—'

'There is one more option,' Warlow said. 'Why don't you talk to Daniel Hughes's wife?'

Gil frowned. Hughes, a local baker, had been Roger Hunt's second victim. Thrown off some steps at a railway station, he'd never woken up from his injuries. Hughes's family had suffered largely in silence while the team hunted for Hunt.

'It's a thought,' Gil agreed. 'Tidy.'

'It's more than that,' Warlow urged. 'It's a different perspective. That's what I think you need. Stop going around in circles.'

Gil turned to Rhys. 'Make a note of that,' he instructed. 'And before you ask, it's why they pay DCIs such exorbitantly large salaries. To see the wood between the trees.'

Rhys did not make a note. He was too busy eyeing the drip, the monitors, the bed, and every bit of ancillary equipment on show with a mixture of fascination and revulsion.

'I don't think I could be a doctor,' he announced.

'Considering a change of career, Rhys?'

'No. Just saying. Understanding the function of all this equipment. And then learning what all this stuff inside does.' He ran his hand down across his chest and stopped somewhere around his belt.

'I noticed your hand stopped somewhere around your midriff there, Rhys,' Gil observed. 'The implication being that your knowledge ends somewhere around there. Does that mean I need to have "the talk"?' He made air quotes around the words.

'No, Sarge, you're all right,' Rhys assured him. 'Last time I checked, everything was in working order.'

'Good to hear it.' Gil nodded. 'But may I remind you, the vegetable aisle in Morrisons was not the best place to do that check. That poor Romanian shelf-stacker will never handle a banana again.'

Warlow held up a hand, wincing slightly at the effort.

'Right, you two can go now because laughter is not the best medicine with this thing,' he wheezed, though there was a glimmer of amusement in his tired eyes.

'Will you be home for Christmas, sir?' Rhys asked.

'Unlikely,' Warlow could only repeat the bulletin delivered to him that morning by a smiling young doctor.

She'd added that his SATS were better and his white cell count was falling. He took both statements at face value as good things, judging by her smile.

'Never mind,' Gil said. 'I'm sure Santa will find you here. If not, watch a film. I hear *No Christmas Tree For Old Men* is quite good.'

The weak chuckle from Warlow was worth the terrible joke, Gil decided.

They stayed a while longer, chatting about how Warlow might have got his pneumonia. There was, of course, a vaccine, and retrospectively, Warlow knew it had been discussed somewhere along the way with Nurse Jenny. Not having it had been pure oversight on his part. Something on his list, but low down. But tears over spilt milk were not his style.

'He looks bloody awful, doesn't he?' Rhys muttered on their way out of the building.

'Patients in hospital are seldom at their best. But let's listen to the Oracle. See if you can dig up an address for Daniel Hughes's widow.'

They edged through hospital traffic and out towards the west, Rhys still distracted, his usual spark muted. 'When the beans are ready, feel free to spill them,' Gil said.

'Sorry. Seeing him… it reminded me of when my dad had his heart thing. My mother had faith in the system. She was the strong one. But my dad…' Rhys shook his head. 'Seeing the DCI like that… it brought back some memories. Not good ones.'

Gil nodded but said nothing, giving Rhys the space to continue.

'I've never seen my dad so… vulnerable. So scared.'

Gil's usual quips died on his lips.

'When I got to the hospital, Dad was hooked up to all these machines. He looked tiny in that bed. And his eyes…' Rhys trailed off. . 'I'd never seen him afraid before. I'll never forget that.'

'It's tough.'

Rhys nodded. 'And now, every time he gets a twinge or feels a bit off, I'm right back in that hospital room. Terrified.'

'It's normal to worry. But your father's still here, right?'

'I know,' Rhys said. 'But sometimes, late at night, I can't help thinking… what if next time—'

'Ah, the dark watches of the night.'

'Yeah, what's that all about? No one ever explained to me why all your worries go on parade in the middle of the night.'

'Nothing the old brain loves more than a good three a.m. disaster party – worst-case scenarios only, of course,' Gil said.

'And there is never any popcorn.'

'If there is, it's existential dread flavour. But your dad got great care, didn't he?'

'Yeah,' Rhys agreed. 'The best.'

'Well, then,' Gil said. 'Focus on that. And on making

memories with him while you can. That's all any of us can do, really.'

Rhys managed a small smile. 'I didn't mean to unload all that on you. But Gina says I should talk about it more instead of bottling it up.'

'Did I ever tell you that girl was a keeper?'

'Once or twice.'

'I remember when I was courting the Lady Anwen.'

Rhys cocked an eyebrow. 'Courting? Was this in the eighteenth century?'

'Mock not. These were the days before phones, no internet.'

'Carrier pigeon, was it?'

'Not quite.' Gil ignored the barb. 'We had to talk to one another and make arrangements we stuck with. Imagine that, George Jetson.'

'Who?'

'I digress. I always remember a piece of advice that Anwen's father once gave me not long after we'd started going out. He was a pharmacist. You could buy sherry from a barrel on the counter in his shop. God knows how fortified wine could ever be medicinal, mind. But this was real old school. The premises had giant spherical flasks full of coloured liquids in the window. Anyway, what he said to me was that you should never squeeze toothpaste out of the tube from the bottom.'

'Why's that?'

'Very unhygienic. Better to use your hands like normal people. Besides, one slip and you'd be having a very awkward discussion with the A and E nurse as she looks at you askance and asks, "I hope the brush is still in the mug on the sink?"'

Rhys laughed. 'I'll have to remember to tell Gina that one.'

'Preferably after she's brushed her teeth.' Gil glanced at his watch. 'Approaching lunch. Don't know about you, but I am hungry and, judging from the noises emanating from your belt region, either you've sneaked in a young polecat or you have some hunger pangs of your own.'

'What do you fancy? Greggs?'

'Not on your nelliphant. I am talking hearty winter veg soup with crusty sourdough from chez Jones.' He, of course, enunciated the z in chez. 'Since we'll be in Llandeilo.'

'Sounds good.' Rhys, brighter following Gil's toothpaste joke, now positively beamed at the prospect of another Lady Anwen lunch. 'Will she mind me turning up?'

'*Mi gaff es su gaff*,' Gil said. 'But let me pull over for a moment to give her a heads-up, or I'll be in the shed *chien* before you can say: give me time to get my curlers out.'

# CHAPTER NINETEEN

WEDNESDAY

Geraint Lane's mobile buzzed in his pocket, the vibration like a tiny earthquake against his thigh. He glanced at the caller ID and smirked. Libby Stonehouse. The editor of the *Western Post*. His former boss.

*Well, wonders never bloody cease.*

He let the phone ring awhile, testing her perseverance – or was it desperation? – on the receiving end.

*Probably squeezing the bejesus out of one of those stress balls she always had on her desk. Pretending it was to help her nicotine addiction when, in fact, it was practice for what she'd dreamt of doing to all her male employees.*

Lane's focus drifted, taking in the sleek desk, a framed cover of his upcoming book prominently displayed on the wall. A far cry from the cramped cubicle he'd been relegated to at the *Post*.

He thought of the advance sitting pretty in his bank account, more money than he'd made in years of chasing down lost cats and covering primary school concerts for that rag.

'Libby Stonehouse,' he drawled with faux surprise.

'Ger!' Libby's smoker's croak crackled through the speaker, bright and brittle.

It reminded Lane of those cheap fluorescent bulbs they'd used at the *Post*, always flickering and giving everyone a headache. 'How are you?'

Lane suppressed a chuckle. Using his shortened name, and her forced familiarity – it was all so transparent. Like looking through a grimy window that hadn't been cleaned in years.

*Ger, my arse. Like we're old pals. Like she didn't toss me out like yesterday's soiled fish and chips wrapper.*

'What can I do for you, Libby?' He kept his voice neutral, but inside, a part of him was a cartoon villain gleefully rubbing his hands together.

'I was hoping we might discuss your book. Isn't it exciting? It's causing quite a stir.'

*A stir? More like a bloody tsunami. And you're just realising it now, aren't you? That must be a tough bit of gristle to swallow.*

'Is it?' Lane feigned surprise, though he'd been carefully orchestrating the buzz for weeks. Planting little seeds of interest here and there, watching them grow into a forest of anticipation. It was like tending a garden, albeit one full of nettles. And he was planning to push Libby face-first into it.

'Absolutely. We'd love to do an exclusive interview. Local talent. *Post* reporter done good. For old times' sake.' Her little laugh ended up in a phlegmy cackle.

*Christ on a moped. Next thing you know, she'll be reminiscing about the good old days. As if there were any.*

Lane settled back, relishing the desperation he was hearing. He closed his eyes for a moment, savouring it.

'Old times' sake? Right.' He let the sarcasm drip.

A pause. Lane could almost see Libby wriggling on the other end.

'Ger, I'm aware things ended... awkwardly between us, but—'

'Awkwardly? Is that what we're calling it now? You fired me, Libby. Budget cuts, wasn't it?'

Memory of that day flashed through his mind. The peeling paint of Libby's office. Her plastic apology. The pitying looks from his colleagues as he'd packed up his meagre belongings into a cardboard effing box.

*Bet she thought I'd fade away. Disappear into obscurity like all the other hopefuls she's tossed aside. Well, surprise, Libby. I'm back, and I'm about to become your worst nightmare.*

'You know what it's like. Everything is online now. The financial situation was, still is—'

'Spare me. The way I remember it is that I was given all the crap to cover. But I bent over and took it. Never botched an assignment. I put together some shit-hot copy. But that didn't matter, did it?'

He thought of all the late nights, the hanging around, the crap diet. All for what? To be tossed aside like a used tissue.

'Of course it mattered. But sometimes, tough decisions have to be made. Surely, you understand that. And it's not as if you've done too badly as an Indie.'

Lane grinned. And there was nothing pleasant in that grin. People said he sometimes had a wolfish expression. One that would have sent shivers down Libby's spine if she'd seen it. Or so he hoped. There she was, somehow twisting the mortification of him being fired into a hard-knocks lesson that ultimately led to his success. As if writing a tell-all about a serial killer was comparable to running a failing local rag.

He pictured her in that claustrophobic office, a corkboard covered in Post-its, photos of *Love Island* hunks in shorts, which, had they been women in bikinis, would have precipitated a micro-aggressive howling storm from the female members of staff. Not that he minded. But the one rule for XX, one for XY fed into her ball-squeezing script.

The image made him want to drag this out even longer, to dangle the possibility in front of her drooling donkey face on a string.

'I have certain contractual obligations, Libby.' He examined his nails, feigning disinterest, even though Libby couldn't see him. It was all part of the performance, the dance of power he'd played out in his imagination for months.

'We can use your time at the *Post* as the spine,' Libby schmoozed, as oleaginous as a snail track over a lawn. 'Your perspective as someone who was so deeply involved in the case—'

'Deeply involved? That's one way of putting it.'

*And so far from the truth as calcium carbonate is from a ripe Camembert. I was in the bloody thick of it. And now you want a piece of the pie? Fat chance, Liberasshole.*

A beat of silence. Lane imagined hearing the gears turning in Libby's head, trying to manufacture the right words to reel him in.

'Ger, I realise it's been a difficult time for you. But that's what makes your story so interesting.'

Lane let the silence stretch, visualising Libby squirming on the other end. Hearing that stress ball squeal out its protest. He savoured each second like a fine wine.

*Chateauneuf de Desperation.*

'I've already signed a contract with one of the nationals. They're serialising the first three chapters.'

He pictured Libby's face falling, her dreams of a juicy exclusive slipping through her fingers like sand. It was a mental image he'd treasure for years to come.

'But surely, a local perspective—'

'Local?' Lane scoffed.

*This is going to be huge. The* Post *is a minnow in a pool full of sharks. And you're about to get eaten alive, Libs. I hope you're ready for that.*

'We have a loyal readership. People trust us.'

'Trust?' Lane laughed, a harsh sound devoid of any real mirth. 'That's rich. *I* trusted you.'

Stonehouse's famous temper sparked, triggering memories of office arguments and slammed doors. 'Oh, come on, for God's sake.' She took a breath. 'There will be a lot of local interest. I hear that the abducted detective, Richards, features prominently. I'm trying to set something up with her, too.'

*Good luck with that. That's one phone call I'd pay money to tap into.*

The thought almost made Lane laugh.

'I'm sure she'd be happy to chat,' he said.

'Can you put in a word?' she breathed.

Lane grinned. 'Happy to.'

'So, that leaves you. Can we work something out? I'm sure we could—'

'I'll think about it.' Lane basked in the power he held over her. It was intoxicating, this reversal of fortunes. 'I might throw you a bone if I'm feeling generous. But don't hold your breath.'

He ended the call without waiting for a response, a cruel smile playing on his lips. The tables had turned indeed, and Lane intended to enjoy every sodding second. He closed his eyes and let the satisfaction wash over him.

*This is just the beginning, Libby. Just you wait until you get to the chapter in the book where it explores how shit-packing useless the local press has been in questioning the actions of the local plod. And for local press, read The Post.*

The thought comforted him, and he turned back to his computer, laughing softly to himself while he replayed and relished the call.

Shit, that had been satisfying.

His gloating didn't last.

The landline's shrill ring shattered the smug moment. Lane's hand jerked, striking a water bottle that sent an arc of fluid spilling off the desk.

He caught the aluminium bottle before it hit the floor, but all he could do was sit there, listening to the phone's shrill call, water slopping over the edge of the desk.

Nobody used that number.

They had the landline as part of a BT Wi-Fi package. Amol enjoyed knowing there was a second means of communication if the hospital needed to get hold of him.

But no one rang it.

Well, only a handful of others were even aware it existed. One other, really.

His stomach knotted. He glared at the handset, willing it to fall silent. Still it rang. Insistent, demanding. Five rings. Six. Seven. On the eighth, his trembling fingers reached for it.

'Hello?' The word stuck in his suddenly parched throat.

'Geraint.' That voice. Smooth as silk wrapped around a razor blade. 'Been a while.'

Sweat beaded on Lane's forehead despite the chill creeping through his veins. 'What do you want?'

'Things are getting awkward.' A pause, pregnant with menace. 'Thought you should know.'

'I don't want to. I'm done with all that.' Lane fought to stay calm, but each word felt like ground glass in his mouth.

A soft chuckle scraped across his nerves.

'Really? Ah, but it doesn't work like that, does it? Something needs doing. Tidying up. Something I can't do myself. So, you have to. You might even enjoy it.'

'No.' Lane's free hand clenched into a fist. 'I told you—'

'Hey. Shut the fuck up.' Steel crept into the voice now, sharp and cold as a morgue drawer sliding open. 'If one of us falls…'

'Don't.' The word escaped as barely more than a breath.

'… we both fall. You know that. I'll be in touch with the details.'

The line went dead.

Lane set the handset down with hands that shook so badly he nearly dropped it.

The spilt water had formed a lake on the table, but he couldn't move to clean it up. Memory of the call with Libby had run for the hills. All he could hear was the echo of those words over the landline, the promise and the threat wrapped together like a noose around his neck. And underneath it all, the certain knowledge that he had no choice.

He'd escaped Hunt's clutches, but he'd been stupid before that. Desperate after the *Post* had let him go.

He'd needed money.

*Sodding Libby*.

And what he'd done had seemed such easy money. But the Hunt case had opened up a door into the labyrinth, and inside that maze was a locked box of horror that needed to stay locked.

*Shit*.

Lane had no choice other than to do as he was told.

# CHAPTER TWENTY

WEDNESDAY

A couple of hours after Catrin's last exchange with Anna Gwynne, the Avon and Somerset detective texted again with some images of the caravan crime scene, plus a link to a touring park to the south of Weston-super-Mare set in wetlands near the River Axe.

> Take a look and let me know when you've seen it.

The links were to a website. Though essentially a sales page, it gave enough information for Jess and Catrin to appreciate the setup. The images, taken on a beautiful summer's day, showed a small saltwater lake only twenty-five miles from Bristol, with two tiers of pitches in a semicircle around it. On the unoccupied half, a jetty led to a marina of sorts with snaking waterways presumably leading to the Bristol Channel, confirmed later on a map. The addition of a second layer of pitches two years previously – cheaper by dint of the poorer views and lesser proximity to the water – spoke of its popularity. Hardstanding pitches for motorhomes and caravans, grass pitches for tents. The reviews were excellent, especially the quality of the shower and toilet facilities and a waste disposal point.

'Your idea of fun?' Jess asked after reading through the details.

'No. Any romantic caravan and camping notions were driven out of my system as a child on the Gower. We went to the beach, rain or shine. More rain than shine, as you might expect. I need a hotel room and a hot shower and a G and T with ice at six on the dot when I'm on hols.'

'Me and you both,' Jess said.

'It says the site is secure, accessed only through the village.'

Jess scrolled through images. 'But the side away from the lake backs onto open fields.'

'My thinking as well, ma'am.'

'Okay, let's see what DI Gwynne has to say.'

The answer was a lot. A few minutes later, Jess and Catrin discussed the Ford case once more, face to face with its SIO via a video call.

'Developments?' Jess asked.

'Exactly that.' Anna stared back at them, looking stern. 'I could share my screen, but I think it'll be easier simply to summarise what I've just received from crime scene techs.'

'Is this after they've given the caravan the once-over?' Jess asked.

'Correct. Let me read you the brochure. The Mandalay 250 is a stylish two-berth caravan with a convertible double bed, compact kitchenette, and wet room. Designed for comfort, it features ample storage, all-season insulation, and an optional awning, making it perfect for couples' getaways.'

'Doesn't melt my butter,' Jess said.

'From what I've been able to find out, this was a 2000 model, bought for cash by the Ford sisters jointly after Covid when many people decided they might never go on holiday again. Louise Ford kept it at her house in Eastville. Or rather, at her partner's garage. He runs a body shop.'

Anna did not strike Jess as someone who liked to waste words. There would be a reason for this explanation.

'The sisters took the caravan to Sunny Lake.'

'I'd put my money on their caravan being in the cheap seats,' Catrin said.

Anna grinned. 'You'd be a winner then. Know much about caravans?'

'Other than they can be towed to spots like Sunny Lake caravan park, then no, I do not,' Jess said.

'This one was twenty-four years old but still had all mod cons. Built-in microwave, a gas hob and oven. Because they often use propane, caravans have vents, both in ceiling and at floor level. You'll read blogs that tell you carbon monoxide is heavier than air and will sink to ground level. It isn't. If anything, it's slightly lighter than air and diffuses to mix evenly with air in any given space.'

'News to me.' Catrin grimaced.

'The forensic report on the barbecue was also interesting. It's a simple tray with foldable legs, available in garages and supermarkets all over the country. I've already told you there was no food in the caravan fridge that could be barbecued. No food on the barbecue. Yet, it had been lit. There were also no fingerprints on the tray or the legs. In fact, unnaturally clean.'

'Much like Kerry's house,' Catrin observed.

'I'm sending you another crime scene photo.'

Catrin's phone chirped. She opened an image that showed what looked like the bottom of the caravan where a silver tray seemed to have spilt over such that it was lying on the ground with wire legs on a stand splayed next to it. The contents of the tray – some ashes and black unburned fuel – had not spilt out.

'Knocked over?' Jess asked.

'At first glance, you would say so. However, in this particular caravan model, the floor-level vents are simple round holes in the caravan flooring guarded by steel mesh on the outside and plastic mesh on the inside. On some models, these are often in storage cupboards and end up getting blocked. In this model, there are six. Evenly distributed and none had been blocked.'

'Don't tell me. One is right above where the barbecue fell over.'

Anna's smile came with an acknowledging nod.

'What's your working hypothesis?' Jess asked.

'It's winter. They had the awning up as an extension of the caravan, but it had been zipped and sealed. The weather the night the sisters died was cold but calm, with very little wind. In fact, an early frost. It's possible they thought about barbecuing—'

'With no food, though?'

'There is that.'

'Could they have had the barbecue for heat?' Catrin asked.

'There were heaters in the caravan. The awning had a couple of seats, but they were folded up,' Anna continued. 'It's unlikely they'd have sat out.'

Silence followed.

'Malice,' Jess said eventually.

'That is increasingly my thought.' Anna's expression stayed deadly serious. 'I think someone, someone very careful, waited until the Fords were asleep. Probably hiding in one of the many fields around the site. Then they crept into the awning with a little disposable barbecue, or brought their own, lit it, placed it so that it appeared as if it had fallen under a vent, and disappeared into the night.'

'Bloody hell,' Catrin said.

'It's the only actual explanation if you consider the lack of stored food and no evidence of any on the grill either.'

'They might have been better off leaving some food residue on the barbecue,' Jess suggested.

'If they had done that, they risked the smell of cooked food alerting the occupants. Plus, post-mortem food contents were consistent with sandwiches. So the barbecue thing doesn't quite fit.'

Jess nodded. It made sense.

'You're not treating this as simply an unnatural death?'

Anna narrowed her eyes as if this succinct statement had been one she'd needed to use herself. 'The bosses aren't happy, but I've asked this to be escalated to foul play. I am not flavour of the month, but that is a status I have long since accepted. My super owes me one. In fact, he owes me several. I'm going to interview Ford's husband later on. Depending on how that pans out, I may need to pay a visit to your patch.'

'We are planning on chasing up the receipt found in Ford's trash this p.m.,' Catrin said. 'We'll inform you of what we find.'

'That would be wonderful,' Anna said, sounding more than grateful.

'If you want to come down, just let us know,' Jess said. 'The red carpet is still in the cleaners, but we'll get the kettle on.'

When they ended the call, Jess did not go back to her desk immediately. Instead, she walked into the stairwell of secrets. At one time, when she was younger, she might have gone outside for a smoke. But that had only lasted between the ages of eighteen and twenty-two. After that, the stink of smoke in her hair and on her clothes bothered her more than the absence of a nicotine rush. And now the death of two sisters was bothering her even more.

Gwynne was no fool. She'd followed her instincts and, increasingly, this felt like something very unpleasant. And yes, their role in tracking Kerry Ford's movements was peripheral for the moment, but bloody intriguing.

If Anna Gwynne found her way across to the Wild West, Jess was eager to meet her. But, despite the morning's *malu cachu* with the bigwigs – one of Warlow's favourite sayings which he translated as "mincing shit" – and the relief, albeit gruesome, of Anna Gwynne and her enigmatic Ford sisters' case, Jess couldn't shake off the concern over Warlow's state. She'd made the self-destructive mistake of consulting with Dr Google when she got home the evening before. Top of page one of a million results for pneumonia was the reassuring statement that most people recovered fully, but the thirty-day mortality rate – whatever the hell that was – remained between five to ten percent.

The key word in all of that was mortality.

Jess did not like those numbers. Not one bit. She needed to know he was feeling better. The easiest and only way was on FaceTime.

'Why aren't you in some boring meeting discussing rumours about my demise?' were his first wheezy words.

'Been there, done that. Everyone sends their best.'

'I bet they do.'

'Well. Mostly, they do. Did Gil and Rhys get to see you?'

'They did.'

Warlow still wore an oxygen mask, and his words came through a little muffled.

'That cheered you up, then.'

'I've sent them packing. I'm paying their salaries, don't you know?'

Jess let out a single huff of air, acknowledging the in-joke they shared from one of the tropes that had infiltrated social media. Or at least some of the police-based social media they came across. One where some entitled idiot wanting to argue or belittle the officers dealing with them reminded said officers it was they, the transgressor, who was paying the officer's salary. It usually went down like a concrete zeppelin.

'How are you?'

'On the mend; they say my temperature's down, so by the time I see you next, I'll be doing the fandango.' He stopped for a bout of coughing. 'And it doesn't hurt as much to bring up the lining of my bronchi as it has.'

'Progress, then.'

'Yup. What bothers me most is that my brain is refusing to boot up. It's taken me all morning not to do the crossword. I spent two hours looking for a word beginning with M that meant beggar.'

'Mendicant,' Jess said.

'Surely, that's just a very unpopular odd-job man.'

Jess refused to grace that one with a laugh. 'You must be feeling better.'

'A bit. No doubt about it. I sense that fandango coming on as we speak. You?'

She told him about Anna Gwynne's two calls and the way she was thinking about the Ford case.

'Sounds right up your street,' Warlow said. Another cough followed.

'It's not as if I don't have other work to do, but she sounds nice and, yes, it is a bit of a puzzle. But I am also glad to hear you're a bit better.'

'I am. Plus, it's giving me a chance to catch up on some reading.'

'Jilly Cooper or Cormac McCarthy?'

'Neither, though I have read both, and they can both string a few words together that make you turn pages. No, I just read a Bosch from Connelly and now I'm riding along with Holly Gibney as a vicarious member of *Finders Keepers*.'

'You've lost me.'

'You need to give both a try. Mr King's Mercedes series is excellent. And you can go back to work knowing that I am not deteriorating.'

'Okay, then.'

'Thanks for ringing.'

'Everyone sends their love.'

'Tell them not to be so soppy and bloody well get on with it.'

She smiled at that because she knew when he was pleased, no matter how hard he tried not to show it.

# CHAPTER TWENTY-ONE

WEDNESDAY

Gil and Rhys, fortified by a lunch of the Lady Anwen's cawl with some sharp Welsh cheddar and crusty bread, walked off any post-prandial lethargy by heading to the Hughes's property on foot.

The town was busy just before Christmas. No rain yet, and with only showers forecast, it meant lots of visitors hunting for late presents or simply strolling the streets, calling in for a quick drink or a coffee and some carrot cake or mince pies.

Rhys was still reminiscing about lunch. 'In college, I told an English friend of mine that he'd love my mother's cawl. He thought I was talking about a kind of headgear, not a meat and vegetable stew.'

'Just as well you didn't mention a wizard's sleeve, then.'

'What's that?'

Gil did not break stride. 'Something best not discussed when there are children about.'

They took the hilly Carmarthen Street to the town's main drag, where the shops had made an effort with windows full of tinsel and baubles and spray-on snow.

Mrs Hughes lived in an imposing property on Crescent Road, near the Civic Hall. Gil led the way, but Rhys had fallen silent. Gil was savvy enough to realise that the last time Rhys had wandered these streets, it had been in pursuit of some miscreants. A pursuit that ultimately ended with the finding of the baker, Hughes, unconscious from the head injury he'd eventually succumbed to. All a consequence of being thrown off a bridge onto the platform of the town's railway station that made up one stop on the titular Heart of Wales Line.

'This bringing back unhappy memories, Rhys?'

'I keep thinking of Hughes on that platform.'

'Did you visit his wife on that day?'

'No, Mr Warlow did that. Do you know her?'

'Only in passing. She nods if she sees me in the town. Her daughter is a different cauldron of sardines, though. And I expect she'll be there when we visit.'

Gil knocked on the imposing front door of the Victorian villa on Crescent Road. Built in the market town's heyday, its granite steps and ornate doorframe spoke of better times.

Mrs Hughes answered quickly, as if she'd been watching for them through the net curtains. A small woman in her late sixties wearing a cardigan, she managed a wan smile. Grief had worked its erosion on her features, deepening the lines around her mouth and dulling the brightness Gil remembered from encounters in town before the attack. Her cardigan was buttoned unevenly, as if done up in haste, and she kept adjusting the cuffs in that nervous way people did in trying to present a brave face to the world.

The contrast between the immaculate house behind her and her slightly dishevelled appearance spoke volumes about where her mind had been. Or still was.

'Sergeant Jones,' she mumbled.

'Mrs Hughes. This is DC Harries.'

She nodded to Rhys and beckoned them inside. The hallway smelled of furniture polish. But there was no bunting or tinsel or mistletoe in the Hughes's house. Not this year.

She led them into the front room, where winter sunlight streamed through bay windows onto displays of family photographs.

Gil's eye was drawn to Daniel Hughes in his baker's apron, beaming at the camera.

'Can I get you anything?' Mrs Hughes asked.

'No, thank you,' Gil replied. 'We won't take up too much of your time.'

Gil and Rhys sat on a floral sofa while Mrs Hughes sat upright in an armchair, her hands clasped tightly in her lap.

'What's this about?' she asked.

Gil nodded. 'We're looking into some matters concerning John Napier and Royston Moyles.'

At the mention of those names, Mrs Hughes's shoulders tensed. 'I see.'

'Did Daniel ever mention a place called *Cân-y-Barcud* to you?'

She frowned. 'No, I don't think so. Though I know about it now. It's where you found Royston, wasn't it?'

'It was.'

'But Daniel knew the two of them. They'd meet, have coffee, or have a few drinks.'

Gil leaned forward slightly. 'Did he ever mention what they talked about? Do the letters "BN" mean anything to you?'

Before Mrs Hughes could answer, the front door opened and closed with a sharp snap. Clicking footsteps in the hallway preceded a woman in her thirties, her face hardening as she saw the officers.

Sarah Hughes had her father's height and her mother's delicate features, but where her mother's face showed resigned sadness, Sarah's was etched with barely contained fury. She wore office clothes – a charcoal trouser suit and white blouse – but her ID lanyard still hung around her neck, suggesting she'd left work in a hurry.

Perhaps someone had called to warn her about the police presence at her mother's house. The way her manicured fingers curled into fists at her sides told Gil everything about how this conversation was about to go.

'What are you doing here?' she demanded.

'Sarah, please,' Mrs Hughes pleaded. 'They're just asking some questions.'

'Haven't they asked enough?' Sarah blurted. 'Haven't we been through enough?'

Gil did not react. 'Miss Hughes, I'm sorry to intrude. We're trying to understand more about a property owned by Royston Moyles.'

'We understand that he and your father were friends,' Rhys added.

That was petrol on a bonfire.

'Understand?' She laughed bitterly. 'Where was all this understanding when Dad needed protection? When that monster was out there waiting to hurt him?'

'Sarah!' Mrs Hughes's voice cracked. 'Please don't.'

But Sarah was building up steam. 'You let him down. All of you. And now you're here asking more questions? For what? So you can fail someone else?'

Rhys shifted uncomfortably on the sofa. Gil remained still. Mrs Hughes's eyes filled with tears.

'Sometimes,' Mrs Hughes said quietly, cutting through her daughter's tirade, 'Daniel would come home troubled. He'd say they were getting into things he wanted no part of. I thought he meant business deals. But sometimes...' She shook her head.

'Sometimes what, Mrs Hughes?' Gil prompted gently.

'Sometimes, the way he said it... it felt different. Like he meant something else. But he never explained, and I never asked.'

'Because it wasn't our business,' Sarah snapped. She moved to stand between Gil and her mother. 'And it's still not our business, Mum. They're just fishing.'

Gil kept calm. 'Miss Hughes, Sarah, I understand your anger—'

'No, you understand nothing. You sit there, asking stupid questions again like they matter. Like they'll make any difference. My father is dead because you people failed to protect him.'

'Sarah, please,' Mrs Hughes whispered.

But her daughter was beyond reach now.

'Have you even the slightest clue what it's like?' Sarah demanded. 'Sitting by his bed, watching him fade away for weeks on end? Knowing that monster, Hunt, was out there all along, planning this?'

Rhys started to speak, but Gil silenced him with a subtle shake of his head.

'Yet here you are, disturbing Mum at Christmas, dragging it all up again. For what? So you can write something in your little notebooks? File another report?'

Mrs Hughes reached for her daughter's hand. 'Sarah, they're just trying to do their job.'

'Their job?' Sarah's laugh was hollow. 'Their job was to keep people safe. How did that work out for Dad?'

Gil stood slowly. Mrs Hughes seemed to shrink into her chair. Her earlier willingness to talk had completely evaporated in the face of her daughter's distress.

'We'll leave you in peace,' he breathed. 'But if you think of anything else your husband might have mentioned…'

'She won't be calling you,' Sarah declared. 'Either of you. We're done here.'

'Sarah,' Mrs Hughes protested weakly, but her daughter was already moving towards the door, holding it open in clear dismissal.

Gil handed Mrs Hughes his card. She slipped it into her cardigan pocket with trembling fingers.

Sarah stomped into the hallway. Gil heard the front door open. He made to follow,but Mrs Hughes stopped him with a hand on his arm. 'I'm sorry,' she murmured. 'She's still so angry…'

'It's understandable,' Gil replied.

'Could it be boys' night? BN? That's what Daniel called it when they met.'

'Could be,' Gil replied. Then Sarah appeared on the threshold. Time to leave.

Outside, the December sun had disappeared behind clouds. The officers walked in silence for several minutes before Rhys spoke.

'That could have gone better.'

Gil nodded. 'Boys' nights. BN.'

'You think Hughes was aware of the filming?'

'I think he knew enough to make him uncomfortable.' Gil halted. 'And perhaps that's what got him killed.'

The winter wind whistled down the street, carrying with it the distant sound of Christmas music from the Civic Hall. But Gil barely heard it, his mind racing with possibilities, none of them pleasant.

———

THE ROAD TWISTED THROUGH HILLS, winding northwards with the fields neatly parcelled off by hedges. Rain threatened from creeping slate-grey clouds that seemed to hang just above the treetops.

Jess kept the Golf at a steady pace, conscious of the sharpness of the bends. It had taken her a while to be totally confident on these narrow, serpentine Welsh roads.

'You didn't have to bring me,' Catrin said, breaking a lengthy silence.

'Got us out of the office, didn't it?' Jess replied. 'Besides, two pairs of eyes.'

They passed a sign for the Dolaucothi Gold Mines. Somewhere beneath these hills, the Romans had once tunnelled for precious metal. Now, tourists panned for specks of gold in muddy streams.

'Heard anything?' Catrin asked quietly.

Jess knew she meant Warlow. 'Tom rang the consultant this morning. They've got him on strong antibiotics. His temperature's down.'

'But?'

'No buts. He's responding to treatment.'

Catrin turned to stare out of the window. Sheep dotted the hillside like dirty cotton wool balls. 'Gil says I'm being stupid.'

'About?'

'Blaming myself. The HIV.'

'He's right.'

'Is he? If I hadn't been so bloody eager to make that arrest—'

'Then someone else would have done it. And possibly they wouldn't have been as careful as you. Maybe they'd have got stuck, too.'

New Cross Garage and Stores appeared around the next bend, a lonely outpost of civilisation. One petrol pump, a small shop with condensation-misted windows, and a faded Castrol Oil sign creaking in the wind.

'His immune system…' Catrin began.

'Is fine. The viral load is undetectable.'

'But pneumonia—'

'Can happen to anyone.' Jess pulled up beside the shop. 'Look at me, Catrin.'

Catrin turned, her eyes bright with unshed tears.

'He would hate this. You beating yourself up. He made a choice that day. To help you. To get that junkie off the street. She was being a menace. And those are his words, not mine.'

'But—'

'No buts. Now, come on. Let's see what Mr…' Jess consulted her notebook, 'Bruce Evans remembers about Kerry Ford buying petrol at eight-thirty on a Thursday night.'

As they got out of the car, the first spots of rain fell. A bell tinkled above the shop door, and an incongruous odour met them.

Patchouli, was that?

Catrin pulled out her warrant card with a steady hand. Jess clocked that. Sometimes, just speaking fears aloud helped dispel them.

Behind the counter, a man with a pepper-and-salt goatee and long hair tied back from his face glanced up from his newspaper. Before either officer could speak, he said, 'You'll be wanting to talk about the woman in the caravan, right?'

Jess and Catrin exchanged glances.

Some days, good days, the job threw you a bone.

# CHAPTER TWENTY-TWO

WEDNESDAY

Gil and Rhys got back to an empty office.

The silence felt oppressive after their fruitless visit to Mrs Hughes.

Gil slumped into his chair while Rhys busied himself, neither man speaking about the widow's distress or her daughter's hostile presence effectively scuppering the interview.

Ten minutes later, Chief Superintendent Bleddyn Drinkwater's bulk filled the doorway, his face set in what Gil privately called his "constipated bulldog" expression.

'Jones. A word.' Drinkwater's eyes flicked to Rhys. 'In private.'

Rhys took the hint. 'Can I get you some tea, sir?'

'No. But make yourself scarce.'

'Right. I'll... uh... right.'

Gil may have sensed a movie moment. An "anything you need to say to me, you can say in front of DC Harries" moment. But this was not the movies. Unfortunately.

Rhys exited.

Drinkwater turned to Gil, nostrils flared. 'I have just come off the phone with a very unhappy and irate daughter of one

Daniel Hughes. Would you care to explain why I've had to listen to her accusing us of harassing her widowed mother?'

'We were following up a lead—'

'A lead?' Drinkwater barked out a laugh. 'About a missing child from how many years ago? While we've still got the Napier investigation hanging over us like Damocles' Sword, as it were?'

Gil's jaw tightened, and his nerves pinged. Whether Drinkwater's tone or his verbal tic triggered the most irritation was a toss-up. 'Sir, if there's any connection between Freddie Sillitoe's disappearance and Napier's activities—'

'Oh, spare me the crusading detective routine, Sergeant. You're chasing shadows and leaving a terrible taste in people's mouths at the same time.' Drinkwater moved closer and dropped his voice. 'Several of my associates used Napier as their solicitor, as I have already explained. We ought to tread carefully. This business is unpleasant enough without you dredging up ancient history.'

'With respect... sir,' Gil deliberately delayed the honourific to imply a hint of irritation on his own part. 'If Napier was involved in anything regarding missing children—'

'If, if, if!' Drinkwater's face reddened. 'Have you made any actual progress? Found any concrete evidence?'

Gil's silence was answer enough.

'That's my opinion, too.' Drinkwater glared. 'You're what? A year or two from retirement? We both know you could go at any time and get a bloody twenty-one-gun salute. It would be a shame to end a distinguished career on a sour note.'

The threat hung in the air like stale cigarette smoke.

Gil said nothing.

Drinkwater hadn't finished, though. 'You've been around the block enough times to realise how bloody pie-in-the-sky this Sillitoe business is. You, of all people, should understand what normally happens to abducted kids. Most of them will be assaulted, and I do not need to tell you how. Only five percent are ever recovered. We both know what has probably happened to the Sillitoe boy and, harrowing as that may be, it is something we need to face up to.'

'Should I put that in writing to his parents, sir? That we've written him off?'

Drinkwater bristled. 'Don't play the clever bastard with me, Jones. Get off your high horse before someone drags you off.'

'Is that all, sir?'

'Leave the ghost stories alone.' Drinkwater turned away but paused. 'Oh, and the next time you want to upset elderly widows, run it past me first.'

The door closed behind him with a decisive click. Ten seconds later, another door on the other side of the office opened, and Rhys stepped in, his face glum.

'I presume you heard all that?' Gil asked.

'Hard not to. Does he have an inside voice? He obviously thinks Freddie Sillitoe is—'

'Sit down, Rhys,' Gil whispered.

'But—'

'Remember what I told you about picking your battles?' Gil managed a wan smile. 'This isn't one of them. Not yet anyway.'

Rhys sank into his seat. 'He basically threatened you.'

'Basically?' Gil snorted. 'Subtlety is not his strong point. But it is not the first time my senior status has been discussed, and I doubt it will be the last time. Our chief superintendent is right about one thing – we have made no progress.'

'So, we're just going to give up?'

'Give up? No, but perhaps we need to be a bit more... discreet in our enquiries.'

'Meaning?'

'Meaning that sometimes, Rhys *bach*, the best way to investigate isn't always the most obvious one.' Gil stood, stretching. 'Now, what are you like with spreadsheets?'

Rhys beamed. 'They call me the Excel gangster.'

'I bet they do,' Gil said. 'And I am glad to see you wear the badge with pride.'

———

THE SEMI ON RIDGEWAY AVENUE, Eastville, wore its ordinariness well. A burgundy door flanked by hanging baskets provided the only splash of colour against pebble-dash walls.

Inside, Brian Ross led DCI Anna Gwynne into a living room that spoke of functionality over comfort. A three-piece suite in faded brown, a flat-screen TV mounted above an electric faux-coal fire, net curtains that had seen better days. The room's sole concession to sentiment hung above the fire-place in the shape of a photo collage in a silver frame.

Anna's gaze was drawn to it immediately.

Among the scattered snapshots of Louise Ford and Brian Ross's life together were several featuring the Ford sisters. In one, they sat on the steps of the caravan, wine glasses in hand, doubled over with laughter at some private joke. Their dark eyes sparkled with identical mischief, their faces mirror images of joy.

But the photo's warmth clashed with the room's utilitarian feel.

Ross perched on the edge of an armchair, hands clasped between his knees. At fifty-five, his face bore the weathered look of someone who'd spent too much time under cars, and his fingers were dark with ingrained tattoos of oil and grease driven into the whorls. But there was no mistaking the raw grief in his eyes as he answered her question about the caravan's purchase.

'They bought it just after the first lockdown,' he said. 'Kerry had some money saved, which came as a bit of a surprise, but I knew this bloke who was getting rid of his Mandalay. Good nick, considering its age. Bargain at eight grand.'

'And they used it regularly?'

'Couple of times a month, weather permitting. Long weekends. Loved it, they did.'

Anna proceeded gently. 'Did they cook much when they were away?'

'Nah.' Ross shook his head. 'They'd walk to the pub, usually. That was half the fun for them. They'd pick sites near somewhere they could get a decent meal.'

'So, they wouldn't normally need something like a disposable barbecue?'

Ross's brow furrowed. 'That's what I thought when I heard it mentioned. Didn't make sense to me. Louise would've said if they were planning a barbie.'

'You drove the caravan up to Sunny Lake for them?'

'Yeah. Done it loads of times. They'd book somewhere; I'd drive it up. For someone who loved the van, Louise hated towing. Then she would get the train or drive up later.' His voice cracked.

Anna waited while he composed himself. 'Mr Ross, I need to ask something difficult. Did either Louise or Kerry have any enemies? Anyone who might want to harm them?'

Ross's head snapped up, grief momentarily replaced by anger. Then understanding dawned. 'You're thinking of that twat, Darren Lister, aren't you? Kerry's ex.'

'He's out, I know, but—'

'You got that wrong. He was out on parole and got rearrested within a week. So, he's back inside. As I say, total twat. And yeah, he was a nasty piece of work. Used Kerry as his personal punch bag until she found the guts to stand up in court.'

'That's why she moved to Wales?'

'Fresh start.' Ross's jaw tightened. 'Louise went with her at first, helped her settle.'

'Does Lister have friends on the outside?'

Ross barked out a bitter laugh. 'Friends? Lowlifes more like. But we're talking petty criminals here, not some bloody mastermind network. Danny was just a thug with fists and a temper.'

'Even so—'

'Listen. My Louise is dead. Her sister's dead. And you're sitting there suggesting what exactly? That some mate of Danny's followed them to a caravan site and…'

He broke off, chest heaving. 'It was an accident. Had to be.'

Anna watched him closely. His distress seemed genuine, but she'd learned long ago that grief could hide many things. And sometimes, the obvious answer wasn't the right one.

But the fight drained out of him quickly. He slumped into his chair. 'Sorry. I just… I keep expecting her to walk through the door, you know?'

Anna nodded. 'I know you told the officers they'd been to the pub in Knibsford that night.'

'Yeah. The Crown. Lou texted me about the sandwiches.' His lips trembled. 'Said they were awful. That was the last…' He couldn't finish.

'One last thing, Mr Ross. Any idea where they bought the barbecue?'

'No idea. Must've picked it up locally. There's a convenience store in Knibsford, I think. I mean, I wouldn't put it past them, but it's news to me. They were thick as thieves together. Kerry was a nosy sod, mind. Gossipy. Worse than Louise. She'd sometimes come across some posh sods in the Airbnbs she cleaned. Once or twice even some minor TV celebs. She'd take snaps of their clothes or their car. That's the sort of person she was. No harm, just full of it. Never fell out with anyone, but she'd be the first to grab a selfie if there was one to be had.'

They talked some more, but Ross had nothing much to say. He had satisfied himself that this had been some awful accident. He'd also already provided an alibi, which had been double-checked. Anna felt no need to revisit that.

After about twenty minutes, she sensed he'd reached his limit. 'Thank you for your time, Mr Ross. We'll be in touch if we need anything else.'

He barely acknowledged her departure.

Anna walked to her car past the pristine front garden and the carefully tended borders. A home that had been loved, now haunted by absence. She thought about the CCTV from the Crown showing the Ford sisters, happy, relaxed, sharing a bottle of wine. Their last meal.

It all came back to that disposable barbecue, standing out like a boil on the case's raw bum cheek.

Why would they buy one? The weather had been cold. And if they never cooked in the caravan... a caravan bought fifty-fifty by the Ford sisters for cash, why would they barbecue?

She made a mental note to check the store in Knibsford, though she already suspected what she'd find.

The Ford sisters had not bought that barbecue.

Had not set it alight.

Had not let it fall under a vent to smoulder and let off its lethal gases.

So, if not them, who?

Behind the lace curtains, a light flickered on. Brian Ross, alone with his memories and his grief. Either genuinely devastated by loss or putting on a very convincing show.

Time would tell which it was.

And then there was the money hidden away by Kerry Ford. A woman who'd saved enough from basic wage cleaning jobs to buy a share in a caravan.

It didn't add up.

Anna decided there and then. A trip to Wales to get a nose for what was going on there had now become a requirement, not simply an option.

# CHAPTER TWENTY-THREE

WEDNESDAY

While Gil was suffering the slings and arrows of Drinkwater's ire, Warlow talked to the boys. He adjusted the nasal cannula – they'd swapped the mask out – as faces populated his iPad screen.

The Perth contingent, as usual, sun-drenched and casual, and Tom and Jodie bundled up against London's winter gloom.

'Jesus, Dad.' Alun's greeting held its usual edge. 'You look like something the cat dragged in.'

'None taken,' Warlow wheezed.

'*Tadcu*!' Leo's toddler face suddenly dominated the screen as he brandished a plastic stethoscope. 'See what Uncle Tom got me!'

'Back up a bit, sweetheart,' Reba called off-screen. '*Tadcu* can't see you when you're that close.'

'I need to listen to *Tadcu's* heart!' Leo pressed the stethoscope against the screen.

Tom's laugh carried across the connection. 'That's not quite how it works, mate.'

'How did you end up there, Dad?' Alun demanded. 'Aren't you supposed to be taking things easier?'

'Anyone can get pneumonia,' Tom interjected. 'It's not like he chose to get sick.'

'Bababababa!' Eva contributed from somewhere in the Australian ether.

'She says you need to rest more.' Reba lifted Eva into view.

'That's quite a vocabulary she's developing. And delighted to see you speak fluent toddler.' Warlow smiled, then coughed for twenty solid seconds.

Everyone waited until he'd finished.

'That doesn't sound too good,' Alun commented.

'Should have heard me two days ago.'

'What have they done to you?' Reba asked.

'Oxygen and antibiotics. They seem to be doing the job.'

'What about Christmas?' Alun pressed.

'I'll be in here, but the spring trip is still on—'

'Why don't you come for longer?' Reba suggested. 'Stay a couple of months. Recuperate.'

'I still work, remember?'

Alun's eyebrows shot up. 'My point exactly. Why are you still chasing bad guys?'

'Al,' Tom warned.

'No, I mean it. Look at him. If this is what it does to you. Hasn't the job done enough to you already? Is the pneumonia related to your HIV?'

*Thanks for that*, Warlow thought. But then Alun had his mother's filters, and they had been a rare commodity. He pulled few punches.

'Bloody hell, Al,' Tom objected.

'Well, is it?' Alun did not back down.

'Apparently not,' Warlow explained. 'In that the HIV remains fully controlled. But I appreciate the concern. In hindsight, I should have got the pneumonia jab, but I was busy when I had an appointment, and then it slipped my mind.'

Alun shook his head with exaggerated irritation.

'*Tadcu*, I can make you better!' Leo thrust his face back into view. 'I'm a proper doctor now!'

'That's his answer to everything lately,' Alun muttered, but his expression softened.

'Bababaaba!' Eva added enthusiastically.

'She agrees with her brother.' Reba smiled. 'Our resident medical team.'

'I'm serious about the job, though, Dad. I mean, you're financially okay, right?' Alun pressed his point home. He didn't add, *since the windfall from Denise.* But he might as well have.

'I'm luckier than most,' was all Warlow said.

'Dad knows what he's doing,' Tom said quietly. 'The job… it's who he is.'

'Yeah, well, what's the point of that when being who he is has landed him in hospital?' Alun retorted.

'I'm right here, remember?' Warlow reminded them. 'And I'm fine. Ask Leo – he's the expert.'

'No, I'm a doctor!' Leo said. 'And you need special blue tubes like mine!'

'He's already got tubes, mate,' Tom pointed out.

'But mine are better because they're blue.'

The argument about Warlow's life choices was temporarily derailed by Leo's insistence on blue tubes being the best, but Alun's concerned frown remained. Warlow recognised it. The same expression his late ex-wife used to wear when worried about something she couldn't control.

Movement at the door caught his attention. Emerson stood there with another doctor, waiting politely.

'Sorry,' Warlow said to the screen. 'I'm going to have to cut this short. Got to go. More doctors wanting to prod me.'

'More tests?' Alun's frown deepened. 'What tests?'

'No idea,' Warlow replied. 'I'll find out soon enough.'

'They're probably just being thorough,' Tom said quickly. 'Standard procedure with pneumonia.'

'Is it?' Alun didn't sound convinced.

'Trust the other doctor in the family, shall we?' Warlow said. 'I'll text you with updates, and I'll definitely call tomorrow.'

A chorus of goodbyes followed; Leo's instruction to "get blue tubes" rising above the general noise.

Warlow ended the call just as Emerson approached with her colleague.

'Evan? This is Dr Phillips from cardiology. We'd like to run some additional tests.'

Warlow studied the newcomer. A woman in her forties with ash-blonde hair pulled back in a practical knot and rectangular glasses that caught the daylight from the window. Her expression held that particular blend of professional concern and quiet competence that consultants seemed to perfect.

'Cardiology?' Warlow's eyebrows climbed his forehead. 'My grandson hasn't been in touch, has he?'

Emerson cocked an eyebrow. 'Is he in the business?'

'Sort of. He's three and a bit and has been given a toy stethoscope.'

'I will send him a report.' Emerson played it straight.

'We're just being cautious.' Phillips smiled, the gesture softening her composed features. 'We like to be thorough with pneumonia patients.'

*Is there an echo in here?* He thought about it but didn't say it. Levity had its place. Probably not this minute, faced with two consultants, though.

Phillips spoke with that careful neutrality that Warlow recognised from his own profession. The tone used when you didn't want to worry someone unnecessarily but weren't quite ready to offer reassurance either.

Warlow nodded.

What else was there to do? Besides, anything was better than lying here dwelling on Alun's words. His eldest son had always been the worrier, wearing his concern like a badge of irritation. Tom understood better; understood that the job wasn't just what Warlow did but who he was.

Still, fifteen minutes later, as they wheeled him towards the cardiac unit, he couldn't help wondering if Alun had a point. Maybe two months in Australia wouldn't be such a bad idea.

———

NEW CROSS GARAGE'S shop interior proved more interesting and cleaner than its exterior suggested, with wooden shelves stocked with an eclectic mix of organic produce and whole foods. A poster near the till proclaimed *No Ultra-Processed Foods Sold Here* in hand-drawn letters. The unmistakable complex rhythms of early Genesis filled the space. Something from *Selling England by the Pound* if Jess wasn't mistaken. She had Warlow to thank for knowing that.

Behind the counter, Bruce Evans cut a striking figure. Tall and loose-limbed with shoulders still broad despite his age, which had seen sixty-five come and go, by her reckoning. His goatee was meticulously trimmed despite its grey, and his long hair, tied back with a leather thong, still showed traces of its original auburn. Turquoise and silver rings adorned his fingers, and a faded Yes T-shirt peeked out from beneath a hand-knitted cardigan.

'I saw the news,' Evans said, folding his paper. He had a slow, soft south-Liverpool accent. 'Kerry Ford. She's one of my regulars. Was, I mean.'

Jess raised an eyebrow. 'You recognised her from the TV coverage?'

'Hard not to. She's been coming here the last Thursday of every month for…' He squinted at the ceiling, his grey-green eyes sharp despite the surrounding crow's feet. Looked like he spent time outside when he was not in the shop. 'Must be going on two or three years now. Could be more. Covid punched a hole in my memory for too many months. Plague years, I call them. She always came in between eight and nine. That's when I shut up the place.'

Catrin pulled out the receipt they'd found. 'We have a receipt. Time stamped nine twenty-two.'

Evans barely glanced at it. 'Yep. She usually got some fuel, a couple of bits from the shop. Liked the organic granola.' He gestured to a shelf of mason jars filled with various cereals. 'Made by my wife. Local honey, too.'

'Your wife's local, then?' Jess asked.

'Met her at Glastonbury '82. Followed her back here like a lost puppy. Best decision I ever made, even if the locals thought I was some sort of drug-crazed hippie.' He chuckled, the sound warm and genuine. 'Which I was.'

The music changed to "Eye in the Sky". Laid-back vocals and rhythm from Alan Parsons. Jess knew this, too.

*Bloody hell, Warlow.*

'Did Kerry ever mention where she was coming from?' Catrin asked. 'Or going to?'

Evans shook his head, his ponytail swaying. 'Never asked. Not my business. She was always pleasant enough. Bit quiet, maybe, but polite. Unlike some who think anything west of Carmarthen is bandit country.'

'Notice anything unusual about her visits?' Jess asked. 'Any patterns?'

'Besides the timing? Always paid cash. Always seemed in a bit of a hurry to get home.' He paused, fingers still keeping time to the music. 'Though now you mention it, she'd been more tired these past few months.'

'Ill, you reckon?'

'Who knows? The autumn and winter can be long and wet down here. Affects some people more than others, don't you think? You know how some people carry stress on their shoulders? Like that.' He shrugged.

'Did she ever mention work?'

Bruce Evans pulled a face. 'She was a regular customer, but that's all.'

Evans nodded towards the shelves. 'You'll want to try my wife's granola before you go. She did.'

'No thanks—' Catrin began.

'No ultra-processed rubbish in my shop,' Evans insisted, pointing a bony finger at the sign, already scooping some into a paper bag. 'Leave that to the supermarkets. They can poison their customers with chemicals as much as they like. I'll stick to proper food, thank you very much.'

Catrin handed him her card. 'If you remember anything else about Ms Ford, please give me a call.'

Evans tucked the card behind the till. 'Will do.'

'Particularly if you can pin down when these monthly visits began,' Jess added.

He handed them the granola with a flourish. 'I'll do my best.'

'Love the music, too,' Jess said.

'You know Parsons' work?'

'I do.'

'Rare thing these days. I mean, this is his own project but—'

'He worked with Pink Floyd and at Abbey Road.'

'Wow. You know your onions.' Evans grinned.

They left the shop to the sound of Yes's "Roundabout" and the dancing bass line.

'Well, that was…' Jess began.

'Different,' Catrin finished. 'Observant guy.'

'They do exist,' Jess said.

'Think the granola's any good?'

'Should be. Lucky Evan isn't here, or we'd have been there for an hour talking albums.'

'I wouldn't have minded, ma'am,' Catrin said as she drove out.

Jess picked up on her wistful tone and echoed it. 'No. Neither would I.'

# CHAPTER TWENTY-FOUR

THE SHARED office space at HQ was once again relatively quiet that Wednesday afternoon. Christmas Eve, no less. The plan was to have a briefing at mid-afternoon to share new intel on the ongoing cases. With a bit of luck, if nothing else turned up, they might all get away late afternoon to stuff their turkey, duck, goose, or nut roast – depending on what floated your boat.

Around 4:30 p.m., Catrin took a call from Tomo.

'Just checking in,' he said. 'And thanks for the information concerning the Marstons. Takes all sorts, I suppose.'

'It does. But everything checks out. If you really want to cut yourself off and be one with nature, having a bit of money as the daughter of a shipping magnate helps.'

'Yes, to that. How's the boss?'

Catrin glanced at Jess reflexively. 'Made good progress overnight. He's off oxygen, seems to be on the mend.'

'Send my regards. I suppose his being away means the shop is less busy?'

'You'd think so. But we've been roped into a case from Avon and Somerset. We're not idle. You?'

'Pretty quiet. At this time of year, people mostly stay away from causing mischief. Too cold, too dark, too much on the telly. We have training ops between Christmas and New Year, though. Search and rescue. Get the dogs out for a run.'

'You'll be busy, then.'

'Best way to be. It'll be PCSO Sharma's first December outdoor course. She's looking forward to it.'

'How are you getting on?'

'She's a good one. I've been lucky. First Hana and now Priya. The gods must be taking pity on me in my old age. Anyway, keep your ear to the ground on the Marstons, won't you?'

'You still have the yips about them, then, Tomo?'

'It'll pass. But I can't help imagining that little kid wandering around, lost. I mean, what were they bloody thinking?'

'Hmm.' Catrin signed off. 'Have a good one.'

'You too. *Nadolig llawen.*'

---

TEA WAS SERVED with the inevitable mince pie accompaniments, all homemade by Rhys's mother.

'Can't beat a good mince pie,' Gil said.

'In some countries, it's gingerbread,' Catrin observed.

'In some countries, it's bloody KFC,' Gil replied.

'What?' Rhys asked, incredulous.

'Japan, apparently,' Jess explained. 'It's dying out. But you can't get a family bucket unless you preorder well in advance.'

'I would.' Rhys's expression took on a faraway look.

'No surprises there,' Gil added.

Jess wiped the pastry crumbs from the corner of her mouth. 'Right, let's run through current investigations. Pretend I'm Evan.'

'Still haunting us, even from a bed overlooking Swansea Bay,' Gil muttered.

'Like Bob Marley,' Rhys said.

It took a moment, and some frozen mince pie chews, before Gil tuned in to Rhys's thought station.

'You mean Jacob Marley,' he said. 'The ghost who haunted Scrooge in *A Christmas Carol*.'

'That's him.' Rhys delivered the qualification with a few sputtered crumbs for effect.

Gil had a twinkle in his eye. 'Of course, Bob Marley would do at a pinch, though. I mean, he could certainly wail.'

'Oh no, please,' Catrin begged. 'No Bob Marley puns. Not today.'

'Don't stress, Catrin,' Gil said. 'Wouldn't dream of it. Relax. Every little thing will be all right.'

Catrin's chin jutted out under a dagger's stare.

'I'll lead off,' Jess said quickly. 'DI Anna Gwynne will visit us from Bristol after Christmas. She's keen to run through what we have, see things for herself. I know the feeling.'

'Does that mean we're definitely thinking unnatural death?' Rhys asked.

'That's as good a way of putting it as any. Obviously, we'll cooperate fully.'

'I read up about the Black Squid killings,' Rhys said. 'Apparently, Shaw, the man they had in prison for killing his daughter's murderer, isn't there any longer.'

'No, he's still at large and on Interpol's list.'

'Is he abroad, then?'

'Who knows,' Jess said. 'Gil, what about the Sillitoe boy?'

The expression on Gil's face probably told the others all they needed to know. Still, he obliged with a summary.

'No joy yet. As you know, I questioned Daniel Hughes's widow only to be met with hostility from his daughter and a subsequent dunking in very hot water from the powers that be.'

'Does that mean you're shelving it?' Catrin asked.

'I wish I could. But I can't. I'll keep things low profile. I'll have another word with Charlie Brewer over the holidays. That way, no one can accuse me of wasting resources.'

'I don't think you're wasting resources,' Jess said. 'And neither does DCI Warlow nor Superintendent Buchannan.'

Gil nodded. 'That's one hell of a five-a-side team, thank you.'

'Right,' Jess said. 'Everyone set for Christmas?'

———

OF COURSE, people were busy on Christmas Eve. Presents to wrap, food to prepare, visitors to welcome. But some people had to work. People who kept things running, who maintained the infrastructure Western civilisation depended upon. Top of that list were nurses and doctors. Nurses perhaps more than their medical colleagues.

There were few routine procedures carried out on Christmas Eve. For one thing, there were less staff around to provide aftercare. For another, the afflicted somehow became less afflicted when tinsel, hot toddies, and pigs in blankets were viable alternatives.

Of course, that excluded genuine emergencies.

But on acute medical wards, staff were rostered.

Warlow chatted with several staff members that day. He learned that Laura, aka staff nurse Pring, had two kids aged seven and eight, and she and her partner were going to her mother's for Christmas lunch and her in-laws' for Boxing Day. She'd wanted to make Christmas dinner herself, but she was doing an early shift on the day, so she'd accepted the invitations. The kids were getting to an age where they wanted to be at home with their new things, though, so next year, that's what she was planning.

Lloyd, another nurse, was going to a Christmas party that began at eight p.m. and would probably meet up with some people at the pub on Christmas morning. He and his partner were off to a late Christmas dinner at friends'. Lots of booze and dancing. Lloyd was twenty-nine with no kids.

The ward was full. Mainly respiratory cases, two pulmonary embolisms, two Covid-related – that bugger wouldn't lie down, would it? – and a terrible case of asthma. Plus, two other pneumonias besides Warlow.

By supper time, around six p.m., everything except the beeping machines and the coughing had quietened down.

Warlow had settled into what passed for an evening

routine: medication, temperature check, a half-hearted attempt at hospital shepherd's pie, and then blessed escape into an audiobook. Settling in with his earphones, he fixed on a flaw in one of the ceiling panels as a handy anchor for his thoughts. He found himself wondering, not for the first time, why Holly Gibney kept beating herself up about her mother when a flash of tinsel pulled him back to the present.

Molly appeared in the doorway, doing an impression of a Christmas decoration that had escaped from the ward's tree.

'Bloody hell, are you a lost elf?'

'Have I still got tinsel in my hair?' Molly asked. She wore a big puffer jacket and a green woolly hat with a red tassel. Welsh colours that would also do for Christmas.

She breezed in carrying two bulging Marks & Spencer bags, her dark hair escaping from a messy bun.

Warlow had propped himself up against the pillows, and though the oxygen mask was gone, the shadows under his eyes told their own story.

'You're still a mess,' she announced cheerfully.

'And hello to you, too. What happened to respecting your elders?'

'Oh, please. If I was being nice, then you'd really worry.' She began unpacking treats onto his bedside table. 'This isn't all for you, obviously. But here are those weird oat biscuits you like, and some Christmas pudding that is definitely not hospital approved.'

'Your mother know you're smuggling contraband?'

'She suggested it.' She perched on the edge of his bed.

'Last shift done?'

'Yep. Good tips today, too. I should be back with Mum by half six. And speaking of Jess, we're definitely coming tomorrow. Do you have a microwave up here? Because she's determined you're having a proper Christmas dinner.'

'There's one in the staffroom. I'm sure the nurses will let you use it. The staff are amazing.'

'Unlike the food, apparently.' She wrinkled her nose at his barely touched tray.

'My appetite's coming back. Slowly.'

'Hence the contraband.' She studied him for a moment, her expression softening. 'You really gave Mum a scare, you know?'

Warlow tried a goofy smile. 'I'm fine now. Just tired.' He forced brightness into his words. 'Tell me about Italy. When do you fly out?'

'New Year's Eve. Nina's got the whole itinerary planned. Though…' She hesitated. 'I still wish Mum would come.'

'That's between you two.'

'Diplomatic as ever. You've got a better colour, though. Even if you do still resemble something from *World War Z*.'

'Brad Pitt and the zombie apocalypse? Anyone tell you your bedside manner needs work?'

'Learned from the best.' She stood and hugged him carefully, mindful of the IV line still in his arm. 'Get some rest. I'll be in tomorrow with some crackers.'

'Something to look forward to. Great.'

As she gathered her coat, Warlow felt an unfamiliar tightness in his chest that had nothing to do with his illness. There were things that needed to be discussed, but not yet. Not over Christmas. He watched Molly leave, her wave bright and confident, and told himself he'd made the right decision.

The coffee she'd brought was still warm. He reached for it, his hand trembling slightly, and tried not to anticipate the difficult conversation that would have to come later.

———

GERAINT LANE DROVE SLOWLY, guilt niggling at the edges of his conscience. He'd told Amol he needed to pop out to meet someone. Not exactly a lie, but the omission felt heavy.

The phone call had come out of nowhere; the instructions were impossible to ignore. But it wouldn't take long, thank God.

Amol was off duty tomorrow, and he had plans for a six-course Christmas lunch at The Grove. And didn't they both bloody well deserve it after the year they'd had? And the publisher was picking up the tab as a Yuletide present.

The A40 stretched ahead like slick black ribbon. The sodium lights at Whitland were the last real brightness he'd see until Carmarthen. His headlights caught the eyes of sheep in the fields, their reflective gaze alien and unsettling. To his left, the Preseli hills were just darker shapes against the night sky, ancient sentinels watching his progress with indifference.

Past St Clears, the road dipped and curved through a landscape of skeletal trees and hedgerows. The occasional farmhouse light appeared and vanished, lonely outposts in the darkness. The garish Christmas decorations in windows seemed to emphasise the isolation rather than relieve it.

'Just get this one thing done,' he told himself, and then he could officially switch off. No more work on the book for a couple of days. Time to yield to the festivities. Why the hell not? Relax and prepare for what the new year promised. He'd be busy then.

*And not with the bloody* Western Post's *parish pump journalism.*

The thought made him grin. He held his speed steady while the road twisted through Johnstown's trading estates and the glowing signs of shuttered car dealerships.

He checked his mirrors compulsively. Christmas Eve meant amateur night on the roads. So, too many office parties, too many drivers thinking one for the road wouldn't hurt.

A set of headlights appeared behind him, too bright, too close, before turning off. The last thing he needed was to become another festive statistic, not when everything was finally falling into place.

Beyond Carmarthen lay unfamiliar territory altogether. But that was where he needed to be.

The thought sobered him. Meanwhile, his sat nav ominously counted down the miles.

# CHAPTER TWENTY-FIVE

CHRISTMAS DAY

Betsi Peters sat in a sea of torn wrapping paper, far more interested in the crinkly sounds it made than the wooden blocks and soft toys scattered around her. Craig watched from the sofa, coffee mug warm in his hands, trying to focus on his twelve-month-old daughter's delight rather than the images that kept flickering through his mind from last night's shift.

'Look at her,' Catrin said softly. 'Who needs toys? Shiny crinkly paper is the star of the show.'

Craig managed a smile.

Catrin sent him a questioning glance. 'Want to talk about it?'

He took a long sip of coffee from the mug. 'Two teenagers thinking they were Batman and sodding Robin. The lorry driver had seconds. They were on his side of the road as he crested the hill. The poor sod was just trying to get home for Christmas. Head-on collision. Seconds later, the Astra was half the size it should have been front to back...'

Betsi crawled over, pulling herself up on Craig's legs. He lifted her automatically, breathing in the baby-sweet scent of her hair.

'Both critical, but stable when I left,' he continued. 'But their poor parents... having to tell them on Christmas Eve.'

'I'm sure you did everything you could.'

'It's just…' He pressed a kiss to Betsi's head. 'Sometimes, it hits home, doesn't it? Every time I go out, I see where it could all go wrong. The speeds people drive, the chances they take.'

Catrin moved to sit beside him. 'But you can't stop the boy racers. Most people are sensible, aren't they? And seeing you on the road makes people even more careful. Every day isn't like last night.'

'Thank God.' Craig put Betsi back down.

'You love it, though. You know you do.'

'I do,' Craig admitted. 'When we get it right, when we prevent something worse happening… it matters. Even the bad days matter.'

Betsi squirmed over to her paper kingdom. She picked up another shiny bit of paper and waved it triumphantly with an accompanying squeal.

'Da!' she declared and offered it to Craig.

He took it solemnly. 'Thank you, Betsi Boop.'

Life and death, joy and tragedy. They lived side by side, separated only by a heartbeat. A split-second decision. A moment's inattention.

'More tea?' Catrin got up and walked to the kitchen.

'Definitely. What time do we have to leave?'

'Said we'd be at my mum's by eleven. Your mum's by half twelve. But we'll be back here by four. I've got everything prepared. Christmas lunch will be at seven.'

'Yes, ma'am.' Craig opted for mock formality. 'I'll try to leave some space, though you know what it's like on Christmas Day at your mother's and mine.'

'Limit it to three sausage puffs in my house and two prawn toasts at your mother's, then.'

Craig moaned. 'That's hard. Your mother made those with turkey and cranberry last year.'

Betsi waved some more paper up and down, grinning and entertaining herself to an accompanying rendition of "Incy Wincy Spider" from the iPad's speaker.

Catrin glanced back over her shoulder and smiled.

Craig grinned. 'She's going to be a conductor, obviously.'

'Llanelli Philharmonic,' Catrin said.

That was worth a Craig chortle. And slowly, his preoccupation with last night's shift lifted just a little.

———

DEAN MARTIN'S velvet voice crooned "Let It Snow" from Rhys's carefully curated Christmas playlist. A mix of old classics and newer covers that avoided the usual clichés with difficulty.

Rhys stood at the stove in his garish Christmas jumper featuring a llama in a Santa hat, flaking smoked salmon into perfectly scrambled eggs.

'Most people throw everything in a pan and hope for the best,' Gina called from where she was setting their small table with a centrepiece made from pinecones and silver-sprayed twigs she'd collected herself.

'Most people don't understand the art of breakfast,' Rhys replied with mock solemnity. 'Besides, it's Christmas.'

A bottle of Prosecco sat unopened in the fridge. A treat for later. They'd both agreed that serving Christmas dinner at the drop-in centre required clear heads.

'Bagels are toasting,' Rhys announced. Ella Fitzgerald replaced Dean as the day's soundtrack. 'Tree looks nice, doesn't it?'

Their Christmas tree was modest—barely three feet tall—but Gina had worked magic with charity shop decorations: glass baubles in deep blues and silvers, strings of wooden stars, and a collection of tiny copper bells that tinkled softly whenever anyone walked past. A paper angel, slightly lopsided, crowned the top.

'It does.' Gina straightened the angel. 'Though your mum's will put it to shame.'

'Mam's tree puts Trafalgar Square to shame. We even used to have a lighting-up ceremony.'

They sat down to eat, knees touching under the small table.

The bagels were perfectly toasted, the eggs creamy, the salmon adding just the right touch of luxury.

'Right, then,' Gina said. She reached for a neat, carefully wrapped package. 'Since we're being sensible this year…'

Rhys grinned. 'One present each. Though I might have a surprise or two for later.'

'Rhys Harries, what are you up to?'

'Wait and see.'

They exchanged their gifts: A birthstone necklace for her, and a Nintendo Switch Sports Accessory bundle for him, which they would both play, and some aftershave. Things chosen with care and knowledge of each other's passions.

'You remembered,' Gina said softly. 'Perfect.'

'Like you,' Rhys replied, then immediately rolled his eyes at himself. 'God, that was cheesy.'

'Absolutely terrible.' Gina leant over to kiss him. 'But I'll let you off since you made breakfast.'

Rhys caught her hand.

Outside, a light dusting of frost sparkled on the pavement, and somewhere a church bell tolled. All combining perfectly with Ella's rich tones to ease them into Christmas morning.

———

Jess and Molly arrived at the hospital at twelve, each carrying foil-covered plates that steamed gently in the winter air. The staff had made an effort and festooned the ward with tired tinsel and paper chains.

Warlow sat propped up in bed, looking better than he had in days.

'Happy Christmas.' Molly placed her plate on the table beside his bed. 'We've brought the whole works, including turkey, stuffing, and roasties. I've mastered the microwave. Not exactly state-of-the-art.'

'Though the sprouts might be mushy.' Jess pulled up two chairs.

'Cadi?'

'Sleeping off her own Christmas dinner.' Jess smiled. 'She's fine. Missing you, but fine.'

They arranged themselves around the bed, carefully balancing plates on laps. Warlow used his bedside table so as not to get the IV line tangled. Passing visitors cast envious glances at the spread.

'This is really good.' Warlow tackled a roast potato. 'Better than good.'

'Molly did most of it,' Jess said.

'Only because you were banned from the kitchen after last year's Yorkshire pudding incident.'

Their laughter felt natural, welcome. Warlow watched them both, something shifting behind his eyes that neither woman quite caught.

'You're looking better.' Jess smiled. 'When do they think you can come home?'

'Twenty-seventh, or twenty-eighth if things carry on like this. The IV comes down tomorrow,' he said.

'And off work for a month?' More a suggestion than a question.

'Well…' Warlow drew out the word. 'See how it goes? Tell me about your caravan case.'

'No,' Jess replied. 'I refuse. No shop today.'

Molly launched into a story about Cadi stealing paper from opened presents around the cottage, but Jess kept watching Warlow, noting the way he was a little too willing to smile. As if he was trying too hard to be his normal self. Of course, that was understandable, as the circumstances were far from normal. Still, there was something she couldn't quite put her finger on.

Outside in a hospital corridor, a local choir were singing "Silent Night".

Warlow joined in with Molly's laughter at all the right moments, ate his dinner with apparent enjoyment, but Jess knew him too well. The illness had hit him hard. Kryptonite indeed.

Had he been shocked into taking a long hard look at himself?

He'd retired once. Could this be the trigger for a return to that state? The force would miss him. She caught herself.

The surroundings were getting to her, too. Time would tell.

But some truths, Jess thought, were like time bombs. The question was, how long until this one detonated?

————

GIL SAT cross-legged on his living room floor, surrounded by wrapping paper and the joyful chaos of family Christmas. His youngest granddaughter, Manon, was attempting to teach him the rules of a new game, which seemed to involve an improbable number of coloured unicorns travelling across rainbows.

'No, *Tadcu*.' She sighed with the infinite patience of a five-year-old. 'Eat something only when the dice tells you to.'

'Ah, of course.' Gil nodded seriously, catching his daughter's amused glance. 'Silly me.'

His phone buzzed. He almost ignored it – he wasn't on call – but years of instinct made him check the screen. He frowned, stood, and wagged a finger.

'Two seconds,' he said. 'And no cheating while I'm away.'

The little girl's smile indicated there would definitely be cheating while he was away.

In the kitchen, away from the warmth and laughter, Sergeant Powell's voice was tight with concern. 'Sorry to disturb you, Gil, but I thought you'd want to know. A man called Charlie Brewer was found in the car park behind the Vic in the early hours. Been worked over pretty good.'

Gil's hand tightened on the phone. 'How bad?'

'No breaks, but his face is raw meat. Said to call you specifically. Said you'd understand why.'

'*Arglwydd mawr*,' Gil muttered. 'Where is he now?'

'Just about finished in A and E. We'll give him a lift home. Says he can't remember much, but…'

'I'll be there in twenty.'

He returned to the living room where his granddaughter

was carefully counting crystals won by her unicorn. 'Sorry, *bach*. *Tadcu* has to pop out for a bit.'

'But we haven't finished the game!'

'Work stuff,' he told Anwen apologetically. 'Won't be long.'

She gave him a wary glance, but he responded with a hands-up-can't-be-helped gesture.

The hospital car park was nearly empty. Most people were at home with their families. Charlie sat hunched on a plastic chair in the waiting area, holding an ice pack to his face. His left eye was swollen shut, his lip split, dried blood crusting his collar.

'They said you'd come,' he mumbled through puffy lips.

Gil sat beside him. 'Want to tell me what happened?'

'Not really.' Charlie lowered the ice pack to reveal the mottled bruising across his cheekbone. 'I left the Sal. I was passing the car park of the old Vic and... shit. He came out of nowhere. Sucker punched me from behind. I went down hard.'

Gil visualised the spot. A place where outdoor seating took up space in the summer. Lots of lurking dark shadows in midwinter. 'Who?'

'From the back?' Charlie said, with an unaccustomed tetchiness. 'He laid into me. I curled up into a ball. All I can tell you is that he was all in black.'

'Did he take anything?'

'No. But he said that he was passing on a message. Said I should keep my nose out of other people's business.'

'The Napier case?' Gil said with genuine surprise.

Charlie's good eye flickered nervously. 'I'm sorry, Gil. I thought I could help, but... I mean, what the fu—. What the hell is going on?'

'It's complicated. We've obviously trodden on somebody's toes.'

'I was ambushed. He was waiting. He knew I'd been in the pub. I reckon they must have seen us together before. Me and you.'

Gil let the cold anger settle in his gut. Amateur thugs didn't do surveillance. This was professional intimidation.

'Let me drive you home, at least.'

Charlie shook his head carefully. 'No offence, but I'd rather not. I'll go in the response vehicle. The driver's a mate.' He sighed. 'And I'd be careful, too, Gil. Whatever's going on here, it's bigger than a dead solicitor.'

Someone came out with some painkillers in a paper packet for Charlie to take home, and Gil helped him shuffle into the gathering dusk of mid-afternoon. Behind him, tinny speakers played 'Joy to the World' while a drunk Santa was wheeled in.

Even on Christmas Day, A&E remained a monument to human folly. But Gil's mind was already racing ahead, connecting dots, seeing patterns.

Someone was willing to send very physical messages to keep their secrets. The issue was, who had that much to lose?

Someone was cleaning house. And they weren't being subtle about it.

# CHAPTER TWENTY-SIX

To be fair to Emerson and the other physicians, they kept their word. Warlow continued to make good progress over the next few days, losing the IV and heading home on the twenty-eighth of December, carrying a raft of medication with him.

He could not drive himself, so Molly drove Jess down to fetch him, and she drove the Jeep home with Warlow as passenger. Other than feeling a little weak, being outside in the fresh air was a welcome change, and he felt a lot better than when he had somehow dragged himself from the car to the hospital several days before.

'I still can't believe you did that,' Jess said when Warlow said as much.

'You know me.' Warlow realised how inadequate an answer that was but hoped his ironic self-deprecation worked as apology.

'At least tell me you'll take it easy for now.'

'Emerson says to make sure I exercise,' Warlow replied. 'Cadi will be pleased.'

Cadi was indeed pleased, transforming into a wagging, wriggling, jumpy black ball of fur when Warlow got down on one knee to give her better access.

'I missed you too, girl,' he muttered.

'Funny you didn't say that to us,' Molly, already home, said from the kitchen.

Tom and Jodie appeared, hugs taken and given, with extra squeezes from both.

'Good to be back,' Warlow said.

'How are you feeling, Dad?' Tom asked.

'Better. Word to the wise. If anyone asks if you fancy a bit of pneumonia, tell them to bugger off.'

'What have they got you on?' Tom asked.

'Don't ask me. It's all in the bag.'

Tom glanced at the large paper pharmacy bag Warlow had placed near the sink and delved in.

'Isn't it lunchtime?' Warlow asked.

'It is,' Molly said.

'Good, because I have a craving for a turkey sandwich and chutney.'

Jess grinned. 'We can manage that.'

They sat around the table, wore paper hats, pulled Christmas crackers, and basically enjoyed a belated and impromptu Christmas lunch. There were turkey sandwiches, coleslaw, cornichons, capers, tomatoes, the lot. And Christmas cake to finish.

'We should do it this way every year, I reckon,' Tom said.

'You'll get no argument from me.' Warlow sat back and adjusted his paper crown. 'However, I have to say Molly's Christmas dinner, which I ate in a hospital bed, tasted wonderful.'

'You were so hungry you'd have eaten a leather boot,' Molly said. 'I could see it in your eyes and in the way you were drooling.'

'That may be the case, but that simply added to the enjoyment. You're getting good at it, Molly.'

She smiled, with eyebrows raised. 'Where is the real Evan and what have you done with him?'

'He's right,' Jess said. 'It was good.'

'Right, now I know someone's spiked the mayonnaise.' Molly delivered the riposte with eyebrows still up.

Tom glanced between mother and daughter, more like

sisters to him, both in the way they looked and the way they interacted with his dad and with him.

'Lovely to see you home, Evan,' Jodie said and held out another cracker for him. He did the deed and lost both the hat and the novelty fortune teller fish that came as a prize.

Warlow insisted on taking Cadi for a quick stroll up the lane to get some air. Molly went with him. He suspected she was more a chaperone than a companion.

Outside, the grey afternoon slid silently into a brief dusk and then full dark. Despite protesting that he felt fine, Warlow couldn't fight the heaviness in his limbs. The walk, though only a mile, had taken it out of him. By nine p.m., he felt his thoughts drifting like autumn leaves in a stream, lids too heavy to take in some turgid TV drama masquerading as prime-time viewing.

The voices of his family became gradually more distant, their laughter and conversation blending into a soft hum that reminded him of his days in hospital. The hours he'd spent in that twilight realm between sleep and waking.

When Jess quietly suggested he head to bed, he didn't argue.

His office bedroom – he'd insisted on not sleeping with Jess because his coughing would undoubtedly rear its head sometime during the night – when he finally reached it, felt both familiar and strange, as if the pneumonia had somehow altered his perception of the space.

The bedside lamp cast odd shadows on the walls, and his familiar books on the side table still didn't quite anchor him to reality. Lying back against the pillows, the ceiling swam, and he felt himself sliding quickly into darkness.

Next thing he knew, he was standing at the back of a church. A familiar musty smell of ancient stone and varnished oak pews filled his nostrils, but something felt wrong. The light through the stained-glass windows cast longer and darker shadows than they should. The air felt treacle thick.

He recognised faces in the congregation: Gil, Jess, Rhys, Tom, and Alun. All the boys without partners. All dressed in black. But their expressions were wrong. All frozen in a rictus of grief reminiscent of waxwork figures.

The click of shoes on stone drew his attention. His breath caught as Denise walked past him, ramrod straight in a full DCI uniform, her silver-streaked hair pulled back severely. She strode to the pulpit without a glance.

It was only then that Warlow saw the coffin.

His legs moved without conscious thought, carrying him down the aisle. He knew what he'd see before he reached it, but the sight of his own face, pale and waxy in death, still sent a jolt through him. The body, his body, wore Denise's favourite blue dress, the one she'd been buried in.

'Evan was never good at accepting help,' Denise's voice rang out from the pulpit with that familiar hint of irony he'd both loved and bristled at during their difficult marriage. 'Always had to do everything himself, even if it killed him.'

A ripple of knowing laughter spread through the congregation.

Warlow tried to speak, to object, but no sound came out.

'He was a good detective,' Denise continued, 'better than he was a husband, truth be told. Always chasing the next case, leaving me to pick up the pieces.'

She paused to adjust her uniform sleeves. 'But he gave me two wonderful sons, even if he wasn't around to see them grow up properly.'

*That's not true*, Warlow tried to shout, but the words remained locked in his throat. He'd been there. Hadn't he?

The memories suddenly felt slippery, uncertain.

The congregation began to sing. Not a hymn, though. Procol Harum's "Whiter Shade of Pale", the song that had played when he and Denise first met. But the melody was wrong, like a record playing too slowly.

'Of course, I took his place.' Denise cut through the singing. 'Someone had to finish what he started.'

She stared at him then, and her eyes were the cold grey of a winter sea. 'Someone had to make things right.'

Warlow stumbled backwards, his heel catching on a proud flagstone. But it wasn't the stone floor of the church, but the linoleum of the hospital corridor he saw. Where he'd nearly died. The smell of incense transformed into antiseptic.

'You can't have both worlds, Evan,' Denise said, suddenly beside him. Her hand was stiff on his cheek. 'Choose. The living or the dead. You can't keep straddling the line.'

He reached for her, but his hand met only smoke. The walls dissolved around them, running like wet paint.

'Denise, I—'

'Time to wake up, Evan. Unless you want to stay here with me?'

The question hung in the air. Warlow jerked awake in his own bed in Nevern, his heart hammering against his ribs. The bedside clock read 3:17 a.m., and somewhere in the distance, a fox screeched. A sound that usually brought comfort but now carried a discordant echo from his dream.

He lay there in the darkness, the ghost of Denise's touch still cold on his cheek, wondering if she had been right.

Had he always tried to inhabit both worlds? The living and the dead? Victims and survivors? Or was it the disease playing tricks with his mind?

Sleep, despite the comfort of his surroundings, despite his recovery, was a long time coming.

In the morning, he was not the first up.

A fresh mug of tea awaited him when he surfaced.

'Heard you get up,' Jess said, already dressed.

Warlow stirred his tea while Jess buttered toast at the counter. She'd already dressed for work.

'Sleep okay?' she asked.

He considered telling her about the dream but decided against it.

'Still adjusting to not having someone wake me every four hours to check my vitals,' he said. 'Or that bloke in the opposite bed doing his best impression of a freight train.'

Molly set a plate of scrambled eggs in front of him. 'You need building up after all that hospital food.'

Tom and Jodie exchanged glances before Jodie suggested, 'Fancy taking Cadi down to Newport? It's not a bad day.'

'Definitely,' Tom added. 'The sea air will do us all good

after all that food yesterday. We need to set off back to London at about two-ish.'

'Anything you say, Doc,' Warlow said, glad of the distraction.

But his mind drifted back to the dream – to Denise standing there in that hospital corridor. The memory felt so real, so vivid, that for a moment he could almost smell her perfume. But he kept that to himself, focusing instead on his eggs and the prospect of a walk along the sand.

While the others got ready, Jess headed for the door.

'Shame you can't come with us,' Warlow said.

'It is. But today's the day I'm meeting Anna Gwynne,' she replied.

'Of course. Three-course lunch at a Spoons?'

'More like a working lunch over sarnies.'

'Give her my regards,' Warlow said. 'What do you make of this caravan case, though?'

'Not sure yet.' Jess's brows crowded together. 'She is convinced there's something not right. Forensics points in that direction, too. And the hidden money in the sister's house is hard to explain. Yet.'

'You sound up for it.' Warlow munched on some toast.

Jess shrugged. 'Always happy to help a fellow DI.'

# CHAPTER TWENTY-SEVEN

CATRIN WAS at her desk when the reception called to say DI Anna Gwynne had arrived. She went down to meet her.

Gwynne was tall, late thirties, smartly turned out in charcoal trousers and a fitted jacket under a camel coat. Her honey-blonde hair was short and emphasised her strong cheekbones.

'DI Gwynne? DS Catrin Richards.'

'Please, call me Anna.' The Bristol detective smiled warmly and clipped on her visitor's badge. 'Thanks for having me over so early.'

'Not even nine yet. You must've left Bristol before dawn,' Catrin said.

'I believe in early starts,' Anna replied. 'Besides, the M4 can be a nightmare later in the day. Though I have to say, it felt strange crossing the bridge and realising I was coming home, in a way.'

'The name gives you away.' Catrin led the way to the stairs.

'I grew up in Pendare, north of Cardiff. My grandparents spoke Welsh—proper first-language Welsh. I always meant to learn, but...' She shrugged. 'Maybe if I ever move back.'

'Never too late.' Catrin smiled.

Inside the office, Jess was back at her desk after a catch-up with Buchannan, who wanted to know about Warlow mainly, while Rhys typed with his usual two-finger intensity.

'Anna.' Jess stood to greet her. 'Welcome to our humble warren.'

'Humble but warm warren.' Anna shook hands before shrugging off her coat. 'Unlike my office in Bristol, where the heating's been on the fritz for weeks.'

'Tea?' Rhys materialised beside them, already heading for the kettle. 'We've got Yorkshire, Earl Grey, or some fancy stuff Sarge brought in that tastes like someone dropped jam in it.'

'Don't knock my toast and jam tea until you've tried it,' Catrin protested.

'Yorkshire would be lovely, thanks.' Anna laughed. 'Strong enough to stand a spoon in.'

'Good to know, ma'am,' Rhys declared. 'Though, if you want proper builder's tea, let Sergeant Jones make it. His brew is like creosote.'

'Speaking of Gil?' Jess cut in with a question.

'Out and about, ma'am. Says he'll be in late morning. Sends his apologies.'

'Probably seeing Charlie Brewer,' Catrin said.

'I heard.' Jess explained briefly about how Gil had been called out to a GBH on Christmas Day. Though, she didn't burden DI Gwynne with too much detail of what implications it had.

That would come later.

They moved to a secure room, steam rising from their mugs, and a sudden surge of satisfaction whipped through Catrin.

Three experienced female detectives. It wasn't often you got this kind of gender imbalance in a major investigation.

Anna pulled out her notebook. Catrin caught Jess's eye and saw the same thought reflected there. This was going to be interesting.

'Right, then,' Anna said, pen poised. 'Tell me everything about Kerry Ford I should know.'

They had a whiteboard in the room, but Catrin summarised their findings so far verbally: how the search of

Ford's property had yielded hidden money, and the investigation into monthly trips north, which included calling into the garage. Of course, this was news to no one.

'But I took a call from the garage owner, Bruce Evans,' Catrin said. 'I think he's going to be a valuable source.'

'Source? How?' Jess asked.

'He's posted photos of Kerry Ford in his shop—not at our request—and got a hit yesterday. A woman returning from her Christmas break immediately recognised Kerry.'

The story, as Catrin had heard it in Evans's own words, had been worth documenting.

'This woman, so Bruce Evans said, sees the photo and says, and I quote, "I know her. She does for me once a month. Three hours' worth of deep clean." I got her name and telephone number.'

Jess sat forward. 'When was this?'

'Last night,' Catrin explained. 'I haven't rung her yet. We waited until you were here.'

'Shall we do it now?' Anna asked, suddenly animated.

'Why not?' Jess shrugged her agreement.

Catrin made the call.

The woman's name was Sylvia Robinson, and from her accent, clearly she wasn't local. West Country, or thereabouts.

After making the introductions, Catrin explained the call was on speaker. Sylvia seemed unfazed, proving to be one of those witnesses who needed less prompting and more reining in.

'Bruce, the hippie, said you might ring because he was going to give you my number,' Sylvia began. 'I had no idea… about Kerry… My God… I nearly wet myself when I saw her photo up in the garage and—'

'Where?' Catrin asked.

'Up behind the till, a colour photo with "do you know this woman" written on it.'

Jess and Catrin exchanged glances. One that didn't escape Anna's notice.

'Sylvia, this is DI Anna Gwynne speaking. Mind if we ask you a few questions?'

'Go ahead. Anything I can do to help. I mean, I've been away up to my cousin's in Dursley for Christmas. I saw Kerry last month—'

'Let's put the brakes on,' Anna said gently. 'Let's start with how you know Kerry Ford.'

What followed was an unremarkable enough story. Sylvia was sixty-eight, her husband had died four years before, and she'd sold up. After inheriting two other properties, she'd sold those along with her own house and bought a six-acre small-holding. She'd moved to Wales because she didn't like where she'd lived before, and she loved animals. So, now she had goats, chickens, dogs, and cats.

'One of my passions is music,' Sylvia continued. 'I went to so many gigs as a kid. Birmingham mainly. Some in Bristol. So, when I heard that a Fleetwood Mac tribute band were coming to Swansea, it was a no-brainer. That's where I met Kerry, in the queue for a warm beer. Just sort of bumped into each other. We got chatting, and she mentioned she cleaned. Well, I jumped at that. I've got a big place, and I hate house-work. She started coming to me last Thursday of the month, regular.'

'Isn't it a long trip?' Jess asked.

'That was the beauty of it. Kerry said she came up once a month to visit friends anyway, so she could make a day of it. She usually stayed for a bit of supper before heading home. To be honest, I did some of the cleaning, too. Better with the both of us. If I didn't, she called me a lazy old git.'

Sylvia's laugh rattled in a throat with what Catrin suspected was years of cigarette damage.

'The last Thursday of the month?' Catrin asked, making notes.

'You've got it,' Sylvia confirmed.

'And who was it she visited besides you?' Anna asked.

'If you ever get a chance to see that band, by the way, you really should. The girl is the spitting image of Stevie Nicks, swear to God. Gave me the shivers—'

'Did Kerry tell you who she was visiting up there besides you, Sylvia?' Jess repeated the question a little louder.

'Oh, yes. Old friends. She said she was like an auntie to their kids. I can't remember their last name... Martin, or something like it. Kerry called it bloody Hogwarts, where they were. The woman was into all this witchcraft stuff.'

In some investigations, there were genuine shivery moments. And here, now, with the three of them around that table, Catrin experienced a "WTF on steroids" moment.

Anna turned a quizzical expression towards her female colleagues.

Jess held up a finger. 'Can you repeat that name, Sylvia?'

'Martin, or Merson...'

'Marston?' Catrin asked.

'Yeah, that's it. Marstons. Like the brewery.'

'When was the last time you saw Kerry?' Anna asked.

'Must've been the last Thursday of November. Yeah, that's the last time.'

'Did she ever tell you about a caravan?'

Sylvia laughed. 'Did she ever. Wouldn't shut up about it. Loved that caravan, she did. Her and her sister were always going off in it, like kids again, she'd say.'

The conversation continued for another twenty minutes but yielded nothing else useful to their investigation. When the call ended, Anna swivelled to face the other two officers.

'Something there struck a chord, right?'

'It did,' Jess replied. 'Just not the one we were expecting.'

She paused as a Warlowism flashed through her mind. 'I know a man, a colleague,' she added quickly, 'who says that cases are like a house of cards. They're delicate and easily toppled. Take the wrong card, and the whole thing collapses in a heap. But if you take the right card, the structure stays, and you have a new one to play with. I think we've found ourselves a new card.'

Anna tilted her head. 'I'm no card player, but I can listen. So, whenever you are ready.'

THE WINTER AFTERNOON pressed against the windows of *Ffau'r Blaidd* like a grey shroud. Inside, Warlow sat in his usual chair, wrapped in a zip-top fleece. What Molly – currently in Cardiff, shopping for her Italy trip – called his "old man cardigan", watching Gil pace the living room floor.

Cadi had greeted Gil with her usual enthusiasm but now lay at Warlow's feet, head on paws, tracking Gil's movement.

'So, someone worked Charlie Brewer over on Christmas Eve,' Warlow said. 'Not very festive.'

'Professional job, too. Quick, efficient, invisible in a balaclava. Left him with a message to keep his nose out.' Gil stopped pacing. 'And Drinkwater's still breathing down my neck about treading carefully with the Napier investigation.'

'Because his golf club cronies used Napier as their solicitor.'

'Exactly.' Gil dropped into the chair opposite. 'But you've seen what I've seen in those images from *Cân-y-Barcud*, Evan. That boy…'

'And someone clearly doesn't like you digging.'

'Which tells me there's something to find. But I'm getting squeezed from both sides here.'

A gust of wind rattled the windows.

Warlow studied the deep lines of worry on his friend's face. 'Be smart about it,' he said finally. 'Work the edges. Build your case quietly.'

'Like the old days?' Gil's mouth twisted in a wry smile.

A tilt of the head from Warlow. 'We haven't always gone in through the front door.'

Gil's phone buzzed. He read the message, eyebrows rising.

'*Mynuffernu*,' he breathed. 'It's Jess. She says they might have found a connection between the Marstons and this case she's helping Avon and Somerset out with.'

'What? The Marstons? Tomo's lost kid?'

'You remembered.' Gil said, impressed.

'I've got bugger all else to think about.'

'A "C" word?'

'No blaspheming in my house. My feelings about coincidence are on record—' A sudden coughing fit cut Warlow short. They were getting less frequent and less violent. But occasionally a good one came back to remind him he'd had pneumonia. And this one was a doozie. He grabbed a tissue, hacking up something substantial.

'Expectorate!' Gil waved an imaginary wand.

'Please,' Warlow wheezed. 'The last thing I need is you pretending to be bloody Dumbledore. Only you could make phlegm sound magical.'

Gil stood to adjust his coat. 'I should head back.' He paused to study Warlow. 'You were going to tell me something earlier?'

Warlow waved him off.

'Not important,' he said.

'If you say so.' Gil headed for the door. 'Get some rest. And you didn't need to add that dramatic coughing fit. Unlike the rest of the force who think you've been swinging the lead, I, for one, realise you've been at death's door. One look at you confirms that.'

'Thank you so much, Matron,' Warlow said but added a grin.

After Gil left, Warlow sat in the gathering darkness, listening to the wind. Crossovers in cases were rare, but when they happened, they could be highly significant.

Jess would no doubt fill him in on all the details. And it was good of Gil to call. To share the problem and keep him in the loop.

Cadi pressed against his legs, offering silent comfort. Warlow pondered what he could do to make himself useful to those left carrying the can.

And so he didn't dwell on the things left unsaid.

# CHAPTER TWENTY-EIGHT

GERAINT LANE STOOD at the kitchen window while Amol arranged takeout menus on the counter. The latter's enthusiasm for their New Year's plans animated his every movement.

'We should definitely order from that new Thai place before heading to Marcus and Sarah's.' Amol held up a glossy menu. 'Their parties are always amazing, but the food is always gone by ten.'

'It's two days away,' Lane said.

'Best to be prepared.'

Lane nodded, managing a mask-like smile. Memory of what he'd done sat as a stone in his stomach. His appetite had not returned since. That phone call forcing him into action. Reminding him of the jeopardy and that he, like the person who'd dragged him into this mess in the first place, had no choice. Not if he wanted to stay out of prison.

*A little favour, a quick bit of paperwork. A snip for someone with your skills.* That had been the invitation. And it was years ago. He'd done it willingly. Got well paid for it, too. He had not expected any of it to come back at him and be a noose slowly tightening around his neck.

'You're quiet today.' Amol came up behind him and

wrapped warm arms around his waist. 'Still thinking about work?'

If only it were that simple.

Lane leaned back into the embrace, treasuring the comfort while hating himself for accepting it under false pretences. The irony wasn't lost on him. He'd finally extracted himself from one nightmare, only to sleepwalk into another.

The Hunt situation had been resolved. Lane's phone and its damning contents now sat decomposing somewhere in the Towy river's murky depths. He should have felt free, unburdened. Instead, he'd merely traded one set of shackles for other, older ones.

*A little favour, a quick bit of paperwork.*

Simple. Clean. Except nothing about it felt clean anymore, not since that follow-up conversation where threats had been wrapped in velvet-soft implications.

'We all need to do what we need to do,' the voice had said. 'Do I really need to explain to you what will happen if anyone finds out?'

Lane watched a neighbour walking their dog across the street, envying the simplicity of their existence. Here he was, planning a dream holiday with the person he loved most in the world, about to celebrate the promise of a fresh start, and all he could think about was how quickly it could all crumble.

The Maldives fund sitting in their joint account felt tainted now, each pound a reminder of his compromise.

Amol moved back to the counter. 'We should book those flights soon. Prices only go up. I mean, your advance for the book is generous and all, but no need to squander money, is there?'

Lane's throat tightened. Every word about their plans was like another brick in the wall of deception he was building between them. He wanted to confess, to let the truth spill out like water through a broken dam. But the consequences were world-ending.

For the both of them.

*Are you trying to tell me that your partner knew nothing about it? About what you did?*

He could hear the accusation in that grumpy DCI's voice if it ever came to it. Or worse, the fat, old sergeant's voice. They'd make a giant meal out of it all.

His silence wasn't only protecting himself anymore.

'You're right.' He turned away from the window and dredged up a smile. 'Maybe we can sort dates after the party.'

The party. Another celebration he'd have to navigate with this secret lodged in his chest.

Amol scrolled through his phone. Watching him triggered a familiar ache of longing in Lane. A yearning for simpler times. A few months ago, his biggest worry had been Hunt and those photos. Now that threat was gone, dissolved in river water, but this other problem, an older problem back with a vengeance, turned the photos on his phone into a minor indiscretion.

Light from the window caught Amol's face, highlighting the smile lines around his eyes, and Lane experienced the familiar surge of protectiveness. He'd do anything to keep that smile in place, to preserve the life they'd built together. Even if it meant carrying this burden alone, letting it eat away at him from the inside while he pretended everything was fine.

But what choice did he have? Some sins, once committed, didn't offer the luxury of redemption. They only left you with the choice of which punishment you could bear to face.

———

ANNA GWYNNE LEANED against the edge of a desk, arms folded, studying the photos Catrin brought up on her screen of Mia Marston, lost in the wilderness, a drone shot of the Marston farmhouse, a front-door shot of Kerry Ford's property.

'Start from the beginning.' She gestured to Catrin. 'The Marston girl.'

'A farmer found her early one morning... uh, the twenty-first. The shortest day,' Catrin explained.

'Is that significant?'

'It is. The farmer was checking his sheep when he spotted the child wandering on open moorland. The girl was hypothermic, dehydrated, not making much sense.'

'And Tomo?'

'Sergeant Thomas,' Jess said. 'Aka the Lone Ranger. Rural crimes.'

'What was his involvement?' Anna asked.

'He was first on scene,' Catrin continued. 'Hadn't been there long when the distraught parents turned up with some odd story of having taken their kids to visit Druid's Moor up that way.' She tapped another photo of the Marston parents. 'Tomo said something was off. Asked us specifically to look into them.'

Anna rubbed her temples. 'And this connects to Kerry Ford how?'

'Good question.' Catrin dropped into her chair. 'The Marstons moved here from the Netherlands with three kids. They homeschool. Off the grid—'

'Something they can afford because Mrs Marston has money from a family business. Still, Tomo's instincts are good.'

'Instincts aren't evidence,' Anna said.

'No,' Jess agreed. 'But we need to establish if indeed the Marstons are who Kerry Ford was visiting. It sounds like it, from Sylvia's description. But it's hearsay until we get acknowledgement.'

The door opened with no knock, and Rhys burst in, phone still pressed to his ear. His face wore the expression they'd all come to recognise. The expression of a man who'd just been handed a missing piece of a puzzle.

'Yes, I'm still here,' he said into the phone. 'Can you send that over now?' He glanced at Anna, eyes wide, then held up a finger in the universal "wait" gesture.

Jess and Catrin exchanged glances.

Anna straightened, watching Rhys's face.

'Right,' he said finally. 'Thanks. Yes, immediately.'

He ended the call and addressed his colleagues. 'That was Financial Crimes. You gave them Kerry Ford's bank details.'

'I did.'

'Something came up on the system. Payments into Ford's account from Janmo Properties.'

'Who?' Jess asked.

'The company name that Royston Moyles used for his rental business. His wife's name is Janet,' Rhys said.

'Moyles?' Anna said. 'Why do I know that name?'

'He was one of Roger Hunt's victims,' Catrin explained.

'Hunt. The bombing in Pembrokeshire, Hunt?' Anna's glance back at her was quizzical.

'That's right.' Catrin, impressed by Anna's knowledge and memory, moved closer to the posted images on the board.

'How is Moyles connected to Ford?' Anna frowned.

Rhys opened his phone and showed Catrin what had come through.

'The payments?' Jess asked. 'Regular?'

Rhys went over to a desk where he logged on and was quickly skimming through the report. 'Uh, no... irregular. Sometimes monthly, sometimes not. And not the same amount each time.'

The silence that followed was treacle thick while Rhys checked something else.

'Flagged up as a business expense by Janmo Properties,' Rhys said. 'It's here in black and white.'

'Was she cleaning for them?' Jess asked.

'It would explain the irregularity of the amount and the frequency,' Catrin agreed.

'I don't understand,' Anna said.

'Don't worry, neither do I. But now we have Ford linked to Moyles and the Marstons, and Moyles is linked to Napier and Hunt.' She shook her head. 'Links in a very sordid chain.'

Anna pushed off from her desk. 'Is there any chance I could talk to some of these people again? The garage owner... what was his name?'

'Bruce Evans,' Catrin said.

'Him first,' Anna said. 'Then Sylvia Robinson. So that I can put a face to the names.'

'You think they knew about the payments?' Jess asked, already shrugging into her jacket.

'I think someone knows something that we obviously do not.' Anna checked her phone. 'And then I'd really like to visit the Marstons.'

'I'm with you there,' Jess said.

'Rhys.' Anna turned to him. 'Can you get everything Financial Crimes has on those payments? Every detail, every transaction.'

He nodded, already reaching for his phone again.

Anna paused to consider each of her colleagues before speaking. 'Am I missing something here? Or is this as bewildering to you as it is to me?'

'None of it makes any sense. At least, not yet,' Jess said.

'Mr Warlow,' Rhys said, 'that's our DCI, he sometimes says follow the money. My guess is he's right.'

Anna tilted her head. 'Sounds like I ought to meet your Mr Warlow.'

Catrin's response was to deliberately not look at Jess at all but to smile brightly instead. 'Perhaps you will, ma'am. If not, I'm sure one of us will tell you all about him.'

Anna narrowed her eyes. 'I'm definitely missing something else here. You lot know how to confuse a DI.'

'We'll have some time in the car for me to bring you up to speed,' Jess said and headed for the door.

Anna followed her, then stopped and turned back to Catrin. Without speaking, she pointed to Jess's disappearing form and then to an imaginary second person somewhere out in the ether, raising her eyebrows in a question.

Catrin nodded vigorously just as Jess's head appeared back inside the door. 'Thought I'd lost you.'

'Coming,' Anna said with just the right amount of manufactured and airy disinterest.

————

THE DOOR CLOSED behind both DIs with a soft click. Catrin

stood at the whiteboard, studying the faces that stared back at her.

Somewhere in this maze of connections was a thorough line. One that linked Kerry Ford to the Marstons and the lost girl on the mountainside.

At his desk, Rhys connected with Financial Crimes again.

In the car park, an unmarked car pulled away from the kerb, carrying Anna and Jess towards what they hoped would be answers.

But, in this job, Catrin knew, answers often just led to more questions. She picked up her pointer, ready to piece it all together.

Again.

# CHAPTER TWENTY-NINE

GIL KEPT the car at a steady sixty-five on the dual carriageway heading east. He had the radio on but wasn't listening. That grainy video image of Freddie Sillitoe flickered through his mind again. A corrupted file that wouldn't delete.

The rain started, a fine mist at first, then more drizzle. Enough to be a bloody nuisance that needed wipers intermittently, and never quite of the right frequency. Just local showers. Indeed, the weather to the north looked clear and cold.

He jabbed at the wiper control with more force than necessary. He still hadn't contacted the South Wales Police. Hadn't dared reach out to the parents. How did you make that call, knowing your words might shatter a family's hard-won peace? Knowing you might be wrong, might be seeing patterns where there were none?

He caught his own eyes in the rearview mirror. Yes, there were dark circles, and wait, was that a slight twitch? Was this becoming pathological? After Operation Alice, when they'd had to wade through all that filth, nobody emerged unscathed. The trafficking, the abuse, the endless transcripts and videos. Some of the senior officers had simply walked away, handed in their badges. He remembered DC Matthews, twenty years on the force, breaking down in the evidence room.

The counsellor they'd made him see – what was her name? Dickson? Jackson? She'd told him it was normal. PTSD, she'd labelled it; common among officers who had to immerse themselves in that kind of darkness.

"It affects everyone differently," she'd said. "There's no shame in stepping back."

Gil had always believed that a kind of fate governed the balance between right and wrong. He never said "good", he preferred "decency". For him, what set humans apart from animals was the will to channel that decency to protect the weak and stand against oppression, criminal or otherwise. Sometimes, he wondered if this made him a foolish old man, but he found deep comfort in knowing that Warlow shared this same belief.

He couldn't step back. Not while Evan was still pushing forward, sick as he was. And Freddie Sillitoe… that case was part of the bigger picture. Had to be.

Gil's phone was linked to the car's infotainment system. He scrolled to Charlie Brewer's number and rang it again.

Nothing.

Straight to voicemail.

*Cachu.*

He couldn't blame the man for switching off. Not after the beating. And his reason for contacting him now was not to pester.

Charlie had done his best, but like Gil, he had no idea what he'd been searching for. The diaries, those calendars with their handwritten scribbles. All typed up on spreadsheets by Rhys now. But no patterns. None of it leading anywhere solid.

Still, it would have been good to know that Brewer was feeling better.

Gil stopped the unanswered call, and the radio came back on. No more Christmas songs, thank the Lord. Now the DJ was wittering on about New Year's resolutions.

'How about promising not to be a banal waste of bloody space?' Gil muttered and flicked to his music library. But no Tom Waits. Not today.

A lorry thundered past, spraying water across his windscreen. Perhaps it was time to admit defeat. He'd meant to tell Warlow that today, had formed the words in his mind on the drive up. But something had stopped him. Evan's stubborn determination, probably. The man was like a mule, sick or not. Always had been.

Gil slowed for the St Clears roundabout, signalled his exit, the indicator's rhythm matching his heartbeat. He'd give it another day or two. Just that. Then... what?

The thought hung unfinished as he headed for Carmarthen. Hanging from the rear-view mirror was a small unicorn placed there by his eldest granddaughter and painted in lurid patterns by all three. Well, scribbled on by all three.

They'd named it Gil. He'd renamed it Gilson Pollock.

His eyes flicked to a playlist. He chose Bill Withers and hoped he had enough breath to join in the chorus of "Lovely Day".

———

A THIN LAYER of frost crunched under Sergeant Tomo Thomas's boots as he surveyed the gathering at the forest's edge bordering Druid's Moor. The weak mid-morning December sun hadn't yet burned completely through the morning mist, and his breath came out in white puffs against the grey Carmarthenshire sky.

The participants in today's exercise would be completely isolated here, where the Caio Forest stretched dark and moody in one direction and the moorland rolled away north towards distant hills in the other. No habitation in sight. They might come across some walkers or cyclists this early, but they were prepared for that. The single-track forestry road they'd followed up here was barely more than a shepherd's path.

'*Anghysbell lawn lan fynyn, Sarge.*' Priya Sharma pulled her police jacket tighter against the cold.

Tomo sent her a sideways glance.

It was indeed properly remote up here. Priya's strong North Wales dialect and accent sometimes made it difficult even for him to understand what the hell she was on about. But he'd grasped the meaning okay. They *were* miles from anywhere.

'Agreed. Wouldn't want to get lost in these hills.'

A flicker of memory danced over his brain. The Marston girl and how lucky she'd been that Rhod Bowen had found her.

'That's why we train here.' Tomo stamped his feet to keep warm.

'Is that Ranger?' Priya's attention suddenly shifted to a magnificent German Shepherd cross being unloaded from a van. 'I read about him last year.'

'The very same.' Tomo grinned. 'Found a woman and her four-year-old on the Beacons in that storm last March. The old *Bannau Brycheiniog* as we are now meant to call them. Though if you ask the dog, he'd probably tell you he was just out for a pleasant walk.'

The dog's handler, Emma Lewis, caught their conversation and laughed. 'More like he was having the time of his life. This one thinks gale-force winds are nature's way of making walkies a bit more interesting. Don't you, boy?'

She ruffled Ranger's ears as he preened under the attention.

'Mind you, the Romans found their way around well enough,' Tomo said. 'We are close to Dolaucothi. Been to the museum yet?'

Priya shook her head.

'You've never been to the gold mines?' Tomo looked scandalised. 'Fascinating place. Spans history, too. They've got these massive Victorian crushing machines used to break up the quartz to get at the gold. And the underground tour goes into tunnels right into the hillside. Some parts are so narrow you have to duck-walk through them. Of course, the Romans didn't have machines. Only hand tools and determination. And big ships full of unpaid labour.'

'Hmm.' Priya bent to pet Ranger.

'Yeah, I'm probably related to an enslaved person,' Tomo said. 'Wouldn't dream of saying it out loud, mind.'

'You just did,' Priya said.

'Yes, I did. But you don't count as polite company. I wouldn't do it there. In polite company, I mean. Ruins the narrative, doesn't it? Us lot being enslaved once.'

Priya stared at him.

'Anyway,' he continued. 'You should see the water systems they built. Bloody ingenious. They'd redirect entire rivers to wash away the hillsides. Some aqueducts are still visible if you know where to wander.'

Their conversation was interrupted by the arrival of two more dogs – a yellow Labrador and a sleek Malinois – with their handler, Dave Weedon's vehicle bouncing along the rutted track that served as a road.

'Morning, all,' DC Weedon called out through an open window. 'Beautiful day for digging up decomposing pork, isn't it?'

'Ah, here are our gravediggers,' Tomo announced.

'Are they really hunting for pork?' Priya asked.

'Not just any pork. This is M&S pork. And for M&S, read manky and stinky. And it wasn't exactly fresh when it was buried five feet under last week by a friendly farmer.' Tomo's grin was a lopsided one. 'You might not want to stand downwind when they find it.'

'Charming.' Priya winced.

Dave had let the dogs have a runabout and the Malinois was practically vibrating with excitement, while the Labrador sat with dignified patience.

'How did you get the dog section?' Priya asked.

'Fell into it,' Dave said. 'Started with regular police dogs, but these… there's something special about cadaver work. They start really young, tested for the right temperament. It's not about breed really. It's about a dog with that mix of drive and focus. There are two of us, normally. Jake's on the way, but he's been off over Christmas. Coming from Leicester today.'

'The training must be intense,' Priya observed.

'Why we're here on this lovely, balmy day between Christmas and New Year.' Dave blew his nose into a tissue.

'They need testing with different odours and different conditions. Lulu here, the Lab, she's also trained for blood work. But both of them can handle anything from collapsed buildings to underwater searches.'

'Underwater?'

'Oh, yeah. Though, this one…' He patted the Labrador's head. 'Thinks every water search is really just an excuse for a swim. I've been to a couple of disaster sites. Spanish floods last autumn, remember them? We went to Poland once. The paperwork was a nightmare, but worth it.'

Tomo cut in, 'Talking of Spain, did you know the Romans used basically the same mining techniques here as they did in Las Médulas in Spain? Probably the same engineers. You can still see the—'

'Sarge,' Priya interrupted gently, 'I will go to the mines, honest. It's on my list. Or even if it wasn't, it is now.'

'Yeah, Tomo. Are you on commission or what?' Dave teased.

'Right.' Tomo clapped his hands together. Three more vehicles were trundling up the track. 'To business. Priya, you're going with Emma and Ranger for the missing person exercise. We've divided it up into sectors. Try not to get too lost on the moors. I've got better things to do than come looking for you.'

'Like what?'

'I,' Tomo puffed out his chest, 'am in charge of the most crucial operation of the day. Tea making.' He patted the water heater in the back of his pickup. 'I'm setting Beryl the Boiler up by the standing stones yonder.' He pointed east. 'There's a good spot for parking just up that old track about a mile from here. Got to love those ancient Celts for creating a perfect tea break location.'

'Shouldn't the sergeant be leading the search exercise?' Priya asked innocently.

'Nah. I've got more of an organisational role. I choose the spots, I get a farmer to bury the treasure, that sort of thing. I'm the only one who knows where the volunteer lost person is hiding. If the dogs can't find him' – he raised a finger – 'or her, it'll be up to me. Besides, any fool can find a missing person. It takes actual skill to brew tea out in the open the way Welsh police-dog handlers like it. It's a sacred responsibility passed down through generations of sergeants.'

He glanced up at the hills disappearing into mist. 'Besides, someone needs to monitor the weather up here. It can turn nasty PDQ.'

'He's not wrong,' Emma checked her radio. 'Last winter, an exercise turned into a real rescue when the fog came down. Couldn't see your hand in front of your face.'

'That's why Ranger is here,' Priya said. The dog had its head up to let her scratch its chin.

'And that's why we have tea,' Tomo corrected. 'Nothing warms you up quite like a brew after you've been playing Tonto.' He held up a hand. 'With apologies to any First Nations people present.'

Priya headed off with Emma and Ranger. Tomo called after her, 'And don't forget, if you get lost, just head north. If you see Snowdon, you've gone a bit too far.'

'Ignore him,' Emma shouted back.

Priya's laughter echoed across the landscape, startling a pair of blackbirds from their perch on one of the pines. The birds wheeled away over the valley, their calls fading into the vastness of the wilderness, where thousands of years of history lay hidden beneath the winter frost.

# CHAPTER THIRTY

JESS DROVE to the New Cross garage, answering as many of Anna's questions as she could and doing most of the talking when they arrived. They stepped in and the bell over the door jangled, releasing a rush of warm air redolent with that patchouli edge. But Bruce Evans had little to add beyond what he'd already told Catrin and Jess during their previous visit.

Anna, however, stared at Kerry Ford's image plastered on the locked cigarette cupboard behind the counter where Evans also stood. He wore a Led Zeppelin T-shirt, the 1980 UK tour dates printed across the back and visible when he turned around to study Kerry Ford's photo with her.

Once again, music filled the space, but Anna ignored it. 'Why are you so interested in Ford?'

'Just trying to help. This is a small community. I wanted to see if I could do more.' He held Anna's gaze with a touch of amusement in his eyes.

'Obviously worked,' Jess said.

'Does that sort of thing not happen where you're from, DI Gwynne?' Evans reached up to adjust a rack of road maps that had started to tilt.

'Not in Hotwells, no.'

'Where's that?'

'Bristol.'

'Truly sorry to hear that, Anna.'

She couldn't remember giving Bruce permission to use first names. But then, there was no law against it. She suspected it was part of his credo. And it was her name, after all.

'Plus, I didn't think it would do any harm,' he added.

'You got a hit,' Jess replied. 'And we're grateful for the information.'

'You talk to Sylvia yet?'

'We did, and very useful she was, too,' Jess said.

'Nice lady. As was Kerry Ford. As I said, I remember her because she always paid in cash,' Bruce noted slowly. 'Always.'

'Didn't you find that odd?' Anna asked.

'Not enough to phone the police. Lots of people use cash around here.'

Outside, a large lorry pulled in to top up on diesel.

'I can't remember the last time I used cash—' Anna began.

Bruce cut in. 'Ah, but you're not a farmer, Anna. You don't go to market.'

He gave them directions to Sylvia's house, his hand waving through the air as he indicated the way.

Back in the car, Anna simply said, 'He's different.'

'I suppose you have to be to run a place like this out here,' Jess explained.

'You believe him?'

'About wanting to help?'

'The whole hippie-hair, rock-T-shirt thing?'

Jess smiled. 'He likes his music.'

'What the hell was playing in there?'

'"Black Cloud" by a band called Trapeze.'

'You've just made that up.' Anna threw her a glance.

'I have not. I'm afraid I've listened to that track too many times not to be correct, as part of my daughter's education in seventies and eighties rock.'

'Were you the educator?'

'I was not. Merely an interested bystander.'

'Is the aficionado DCI Warlow, by any chance?'

Jess concentrated on the road. 'Might be.'

'How long have you two been…' Anna searched for the correct word, only to leave it open-ended.

'About a year.'

'How is he?'

'Much better than he was but thinks he's twenty years younger than he is and indestructible.'

'Shame. I think I would've liked to meet him.'

'He would like you,' Jess said. 'You'd get on well. Now, did Bruce say straight on at this junction or left?'

———

TOMO WATCHED from his position near the Land Cruiser, steam rising from the boiler on the folding table. The empty moorland surrounded him, broken only by the occasional gorse bush and weather-beaten rocks. The wind, constant here, whispered through the coarse grass, carrying the scent of earth and heather.

He walked over to where the three ancient standing stones rose into the pearl-grey sky. A sky stubbornly resistant to the sun's pathetic attempts at breaking through.

They weren't massive stones, but their orange and pale-green lichen-mottled surface added colour to the drab back-drop. The tallest, perhaps twelve feet high, listed slightly to one side as if tired after its millennia of vigilance. Its compan-ions, shorter but no less imposing, created a rough triangle. Their surfaces were intriguing, in places pockmarked by countless winters, elsewhere smooth where sheep had rubbed against them over centuries.

*Bloody strange place for the Marstons to bring their kids*, Tomo thought. He'd done some reading after they'd mentioned their Yule visits. Something about ancient alignments and the midwinter sun. These stones were old, proper old, like a couple of thousand BC.

Neolithic, the books said, though that meant little to

Tomo beyond "bloody ancient". He'd read about similar stones in France being even older than anyone thought, but these three sentinels kept their secrets close. Exactly what they meant was anyone's guess, though.

Places of worship, sacrifice, burial, take your bloody pick, was what he'd gathered. And yes, he'd chosen this area as a late choice for the exercises because of Mia Marston. He'd wanted a better look, and the added advantage of cajoling the farmer, Rhod Bowen, into using some of his machines to bury the treasure had sealed the deal.

Between the gusts, the distant bark of a dog reached him.

He searched for them. Priya's fluorescent jacket appeared first, then the dog's harness. The other search party was still out there somewhere with their animals, working in the northern sector. The cadaver dogs were returning, too, their handlers visible as bright spots of colour on the moor's muted palette nearer the forest edge.

'All good?' Tomo shouted across the wind to the cadaver team when they got near enough.

Dave Weedon raised a thumbs-up.

Priya approached, her cheeks windburned, Ranger between her and his handler, Emma. The "missing" volunteer had been found after an hour and trudged along with them towards refreshments.

'Tea's all ready,' Tomo called out, pushing thoughts of ancient stones and their mysteries aside. 'Should still be hot.'

The wind tugged at their jackets as they gathered around the big Toyota. Behind them, the stones stood as they had for thousands of years, indifferent to the humans who'd come and gone in their shadow over the centuries. A sheep bleated forlornly somewhere in the distance. Another gust swept across the moor, bending the tough grass and sending ripples through the puddles left by last night's rain.

'Bloody bleak up here today, Sarge,' Priya accepted a steaming cup.

Ranger sat near her leg, nose twitching at the biscuits she was unwrapping.

'Always is.' Tomo said. 'Always has been, I reckon.'

'Any chance you could schedule this for July on the beach next time around?' Emma asked.

'How much fun would that be, though?' Tomo grinned and offered her a steaming mug.

———

THE WHITEWASHED FARMHOUSE sat surrounded by rolling hills, its slate roof green with moss. Neat wooden outbuildings, their dark timber weathered to silver-grey, formed a protective horseshoe around a courtyard where cats wandered between carefully tended flowerpots. The whole place had the well-loved feel of a property whose owner took quiet pride in maintaining order.

Three dogs announced Anna and Jess's arrival before Sylvia Robinson opened the door – a Border collie, an elderly Lab, and what appeared to be a terrier mix who maintained a constant commentary of excited yips.

'Hush now, you lot.' Sylvia chided the dogs and ushered the humans inside. She was short, stick thin, silver hair held up in a pile on her head in well-worn jeans and a fleece bearing the Canada Goose name on the zip. 'Come in, come in. Mind the blankets on the sofa. Someone thinks they're for dogs rather than furniture.'

The house was warm and smelled of coffee and something baking. Through the kitchen window, Jess could see the raised beds of a vegetable garden and, beyond that, paddocks where a few sheep grazed contentedly.

'Nice to put faces to the voices. I've got to say this has all come as a bit of a shock. Poor Kerry…' Sylvia swallowed loudly, recovered and asked, 'Coffee? Bean to cup. None of your freeze-dried rubbish.' She took them through to a kitchen. 'I've been doing some research since we last spoke. I looked up the Marstons. Fascinating case. Have you considered—'

'We can't discuss ongoing investigations,' Jess said.

'No, no, of course not.' Sylvia sighed. 'But I watch all

those true crime shows, you know. Sometimes, an outside perspective—'

'Mrs Robinson,' Anna interrupted, 'thank you for seeing us and for talking to us about Kerry. Did she ever mention her ex-husband, Darren?'

Sylvia scratched the Lab's ears. 'Not by name, no. But...' She hesitated. 'Kerry said something once about being glad to be out here. Said no one would find her. I thought little of it...' Her face suddenly lit up. 'Was she hiding?'

Anna didn't answer.

'She never said why she was here. Not exactly.' Sylvia got up to fetch milk. Through the window, a tractor rumbled past. 'That was what made our arrangement so nice, really. She'd come for her two hours of work, but then we'd sit for another two hours just chatting. Sometimes, we'd share a supper. She never said no to a glass of wine. Broke up the monotony, you know?'

She smiled at a flash of remembered pleasure. 'Don't get me wrong—I miss Richard terribly, but there's something to be said for being *sans homme*. Kerry understood that. She'd help me with the heavy lifting upstairs. I mean, it isn't hard to keep the place clean, but a once-a-month thorough blast does wonders. Did wonders.' She paused again, another swallow. 'Then we'd sit here and put the world to rights.'

The elderly Lab huffed and rolled over, exposing his belly to Sylvia's visitors. More cars drove by.

'It's surprisingly busy,' Jess said.

'Holidaymakers at the cottage complex. They have five near the river. Lovely spot. People come to walk. Will you be heading to the Marston place next?' Sylvia asked.

'Kerry was a lot younger than you,' Anna said.

'Yes. Reminded me of myself at that age.' Sylvia settled deeper into her chair. 'Though I had Richard then, of course. Did I mention we met in Bath? 1982 it was, at a folk festival. He was playing banjo in those days. Terrible musician but very handsome. We always came down here for breaks. I bought this place twenty years ago. You wouldn't believe what I'd get for it now—that new holiday complex down the road? The land alone went for four hundred grand.'

The Lab had dozed off, snoring gently, while the collie watched the visitors with unwavering attention. The terrier had finally settled, curled up on one of the blanket-draped chairs.

'Mind you, Kerry never talked much about her past. Unlike me.' He laughed. 'I'm an open book, always have been. Richard used to say I'd chat to a fence post if it would listen.'

Her gaze drifted to a framed photo on the mantelpiece; A man's broad smile captured in the summer sunshine. 'Though, I suppose that's what comes of living out here. You learn to talk when you have the chance.'

'And you always paid her cash?' Anna asked.

The question stalled Sylvia Robinson. 'Umm, yes. Is that—'

'Did she ever mention getting paid cash from any other source?'

'That's an odd question.'

And it was. But it needed to be asked. Sylvia wanted to give the impression that Kerry Ford and she were mates. If so, how much had Ford confided in her was the real question?

Anna waited for an answer.

'No,' Sylvia said. 'No mention of cash, as such. I wasn't the only person she did for. She had regular slots in the week, I think.'

It all smacked of the truth.

Anna caught Jess's slight shift in posture. The almost imperceptible signal that they'd learned all they could.

'We should be going,' Jess said. 'Thank you for the coffee.'

'And thank you for your time,' Anna followed Jess's lead.

'Oh, but I haven't told you about the time Kerry helped me with the goats last spring. She had such a way with the animals, you know?'

But neither officer took up the offer of another anecdote.

Sylvia saw them to the door with no let-up in her chat, her three dogs forming an honour guard. 'Let me know if you need anything else,' she called after them. 'I have quite a good eye for detail. I could show you my journals. I write everything down, have done since 1985…'

Anna and Jess kept walking. The dogs watched them with the same predatory gleam they might watch scurrying rodents.

'No sign or mention of the wayward ex.' Jess drove the car out along the farm track.

'No. And she'd remember if there had been. She's chatty.'

'Lonely?' Jess asked.

'No doubt. But at least she still has the dogs.'

# CHAPTER THIRTY-ONE

DAVE WEEDON HAD Max and Lulu's leads tucked into his belt. Max, the Malinois, moved with characteristic intensity, his amber eyes sharp and focused, while Lulu, the Lab, trotted beside them with a more relaxed gait.

'No problem with the buried treasure then?' Tomo had his hands cupped around a steaming mug of tea.

'No problem at all,' Dave replied. 'These two could find a rasher in a hay barn.' He unclipped both leashes to allow the dogs some freedom.

Max quartered the ground, nose working, while Lulu flopped down near the Land Cruiser, clearly considering her work done for the day.

Priya watched Max's movements. 'How do they signal when they find something?'

'Bark and sit,' Dave scratched Lulu behind her ears. 'Won't move until I come to check. Want to see them search? I can get them to do a sweep.'

At Priya's eager nod, Dave called the dog and rubbed Max's chest—the signal to begin searching.

'Seek,' he commanded.

Max shot off, his muscled body low to the ground, sniffing the air currents that swirled on the wind. He headed out towards open ground before circling back towards the standing stones.

'Beautiful to watch, isn't it?' Dave said. 'The focus they have when they're—'

Max's sharp bark cut through the wind.

The dog sat rigid, about ten yards from the tallest of the three stones, his entire body vibrating with tension but holding the position perfectly.

Dave's smile faltered. 'Tomo, you taking the piss? Did you bury more pork out here?'

Tomo lowered his mug slowly. 'No. They wouldn't bury anything this close to the stones.'

Dave strode over to Max, who hadn't moved a muscle. Kneeling beside his dog, he pushed aside some dead grass and heather. There, half buried in the peaty soil, lay a smooth river stone, flat and grey—the kind you'd find in the valley streams, not up here on the moor. It was barely visible unless you knew to look for it.

Dave straightened up and called to his other dog; he repeated the touch signal. 'Lulu, seek!'

The Lab's transformation from relaxed to focused was immediate. She worked in a different pattern from Max, in broader sweeps across the ground. Five minutes passed, then her bark, too, echoed across the moor. She sat rock-steady several yards west of another standing stone.

Tomo walked over, the tea forgotten on the tailgate. Another stone marker, round and flat, half-hidden again, but similar to the first.

'Could they be picking up… you know, ancient remains?' Priya asked. 'Neolithic burials or something?'

Dave shook his head. 'No chance. Way too old, and too deep.' He turned to Tomo again, his face tight. 'This isn't funny, mate. If you're having us on—'

The expression on Tomo's ashen face stopped him cold.

'I've got a pick and shovel in the car,' Dave said.

The next half hour passed in grim silence, broken only by the scrape of metal against earth and the mournful wind around the stones. The dogs watched, still alert. Four feet down, Dave's shovel struck something that wasn't stone or earth. The hollow sound froze them all.

Tomo dropped to his knees, using his hands now. Carefully, terribly carefully, he brushed away the dark soil to reveal something pale and curved. A bone.

A long, thin bone with a flat rounded head.

'Is that an arm—' Priya began.

'I'd say a radial bone,' Dave Weedon muttered.

'Oh, God.' Tomo's voice was rough with emotion. 'That's it. Nobody touch anything else.'

He stood, wiping his hands on his jacket. The movement left dark smears. 'We need to call this in.'

'But two?' Priya whispered. 'I mean… What if there are more?'

'Wait,' Dave said. He went to Lulu and instructed her again, this time directing her towards the third stone. Another sit, another bark.

'Oh, God,' Emma whispered.

The earlier laughter about buried pork seemed obscene now. A moment of innocence shattered by what lay beneath their feet.

Tomo pulled out his phone and dialled. The wind carried away his words, but they could all see his face. The face of a man who knew this was just the beginning of something bad.

———

JESS HAD VISITED some remote spots since joining the Dyfed-Powys force from Manchester. Parts of Powys, which took up most of the middle of Wales and the border with England, were especially thinly inhabited. The coast, of course, had drawn industry even before the Industrial Revolution reshaped South Wales. But Mid Wales had been – and remained – rural. As the land rose and fell, it earned names like the Black Mountains, the Beacons, and the Cambrians.

They were almost twenty miles north of the *Bannau Brycheiniog* here, south of the Cambrians and still in Carmarthenshire. They retraced their steps, passing, ironically, the National Trust Park where the Dolaucothi mines were situated. But they turned east at *Cwrt-y-Cadno* and the unforgiving land gave up its tended fields and yielded to coarse grasses suitable only for grazing sheep. Where forest plantations had been established, sheep did not graze. But on the moors, farmers still had stewardship and allowed flocks to roam freely.

These large, high spaces were often spots where people, if they so wished, could retreat from civilisation.

The route to the Marston property had the forest to the north and open moor to the east. The way was narrow, following farm tracks with few places to pass and only a handful of properties. They eventually stopped, took a turnoff onto an even narrower lane, and followed a track that swept down to reveal the name of the farm, *Dôl y Derwyddon*, on a wooden gatepost.

The Marstons had clearly invested heavily. The property nestled in a protected hollow. New metal roofing gleamed on the weathered stone barns, and fresh post-and-rail fencing traced neat lines across the property. Behind the main buildings, a cluster of permanent yurts dotted the landscape, their canvas walls taut against wooden frames. The "petting zone" no doubt housed a menagerie of Instagram-worthy animals. Several placid llamas watched their approach with mild interest, while goats pushed their faces through the fence railings, hoping for treats.

Taran Marston met them in the immaculately swept yard, all smiles, as if he'd rehearsed this moment and they were a visiting group in a charabanc.

'Welcome to our sanctuary,' he said, the words flowing with the smoothness of frequent repetition.

Catrin had already phoned to say that the officers were on their way, and he'd made an effort.

His shirt was crisp organic cotton under a waxed jacket. He was on home ground here, and his manner spoke of someone who'd found enlightenment and wanted everyone to know it.

He led them into what had once been a traditional farmhouse kitchen. Now it was a study in carefully curated bohemian charm – mismatched vintage furniture, dried herbs hanging from ceiling beams, and crystals catching the light on every windowsill. The walls were adorned with a mixture of pagan symbols and framed inspirational quotes about Mother Earth.

Noor Marston stood next to a fireplace stacked with logs ready for burning. No doubt culled from their own trees. She had her blonde hair pulled back in a braid, wearing flowing loose-fitting clothes that looked both expensive and organic. Her boots had thick industrial soles.

Jess could hear Warlow's voice in her head whenever they had to interview someone dressed like this. 'The colour-blind clown vibe,' he called it and generally added as a follow-up growl, 'Not judging, mind.'

'Please sit,' Noor said, her Dutch accent precise and measured. 'Would you like some herbal tea? We grow everything in our garden.'

'Thank you, but no.' Jess settled onto a wooden chair that had been deliberately distressed to add an aged appearance. 'Thanks for agreeing to meet with us.'

Anna did not stand on ceremony. 'We're here to ask you about Kerry Ford, Mrs Marston.'

'Of course.' Noor's response snuffed out her smile, and her pale eyes became serious. 'Such a tragedy. She was very helpful to us when we first established ourselves here.'

'You employed her for cleaning?' Anna prompted.

'Yes.' Taran exchanged a quick glance with his wife. 'It's difficult to find reliable help this far out. Kerry would come up, sometimes twice a month. Lately, once monthly. Cash in hand. She preferred it that way.'

Their answers had a polished feel. Perhaps not of a well-practised script, but chosen to paint a picture of casual, unremarkable employment.

'So, twice a month, you said?' Anna asked.

'Not always. Regularly, the last Thursday of the month, but in the busy season, when we have visitors, twice at least.'

'You have visitors now?' Jess asked.

'No. We are closed until February,' Noor said.

'Was it Ms Ford's choice to be paid in cash, or yours?' Anna asked.

'Hers. Look, I know the powers that be prefer every transaction to be traceable. But I do not work for the taxman—'

'That's not why we're here, Mr Marston.'

'Glad to hear it.' There was no belligerence in his delivery. More amused relief if anything.

When Anna asked about Kerry's ex-husband, their responses were equally measured, equally empty of useful information. Everything they said projected an image of vague, harmless eccentricity cushioned by not having to depend upon the business entirely for their survival.

'Can I ask about the morning you visited the standing stones?' Jess studied Noor's face carefully. 'When your daughter Mia wandered away?'

'What has that to do with Kerry Ford?' Noor stiffened.

'Nothing,' Jess said. 'Curiosity, that's all. My geography isn't brilliant, but where are they in relation to the farm?'

'A couple of miles as the crow flies. Southeast,' Taran said. 'It's a trek over rough ground. No path as such. At least, not on any map.'

'And we hiked that morning. In the dawn light. An adventure for the kids.' Noor's hands fluttered to her throat, the gesture almost theatrical. 'Mia has always been… how do you say… a free spirit? She feels the call of nature.' She gave a small, rehearsed laugh. 'We encourage our children to connect with the earth's energy.'

'Is Mia here now?'

'No.' Taran smiled. 'The children are with Noor's sister in the Netherlands. It's our New Year tradition. It gives everyone a break, helps them appreciate each other more when they return. And I get a chance to do some maintenance on the property.'

'Your place is fascinating,' Jess said. 'Very… unique.'

'I'd be happy to give you a tour,' Taran offered, his sales pitch slipping into place. 'Show you our meditation spaces, the crystal alignment garden…'

'Perhaps another time,' Anna said, already standing.

Outside in the crisp air, the llamas still stared, but their gaze seemed knowing rather than placid.

'Impression?' Anna began once they were seated.

'Strange,' Jess finished. 'Very. But strange doesn't make them criminal.'

'Given what we know about Kerry Ford, it all fits. But did you get the impression that they were putting on a show?'

'Probably because they are. That's their business model, isn't it? Being professional earth children.' Jess started the engine. 'I'm glad we came, but this hasn't got us any closer to understanding who killed Kerry and her sister.'

Anna said nothing, but Jess knew she was thinking along the same lines.

They'd driven barely a mile when Jess's phone rang.

'It's Catrin.' The sound crackled with urgency across the car's speakers. 'I've taken a call from Tomo. He's up at the standing stones north of Caio Forest.'

'What?' Anna shot Jess a bewildered stare.

'He's found something, ma'am. Something bad. I know you're up that way and you'd want to know.'

Jess caught Anna's eye and pulled over. 'Can you send me a pin and directions?'

While they waited, Jess quickly explained to Anna what the call was about. 'Tomo runs exercises this time of year with dogs. He was the one who responded when the farmer found Mia Marston wandering.'

'Why is he up there, though? Isn't that a bit of a coincidence?'

'Knowing Tomo, he's wanted to scratch an itch.'

Catrin came back with directions within two minutes.

Jess stared at the text. 'Damn. No direct route. We have to go south and then north.'

She took off again and rang Catrin back on the speakerphone. 'Got them. What exactly have they found?'

Catrin sounded odd when she spoke. 'They have cadaver dogs, ma'am. The dogs… they've found some bodies. Small bodies.'

For a few seconds, the only noise was that of the car's engine ticking efficiently.

Anna stared first at the radio, then at Jess, but said nothing. As if she'd lost the ability to speak.

'CSI should be almost there by now,' Catrin broke the silence. 'Tomo has requested ground-penetrating radar.'

'I do not like the sound of this,' Anna muttered.

'We're on our way,' Jess said. But all the while, her brain whirled with unconnected fragments.

A woman with violence in her past, murdered. A woman who'd hidden money in her home, who'd visited a secluded farm and got paid in cash. A farm kept by people who took their kids to visit standing stones on a day celebrated in the pagan year. Stones where cadaver dogs had now found bodies. None of it made any sense.

She wished she could talk to Warlow.

But he wasn't here, and she wouldn't bother him until she knew more.

'I thought I was coming over here on a fact-finding mission,' Anna said with a shake of her head. 'This has taken a real *The Hills Have Eyes* turn.'

Jess didn't buy into that. But Anna was right about one thing. There was nothing at all to like about the way this case was heading.

# CHAPTER THIRTY-TWO

JESS AND ANNA drove through the dense forest. Reaching the open moorland was like emerging from a tunnel. Jess stayed tight on the steering wheel to negotiate the track. A quick call to Buchannan and he'd given his blessing for her to attend the scene. She decided not to hypothesise about links to anything else. After all, they had no hard evidence, just an increasingly unnerving number of links, and she said as much to Anna.

'I prefer links, too,' Anna commented. 'Screw coincidences.'

'That has been drummed into me and the rest of our team.' Jess's voice was tight. 'Say "coincidence" three times in the mirror and you turn into a pillar of salt.'

'Isn't that some sort of biblical warning about not looking back?'

'Yes, well, the man who coined the phrase isn't precious when it comes to mixing motif and mythology. It doesn't take a Lott – excuse the pun – to get Gil Jones warmed up.'

'He's another one I'd like to meet, then.'

'Careful what you wish for,' Jess joked.

They parked up to the sound of CSI tents snapping in the wind. The ground was treacherous underfoot. They had to walk the last fifty yards over patches of boggy earth hidden beneath deceptively firm tufted grass from where they had parked. The light was fading from a day once again shrouded in grey clouds. The distant hills faded into smudged charcoal drawings. A crime scene manager checked them in and they went in search of Tomo. Dave Weedon, Max, and Lulu were still there, too.

Tomo observed their approach.

'Is it a child?' Jess asked, her words half carried away in the wind.

Tomo looked as if he might throw up at any moment. When he pulled off his latex gloves, his hands trembled, and a fine sheen of sweat covered his forehead despite the chill. Jess suspected he might already have been sick; there was a sour edge to his breath when he spoke.

'Yes, though not sure yet about male or female.'

'Is the HOP on their way?'

'They are.'

'This is Anna, by the way.' Jess realised she had forgotten the introduction. 'DI from Avon and Somerset.'

They shook hands.

A small army of trucks, cars, and vans had pulled up, their searchlight headlights already cutting through the gathering gloom. Despite the lighting, it wasn't hard to see they were far from any kind of habitation. The nearest farmhouse was a lonely dot on the horizon; a geometrical shape breaking up the natural curves, its windows dark and unwelcoming, possibly abandoned.

'This spot…' Anna's boots squelched in the mud. She pivoted, taking in the isolation. 'Did you choose it?'

Tomo squeezed his eyes shut, the skin around them tight with stress. 'I did.'

'We've just been up to see the Marstons,' Jess said.

'What?' Tomo looked bemused.

'It's a long story,' Jess explained.

'I don't come up here often. But the kid, Mia, I couldn't forget her. It's as good a place as any for a training day. I never expected to find something like this.'

His last words were almost lost in a sudden gust of wind that made the big truck he was leaning against shake.

'And we think there are more?' Jess asked.

'The dogs found two more.' His words fell like stones.

'Povey in the tent?'

'Yeah,' Tomo said, sounding hollow. 'Priya's with her.'

More floodlights flickered on as darkness regained the moor. Distorted shadows seemed to reach for them with grasping fingers. The temperature was dropping, and Tomo's breath snaked out his words in a visible trail of vapour.

Jess squeezed Tomo's arm. A tremor ran through the sergeant beneath her hand. 'It must have come as a shock. It's no consolation, but if you hadn't been the stubborn, curious old bugger you are, we'd never have found these.'

Tomo's eyes, full of pain, cleared a little at that.

A nearby generator coughed and spluttered into life, a jarring backdrop to their grim discovery.

'No.' He drew his jacket tighter in the biting wind. 'Suppose not.'

Povey was indeed in the tent, with Priya and another tech. They'd placed a wide cordon around the stones, and other snow suits were examining the ground nearby.

The CSI looked up from where she was down in the hole dug by Tomo and Dave. Below her, a few bones were on display. She held a trowel and a brush.

'How long have they been here?' Jess asked.

'Years more than months, I'd say. You'll have to wait for the numbers.'

'Looks more like an archaeological dig,' Anna said.

Jess quickly made more introductions.

Povey waved a horsehair brush. 'This might take a couple of days. Radar is on the way for the others.'

Jess nodded. 'Anything else?'

Povey let her eyes drop towards the skeleton. 'You'll need to give us a few hours, at least. May even be a day or two here. It's slow going.'

Jess walked back out and sighed. 'We're cluttering up the place here.'

Anna agreed.

The car's heater slowly pushed back the bone-deep chill

which had seeped into them on the moor. Neither woman spoke for several minutes. The forest closed in. Jess suspected Anna was, like her, trying to process what they'd just witnessed.

'I've never seen Tomo like that,' Jess finally said. 'And I've seen him at some rough scenes.'

Anna shifted in her seat. 'He seemed... haunted. Not just by what he'd found, but something else. That business about the girl, Mia?'

'Yes.' Jess navigated a sharp bend, her headlights catching the eyes of something that froze at the roadside. 'He's always been one for taking things personally, animals especially. But they were children's bones...' She let the thought trail off.

'Will he be okay?'

Jess flicked on the wipers as a fine drizzle fell. 'He'll be fine. But it's got to him. That's the reason the training day is up here anyway. That's all down to him wanting to see the stones again.'

'Like he was drawn back?'

'Exactly.' Jess checked her mirrors, more out of habit than necessity, on the empty road. 'As I said before, I trust Tomo's instincts.'

They drove on, chatted a bit, but mostly drifted into silence, pondering their own thoughts. Eventually, the lights of Llandeilo appeared, warm points of gold in the darkness. On the outskirts of the town, Jess took the road back up towards Llandovery. The Plough at Rhosmaen glowed ahead. A beacon in the December night. Christmas lights still twinkled along the eaves, repurposed now for the New Year, creating an incongruous brightness that jarred their sombre mood.

'God, I need a drink,' Anna murmured as they pulled into the car park.

'We all do.' Jess killed the engine. 'Gil's meeting us here.'

They sat for a moment longer in the car, watching guests hurry through the rain into the hotel's warmth, their holiday cheer a world away from the grim scene they'd left behind.

'Ready?' Jess asked.

Anna nodded, gathering herself. 'As I'll ever be.'

She hoisted out a holdall from the back seat.

Inside, the bar and restaurant buzzed with the merry chatter of tourists and families, the clink of cutlery, and festive music playing softly in the background. The aroma of roasted meats wafted through the air.

'Have you booked in?' Jess asked.

'I rang through to tell them I'd be late.'

'Over there.' Jess pointed to a quiet corner in the lounge, where deep armchairs clustered around a low table.

Gil was already waiting, nursing a pint.

A young couple at a nearby table laughed over their cocktails, smartphones out to capture their holiday memories. But the day hung heavily on Jess; their easy happiness felt distant, a thin veil over the unsettling image from the moor that lingered in her mind.

Jess introduced Gil. He immediately went to the bar and came back with a G and T for Anna and a small glass of wine for Jess.

'Time's getting on,' Jess said. 'I suggest we include Evan in the discussion. We could do with his input. Do you mind?'

Anna shook her head above the glass at her lips. 'Anyone who can shed some light on all of this is more than welcome.'

Gil raised his phone, connecting to Warlow on video chat. The DCI's familiar face appeared, backdropped by his living room's soft lamplight and the glow of his own Christmas tree. He was wrapped in what Jess recognised as his favourite fleece, a glass of red beside him.

Once again, Jess introduced Anna.

'Sorry to hear about your illness,' Anna said.

'What illness?' Gil frowned. 'Have you been ill? No one said.'

'Nice to meet you, Anna. Strange circumstances, I know. Ignore Gil. Being a clown is his default mode.'

'Right, then.' Jess kept her voice low. 'Let's start with the Marstons.'

They discussed their impressions of the "odd" couple, which, by consensus, was what Anna and Jess had decided they were. Nothing illegal about that, of course. Anna shared her instincts about Noor Marston's earth-mother vibe, while Jess described Taran's controlled responses.

'Were you happy with their explanation of the link to Kerry Ford?' Warlow asked.

'It works, but it's not what Sylvia Robinson said to us. Her impression was that Ford had become a family friend.'

Warlow considered this but said nothing.

When they moved on to Tomo's discovery, his face darkened visibly, even over the screen. 'Three bodies? And you say it's nowhere near any roads?'

'Middle of sodding nowhere.' Jess watched a family with young children pass their corner, the kids wearing reindeer antlers and giggling. Her throat tightened. 'But we can't now ignore the link to the Marstons either, though I'm clueless as to what the hell it all means.'

Warlow laid it out. 'Ford's dead. She knew the Marstons. At least three bodies out at those standing stones, and the Marstons are linked to that site as well. I know I'm stating the obvious – but how does Ford fit into that picture? And what about her property? Anything there?'

'That's where I think we need Tannard again.' Gil leant forward. 'She's got a knack for finding things people think they've hidden well. We should search the place again.'

Warlow nodded. 'Agreed. I'd get Tannard and some uniforms back out there tomorrow. The money doesn't add up. Even if she took cash from everyone she worked for. She bought half shares in a caravan, for God's sake. They aren't cheap.'

A burst of laughter from the corner drew their attention. A group of friends were toasting something; their faces flushed with celebration and wine.

Gil grimaced slightly before turning back to their discussion.

'There's a connection here somewhere,' Warlow mused. 'You… we… are just not seeing it yet. I'd wait for Povey and the HOP to process the crime scene and get forensics on the bodies. Meantime, I'd go back and dig into Ford.'

Anna nodded, and there was a spark in her eyes.

As they wrapped up, Jess moved away from the others to speak privately with Warlow. 'Thanks for that.'

'We both know it's exactly what you would have done anyway. But I appreciate you involving me. I won't lie, recuperation is boring.'

'I'll be late,' she said.

'I know. I'll be in bed. Molly texted. She's on her way back from Cardiff. Said something about finding a couple of bargains.'

Jess smiled, her first genuine one of the day.

Gil offered her a bed for the night, but Jess declined. The thought of seeing Molly, hearing about her shopping adventures, and crawling into her own bed was too much of a draw, despite the long drive to Nevern ahead.

'I'll pick DI Gwynne up tomorrow, take her into HQ to fetch her car before we go out to Ford's place first thing.' Gil finished his drink. 'I'll get some help, rope in Rhys as well.'

He glanced at Anna. 'We'll make a proper job of it.'

They said their goodbyes in the car park. Jess waved Anna and Gil back inside, then climbed into her car, chilly now after the warmth of the hotel.

The road ahead led back to family and the comfort of home. A few hours' respite to shake off the day's darkness. She turned up the radio, letting holiday tunes fill the car, a small buffer against the thoughts of where on earth this case was leading them.

# CHAPTER THIRTY-THREE

GIL TOOK out his phone while Anna checked in. He scrolled through his contacts. He'd need to coordinate tomorrow's visit carefully. First call was to the station, arranging a uniformed presence at Kerry Ford's property. Then a direct call to Tannard. She was busy, so he couched it in terms of his team doing the heavy lifting. But she'd been to the house already, and having her there would save a lot of time.

'Sorted?' he asked as Anna returned and slid back into the chair at the table.

Her glass still had some unmelted ice at the bottom, slowly diluting the gin. 'Half hour for some food. They're packed but sympathetic to a hungry detective.' She nursed her drink. 'You're based nearby?'

'Llandeilo. Only a few miles down the road if you need anything.' He pocketed his phone but handed her a card. 'And we're all set for tomorrow morning.'

'Jess filled me in about Freddie Sillitoe.' Anna's eyes were sharp with interest. 'Dead end?'

Gil sighed. 'Not getting very far on that, I'm afraid. Every lead gone cold. Sometimes, they just…' He shrugged. 'More than happy to help with this Ford business, though, good timing for me. Fresh eyes, fresh case.'

'I feel bad pulling you away from your cold case, though,' Anna said softly. 'It can't be easy setting it aside.'

'Don't apologise. Not for this. Whatever this is.'

'I wish I knew,' Anna muttered.

'Anyway, Evan would have fought to be first in line. He's spitting feathers not being here to help.'

Anna nodded, clearly understanding.

'Let's see what tomorrow brings,' Gil said.

'Speaking of Warlow, it's unusual to see partners working together. You know what I mean?'

Gil smiled. 'Good match, those two. Both been through the mill. Jess with that business up north with her ex; Evan, after losing Denise.' He took a thoughtful sip of the last inch of his pint.

'He lost his wife?'

'To alcohol several years ago. But she died only a year or so ago. They were separated, Evan and his wife. It's nice seeing him and Jess happy.'

'They seem solid.'

'They are.' Gil studied her. 'You're not a stranger to the odd tough case, though. The Black Squid murders made headlines everywhere.'

Anna's expression remained neutral, but something flickered in her eyes. 'It was an interesting few years.' She traced the base of her glass with a finger.

'Any family in Bristol?'

'I'm a walking cliché, since I ended up living with one of the witnesses in that case you mentioned. So, I have no leg to stand on when it comes to mixing professional and personal and procedural complications.' Her smile was wry.

'A keeper?'

Anna smiled. 'So far.'

'Ah well. That's the job for you. Bleeds into everything you do.'

'Occupational hazard.' She shrugged. 'You've been married long?'

'Forty-odd years. Some of them very odd. But happily married for several of them.'

Anna rewarded that with a smile.

'Two daughters, three grandkids.' His face lit up. 'Youngest just started school, whip-smart, the tinkers. Take after their grandmother, thank God.' Gil glanced at his watch. 'Better let you get to your food. We'll head out around half eight tomorrow?'

Anna nodded. 'Perfect. Thanks for the drink. And the welcome.'

'Honorary team member, ma'am.' Gil stood.

'Anna, please.'

'Okay, Anna. Restaurant's decent here. You'll enjoy it.'

'I usually do. Eating alone agrees with me.'

'You'll get on with Evan, then.' He smiled. 'Goodnight.'

'Night, Gil.'

⸻

ANNA WATCHED HIM LEAVE, quietly satisfied with the day. It was good territory she'd landed in—good people fighting the good fight. Her food would be ready soon, and then a long sleep in a strange bed. Tomorrow, they'd start digging in the weeds.

She'd always enjoyed a bit of gardening.

⸻

WARLOW SAT at the kitchen table at *Ffau'r Blaidd*. Molly spread her purchases across its surface while Cadi's head rested on his knee. The Labrador's eyes were half shut in relaxed ecstasy. Her go-to response to having her ears fondled.

'Look at this!' Molly was holding up a cream thick-wool sweater. 'Perfect for Milan in winter, don't you think? And this...' She produced a tailored black jacket.

The click of the back door announced Jess's arrival, bringing with her a blast of night air. She shivered and let out a 'Brrr' before noting the display.

'Successful day, then.' She dropped her bag and bent to ruffle Cadi's fur.

The dog's tail beat a rhythm against the chair.

'Everything was in the sales. Well, almost everything.'

She revealed a pair of leather boots with sturdy soles that definitely hadn't been on any sale rack. 'But these will last forever, and they're waterproof for all the slush they'll encounter.'

Jess picked one up, examining it with exaggerated seriousness. 'They're gorgeous. Just don't tell me how much forever costs.'

Warlow observed, amused. This easy interaction between them still tickled him sometimes.

'And this—' Molly dug deeper into her bags, producing a cashmere scarf in deep burgundy and charcoal. 'The woman in the shop said these are this winter's colours.'

'It suits you,' Warlow agreed. He pushed up, steadying himself against the table's edge. 'You hungry, Jess? I can heat up that chilli from yesterday.'

The kitchen tilted slightly. He gripped the table harder, hoping neither of them had noticed, but Jess's sharp intake of breath told him otherwise.

'Evan?' Molly paused in her show-and-tell.

'I'm fine,' he said automatically. 'Just stood up too fast.'

'Sit down.' Jess's ordered. 'I can sort out my own food.' She waited until he complied. 'How long has this been happening?'

'It's nothing. I've been sitting around too long. That's all.'

Molly gathered her purchases, suddenly subdued. 'I should finish packing anyway. Still need to work out how to fit everything into a carry-on bag.' She walked towards the passage but stopped. 'Don't let him convince you he's fine if he's not.'

Cadi followed her upstairs, leaving Warlow and Jess alone in the kitchen. Through the window, the lights they'd strung up around the eaves danced madly in the breeze.

'How's your visitor from across the bridge working out?' he asked.

Jess's expression made it clear she wasn't fooled by his

change of subject, yet she answered anyway, moving around the kitchen to find plates. 'Anna? She's good.'

'You saw her on the call. She comes across as a straight talker.'

'Gil likes her.'

The microwave hummed. 'She's on the ball. I feel bad roping her into this case up in the forest.'

Warlow nodded, still slightly disconnected, aware of Jess's keen eye on him. He'd have to be more careful. The spells were getting harder to hide, and between Jess and Molly, he was running out of excuses.

'Yeah. What do you make of that?'

Jess's phone rang and she glanced at the number.

'Povey,' she said and put it down on the table with the speaker on.

'Alison. I'm with Evan on speaker. So, do not reveal any dark secrets.'

'I'm definitely going to disappoint you there.'

'What do you have?' Jess asked.

'HOP's been. It was Tiernon, by the way. We've had the forensic anthropologist out. He thinks these graves are not that old. That is, not ancient old. A few years at the most. Tiernon has asked us to exhume as soon as possible. We'll probably work through the night. There is still some flesh, so we'll get DNA. But it isn't the bodies as such I was ringing about.'

Jess threw Warlow a glance. 'What else?'

'The marker stones. When we lifted them, there was something underneath. Written on all three in marker pen. One was better preserved than the others. I'm sending over a photo.'

Jess's phone pinged, and an image appeared. She enlarged it, and the curved surface of a river-smoothed stone appeared, followed by the handwritten remnants of a word.

'What does it say?' Warlow asked.

'We aren't sure yet. We think eight letters. Begins with a G, we can see that because it's larger. Ends in E. Same on all three, but the one I've sent you has the most letters. You can make out an L and an F and a D. And there's an I and an E on the other stones. It's a mix and match.'

'The same on each stone?' Warlow asked.

'Looks that way,' Povey replied. 'We've transported them back to the lab. We'll clean them up and photograph them under filters. In fact, that is being done as we speak. I wanted to let you know before it gets too late.'

Jess checked the time. 8:33 p.m.

'So, ground radar—' Warlow began.

'Confirms bodies in the other two. We're well on the way towards exhumation now.'

'And there was nothing buried with the first corpse?'

'No. No casket. Just in the earth.'

'All at the same depth?' Warlow asked.

'Give or take. Between four and five feet. Grass had regrown over the surface.'

'Thanks, Alison,' Jess said.

'How is the sick man of Dyfed-Powys?' she asked.

'Alive and kicking,' Warlow said. 'Alive at any rate. The kicking is still a work in progress.'

'Good to hear. Right. I'd like to be out of here by midnight, so I'm going to get to it.'

Jess thanked her and returned to the pinging microwave to give the chilli another blast.

'Jacket potatoes have been in long enough,' he said. 'I managed that.'

Molly joined them, and they all ate hungrily. Warlow's appetite had returned with a vengeance, but Molly excused herself shortly afterwards to take a shower, leaving Jess and Warlow to clear up.

Jess's phone beeped another message. She frowned at it.

'What is it?'

She showed him. Another image from Povey of the stone, this time under an odd blue light and showing up a complete word, albeit with some of the letters faded.

'Gelifed?' she said.

'No, there's no vowel after the F. *Geliefde.*'

'Is that some kind of made-up Tolkien thing?'

Another notification. This time a text message:

Geliefde. Dutch word for beloved.

'Shit,' Jess whispered.

Warlow read the message too, and for a moment, all they could do was look at one another in silence as the meaning sank in.

Jess texted back a thank you to Povey. Then she dialled Gil, who answered promptly and listened without comment when she told him what she wanted him to do.

# CHAPTER THIRTY-FOUR

THE NEXT MORNING, after arresting them at their property at 07:30, the Marstons were taken to the custody hub in Llanelli where they were offered legal support and accepted it.

Two different solicitors. Because Jess wanted to interview them separately. She took Catrin with her, and they began with Noor Marston at three minutes past nine in the morning.

The interview room carried the whiff of a cleaner's mop – the place's usual miasma of stale air and nervous sweat banished by chemicals. Two cameras recorded from opposite corners, their red lights steady and unwavering. The table was fixed to the floor, its surface already bearing a few scratches despite its relative newness. A fly buzzed against the sealed window, trapped between glass and blinds.

'This is ridiculous,' Noor Marston snapped. Her fingers did not stop moving, one hand playing at a hangnail on the other. The skin looked coarse. Not a manicured hand, one used to hard work. 'I was in the middle of making breakfast when your... people barged in.'

'Everything was recorded, Mrs Marston. No one barged in on the video that I saw. I think our officers were polite. Gave you ample time to dress and get prepared.'

'They watched me.'

'A female officer stood at an open door and let you gather your clothes and dress.'

Twenty years on the force had taught Jess that the angriest suspects were often the most afraid.

Beside Noor, a duty solicitor by the name of Scott shifted in his chair; his suit had a rumpled, slept-in appearance. A coffee stain marked his tie, and his briefcase bulged ready to burst, stuffed with badly organised papers. He'd already interrupted twice to ensure that his client had water, and the cup was refilled for the both of them.

Jess knew him, knew all his little self-referential foibles – the procedural pedant who'd rather argue about half-filled water cups than actually defend his client.

'Interview commenced at 09:07,' Catrin stated clearly, her lilt precise and measured. She'd positioned herself slightly sideways to the suspect—less confrontational, more approachable. It was a technique that had served her well over the years. 'Present are Detective Inspector Jessica Allanby, Detective Sergeant Catrin Richards, the suspect Noor Marston, and duty solicitor Dion Scott.'

She delivered the caution with practised efficiency: 'You do not have to say anything, but it may harm your defence if you do not mention when questioned something which you later rely on in court. Anything you say may be given in evidence.'

Scott nodded, satisfied with the procedure, though he stared only at the recording equipment. He wrote something down on a notepad until Noor shot him an irritated glance, at which point he stopped.

'I don't understand why I'm even here,' Noor said, her accent catching on the R's and S's, but the intensity in her voice had softened to something closer to anxiety. Fed up with the hangnail, or perhaps not wanting to make it worse, Noor found a loose thread on her voluminous sleeve and worried at it instead.

'Mrs Marston,' Catrin continued, 'you're here today in connection with the discovery of human remains found in the Caio Forest area. Do you understand?'

Noor's 'Yes' was barely above a whisper, her earlier bravado evaporating. She reached for a silver pendant that disappeared beneath her blouse before she could grab it.

Jess sat back, her manner deliberate and calm. She'd positioned the case file half open but with its contents obscured by a blank sheet. Its presence would be a silent pressure point. 'I'd like to ask you about the standing stones on Druid's Moor. They're about two miles from your home, aren't they?'

'Yes.' Noor continued worrying at the loose thread. Her nails needed attention. The blue varnish was badly chipped.

'How familiar are you with that location?'

'We…' Noor glanced at Scott, who gave an almost imperceptible nod. The solicitor held his pen poised in case something of great importance emerged, it seemed. 'We visit sometimes. For the sabbats. The wheel of the year. It was a sacred site once. It has been there for millennia. That's something to treasure, isn't it? I explained all of this when Mia got lost.'

Jess let the silence stretch for a moment, allowing Noor to squirm in it, the thread getting slightly longer by the minute. 'Just for religious observations?'

'Certain times of the year. Of significance. Equinoxes, Yule. That's all.' Noor moved her hand to her pendant again, clutching it like a lifeline.

Jess reached into the folder and withdrew a photograph, sliding it across the table with deliberate slowness. The image showed the weathered river stone with the word *Geliefde* highlighted by Povey's magic light.

'Can you tell me what this means?'

Noor's hands stilled. Her face drained of colour, but she remained steady. 'I'm sorry, I don't know.'

'You're certain about that?' Jess's eyes never left Noor's face. Behind her, Catrin had shifted position slightly, boxing Noor in psychologically.

'Yes.' The word caught in her throat, but her eyes, meeting Jess's for the first time, were steel-hard with determination.

Was that a flash of fear she read there, or a warning?

Noor's accent had shifted again, too—perfectly controlled now, each syllable precise.

Catrin leaned forward. 'It's Dutch, Mrs Marston. It means "beloved".' She paused, waiting to see if Noor's composure cracked even slightly. 'And I think you were already aware of that.'

Noor Marston's gaze darted to the door as if calculating escape routes. The pendant had slipped free of her blouse—a small silver tree, its roots tangled around what looked like a Celtic knot. Jess understood the signs: they were getting close to something, and Noor Marston was terrified.

The fly stopped buzzing behind the blind.

In the sudden silence, Noor's breathing quickened, shallow and irregular.

When she spoke again, her voice had changed entirely; younger somehow, almost childlike. 'I want to go home now. Please.'

Scott cleared his throat. 'I believe my client has made it clear she has nothing more to say about this matter.'

But Jess had seen it. The moment when the mask slipped. And in Noor's eyes, there had been something more than fear. There had been recognition.

Scott, on the other hand, was posturing in order to give her time.

'That's as may be,' Jess said. 'Unfortunately, we haven't quite finished. Would it surprise you to learn that three bodies have been discovered buried close to these standing stones, Noor?'

No response.

Scott leaned across to whisper to Noor.

'No comment,' Noor spoke slowly.

'Really? A marker stone with a Dutch word written on it, and you don't want to tell us anything?'

'No comment.'

'Small bodies. Children's bodies,' Catrin said.

'No comment,' Noors whispered.

'I would think about that very, very carefully if I were you.

We are going to find out who those children are. It is only a matter of time.'

'No comment.'

'Did you know those children, Noor?' Jess asked.

A moment's hesitation before Noor said again, 'No comment.'

It went on like that for another five minutes until Jess put an end to it. 'Let's pause things. We'll get you a cup of tea, Noor. And then we'll be back after we've chatted with Mr Marston. How about that?'

Noor did not lift her eyes from the desk.

———

'DOING anything special for New Year, Gil?' Rhys asked, defaulting to the first-name exchange they'd now adopted when alone, as they were this morning, on their way to the mill and Kerry Ford's rented property.

'Only shouting hallelujah from the rooftops when I wake up January first knowing I've made it through another year. You?'

'A group of us are going to the pub. There's a quiz, some food, and then a DJ.'

Gil watched as Rhys finished a long and noisy Greggfast. He had offered to drive, giving his younger colleague a chance to eat his bacon and omelette breakfast roll, bacon and sausage breakfast roll, and garden variety (not) sausage roll, washed down with coffee and a bottle of water.

'Ultra-processed food is bad for you. Toxic. Poison. The Lady Anwen has told me all about it…' Gil paused before adding, 'More than once.'

Rhys took on a hangdog expression. 'It's a treat. Once a month, max. Rest of the time, I'm healthy. Lots of veggies. Just ask Gina.'

'I don't need to ask Gina. I've seen her collection of designer gas masks.'

'Not fair.'

'Very fair. Since I am forced to spend many hours next to you in the enclosed space of a motor vehicle.'

They drove on in silence until Gil added, 'The Lady Anwen listens to lots of podcasts.'

'Sorry to hear that.'

'Which means,' Gil said, ignoring the sarcasm, 'that I am well-informed, or misinformed, as the case may be, on many trends. Especially food trends. No UPF in our house. And, so I've been told, we now must eat thirty different plant varieties every week.'

That earned him a sceptical side-eye from Rhys. 'That's a lot.'

'It is. I've told her it might be easier if she just dragged me through the fruit and veg section of Tesco face-first, like a basking shark.'

'Nice image.'

'She keeps banging on about fibre and stools as a health measurement, apparently.'

A stricken Rhys elaborated. 'And we're not talking about breakfast-bar furniture here, are we?'

'Definitely not. We're talking stool-to-forearm length for comparison. Though that sounds more like carpentry than I want it to—'

'Did you say forearm?'

'Apparently.'

Rhys stared at the packaging at his feet. 'I've just eaten that sausage roll. Maybe I should compensate by munching on the nearest bush.'

'Now that is a sentence I do not suggest you use on your night out with friends,' Gil said.

Rhys let out a laugh. 'No, you're probably right.'

They pulled up outside the rental cottage. A marked police vehicle and a CSI van were already on site. Anna Gwynne's green Peugeot pulled up behind them.

'Here we are. Haystack House,' Gil said. 'Time to play hunt the needle.'

# CHAPTER THIRTY-FIVE

AN ALMOST IDENTICAL INTERVIEW ROOM. An almost identical solicitor. Except that Lewin was older, his suit not so rumpled, and he did not have a pen poised.

Taran Marston appeared more composed than his wife had. Jess thought he might. After all, he'd had the where-withal to come to the station to express his concern over their daughter, Mia's, wanderings. Keen to suppress any worry over how that might be construed. Anxious to reassure. She wondered if he'd be playing that card today.

Catrin did the needful. Time, those present, the PACE caution prerequisites.

Marston sat upright, arms folded across his chest like a barrier.

'We've spoken to Mrs Marston already,' Jess said.

'How is she?'

'Anxious. Nervous.'

Marston nodded, his shoulders relaxing slightly. 'She doesn't like being away from our home.'

'Agoraphobia?' Jess waited, letting the silence stretch.

'Interesting word, agoraphobia. The Welsh word for open spaces is *agored*. Probably the same origin.' Marston spoke as if to edify himself rather than anyone else. 'But it's more away from home than the outside that she hates. Home-ophobia.' He laughed at his own joke. 'I don't suppose anyone would ever use that, though.'

Jess did not respond. Instead, she pressed on with the business of the day. 'As I explained to Mrs Marston, you're here because of what we've discovered at the standing stones.'

Marston frowned, the lines around his mouth deepening.

'Three bodies.' Catrin leaned forward. 'Children, most likely.'

'Oh, God.' Marston dropped his arms into his lap, his composure cracking. 'That's awful.'

Jess nodded, her gaze unwavering.

'They've been there some time. Years, most likely.' She let each word land deliberately.

Povey had sent through an updated report.

According to the forensic anthropologist, in exposed conditions like these, a human body would typically be fully skeletonised within seven years. Of the three found at the site, one was consistent with that timeframe—little remaining beyond bone and remnants of clothing. The other two showed less advanced decomposition: partial skeletonisation, some preserved tissue. Their condition suggested they'd been there for a shorter period—likely between five and seven years. The peaty soil, with its natural preservative qualities, had slowed the process. But this was no exact science. Temperature, moisture, insect activity—all played their part. The timelines were estimates. Nothing more.

Jess continued in a harder tone. 'What can you tell us about them?'

'Tell you about them?' Marston's hand found its fellow in his lap. 'I can't tell you anything.'

He paused, taking on a defensive edge. 'Except that Noor and I enjoy the outdoors. The standing stones have a significance. Not only to us, but to many people who have come before us. Surely, you know that.'

'We know you visited at certain times of the year.' Jess folded her hands on the table.

'We do. As do other people. As do our children.' His glance skittered between the two officers.

'Where are your children again?' Catrin asked, her pen hovering over her notepad.

'With my sister-in-law. In the Netherlands.' The words came quickly.

'Do you have a contact number?'

'What? Why?' His face flushed red.

'So that we can make sure they're okay, Mr Marston.' Catrin's voice remained steady, professional.

Marston's face contorted. 'Hang on. My daughter, Mia, got lost a few days ago. Someone found her, and she was returned. I've explained what happened, and yes, we were visiting the standing stones at Yule. Now you want to scare the living daylights out of my sister-in-law?'

Jess noticed that little white concentrations of frothy spittle accumulated at the corners of Marston's mouth. Something she'd not seen before.

She wanted to offer him a tissue to wipe them away. Instead, she lifted her eyes to his and fought down her disgust.

'Your wife isn't saying anything to us. Not even when we showed her this photograph.' Jess repeated the manoeuvre she'd used with Noor Marston, sliding the images of the marker stones across the table with deliberate slowness.

Marston studied them, giving nothing away until eventually he shrugged. 'Look, my wife… she has certain beliefs. Beliefs that could seem different, even odd, to you. It's possible she may have placed these near the standing stones. She does that kind of thing. You might find other totems dotted all over the farm related to Wiccan beliefs. Sometimes animal bones, or even stones like—'

'What do you know about the bodies?' Jess's cut through his explanation like a blade.

'This is insane.' Marston pushed back in his chair.

Jess waited. Silence drifted into the room. A vacuum needing to be filled.

'I am not letting you frighten my sister-in-law to check on my kids,' he said.

'You're refusing?' Catrin's pen scratched against the paper.

'I am refusing.'

'Why?'

'Because what you're asking makes no sense. You bring us in on some trumped-up accusation. And now you want to embarrass me and my wife with her family?' Sweat beaded his upper lip.

'We haven't accused you of anything,' Jess said softly, dangerously.

'Exactly. But you want to ring my sister-in-law anyway? Forget it. In fact, forget all of it. I am not answering any more of your questions. Not that you really had any.'

'Does the word *"geliefde"* mean anything to you?' Jess tapped the photograph with one finger.

Marston sat back with his mouth flat, having gone full umbrage, his chest heaving. 'No comment.'

'That's simply going to prolong the process, Mr Marston.' Catrin's words hung in the air between them.

'No comment.' His reply came out through gritted teeth.

———

GIL'S SHOULDERS ACHED. He'd been peering at bookshelves for an hour, methodically checking each volume for hollowed pages.

Ford was smart. Too smart to use such an obvious hiding place, but they had to be thorough.

The cottage's dim interior pressed in around them despite the brightness of the day. Dust motes swirled in the beams of light through low windows.

Three uniformed officers worked systematically through the kitchen and living areas while Rhys examined the fireplace for the third time.

'Nothing in the bathroom either,' Tannard called from the landing. The CSI had been checking every beam and joist, her expertise pointing her in directions the officers would have never thought to look. 'Though, I'll tell you what, these beams are genuine fifteenth-century oak. Magnificent things.'

Gil grunted, closing another volume of a Lisa Jewell blockbuster. The floor was looking like a house clearance sale.

'Sarge?' Rhys appeared in the doorway, face smudged with soot. 'Found something odd behind the hearth, but it's just old pipework.'

'Keep searching.' Gil straightened, pressing his hands into his lower back. 'Maybe you should go outside with DI Gwynne, see how she's getting on in the garden shed. Though exactly what we're searching for is anyone's guess,' he added in a mutter.

Tannard moved across the upper floor, making the cottage creak. Then a silence before she called down, 'Someone bring me the stepladder.'

Gil's pulse quickened. He took the stairs two at a time, Rhys close behind, with Anna Gwynne in his wake. She must have heard the shout, too.

Tannard was balanced precariously on a chair, the torch beam focused on one of the exposed beams near a light fitting.

'See it?' She pointed to a slightly darker patch. 'Wouldn't spot it from below. But the grain's wrong.'

Gil squinted. Yes, there was something not quite right about that section of wood.

A Uniform appeared with the stepladder.

Tannard clambered up, a toolbag hanging from one shoulder.

'Clever.' She probed the spot with gloved fingers. 'Used wood putty mixed with sawdust, stained to match the dark wood, but…' She pressed harder. 'It moves in the middle.'

The room went quiet. Even the cottage seemed to hold its breath.

Tannard used a screwdriver to force the blade underneath the section and worked it carefully, easing the patch away. 'Got something.'

She dug a finger into the small cavity, then used the screwdriver's blade to fish. A moment later, she withdrew an inch-long thumb drive, holding it up to the light. No larger than a postage stamp, it had been perfectly concealed in the beam's heart.

'Rhys.' Gil's voice was tight. 'Get your laptop.'

'I haven't got it, Sarge.'

'I have mine,' Anna said and hurried out to the car.

They waited in silence while Anna set up on the table downstairs. Rhys had been out to the kitchen to fetch some water twice, barely able to contain his impatience. But Anna's fingers were steady as she plugged in the drive.

'Copying it first,' she murmured, creating a secure backup. 'Just in case.'

The drive contained a single video file. Nothing else.

Gil, Rhys, and Tannard crowded around. Anna opened the file.

An outdoor scene, wobbly, taken on a phone's camera, viewed between the leaves of some branches, which occasionally drifted over the lens. In response, the camera operator shifted for a better view.

'*Aros funed.* That's *Cân-y-Barcud*,' Gil said, his plea for them to wait a minute slipping out in his native tongue.

No one in that room needed an explanation of where Gil was referring to except Anna, and Rhys obliged now, reiterating quickly how they'd all been there. Even the uniforms. Either when it was the site of a murder crime scene when Royston Moyles's body was discovered, or the site of an abduction when Hunt took Catrin Richards hostage and triggered a manhunt.

On the screen, a figure stepped out of the building, heading towards a vehicle.

A young Charlie Brewer moved into shot. Then another figure emerged, and Gil's breath caught in his throat.

'Is that—' Rhys began.

'Yes. It is,' Gil said.

On video, through the cottage doorway, a third man emerged, smiling.

'*Arglwydd Crist.*' The words escaped Gil's lips before he could stop them. He was already pulling out his phone, hitting speed dial for Jess.

'Sarge?' Rhys's face had gone pale.

Gil turned away once the call connected, his free hand clenched into a fist. 'Ma'am? We've found something. No, say nothing yet. Just listen to what I have to say. When I've finished, Rhys is going to send you a file.'

Through the window, the garden sat in bright sunlight, echoing the vibrant day that the video had been taken on. For now, on screen, there was no movement, just a constant view of *Cân-y-Barcud*'s back door and the little wall at the side that continued along the rear of the garden until... a woman came around the corner, hand in hand with a small child.

Not everyone in that room knew everyone in the clip. Not everyone had met the woman, for example.

'What sort of file?' Jess demanded, but Gil did not respond. The phone, still in his hand, dropped away from his face. Something on Anna's laptop screen had grabbed his disbelieving attention.

The woman was holding a child's hand.

Gil knew exactly whose hand it was.

And that knowledge burned within him, rendering him momentarily unable to reply.

# CHAPTER THIRTY-SIX

A TENSE ATMOSPHERE permeated the observation suite at the Llanelli custody hub. On the large monitor, Geraint Lane sat beside his solicitor, Jeffreys, whose carefully neutral expression appeared in stark contrast to his client's visible agitation.

'You're sure about this?' Jess asked Anna, though she remained completely focussed on Lane. 'Taking the lead on questioning?'

Anna nodded, her case file clutched tight. 'The Kerry Ford angle's mine. I know the details inside out.'

Gil hadn't spoken since they'd gathered. He stood closest to the screen, shoulders rigid, watching Lane with an intensity that made Jess uneasy.

The video they'd found at Ford's place had burrowed under his skin in a way she'd rarely seen.

'Gil?' Jess touched his arm lightly. 'You good?'

He gave a curt nod, already moving towards the door. 'Let's get started.'

Anna followed, but not before exchanging a concerned glance with Jess.

The observation suite door clicked shut behind them, leaving Jess alone just as her phone vibrated. She looked at it, hesitated, but then accepted the call.

'Evan,' she answered. 'Everything okay?'

He laughed. 'You don't have to assume every time I call it's to tell you I've relapsed.'

'Have you?'

'No. Been out with Cadi. And I happened to text Rhys about his end-of-year assessment and I get a "guess who's come to dinner" quiz question.'

'Rhys,' Jess said with a snort. She should have known.

'You've really brought Lane in? What's his involvement here?'

'That's what we're about to find out,' Jess said, leaning closer to the screen. 'He didn't come quietly, I can tell you that much. Ford had concealed a video of *Cân-y-Barcud* with the Marstons and Brewer and Lane together—'

'Keep Catrin away from him if you can. Last thing we need is those two in the same room.'

'She's working on tracking down Noor Marston's sister. Gil is—'

The interview room door opened on-screen.

'They're going in. I'll call you back.'

'Fine,' Warlow said, with that flatness that always made her wonder what he wasn't saying. 'Later, then.'

Jess ended the call, her attention caught between the unfolding scene before her and the nagging worry about Gil.

She'd never seen him like this. So contained, so focused. Like a coiled spring. Or a coiled rattlesnake. But then, she'd also seen what was on that video, so she wasn't entirely surprised. But it did nothing to ease her anxiety.

On the monitor, Gil took his seat, and this time, he did the required formalities for ticking the PACE boxes and then turned to Anna.

She took her cue. 'Hello, Mr Lane. I am DI Anna Gwynne. Did you know a woman by the name of Kerry Ford?'

Lane, his normal belligerence after having been brought in from home, now hovering at the maximum, sent Anna a loathsome glare and said, 'Kerry who?'

CATRIN AND RHYS were doing what he'd tried to rebrand as "scut work"—a term that had died a quick death, everyone reverting to the time-honoured "donkey work" within days. Catrin couldn't blame them. Wasn't "scut" related to jazz, or worse?

She'd been methodically working her way through the slim leads they had on Noor's sister. She had a name: Greet van Oppen. A name that should have made things easier but, of course, hadn't. The van Oppens moved in circles where privacy wasn't just expected; it was bought and paid for at a premium.

In the old days, if someone was ex-directory, that was that. Try explaining that concept to anyone under thirty now, when you could find people on any number of social media sites and they'd assume ex-directory was some underground music scene.

Money couldn't buy invisibility anymore, not in the Instagram age.

Greet van Oppen had carved out a niche for herself in sustainable fashion, her socials a carefully curated blend of images, mainly of vintage designer pieces and ethical brands. No flashy product placement or typical influencer poses. Her content comprised thoughtful posts about fabric conservation, traditional tailoring techniques, and the craftsmanship behind high-end fashion. The kind of content that attracted serious collectors and industry insiders rather than casual followers.

Her latest post featured a 1950s Dior piece she'd had restored, discussing the importance of preserving fashion history. It wasn't the usual influencer fare of unboxing videos and discount codes – this was measured, educational, pitched perfectly to an audience who understood that true luxury whispers rather than shouts.

Bit of a contrast with her sister, who favoured druidic rituals at the standing stones.

Still, that carefully maintained social media presence had given Catrin an in. A direct message from the police might have been ignored, but Catrin had written something appropriately formal and deferential. Twenty minutes later, she'd received a response—not from a PR team or assistant, but from Greet herself, and a call routed through HQ's switchboard.

'Hello?' Greet's accent had been modified. Almost American unless you listened closely.

'Ms van Oppen,' Catrin began, keeping her tone professionally neutral. 'Thank you for speaking with me. I'm calling about your sister, Noor Marston. She's currently helping us with inquiries into a serious matter.'

'Noor? What has happened?' Greet's cultured voice had an edge to it.

'I'm afraid I can't discuss the details. However, we do need to establish the whereabouts of Noor's children.'

The silence that followed was so complete that Catrin checked to see if the call had dropped.

'Is this someone's idea of a joke?' Greet's response, when it finally came, was barely above a whisper.

Catrin frowned, caught off-guard by the response. 'I assure you, Ms van Oppen, this is a serious police inquiry.'

'Serious?' The word came out as a hiss. 'You think this is serious? Well, Detective…'

'Richards.'

'Detective Richards. Let me explain something. This isn't only serious; this is cruel. And in very poor taste.'

Something cold settled in Catrin's stomach. She caught Rhys's concerned eye across the desk. He'd picked up on her reactions. She saw her own unease reflected there.

'None of us – not me, not my parents – have seen Noor in five years. We begged her. Wrote letters. Sent emails. Tried everything to stay in contact with those poor children. To at least know they were all right. Or to know when the…'A sharp intake of breath. 'Do you know what it's like to have part of your family simply cut themselves off completely? To wake up every morning wondering if today might be the day you finally hear something?'

Catrin's pen had stilled on her notepad. Rhys was now standing, hovering near her desk, picking up on the shift in atmosphere.

'And now you call, asking about the children as if… as if we hadn't been trying to find out ourselves for five years?'

'I don't understand,' Catrin said.

'Obviously… what has my sister told you?'

'Not a great deal. Neither she nor her husband was willing to give us your contact details. All they said was that the children had gone to you for their usual New Year break.'

Greet choked back a sob before she whispered, 'If I find out that this is some kind of prank—'

'No prank, Ms van Oppen. This is an extremely serious matter.'

Greet was crying openly now. 'My sister… her children…'

The next inhalation ratcheted in her throat.

No words came across for several long seconds. Finally, Greet recovered enough to speak, though the words warbled a little. 'Have you ever heard of Sugawara's congenital muscular dystrophy?'

Catrin had not. In a few short minutes, she would wish she still never had.

———

Lane denied.

He denied ever having met Kerry Ford. Denied having left Wales in the last month. Denied even having read about the death of two people in a caravan in Weston-super-Mare. It was at that point he went into Lane rant mode.

He leaned forward, index finger jabbing at the tabletop, his face flushed with righteous indignation.

Jeffreys, his solicitor, po-faced, balding, with glasses, seemed unable, perhaps even unwilling, to temper his client's growing anger. He was enjoying the spectacle.

'This is exactly what I'm talking about,' Lane spat, stabbing his finger now at Gil, slapping the table in his temper. 'Pure intimidation tactics. You people can't stand the fact that someone's finally holding up a mirror, can you? Three weeks before my book comes out, and suddenly I'm dragged in here like some common criminal.'

Anna glanced at Gil, but his face remained impassive.

'Years and years of research,' Lane said. 'And then the Hunt fiasco. Clear evidence of systemic failures, institutional incompetence that will make people's blood run cold. What you lot allowed to happen to Catrin Richards... Christ, the misogyny runs so deep you probably don't even see it anymore.'

He let out a bitter laugh. 'And now this. What is it – a warning shot? A friendly reminder to maybe tone it down a bit? Because I'll tell you something for nothing, Sergeant.' He sneered the word at Gil. 'If you think this little display of power is going to stop me—'

'Kerry Ford.'

Gil's voice, when it finally came, was quiet. So quiet that Lane actually stopped mid-rant, his mouth still partly open.

'My God. How many times do I need to say this?' Lane blinked, clearly thrown by the interruption.

'Kerry Ford,' Gil repeated, in the same measured tone that had steel beneath the even timbre. 'You say you don't know who she is. But she knew who you were.'

'A great many people know who I am.'

Gil's jaw tightened. The closest to a smile he'd come to since the visit to Ford's rental property. 'Don't kid yourself. Kerry Ford is dead. But she left a legacy. A video. You're in it. Along with some other people of interest.'

'What are you talking about?' Lane's irate bluster faltered an iota.

'Why don't we watch it together? Then I'll tell you about the other reasons we brought you in.'

The colour drained from Lane's face so quickly that even Jeffreys, when he caught sight of it, shifted uncomfortably.

# CHAPTER THIRTY-SEVEN

GIL PLAYED THE VIDEO. He provided a commentary, too. Brief and, astonishingly enough to all who knew him, controlled.

But barely.

He pointed out people as they appeared: Charlie Brewer, Taran Marston, Lane himself, but he stopped both the words and the imagery before the woman and child appeared.

'This video was shot, we think, on her phone, by Kerry Ford. We're not sure of the date yet, but we may get that from her metadata or the cloud. It'll be floating out there somewhere. Or you can save us the trouble and tell us.'

Lane had shrunk. He was not the same person who, moments before, had ranted and jabbed his finger like a weapon. This was a very different Lane. A Lane who stared at the screen, arms clasped around his chest, hunched in on himself.

'No comment,' he muttered.

'Wow,' Gil said. 'But then it may be that your comment bin is running on empty after everything that's poured out of it this morning. I mean, it's obviously you. There's no denying it. You're certain you have nothing to say before we continue with the video?'

'No comment.' Lane kept his eyes down.

'You'll want to see this next bit. This is the best bit. The clinching scene.'

Even Jeffreys, normally a study in professional boredom, sat up now.

Gil ran the tape. A thirty-second section of nothing but tweeting birds and rustling leaves followed until the woman and the little boy appeared.

Noor Marston was smiling. The child she was holding hands with was not. The child looked frightened. Lost.

Gil let the tape run to its end. Five seconds from that end, Kerry Ford's face appeared on the screen. Grinning. Full of mischief. Totally unaware of the fact that her snooping would ultimately lead to her death.

'I am giving you one more chance to speak to us, Geraint. Do you know who that child is?' Gil's voice was suddenly hard as iron.

'No comment.'

'Then I'll tell you,' Gil said. He was icy calm on the outside, but a dangerous light shone in his eyes, like the flickering red of boiling lava. 'That child looks very much like a boy called Freddie Sillitoe. Taken from a Barry Island beach. Taken and stolen from his family. Any idea what that feels like? You don't. No one, other than the parents and siblings and the child themselves, can ever truly understand. I'll ask you again. Obviously, you had knowledge of what was happening and who those people are because you were there. And you are going to have only one chance to tell us, because apart from Kerry Ford's death, you are now facing kidnapping, abduction, and conspiracy. There isn't much you can do to help yourself, Geraint, I'll be honest with you. But there may be something.'

Lane's eyes had become white ovals, the look a cornered animal might give to its hunter: wild and hopeless. He shivered where he sat, paralysed by fear and an awareness, no doubt, that his entire world had just collapsed around him in the time it took to play an amateur video clip, shot by a woman whose curiosity had finally come back to bite her and all those involved.

Even Anna appeared surprised when someone knocked on the interview room door. Whoever it was must not have realised that this was a crucial juncture in the interrogation. It flew in the face of all taught techniques.

Gil's face tensed.

Jess's head appeared around the door, apology etched into her rictus expression. 'I am sorry. Truly. But we need to talk. Now.'

Gil, as calm as a sea before the tsunami, kept his eyes on Lane as he stood from his chair. 'Might be best if we let you and your… adviser chat for a few minutes. We will be back. And when we are, it will give me immense pleasure to charge you with a full deck.'

Jess gave Lane one glance. He did not return it. Whatever he was staring at was dark and bottomless.

———

JESS TOOK them back to the observation room and shut off the monitor so that they would not be distracted. Anna looked intrigued. Gil looked angry, barely controlling his disgust. Jess could see that. But this was too important.

'Catrin got hold of Noor Marston's sister,' she said. 'Catrin's waiting for a video call from us.'

They clustered around a screen where Jess had already logged on. She put through a Teams call.

Catrin's face came into view. Her expression was a difficult one to gauge. Under other circumstances, Gil might have quipped that she looked a little excited, but at the same time, a little sick.

'Go ahead, Catrin,' Jess said.

'As I explained, I spoke to Greet van Oppen… I recorded the call. It's gone through to you, ma'am. Might be easier to play it on your phone. I suggest you start the file at two minutes in.'

Jess opened her phone, found the file, and they listened, thanks to the wonders of modern technology, whilst the exchange between Catrin and Greet played. It was the latter they heard first.

———

'HAVE you ever heard of Sugawara's congenital muscular dystrophy?'

'I'm afraid I haven't.'

'It's… cruel. A horrible, terrible thing. I'm no expert, though I now know much more than I ever wanted to. It's genetic. A child with this condition appears completely normal for the first couple of months, or perhaps weeks. Then there are feeding problems. The muscles, they don't grow properly. They… harden. Fibrosis, they called it. It sounds not too bad, but there are brain abnormalities, eye abnormalities, cardiac changes that get worse as the child ages.'

'Oh, God,' Catrin whispered.

'As I say, it's genetic. What they call a recessive disease. Both parents need to carry the gene for it to have an effect. Are you aware of alleles?'

'Not really—'

'Unfortunately, now I am.' Greet paused there, gathering herself before continuing. 'A gene is a strand of DNA. The double helix we all know. But genes are always in pairs, or alleles. If one allele carries a disease like this but the other gene is normal, you will be healthy, but you can carry the risk on the abnormal allele. If there are two normal people who carry the damaged alleles… the statistics are stark. Every pregnancy in that case has a one-in-four chance of a child developing the disease by getting one faulty gene from each of the parents.'

Greet paused again, swallowed, the noise loud over the recording. 'That also means that there's a one-in-four chance that a child could be completely normal if they get the healthy gene from their parents, and a one-in-two chance they get one healthy and one bad, so they too would be carriers, but not get the disease. Noor knew after their first, Mia, that they could get the same thing again. Because the chance is the same every time, do you understand?'

Jess wondered how Catrin would have felt hearing this, having just had a healthy child of her own. Bad enough hearing it with a grown-up healthy Molly at the back of her mind.

'Noor and Taran, they understood the chance of it happening again, but more of a chance of it not happening. They tried again. Lieke was beautiful, but she also had the disease. And of course, genetic testing told them that, but they didn't believe in... none of us believe in termination.'

There was a noise on the phone there. A stifled gasp of horror. Jess assumed it had come from Catrin as part of the conversation. She glanced at the screen where Catrin looked out at them, her expression composed in a controlled neutrality. She had the advantage of having listened to this more than once. A chance to compose herself to a degree. Which was more than could be said about the others.

Greet continued speaking. 'I said they should not try again. But they wanted a boy. A normal little boy.' A pause in the dialogue was interrupted by Greet blowing her nose. 'But Mats had the disease, too. You see, there is no guarantee. The odds do not change. One-in-four chance. It was severe in all three. Very progressive. The doctors thought that the children might live until they were nine or ten, but when they saw how quickly Mia deteriorated... they said five or perhaps six. But they could not know for certain.'

'I see...' Catrin said and paused as she choked back tears into a cough. 'I'm so sorry.'

'We did all we could. All the best doctors in Europe and America for two years after Mia was born, but there was no treatment. It affected Noor badly. How do you cope in such situations? She did not. She went somewhere else in her head. The cosmos, the universe, nature. There were no answers in science, so she sought solace somewhere else. And Taran... he did everything possible, too. But Noor wanted to escape. They took the children, their three sick children, eighteen months between the three of them, back to the UK. Late

2017 Mia was four, Lieke not yet three, and Mats a year and a half. She said she wanted them to have somewhere peaceful to… to…'

A long pause followed. Eventually, Catrin spoke again. 'I am truly sorry that you have had to tell me all that, Ms van Oppen.'

'My father tried to visit once. They sent him away. Wouldn't let him into the property. It broke his heart. He was the carrier on our side. The guilt ate at him. I can't speak for Taran's side of the family.'

Nothing but breathing came over the line for the next seconds but Greet eventually returned to Catrin's original question. 'What is this about me having the children?'

'It's a long and complicated story. I realise now how you might have found my question… distasteful. But there isn't much I can say at this stage. I am going to have to talk all this through with my superiors.'

'Is Noor… is she okay? Why would she say such a thing?'

'I don't know, is the honest answer.'

'Should I come over to… where is it again? Carmarthen. Wales? Are you close to where Noor has the farm?'

'Close enough.'

'Perhaps I should come over.'

'I'd wait if I were you. I promise to get back to you when all this is sorted out.'

'Are you sure? Where are Noor and Taran now? Can I speak to them?'

'No, you can't. Not at the moment. As I say, they're helping with our inquiries.'

'Please ring me if I can help. You have my number now.'

'I will. I promise.'

The call ended there.

―――

JESS MET Catrin's eyes on the monitor.

'Well done,' Jess said. 'That was a hard listen.'

Catrin nodded and pursed her lips, fighting tears. 'I'm still not sure what to make of all this, ma'am. I mean, I saw the video from the thumb drive. Has Lane said anything?'

'Not yet,' Gil said, and once again, his voice sounded odd. 'But I think I know who is buried near those standing stones on Druid's Moor now.'

'Noor and Taran's children,' Anna said.

'If it is them, then who is the Mia who got lost on the hills, and where are the other two, if there even are another two?' Jess said.

Gil's breathing was loud. 'We need to get back in the room with Lane.'

'Not the Marstons?' Anna asked.

'No,' Gil said gruffly. 'Lane first. But then maybe you and DI Allanby should talk to the Marstons. How old did Tomo say Mia was? The Mia who was found?'

'Eleven, give or take. Why?'

He didn't answer directly. 'What about Brewer?'

'His phone's off. He was not at home when uniforms called.'

'I want him found,' Jess said.

'What was it Tomo noticed about Mia again?' Gil asked. 'I can't remember.'

No one could remember.

'We'll get Rhys to give him a ring. And then he can start filtering missing kids from say, 2018 onwards. Concentrate on just before or after lockdown. Cross-reference from there on,' Jess said.

'You think Mia is a surrogate?' Catrin whispered the question, brittle shock in her question.

'And not the only one,' Gil muttered. 'Now, anyone mind if we recommence our little chat with Lane? He's been marinating in his own juices for long enough.'

He turned.

Jess caught his arm. 'Are you sure you can do this?'

She wasn't questioning his skill as an interviewer. She'd been in enough interview rooms with him to appreciate how capable he was. But she sensed that boiling red lava.

'I won't lie to you. I'm sitting there fantasising. Hoping he might lose it, spring up from his chair and try to break for the door. That would give me an excuse for laying hands on him.' Gil squeezed his eyes shut for a brief few seconds, like someone breathing in a waft of delicious cooking or their favourite wine.

'But that isn't going to happen, is it?' Jess said.

'No, ma'am. It isn't. But a man can dream.' He walked out of the room.

Anna followed.

'Keep an eye on him,' Jess said.

Anna nodded. 'I will, but if Lane ever did make a break for it, I think I'd be piling in right behind Sergeant Jones.'

# CHAPTER THIRTY-EIGHT

WHEN ANNA and Gil walked back into the interview room, something had happened. Lines of untidy writing covered the solicitor's legal pad for starters.

Gil restarted the interview. The solicitor spoke first.

'My client would like to speak to the senior officer in charge.'

Gil glanced at Anna. She nodded.

Gil then stared directly at Lane. 'Geraint Lane, I am arresting you in relation to the abduction—'

Lane sat up, eyes wide. 'Wait, wait, wait.' He threw Jeffreys a glare of disdain. 'You said they'd—'

Jeffreys waved a hand across his throat in a "shut up" gesture.

'He said what, Geraint?' Anna said. 'That he could make demands? Show these stupid coppers who is in charge?'

Lane's expression said it all.

'It doesn't work like that. You're not in a TV drama. These are serious charges. What is it we have so far, Sergeant?'

'Abduction, kidnapping, possible murder, ma'am,' Gil said, drilling his gaze into Lane's face.

'I advise you to say nothing,' Jeffreys said.

But Gil's words might as well have been a gorgon's glare.

Lane was shaking visibly. 'I'll tell you what I know. If I do… if I tell you everything I know… can the charges be reduced?'

Anna answered, 'No, you will still be charged. But a guilty plea always helps. Where children are concerned, prison is not a terribly healthy place to be. If you cooperate, segregation might be an option.'

'I never harmed any children.' Lane's protest was delivered almost falsetto. 'I had no idea what was happening. He tricked me into it.'

'I still advise no comment—'

Lane turned on Jeffreys. 'Shut up.' He turned back, his expression full of pleading. 'I have a lot to tell you. But I need to know if it will help. I don't want to go to prison.'

Gil shook his head. 'That will be up to a judge, Geraint. All I can tell you is that if you don't tell us, it will go badly for you. Because we will find out. We have three bodies buried on a mountain.'

'What?' Lane threw up his hands, his breathing heaving in and out of his chest. 'Oh fuck, oh fuck.' His gaze swept the room, seeing nothing but the abyss he teetered on the edge of.

Neither Gil nor Anna moved. They let him have his meltdown. It took a while, but eventually, he settled.

'I swear to God, I know nothing about any buried bodies,' he said. The whole of him trembled: body, face, lips, voice.

'Then what do you know?' Gil asked.

Lane was crying. Big tears running down his face.

Jeffreys produced some tissues from his bag. Lane snatched them off him.

Gil and Anna waited for the victimhood card to come into play. Lane was simply the type. They'd have to wait for him to wade through that first, no doubt.

They were not mistaken. The words poured from Lane, and they let it happen, controlling their disgust because they'd been trained to do so. Still, it was like watching filth dribbling out of a broken sewer pipe.

'I'd just lost my job with the local rag. I was low. I had no money. I hadn't met Amol yet. I didn't even have enough money to pay the rent.' If he was looking for sympathy, he found none in the icy stares Gil and Anna gave him.

'Charlie Brewer said he had some work I could help him with. Lucrative, he said.'

'Ah, yes, Mr Brewer.' Gil repeated the name, and a dark flush spread slowly up from his neck to his face. Though well aware of Brewer's involvement after seeing Ford's video, hearing it from Lane's lips, and uttered so casually, compounded the realisation of how they'd all been taken in by the younger man.

'Charlie, yeah. I'd done a piece for the paper on NON properties—'

'NON?' Anna interrupted.

'It's a rental website,' Gil explained. 'Specialises in out-of-the-way places. "No One Near". Some people like that kind of thing.'

'Charlie worked with Moyles. They had a couple of properties, so I knew about them. One day, he said that he needed some papers signed, some photos for a passport application. He said that the family were customers and were desperate.'

'And you didn't find that strange?'

Lane shrugged. 'Yes and no. Ironically, one of the occupations that new government regulations recognised as potential signatories for passport applicants were journalists.'

'So, you went there to sign?'

Lane continued to tremble. 'Charlie had helped me out. With drugs and that… before. I owed him some money. He said that this way, I could wipe my debt and make some more. The people who had the photos were desperate and willing to pay, he said.'

'And you believed all of this?' Anna asked.

Lane squeezed his eyes shut. 'I needed the money. I needed some drugs. I was in a dark place.'

Gil had his hand around a pen. His knuckles were pearly white.

'It didn't sound that bad. They'd come over from the Netherlands: Dutch mother, British father. And they wanted British passports. That's not illegal. Charlie said we'd meet these people at one of the NON properties, *Cân-y-Barcud*. About halfway between Carmarthen and where these people lived. The property was vacant at the time and ideal. Out of the way. No One Near, right? When we got there, Charlie got pissed off because the cleaner he'd booked hadn't finished. He told me to stay in the car, and ten minutes later, I saw a woman leave and get into a car and drive off. I did not see her face. Wouldn't recognise her. I saw her for maybe half a minute, carrying cleaning stuff, before she drove off.'

'What car?'

'I can't remember. God's honest truth.'

'Then?'

Lane sipped some water from a cup. He used both hands to steady it. Some water spilled.

'Shit,' he muttered.

'And then?' Gil repeated.

'Some people came. A couple in a Land Rover. Three kids. Two girls and a boy.'

'Who were they?'

'I remember the name was Marston. The woman had a Dutch accent. Charlie had photos of the kids. I remember the girls stayed in their car. But it was them, I swear it was. The boy was restless and came into the cottage. I signed the photos and wrote something down. I can't remember exactly. Something along the lines of a true likeness or some shit. Standard wording. And it was. A true likeness. Marston, the father, explained they needed passports for the kids but that they were wary of Covid exposure. It all seemed kosher to me.'

'And you signed it?' Gil asked.

Lane nodded.

'How much did they pay you?'

'A thousand. Cash.'

'And you didn't think that strange?'

'This was in early 2021. Everything had gone to shit. There were threats of more lockdowns. They said they wanted a passport ready for going back to Europe once restrictions lifted. And Charlie's explanation sort of rang true.

Vaccines were rolling out. There was something about shielding the kids. Plus… they paid.'

'What about the boy?' Gil asked.

'What about him?'

'What did he seem like?'

'Didn't say much. Whined a bit. He'd been crying. I assumed there'd been a falling-out on the journey. I thought nothing of it. His mother, she was stern with him. On the one hand cajoling, on the other, warning him to behave.'

'Have you had any contact with the child or the Marstons since?' Anna asked.

'No, none. I swear.'

'And you were not aware of this video taken by Kerry Ford?'

Lane shook his head. 'She must have doubled back through the woods or something. As far as I knew, she'd gone.'

'Did Brewer ever mention Ford to you?'

'No.'

'Have you ever bought a barbecue?' Anna asked.

Lane shook his head as if he was clearing his ears. 'A barbecue?'

Anna did not repeat the question.

'We have a barbecue. A gas barbecue,' Lane said.

'Never bought a disposable kind?'

'No. Why?'

'Kerry Ford died from carbon monoxide poisoning.'

Panic flared in Lane's face. 'Whoa, whoa, what?' He uttered the protestations between rapid breaths. 'I don't know this woman. I swear. I only did what Charlie asked.'

He started to cry again. 'Shit, oh shit, I'm sorry. I know nothing about a barbecue. I know nothing about this video. Or the other videos.'

'What other videos?' Anna asked.

Lane wailed. Self-pity turned up to the max as he whined out the information. 'The ones Moyles secretly filmed inside that bloody cottage. I swear I knew nothing about them until

Hunt told me when he threw me into the boot of my own bloody car in Kidwelly Quay—'

Lane stopped, chopped off the sentence, and sucked in a breath. He glared at Gil. In that glare writhed a horrified realisation that he'd just said something he should not have.

Both he and Gil knew Hunt had locked him in the boot of his car on another occasion. The day Catrin Richards had been abducted. But only Lane knew about what happened at Kidwelly Quay. He'd told the police that he'd been mugged and that the mugger stole his phone and locked him in the boot of his car. They'd reluctantly accepted his explanation that he'd never seen his attacker.

Until now.

'What do you mean—'

Gil put a hand up to stop Anna and demanded another answer from Lane. 'You told us you didn't know who mugged you that time.'

'I...' Lane spoke now in a breathy grunt. 'I... uh... I'm confused.'

'I don't think you're confused. I think your control has slipped enough for the truth to come out. You just said Hunt stole your phone.' Gil's face had become stony. Only the way his bushy eyebrows lifted gave away the fact that he was quickly putting all the missing pieces together in this whole sorry mess. 'You'd already met Hunt. And then you arranged for Catrin Richards to meet you at *Cân-y-Barcud* the day he abducted her. You were in it with him, weren't you? Up to your ugly neck.'

Anna frowned. 'I'm sorry. What has this to do with Kerry Ford?'

It took a long twenty seconds for Gil to respond. When he did, he'd pulled his lips back from clamped-together teeth in a terrifying parody of a smile. 'Theoretically, nothing, ma'am. It's a different case. At least, we thought it was. But it is one we will need to take into consideration when we charge Mr Lane.'

'No, no, no. I'm confused,' Lane back-pedalled. 'I swear. I

don't know this Ford woman. I didn't buy a barbecue. I got confused about Hunt, I swear.'

Gil's words were unforgiving. 'You collaborated with him, didn't you?'

Lane's expression had morphed into cartoonish terror. He must have considered all his options in five seconds flat before capitulating. 'All right, all right, I was scared, okay?' he yelled. 'I was scared for my bloody life. That psychopath threatened me and Amol. I had to.'

'Where is Brewer?' Gil asked abruptly.

'No idea. I swear.'

'When was the last time you saw him?'

Lane rocked back and forth, looking at the ceiling, his face contorted in a half cry. 'Oh, God.'

'When?' Gil repeated.

'He rang me a few nights ago. Said he had another little job for me.'

'What kind of job?' Gil threw out the question as a staccato burst.

Lane moaned. 'He wanted me to beat him up.'

'*Mam fach,*' Gil uttered. He glared at Jeffreys. 'I suggest your client prepare a written statement.'

He turned to Anna. 'We need to talk to DI Allanby again, ma'am. And to DCI Warlow.'

# CHAPTER THIRTY-NINE

ANOTHER TORRENTIAL DECEMBER shower hammered against Catrin's windscreen. Llanelli-bound on the A48, she was already rehearsing her interview for the Marstons. Immediately after the video call she'd had with DI Allanby and the team, Jess had asked her to come over.

Her phone's chirp broke through the rhythmic sweep of wipers. DCI Warlow's name flashed on the display.

'Pull over somewhere safe. Best to do this over video.'

She guided the car into a lay-by and shut off the engine.

Warlow's face appeared on her screen, drawn and pale from his bout of pneumonia, but his eyes shone bright with purpose.

'You're looking better, sir,' she offered.

He waved away the pleasantry, his hand trembling slightly with the effort.

'Just got off the phone with Gil,' he said.

She tensed at something in his tone.

'It's about Lane,' Warlow continued. 'But Gil wanted you to hear this from me first.'

Her fingers tightened imperceptibly on the phone resting on the steering wheel. 'Go on.'

'Lane's been talking. In fact, he can't shut up. He's in all of this, whatever *this* is, up to his filthy neck. And in the middle of his "I'm a victim" spiel, he let on that Hunt was threatening him, that they were working together on your…'

He paused, choosing his words carefully, his breath catching, '… on what happened to you.'

The silence in the car grew long and dense.

Catrin stared at Warlow's face on her phone, a muscle working in her cheek. Her voice, when it came, sounded controlled but carried an edge sharp enough to cut glass. 'I see. Thank you for telling me that, sir.'

'I don't need to say that you did not deserve what they put you through. Lane should never have been allowed to get anywhere near the investigation into Moyles, or you.'

She nodded. Quick little movements to match the vivid memories of those early conversations with the higher-ups that exploded like fireworks in her head. Drinkwater had been the shooter, but the bullet had Superintendent Goodey written all over it.

Catrin remembered the conversation clearly. An almost throwaway suggestion:

*I promised I'd get back to you regarding the press. There's a chap called Geraint Lane who's been persistent. He wants to do a kind of day in the life of a detective. Well, you in particular as one of our rising stars, as it were.*

That had been Drinkwater's "suggestion". The faux casual "rising star" flattery. And of course, he'd deftly side-stepped when she'd tried to resist. She'd even directly challenged him.

*Do I have a choice whether I do it or not, sir?*

But he'd pulled that trick about assuming she'd already agreed from their last chat. Classic Drinkwater, rewriting history to fit the agenda. Then he'd laid it on thick about the Probert case and the documentary a TV company – again, with the blessing of the force – made about their success in finding an ex-rugby icon's killer and her role in that. Though her role had simply been the same as that of the team.

Warlow had laughed about that, putting her and Rhys centre stage as both by far the best-looking options for TV. Jess had shied away, too, because that was her nature.

But with Lane, Drinkwater had made it sound like she'd be letting the team, or even the whole force, down if she refused. By the time he'd wrapped it up with that "just a couple of hours" line, making it sound like she'd be unreasonable to object, she'd been thoroughly outmanoeuvred. The worst part was she'd seen every manipulation for what it was and still ended up saying yes.

Warlow shifted in his chair. It made the laptop jerk. He corrected it but not before it revealed a different angle in the room and a blanket across his lap. It prompted her to ask a question.

'How are you really doing? And Cadi?' She always softened at mentioning the dog who'd found her when all hope seemed lost.

'I'm fine. Stop fussing. Cadi's spoiled rotten, as usual.' He leaned closer to the camera. 'Now get yourself to Llanelli and help Jess sort out this Marston mess. God knows what's at the bottom of this one.'

'Yes, sir.'

The call ended, but Catrin sat for a moment longer, rain beating on the car roof. She needed a moment to process what had just happened.

Warlow, as always, went straight to the point with no fluff. But in replaying the conversation, what emerged, to her surprise, was a spurt of something strengthening her resolve. She started the engine and pulled back onto the road with renewed purpose.

God, the universe did surprises so well. The steady, slow dread of anticipation over the book, a dread that seemed to grow larger with every passing day, remained a knot in her stomach. But this... this revelation that Lane and Hunt had been working together triggered a sudden burning sense of anger and injustice.

'Bastard,' she muttered. 'You snivelling, lying, cowardly bastard.'

———

GIVEN the discovery of human remains, it hadn't been difficult to get a magistrate's extension to hold the Marstons. They'd been in custody now for over twenty-four hours. This time with Catrin next to her, Jess began with Noor.

'We know about your children.'

Noor did not seem to cope very well with her confinement. She seemed to be unravelling, both physically and mentally.

'We spoke to your sister, Greet. We know about the condition, the Sugawara's.'

Noor's mouth hardened, her fingers twisting in her lap.

'Are they who are buried near the stones, Noor? Is it Mia and Lieke and Mats?'

Noor shut her eyes. The lids trembled in tandem with her lower lip, but she didn't speak.

'How did they die?' Catrin asked. A question that needed asking, loaded as it was with a ton of implications. But she managed to temper it with enough sympathy to allow some room for honesty.

Even so, next to Noor, her solicitor flinched.

'Was it the disease?' Jess persisted. She had to ask. She'd need some expert input in explaining how this horrible condition caused children to die, but she also had to ask if Noor and Taran Marston had hastened the end.

'*Geliefde*,' Noor whispered. Her hands shook.

'Where are the other children, Noor?' Catrin asked, watching the woman's face intently.

'*Geliefde*.' she whispered again.

'I can see you're not doing great, Noor. And I'm sorry about that. I'm sorry about the ordeal you and your children have been through. But the others, they're someone's children, too.'

'*Geliefde*,' came the whispered reply, her focus on some distant point that was not in this room.

'My client needs some medical help,' Scott said. He reached for Noor's trembling shoulder.

Jess nodded to Catrin. 'Interview ended at 18:30 hours.'

They immediately re-interviewed Taran Marston. With

him, Jess took a much firmer approach. She played him Kerry Ford's video.

He watched it in silence, his face an expressionless mask.

'Lane, the man who signed the boy's photograph for a passport, is also in this hub. He is talking and talking quickly. I am giving you an opportunity to do the same,' Jess explained, her tone sharp.

'How is she doing?' He flicked his gaze between the two officers. 'Noor, I mean.'

'Not great,' Catrin answered bluntly. 'I'm no expert, but I'd say your wife is not coping at all well.'

Taran nodded, something finally cracking his composure.

Catrin reiterated the fact that she'd spoken to his sister-in-law. That they knew about the Sugawara's. Jess then repeated the question about how they'd died.

'We didn't…' His shoulders sagged. 'They died naturally. Mia made it to six, Lieke four and half, Mats four. And before you ask, could we have stopped any of it? No, we could not. And neither did we do what I often thought about doing. The merciful thing. We did not… though it was very hard.'

'Whose idea was it to bury them where you did?'

'Noor's. If you say she isn't coping, then you're seeing what I saw.'

'What about the other children?' Jess demanded.

Taran let his head drop. 'A man called Moyles called at our place uninvited. He wanted to know if we had any properties, outbuildings, and the like. To rent. He said he specialised in renting out remote properties. He came at a bad time. Noor was not doing well… we'd just lost Mia. This was early 2018. I got to talking. We had a drink. Moyles said he could help.'

'How?' Jess asked.

Marston signalled his disapproval. 'He didn't give me all the details. All he'd say is that he had access to a system. Children who'd been abandoned, in foster care, where the home environment had become too compromised to reclaim them. Adoption ready, in his words. For a fee, of course.'

'What about papers?'

'There wouldn't need to be in our case. He said we already had paperwork. I didn't understand what he meant at first, but then I realised he was talking about our children. They had birth certificates. Moyles, and then Brewer—'

'Brewer was a part of this?'

Marston nodded. 'He suggested we keep the authorities away from the farm. We had Mia at home, though she'd passed. Noor couldn't bear to give her up… that was when we buried her near the stones.'

'Are you saying that through Brewer and Moyles, you replaced all three of your children after they'd died?' Catrin asked.

Taran nodded, his face ashen. 'Mia from somewhere in Scotland. Lieke from Shropshire, I think. Mats was more local. Brewer said he could try and match their ages for when our children passed. Not exactly, but near enough. Surrogates for Noor.'

'Did it work?'

'It did. Not completely, but we homeschooled them so no one would know. Changed their hair colour to light, like Noor's. Though Mia hated it, so we stopped doing that with her. As far as the authorities were concerned, we'd come across from Holland with three kids in 2017. Covid hit. No one asked questions. By the time it was over, we had applied for new passports with the children's images. It felt almost like divine intervention.'

'Except they did not come to you through divine providence or of their own free will. These children were taken,' Jess said.

Marston paused a beat and then went on. 'I swear, I did not know. That was not what Brewer and Moyles told us.'

'Tell me about passports.' Jess was not in a sympathetic mood.

'The hard part was getting someone to certify the children's photos. We thought we might start to travel again. To do that we'd need passports. I spoke to Charlie Brewer.'

Jess's head snapped up.

'He was already a fixer. We worked with him on some of

our properties. Before the pandemic. I told him it was hard finding someone, because of lockdown and because we were new to the area, to sign the photographs. He said he had someone. For a fee. We paid.'

'Did you know the signatory?'

Sweat beaded on Marston's upper lip. 'No. Only that he was a journalist of some kind. A friend of Brewer's.'

'What about Kerry Ford?'

Taran shook his head again. 'She turned up out of the blue. Said she had a video of us all at *Cân-y-Barcud* and was I interested in keeping it from the press? I don't think she had any clue what was going on. She only knew that she might get some money out of us. I got the impression we were not the first. People who arranged meetings in No One Near properties often had things to hide, she said. She was chancing her arm. But I paid. Regularly. She would come up and get her cash every month, and I'd pretend that we were hiding from the Dutch Mafia. I'm not sure if she believed me.'

He paused, calm as anything. 'You think that we are monsters? We are not. What Noor endured with our beloved three, no one should have to go through that three times.'

'When did they die?' Catrin asked.

'Mia in January 2018. Lieke in August of that year. Mats in June 2019. Statistically, that should never happen, but it did.' He paused again as if hearing what he was saying for the first time. 'People will hate us. But I did it for Noor.'

Jess's expression was ice. 'You stole someone else's children.'

'We did not know that. Moyles told us these were children who needed homes.'

'These are children. Not dogs.' Catrin's words trembled on the edge of a shout.

Jess shook her head. 'You're right. No one's going to forgive you for that, no matter what you'd gone through. Did you kill Kerry Ford?'

'No.'

'Where are the children now, Taran? Where are the ones you stole?'

For once, Marston looked scared to speak. But he did, finally, his words coming out in a rush. 'Brewer came to us two days ago, the night before we were arrested. He said that you'd come. The children were outside feeding the animals. Or they were supposed to be. But Brewer had taken them somewhere and come back to confront us. He told us to say my sister-in-law had them. Told us to lie or we'd never see them again. This had a dreadful effect on Noor. She considers them her children now. She became hysterical, inconsolable. We had no choice but to lie.'

'There is always a choice, and you should have chosen to tell us this yesterday,' Jess hissed, half rising from her chair.

'I couldn't. He said he'd...' Marston's words, at last, dried up.

'Have you any idea where he's taken them?'

Marston shook his head.

Both Catrin and Jess got up simultaneously.

Catrin said, 'Interview paused at 15:45.'

They almost ran out of the room.

# CHAPTER FORTY

WARLOW EASED himself into the kitchen chair, grateful for the solid wood beneath him. The house was quiet except for Cadi's occasional snuffling in her bed in the corner. Strange how silence could feel so different depending on circumstances. Sometimes peaceful, sometimes oppressive. Today qualified as... useful.

He tossed his head, trying to clear it, but the movement triggered more dizziness. His cough had improved. He no longer sounded as if there was a marble rattling around in a tin can behind his sternum. But these spells of lightheadedness had not got better. Not at all. Not that he'd mention that to anyone. Not even to Molly, who was currently browsing those little shops in Narberth, gathering last-minute items before her trip.

He scanned the whiteboard mounted on the kitchen wall. Jess used it for shopping lists, meal planning, the mundane organisation of daily life. But at this moment, blank. A clean slate. He pushed himself up carefully, a steadying hand against the table until the kitchen stopped swimming around him. The marker felt familiar in his hand. How many similar boards – larger, admittedly – had he stood before throughout his career, mapping out connections, building cases?

He wrote the name: LANE.

The marker squeaked against the surface. Such a small sound, but Cadi's ears twitched in her half sleep.

Lane.

The man was like mercury. Impossible to pin down, shifting shape depending on which angle you viewed him from. Victim or perpetrator? Both, probably. Like so many of them.

NAPIER went up next.

*Pieces of him scattered across half the valley. We never did find all of...*

He forced the idea away, adding MOYLES to the list. Another name that defied simple categorisation. Victim and perpetrator again. Until he wasn't anything at all, except a rotting body in that cottage.

*Cân-y-Barcud.* The place kept drawing them back, like iron filings to a magnet. Or flies to...

*No. Focus.*

BREWER.

FORD.

He stepped back, studying the names.

In any normal investigation, they'd sort themselves neatly into columns. Victims here, suspects there. But nothing about this struck him as normal.

These names wove back and forth across the case in a drunken stagger.

Lane played victim when it suited him, but Warlow had seen enough of his type over the years to know better. A man who could convince you black was white while picking your pocket and selling you your own watch.

*And he'd signed away Freddie Sillitoe with his signature. Transferred ownership to the Marstons as if they were secondhand cars. Freddie. Gil's obsession. The way he looked in that video, up in the loft. Lost...*

His hand tightened on the marker. He hadn't been in on the interviews this time. All he had was what Jess had shared, her impressions, her instincts. Good instincts, usually. But something didn't fit.

He was her sounding board, nothing else. She was not

expecting him to do anything. But he needed to do something.

Something useful.

As with all cases, the pieces were there, but they'd been assembled wrongly. A jigsaw forced together by a child's impatient hands.

Normally, at this point in a case, he'd drive out somewhere quiet. Back to the scene perhaps. Let the place speak to him, as places often did if you listened properly. But he was trapped here, confined to this kitchen with its whiteboard and its silence, its sleeping dog and its memories that wouldn't stay buried where they belonged.

*The loft. Always back to that loft. The way the light came through the skylight, making patterns on Freddie's face as he played with the toys.*

He added another name: SILLITOE.

Cadi whimpered in her sleep, probably chasing rabbits in her dreams. Simple dreams, uncomplicated by the memory of past cases, of bodies found, and lives destroyed. Of explanations that explained nothing.

The names stared back at him from the board. Written in blue on white since he hadn't been able to find a black marker. This was a tech-free exercise. Names on a board.

Simple. Except nothing was simple, was it? Lane claiming he'd only been helping for cash. Napier's remains scattered by the bomb like bloody confetti. Moyles, who everyone thought was the victim until they'd found what he'd been filming. Brewer swearing his ignorance, understanding nothing, while his eyes said something else entirely. And Ford… no matter how hard he pondered her, he came up short on ideas.

*As if they were pieces from different puzzles all jumbled together. But which pieces belong to which puzzle?*

The light-headedness came again, stronger this time. He gripped the countertop, waiting for it to pass. Shouldn't be happening this often. Shouldn't be getting worse instead of better. But then, a lot of things that shouldn't be happening were happening lately.

*Come on, Evan.*

Something was missing. Something obvious, probably.

That's how it usually worked with the crucial detail hiding in plain sight. Brewer had been good at that. Faking an attack, using Lane as a tool. All to buy time before he made a run for it.

*But where are you going, Charlie? Where is there to hide?*

Someone had lied. That much was a given. Perhaps more than one. But then, when had any of them ever told the whole truth?

Lane would lie about the weather if it would yield an advantage. Brewer kept his secrets wrapped in layers of half-truths and misdirection. Warlow no longer believed that the PPs and the BNs scribbled in diaries and calendars meant anything at all. Brewer obfuscating to the maximum. Even Moyles, long since buried, still keeping secrets. Dead men could do that, sometimes. Hide the truth even after everything else had been taken from them.

The marker hovered over the board.

He wanted to draw connections, arrows linking name to name, crime to crime. But that would mean committing to theories, and right now, theories were dangerous. Better to let the names float free, let the patterns emerge on their own.

His fingers traced the edge of the board, and he remembered other cases, other boards. The satisfaction of drawing that last line, the one that made everything clear. When the pattern suddenly revealed itself, like one of those magic eye pictures Molly was so good at seeing.

*But some patterns you don't want to see. Some connections you wish you could unmake. Like that video. Like Freddie in the loft...*

Cadi stirred in her bed, stretched, and padded over to him. Her cold nose pressed against his hand, grounding him in the present. Away from lofts and explosions and bodies in cottages. Away from Lane's plausible lies and Brewer's careful evasions.

'What do you think, girl?' he murmured, scratching behind her ears. 'What are we missing?'

But Cadi, like the list on the board, kept her secrets to herself.

He stood there, letting his hand rest on her warm head,

staring at the names until they blurred. Until they stopped being names at all and became something else. Markers on a map, maybe? A map of destruction and deception that stretched back years.

LANE
NAPIER
MOYLES
BREWER
FORD
SILLITOE

One more to add. MARSTON.

Seven names. Seven pieces of a puzzle. Or puzzles. Mixed together by someone's careless hands.

Or careful hands. Very careful, deliberate hands.

He lowered himself back into the chair, Cadi pressing against his leg in silent support. The board peered back at him from the wall, its names holding their secrets close.

He shut his eyes, but the names were burned there, too, floating in the darkness behind his eyelids.

The house creaked around him, settling into afternoon silence.

Soon, Molly would be home from Narberth, full of stories about the shops and plans for Italy. Soon, the kitchen would fill with normal sounds, normal life. But for now, there was just him and Cadi and the names on the board.

Stuck there.

Except for one. Charlie Brewer wasn't stuck there. He'd made his move. Run for it. A young man's folly.

Warlow frowned. The thing that was in front of him, that wasn't fitting, coalesced from a vague awareness into something solid.

He reached for the phone.

———

GIL KEPT one hand on the wheel. The other scrolled for Warlow's number on his displayed phonebook. The car sped east, towards his hometown of Llandeilo. He had Rhys with him, but they were not going to Gil's house, as welcoming as that thought might be. They were heading for a different address, Charlie Brewer's flat.

Already a call had gone out to ports and airports, and Border Force were checking records to see if he'd already slipped through the net and reached Europe.

Rhys was busy on his laptop. He looked up at Gil fiddling with the information on the centre display. 'Mr Warlow?'

'I know he's unwell, but he'll only give us an earful if we don't.' Gil found the name, but before he could punch the call button, the phone rang with the man himself as the caller.

'I tell you, he is bloody psychic,' Gil said.

'Better than psychiatric,' Rhys muttered.

An old joke, and one of Gil's. This time, all it earned was a wry smile from the senior detective.

'I've just come off the phone with Jess. Where are you two?' Warlow launched right into it without even a hello.

'On the way to Brewer's place. Not that we're expecting to find him. He's flown the nest.'

'So I heard,' Warlow said. 'White cliffs of Dover?'

Rhys, who was bent over his laptop, shook his head. 'Nothing from Border Control, sir.'

'So, that means either he's buggered off on a different passport or…'

'He hasn't gone yet,' Rhys said.

Gil had worked with Warlow long enough to suss when the detective chief inspector was onto something. He said as much now. 'What isn't adding up in that brain of yours?'

'Brewer. He got Lane to beat him up to make himself the victim. To give himself a reason to back off and get you off his back.'

'Agreed,' Gil said. 'Devious little sod. He played me. Right from the very start. All that crap about PPs in Napier's diaries. All *malu cachu*.'

Mincing shit indeed.

'Then why return to the Marstons? He was off the radar with good reason to be. Why risk going back?' Warlow asked.

'To threaten them with the ultimate. To get them to lie by stealing the kids.'

'Right.' Warlow made the word sound dubious.

'Or he wanted money,' Rhys volunteered. 'For services rendered. Like getting Lane to do that favour.'

'Far more likely,' Warlow said. 'Do you have Brewer's phone records yet?'

'We do, sir,' Rhys said. 'I've reviewed them. Marston and Brewer communicated the morning after he was attacked.'

'That's what, at least a day before Marston says he visited them?'

Rhys made some noises, suggesting he was using his brain as a calculator. 'It is.'

'That definitely doesn't add up. Why would Brewer wait?'

'He wouldn't,' Gil said. 'He'd want to get away. He'd be losing all his advantage by hanging on.'

'What if he didn't wait?' Warlow asked slowly.

'But Marston said—'

'I think Taran Marston is lying,' Warlow cut across him. 'I think he's lying through his teeth. I think his only connection to Brewer was to ask him to arrange for a passport photograph to be signed. Not illegal, but dicey enough when neighbours snoop on you.'

'But he said Moyles got him the children.'

'I know he did,' Warlow said. 'And who are the only people in this case who really know the truth about that? Moyles is dead. Napier is dead. Brewer is missing. That leaves only one other source.'

'Kerry Ford?' Rhys said.

'No. Think again.'

'The kids,' Gil said.

'There's something else about the children, well, child, I found,' Rhys said. 'I've been going through missing children's reports since 2018. There was a four-and-a-half-year-old girl who disappeared in March 2018 – she has nystagmus.'

'Hang on. Is that another disease?' Gil asked.

'More a condition.'

'Rhod Bowen, the farmer who found her, said she had a stigma.'

'People get confused,' Warlow said. 'If I remember rightly, Tomo said that she had dancing eyes?'

'I remember that,' Gil said.

'That's nystagmus. Now you're going to ask me how I know about it?'

'How do you know about it?' Gil duly obliged.

'Because my son is an ENT surgeon. People with severe ear infections can get it. Your eyes flit restlessly. Makes you dizzy and feel sick. But sometimes, it's congenital. That author, the very tall one.'

'Richard Osman, sir?' Rhys obliged, still bent over the laptop.

'That's the one. He has it, too.'

'Girl's name is Bridie Crieran. From Dundee,' Rhys said, reading the information from his screen. 'She was not in care, sir. Moyles lied. She was near a river with her brother playing hide-and-seek. They found a school jumper. They assumed she'd fallen in—'

'And Freddie Sillitoe was not in care either,' Warlow added.

'So, either Moyles lied to Taran Marston, or Marston lied to us,' Gil said.

'Ring Tomo, see if he's about. If he's anywhere near the Marstons' place. With a bit of luck, he may still be up coordinating the crime scene access on Druid's Moor. If he is, tell him to get over to the Marston property and have a sniff around,' Warlow said. 'And then get some uniforms to follow on.'

'We'll do it as we go,' Gil said, sounding suddenly croaky. 'We're on our way.'

# CHAPTER FORTY-ONE

THE AFTERNOON SHOWER swept rain across *Dôl y Derwyddon* in sheets, drumming against the slate roofs of the old stone barns. Gil stood in the farmyard, reading the note someone had stuck to the main house door with electrical tape. The paper was already soggy, the ink beginning to run.

**Gone to feed animals before I go. Happy New Year wherever you've got to! See you when you're back!—Llyr**

The farmhand's cheerful ignorance was not helpful and did nothing to ease the twisting tension in Gil's gut. Llyr, clearly not in the loop, had carried on as normal.

Rhys appeared at his shoulder, rain dripping from his hood. 'Whole place is locked up tight.'

The farm buildings hunched around them like sleeping giants. Thick stone walls darkened by rain, moss growing in the mortar lines. Celtic knotwork had been carved into the lintels above each door, and strings of prayer flags, sodden and heavy, hung between the buildings. A wooden statue of *Ceridwen*, the Welsh goddess of rebirth, stood guard by the main barn entrance, her carved face weathered by years of rain and wind.

Tomo's Land Cruiser pulled into the yard, tyres hissing in

the wet, Priya in the passenger seat. They both emerged into the downpour, Tomo already putting on evidence gloves.

'Fill us in,' he called over the wind.

Gil moved under the shelter of an overhanging roof, the others following. 'Warlow's been doing some thinking. Reckons Marston's been lying from the start. The story about the kids being taken? The threatening messages? All of it. And now Brewer's disappeared.'

'Brewer?' Tomo asked, frowning.

'He's a link between the Marstons and *Cân-y-Barcud*. We found a video at Ford's place.'

'Ford, the dead woman? Here, too?'

'It's complicated,' Gil said.

'Yeah,' Rhys put in. 'Brewer got beaten up, but that was a setup. He bought himself some time, and Marston claims he came here and took the children.'

'What?' Tomo barked out the word in disbelief.

'But Warlow has called BS,' Gil said. 'He doesn't trust Marston. And neither do I. We think Brewer might have worked out what was really going on. Maybe even helped plan whatever this is. But something went wrong. Either he got cold feet, tried to back out…'

'Or Marston decided he was a liability.'

'Exactly. Problem is, we don't know what we're looking for.'

'Or where to look.' Rhys gestured at the sprawl of buildings. 'Place is huge. They run yoga retreats, mindfulness sessions. There are barns, meditation spaces, storage sheds…'

'And livestock.' Priya wrinkled her nose at the chickens hiding from the rain in an open shed. Beyond them, shapes moved in the fields. Donkeys and llamas huddled against the rain.

The buildings formed a rough square around the central yard. The main barn dominated one side, its huge double doors shut. Smaller outbuildings, converted for the retreat business, lined the other walls. Crystal wind chimes tinkled from the eaves. Dreamcatchers swung in the wind. A mural of the Green Man peered from one whitewashed wall, his leafy face somehow sinister in the failing light.

'Let's work our way around towards the barn.'

They did exactly that. It took twenty minutes before Gil pushed open the big double doors to reveal what was essentially a storage area for wrapped bales of silage on one side and hay on the other.

It was still light, but barely at mid-afternoon, and the interior of the barn was dim and dusty. The burnt tobacco smell of silage met them.

Rhys's phone didn't cast enough light to see much further than a few yards into the dark corners, but Gil's powerful torchlight showed up the stacked bales almost to the roof. The stone walls rose to heavy wood and steel beams far overhead. A small tractor with a bale handler attachment sat silent in one corner.

The flags on their phones showed only one bar of signal. The barn's thick walls seemed to swallow sound, leaving them with just the drum of rain on the roof and their own breathing.

Tomo's torch beam swept the floor.

'Hold up.' He crouched, studying dark patches on the concrete. 'Something's been moved here. Recently.' He pointed to scrape marks, then to the stack of round bales. 'Those bales have been shifted. Look at the dust pattern.'

Gil's pulse quickened. After so many dead ends, false leads, wild goose chases...

'I can work that handler.' Tomo crossed to the tractor. 'Let's hope there are keys.'

Five seconds later, levering himself into the driving seat, he called back a, 'Yup. Under the seat.'

The tractor's engine boomed in the barn's vastness.

One by one, Tomo extracted the round bales, each weighing nearly half a ton. The stack was six high against the wall. He'd moved ten when Rhys shouted.

'Light! There's something reflecting!'

Their torchlight converged on the gap Tomo had created.

Metal gleamed dully in the beams. The curve of a car's boot lid. The tobacco smell filled the air from the disturbed bales.

'Keep going,' Gil ordered.

The car emerged from its hay cocoon like an excavated fossil. A black Vauxhall.

When the registration plate appeared, Rhys called it in. 'It's Brewer's car. The one that—'

The words died as their lights found the back seat.

Charlie Brewer sat there, or what was left of him. The back of his head was a cave of bone and blood. He stared at nothing through dead eyes.

'Bloody hell,' Priya whispered.

'Tomo,' Gil shouted up at the cab. 'Keep going.'

More bales came away.

Gil forced himself to focus, to think past the horror. 'The kids aren't here. Keep searching. Every corner.'

# CHAPTER FORTY-TWO

But the silage bales held no more surprises. The searchers spread out, checking the rest of the barn, opening feed bins, looking anywhere a child might be hidden. The barn seemed to grow larger with each passing minute, shadows deepening as twilight gathered.

'Here!' Tomo boomed across the space. He stood by another stack of hay bales, rectangular this time. 'These have been shifted recently, too.'

He ran back to the tractor.

These were lighter, easier to manoeuvre. He'd taken four away when Rhys shouted.

'Hang on! Hang on! I see something moving.'

He was right. Something was moving. Or was that... waving? A hand thrust through a gap in the hay, fingers spread wide.

A child's hand.

'Get them out! Now!' Gil yelled.

They tore at the last few bales, heavy enough to require two officers to drag each one away, throwing them aside to tumble down to the barn floor until a space was revealed, black as pitch until their torches lit it up.

What the light revealed was three children huddled against the back wall, chained to metal rings set in the stone.

A few bottles of water lay scattered around them. Some empty crisp packets. A bucket just about reachable in the corner.

'It's all right,' Gil called. 'We're the police. You're safe now.'

The two girls – Mia, who was in actual fact Bridie Crieran, and Lieke, real name Amy Landon – blinked in the torchlight, faces dirty and tear-streaked. But the third child, the boy, pressed himself further into the corner, hands over his face.

'It's okay,' Gil tried again. 'We'll get those chains off. No one's going to hurt you.'

The boy just shook his head, burrowing deeper into the shadows.

'He's scared,' Bridie whispered. Her voice was hoarse from disuse. 'Taran said if we made noise, the *Cŵn Annwn* would come for us.'

The Hounds of Annwn. The Wild Hunt of Welsh legend. Supernatural beasts that pursued their prey across the night sky.

'They're not real,' Bridie added. 'I know that. But Mats… he believes it.'

Tomo was already working on the chains with bolt cutters he'd got from the truck. Priya helped the girls out as they were freed, using reassuring words, holding their hands. But the boy remained pressed against the wall, shaking with fear.

Gil crouched, spoke gently. 'Mats?'

The boy shook his head again. He could have been anywhere between eight and ten years old. Small for his age. But something clicked in Gil's mind. 'No, not Mats. That's not your name, is it? It's Freddie, right? Is that your real name?'

The boy's hands lowered slightly. Eyes peered out from behind dirty fingers.

'The hounds aren't coming, Freddie,' Gil promised. 'And neither is Taran. Never again. You're safe now. I swear it.'

Slowly, so slowly, the boy lowered his hands completely. Tears had cut tracks through the dirt on his face.

'Promise?' he whispered.

'Promise,' Gil said.

The chain fell away under Tomo's bolt cutters.

For a moment, the boy didn't move. Then he launched himself forward, wrapping his arms around Gil's neck, holding on as if he'd never let go.

Gil held him close, the child's heart hammering against his chest to match his own thudding pulse.

The rain continued to fall. Wind moaned through the barn's eaves. Somewhere in the darkness, a chain clinked against stone. But here, in this moment, was something pure. Something rescued from the darkness.

Gil thought of all the lost children he'd searched for over his career. All the ones they hadn't found in time. All the empty rooms and false hopes.

'It's all right,' he murmured, as much to himself as to the boy. 'It's all right now.'

Tomo was already calling for backup, for ambulances, for scenes of crime officers. Rhys stood guard over Brewer's car, preserving what he could of the crime scene. Priya helped the girls towards the barn entrance, where the first hints of blue lights approaching strobed through the rain. Somewhere, a llama called mournfully into the darkness and the wooden Ceridwen looked out with blind eyes. From the rafters came a long, low moan, the sound of age and wear, of a structure that had stood too many winters and knew too well there was no escaping time's onslaught.

But Gil stayed where he was, holding the boy who had been Mats but was really Freddie.

———

A SHORT TIME LATER, in a cottage in Pembrokeshire, in a custody suite in Llanelli, and soon, in houses in Scotland, Shropshire, and on the outskirts of Cardiff, a clutch of officers and, more importantly, three families that had been through more than their fair share of hell, would remember a moment.

A singular moment when the phone rang, or a door knocked, and a voice would tell them that what was lost beyond all hope and expectation was now found.

———

THEY QUESTIONED THE CHILDREN. Both girls could identify Taran Marston from photos as their abductor. In each case, he had chosen spots within two miles of their homes, always close to water to suggest a drowning accident. He'd deliberately left behind a small item of clothing: a shoe for one, a school jumper for the other.

Gil despised the man for that.

In Freddie Sillitoe's case, Marston had left nothing. He hadn't needed to. The anonymity of the massive bank holiday crowd on the beach that warm day in 2019 had done the work for him.

Freddie couldn't remember much about it, yet he seemed to bear the heaviest psychological scars.

Back in Bristol, the team continued to piece together the Ford case. During a search of *Dôl y Derwyddon*, they found a stash of disposable barbecues identical to the one found near the crime scene. Marston had bought a batch on eBay, supposedly for the occasional campers at his property.

The evidence was circumstantial, but there was more: Marston had crossed the Severn Bridge the day before Amy Landon vanished and crossed back the following morning. He had also crossed the day that the Ford sisters died in their caravan.

The case was slowly building. Still, Taran Marston admitted nothing. But the consensus was that Kerry Ford's luck had run out, finally. Perhaps she'd simply upped the blackmailing ante not even knowing why Marston had been willing to pay her hush money all this time. But it was possible that she'd also found out that Noor Marston had more money than she'd let on. Or she'd simply chanced her arm and squeezed them a little too hard. But both Anna and Jess wanted to believe that she did not know the whole story: that the Marston children had been abducted.

Kerry Ford was a lot of things, but she had been no monster.

At the beginning of the second week in January, the parents of Bridie and Amy came to meet the team who had brought their daughters home. No press. No fanfare. The day carried a quiet intensity, marked by hesitant smiles, tears that came easily, and the kind of gratitude that needed no words. For the officers, it was a rare moment of release. An acknowledgement that their long hours and hard choices had ended in something good. Freddie and his parents did not join them; for the boy, it was taking much longer to accept that his nightmare was truly over.

A week later, Anna said her goodbyes to Jess and Catrin.

'Good to have worked with you both,' she said with a genuine smile.

'The feeling's mutual,' Jess replied. She looked down at the offered hand but then pulled Anna into a hug instead.

Catrin followed suit.

Anna wasn't a natural hugger, as both Jess and Catrin would later attest, yet she didn't object on this occasion.

'If there's anything we can do…' Jess offered.

'Oh, I dare say there will be.' Anna's smile turned serious. 'But you've got him for the kidnappings and Brewer, right?'

'We do. We're still looking for the murder weapon, though. I know you'd like full closure for the Ford family.'

'It would be nice.' Anna nodded. 'But even with what we have, it should at least shut my bosses up.'

The officers walked her out to her car and waved her off.

'I like her,' Catrin said as the car disappeared around the corner.

'So do I.' Jess grinned. 'Rumour had it she was difficult.'

'Spread by who?'

Jess smirked. 'Someone who doesn't appreciate thorough investigators, I expect. No doubt of the male variety.'

Catrin laughed. 'I doubt DI Anna Gwynne gives a stuff, though.'

'I'm with you there.'

Catrin pursed her lips. 'I've also decided to change my name. Take Craig's surname. Become Catrin Peters, officially. Driving licence, job, et cetera.'

'Is there a reason other than an act of commitment with Craig?'

'Partly that. Betsi is Peters anyway, and I want that, too. Craig isn't bothered either way, but the press officer got hold of what Lane had been working on. They were going to serialise his book, you know that?'

'I'd heard,' Jess said.

'That might still surface in some shape or form if and when all this goes to court. I want to put some distance between me now and me then.'

'Understandable,' Jess said. 'I did it. I never changed back when Ricky and I split. Too much paperwork.'

'I don't mind paperwork,' Catrin said, paused, and then added, 'I know it sends some people into meltdown. I have friends who say they'd never take their partner's name because it's somehow subservient and a patriarchal construct.'

'What do you think?'

'I think I will do what I want to do.'

Jess grinned. 'Sergeant Catrin Peters. Has a certain ring to it.'

---

THAT SAME AFTERNOON, Gil and Rhys were halfway down the corridor when Superintendent Buchannan boomed behind them.

'Ah! The men of the hour!'

Buchannan was beaming, his big face flushed with pleasure. Beside him, Chief Superintendent Drinkwater forced a smile.

'Absolutely outstanding work, both of you.' Buchannan clapped Gil on the shoulder. 'The kind of old-fashioned copper's nose that you can't teach.'

Drinkwater shifted his weight, his expression suggesting

he'd rather be having root canal work. 'Yes, well,' he managed. 'The result was… highly satisfactory.'

Buchannan laughed. 'Three children rescued, a killer caught? Give credit where it's due. If Gil hadn't kept pushing, kept following his instincts…'

'Indeed.' Drinkwater looked like the words were being extracted with pliers. 'Your… persistence… was justified, Sergeant Jones.'

'Thank you, sir,' Gil said blandly, his expression a study in barely restrained laughter.

'And young Rhys here,' Buchannan kept going. 'Remarkable maturity.'

'Quite.' Drinkwater checked his watch. 'Now, if you'll excuse me, I have a meeting…'

They watched him stride away, his back rigid with what he no doubt hoped was dignity.

'Well done again, both of you.' Buchannan gave them a knowing wink before heading in the opposite direction.

When the corridor was empty, Rhys grinned. 'That was nice. Getting praised by the top brass.'

'Was it?' Gil's mouth twitched. 'I was too busy watching Drinkwater's face. Like a man trying to pass a brick sideways.'

Rhys snorted. 'Lovely image, Sarge. Where are we with Lane?'

'Good question. We have him tied to the kidnapping through forgery on the passport, though he's pleading innocence. You can get two years just for that. And he'll be formally questioned about his involvement with Hunt. He's still claiming coercion there. But I have the CCTV boys working on seeing if we can link Hunt's movements on his bike to Lane's. If they were in communication, I suspect they'd use disposable phones, but all it takes is for Lane to have been sloppy once or twice. If we can put them together somewhere…'

'Bingo,' Rhys said, and he smiled when he said it.

'I daresay someone will be digging up the dirt on him soon, and he'll be the subject of someone else's book, or podcast, or Netflix special. You know that lot; they're like that worm, ouroboros. They eat themselves.'

'I'm still trying to process it all. I'm thinking that Moyles didn't even know that Brewer had suggested using *Cân-y-Barcud* for his side hustle with the Marstons.'

'And Brewer didn't know about Moyles's little videoing habit. Otherwise, he'd have stayed well clear.'

'Both hoisted by their own Cunards,' said Rhys.

That earned Rhys a quirked Gil eyebrow. 'That one of mine, is it?'

'It is, Sarge. And I used it for far too long until someone explained what a petard is. And that's even more ironic, given what happened to Napier and Hunt's bomb-making skills.'

Gil sighed. 'I'm heading down to see Evan this week. Take him for a pint, let him know how it all played out. He'd have enjoyed watching Drinkwater just now. Want to come?'

'I'll drive,' Rhys offered.

Gil grinned. 'I knew there was something I liked about you.'

# CHAPTER FORTY-THREE

THE OLD ONES.

They'd all missed it. And it was Tomo, in a tortured moment of mental self-flagellation, who reminded them all.

'The girl... Mia. That was what she said to the farmer who found her. That they'd been to visit the old ones. We thought it was the stones. It wasn't the bloody stones, though, was it?'

No one had answered him. Of course they hadn't, because who in their right minds would have made that kind of leap? The old ones could have been the standing stones. Should have been those stones, not children. Not the children who the kids had been taken to replace.

———

THE GIRLS IDENTIFIED and described Taran Marston as their abductor. When shown images of Moyles, neither of them knew who he was, exposing Marston's version of events as the tissue of lies that it was.

But there was worse. Bridie, the oldest at almost eleven, was the most articulate.

'We never knew when we'd get food. That was the worst thing. Some days we'd have to sit and watch Noor and Taran eat their dinner. Proper hot food that made our tummies hurt from wanting it so much. We just got bread and pasties mostly. Sometimes, nothing.

'Amy was too little to understand at first. She wasn't quite five when she came. She kept asking when we could go home. We all learned quick, though. Learned to hide when we heard cars. Learned to stay away from the windows. Learned to let them put the horrible burning stuff in our hair that made it go lighter.

'Mats's real name is Freddie. He cried a lot. I don't blame him. But they hated it when he cried. They'd take him to the hayloft, right up in the dark part where all the scratchy sounds were. Sometimes, he'd be up there for ages. When he came back down, he was different. Quieter.

'We were most scared of Noor, though. Not because she hurt us. They never hit us or anything. But because you never knew what she'd do. One minute, she'd be nice; the next, she'd be screaming about the monsters in the forest that only she could keep away. She'd do these weird dances at the stones and put herbs everywhere. When you're scared and hungry enough, you start believing in monsters. Even when you know it's silly.

'But I wouldn't let them dye my hair again. When we went to the stones that morning and I ran away through the trees, I didn't care anymore. And if there were monsters chasing me, they might be better than staying in that place. The farmer was nice. So was the policeman. But Taran and Noor came to get me. It wasn't nice after that. I was in the hayloft all the time.

'I still check sometimes, even now, to see if there are monsters in the woods. I know there aren't, really. But sometimes, I'm not sure what's scarier – monsters, or people who make you believe in them.'

Freddie was too traumatised to speak to anyone, and no one pushed for that. It would come. They could wait.

———

ON THE MORNING of the eighteenth of January, Buchannan strode into the office. He looked triumphant.

'Been a busy morning. I've been with the chief constable and press office. They've been in talks with CPS. Ten minutes ago, the press officer took a call from Lane's agent.' He allowed himself a small smile. 'The book is being pulled.'

Everyone made noises of delight. Everyone except Catrin. Something had given in her. The tension in her shoulders released suddenly, like a bowstring cut. Her exhale was shaky, but her eyes gleamed with fierce satisfaction. 'They're pulling it, sir. Really?'

'Complete withdrawal. No publication, no press, nothing.'

'Sir, I…' She shook her head, tears rushing out in an over-whelming tsunami of relief. 'Best New Year's present I could have asked for. Thank you, sir. For everything.'

'Don't thank me. This is down to Gil and Jess and Rhys, and I suppose Mr Warlow should get a mention. As does our temporary recruit, Anna Gwynne. If she wasn't as tenacious as she is, we might never have had the opportunity to get Lane in that interview room.' He paused and then added, 'And we'll need to get him back in. Soon. We've confiscated his passport. He won't squirm his way out of this. Well done, everyone.'

When he'd gone, they all stared at one another.

Rhys was the first up, punching the air.

Jess gave Catrin a hug.

'I wish Mr Warlow was here to hear all that,' Catrin said.

'I'll get him on the blower now,' Gil said. 'Rhys, get that kettle boiling.'

———

DARKNESS HAD ALREADY SWALLOWED the evening when Jess parked up at *Ffau'r Blaidd* on the night of January eighteenth. Warlow was in his usual chair, laptop open on the small table beside him. *He looks tired*, she thought. More so than usual, and despite the pneumonia that had given him dark rings under his eyes.

'You'll never guess.' She shrugged off her coat. 'They found it. The murder weapon.'

Warlow raised his eyebrows, gestured for her to continue, but there was something subdued about his response that wasn't like him.

'Hidden under an old tarpaulin in one of the outbuildings. Big hammer, like you'd use for fence posts. One of Povey's team found blood in the crevices where the head meets the handle. Same blood type as Brewer. They're running DNA as we speak. And brilliant news about Lane's shitty book. Catrin is over the moon...' She trailed off, noticing his distant expression. 'You okay? How was your appointment?'

'Interesting,' he said after a pause.

She sat in the chair opposite, her suspicions raised. 'Interesting how exactly?'

'As in it wasn't just Emerson I saw today. I also saw a consultant called Benedetti. A surgeon this time. Bottom line, they found something else whilst I was in hospital.' He turned the laptop for her to see. The British Heart Foundation site with a bold heading:

**Heart Valve Disease**

'I have a dodgy ticker. Aortic valve, to be precise. It's leaking.'

'Oh, God, Evan.' She reached across and took his hand.

His fingers were icy.

'Light-headedness is apparently a classic symptom. I thought it was all the coughing. But it wasn't just that. I get light-headed because my blood is not getting where it should get to. We both know my heart is icy cold at the best of times. Now it's becoming lazy, too.' He waited for Jess to smile, but his joke fell flat. On its face.

'Makes you more susceptible to infections, apparently.' He shrugged. 'Hence the pneumonia.'

'But they can fix it?'

'Surgery.' He managed a small smile. 'Surgeon says it'll be fine. Though he had to mention there's a small risk of... well, you know. Begins with D and ends in H with T, an E, and an

A in the middle. Though not in that order. I mean, that would make no sense—'

Tears welled. She tried to blink them away, but Warlow saw them and curtailed the silly talk.

'Hey, none of that,' he said. 'I need more tests first. Scans and the like. Then they'll decide exactly what to do. Might be a pig's valve... Imagine that, me part pig. Some would say about time in that it goes with the uniform. I can think of someone who would say it'll put a tin hat on my eating habits.'

Still, Jess wasn't smiling.

He sighed. 'Or there's this newer thing called a TAVI. Less invasive, apparently. They don't even have to cut you open. They deliver a new valve through your tubes. A bit like Amazon—'

'Why didn't you tell me sooner?' There was a hint of anger in her now. 'How long have you known something was wrong?'

'You've had enough on your plate, and today was the appointment with the surgeon, so I haven't had the details until now.' It was a lousy defence, and he knew it. 'I didn't want Molly to worry either. What with Christmas, and it's her last day in Italy today. I didn't want to spoil her trip. She can find out when she comes back. It'll be soon enough.'

'Evan Warlow, you stubborn—'

'I know, I know.' He squeezed her hand. 'I get to do all this again tomorrow morning, too. A New Year's Zoom call with the boys, thanks to the time difference. Not looking forward to that conversation either. Though, I have a sneaking suspicion Tom knows something's up.'

He leaned back in his chair. 'It actually feels better, having it out in the open.'

'And it explains the tiredness these past few months?'

'It does. Nothing to do with the HIV, thank God, nor just getting older, which is what I'd convinced myself it was.' He gave a short laugh. 'The surgeon, Mr Benedetti, my new BFF, has even given me a provisional date, would you believe? February fourteenth.'

'Valentine's Day?'

'Romantic, isn't it? Thought I might ask them to carve little hearts on the valve, really get into the spirit of things.'

'Evan,' she said with genuine horror.

'Sorry.'

Cadi padded over and laid her head on his knee. He scratched her ears absently.

'Won't be able to walk you for a while afterwards. Jess will have to do all that.'

'As if that's a hardship.' Jess wiped her eyes. 'Anything you need. You know that.'

They sat in silence for a moment, listening to the cottage settle around them. The Heart Foundation page dissolved as Warlow's absurd underwater jellyfish screensaver kicked in.

'Now it makes sense.'

Warlow looked up sharply, the jellyfish screensaver glinting off his glasses. 'The dizzy spells, you mean?'

Jess shook her head, a half-smile flickering before fading. 'No. Molly told me she heard you playing Genesis on a loop before she went to Italy. "Hold On My Heart".'

He gave a low, embarrassed chuckle. 'Ah. Yes. I do cliché pretty well, don't I?'

'You know what that song's about, Evan?'

'Soft rock cheese? Phil Collins getting another mortgage payment?'

'I should know. I've listened to it enough times. I have it on my playlist.'

'I didn't know—'

'It's about fear. Fear of opening yourself up again, even when you want to. Fear of letting someone in because it might hurt. It's about us, isn't it? You, the widower who never let go, me, the divorcée pretending my marriage never mattered.'

'Some of the lines,' he said eventually, 'they got under my skin a bit. That's the trouble with having nothing to do. And I know it was unfashionable to like Genesis at one time, but I couldn't give a stuff. And Collins can be a poet. Plus, the reference to a failing organ in the title tickled the punster in me. "Hold On My Heart". I mean, come on.' He shifted his face into a smile.

She sat across from him, elbows on knees, not smiling. Not yet.

'You don't have to go through this alone. You don't have to hold on so tight it stops you living. You can let yourself feel something, Evan. It's okay.'

He met her eyes, and for a moment, the familiar deflection was absent.

'Scares the hell out of me.'

'I know,' she said softly. 'Me, too.'

The wind caught the eaves, the old cottage creaking as it settled. Cadi shifted at Warlow's feet, sighing in tandem, as if to remind them there was warmth in simply being together.

'Well.' Warlow cleared his throat. 'You'll be relieved to know my next track was going to be "I Will Survive".'

Jess let out a small, damp laugh and wiped her eyes. 'Molly has a take on it. The "Hold On My Heart", I mean.'

'I can't wait.'

'According to her it's an ironic, existential reminder of how hard it is to let go of past hurt while wanting to feel something, *anything*, again.'

'Bloody hell. Nailed it, then.' He raised his glass to meet her gaze.

And for a moment, neither said anything more, letting the silence hold them, letting it mean what it needed to mean.

'So,' he said finally, 'tell me more about this hammer. Proper evidence this time, not just circumstantial?'

'You sure you want to talk about work?'

'Rather that than sit here thinking about pig valves and surgical risks.'

She shook her head. 'You're hopeless, you know that?'

'The other thing of note is that red wine, in moderation, is good for me, apparently.'

Jess got up and went to fetch some glasses.

'I'm still capable of making food, though,' he called after her.

'Something smells nice,' Jess said, reaching up into a cupboard.

'I was going to make pork medallions, but somehow or other it doesn't seem right given the options open to me. So, it's chicken stuffed with ricotta.'

She turned with a very old-fashioned expression. 'Am I going to have to put up with porcine humour now for the next, how many weeks is it?'

'A bit. I mean, you reap what you sow, right?'

Jess let out a long-suffering sigh of her own. But she brought a bottle of Appassimento over to the table, already opened, and poured them each a glass without comment.

'Will you come back to work afterwards?'

'Bloody hell, I'm bored here alone already. I hadn't planned on kicking back just yet.'

'Funny, I spoke to Gil today, too. He definitely seems to have a new lease of life after finding Freddie.' Jess handed him a glass.

'I'm not surprised. Finding three kids… that's a hole in one on the eighteenth at St Andrews while wearing a blind-fold and using a Happy Gilmore technique. He'll be dining out on that for a while.'

'He says he's already looking forward to the new year.'

'Oh well, I'm certainly not going before him, then.'

'Good.' Jess raised her glass. 'I think there's still a bit of the old dog left in you, too.'

'Woof!' Warlow affected a bark.

Cadi pricked up her ears.

'Sorry, Cadi. I expect that means something highly inappropriate in Labrador.'

The dog wagged her tail as if to say she accepted his apology.

Warlow smiled and took a sip of his wine.

Jess had her phone open and pressed the screen. A moment later, the soft, padded electronic drum pattern at the opening of Genesis's wistful ballad came through the Bluetooth speakers in the room, followed by the airy synth of the first few notes. Not a driving beat, more an invitation to a softly lit room to explore some emotional contemplation.

'Really?' Warlow said.

Jess shrugged. 'Shut up and sit next to me on this sofa, Evan Warlow. Just put your arm around me and let the world spin on its axis for a while.'

'Yes, ma'am. Anything you say.'

———

THANK you for reading this book. I hope you enjoyed it as much as I enjoyed writing it... BUT ARE YOU READY FOR MORE?

DCI EVAN WARLOW and the team are back in... CROSS CUT.

**The dead don't haunt Warlow. The living do.**

When a refuse worker discovers the body of media student **Nicholas Vernon** in a quiet Welsh town, Detective Evan Warlow and his team are drawn into a case that spirals from routine enquiry to nightmare. Behind the whispers and online rumours lies a truth far darker than anyone is ready to face in the form of macabre obsessions and the homeless.

With forensic evidence thin on the ground and local loyalties running deep, Warlow must confront both a killer—and a truth about his own mortality he's long avoided.

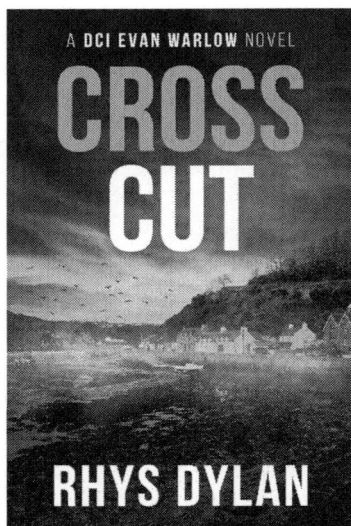

A DCI EVAN WARLOW NOVEL

# CROSS CUT

**RHYS DYLAN**

## CROSS CUT
### Chapter 1

The first week of February, the very heart of late winter in West Wales, began cold and dry. The last of January's destructive gang of Atlantic storms had spent itself the day before over the Irish Sea and the harbour town of Fishguard, 250 miles west of London. High pressure had settled, leaving this morning bright and brittle with frost. At 06:50, it was still dark as the refuse collection vehicle trundled down Tower Hill in the old town, its orange lights rotating in a steady rhythm, casting fleeting halos on the frost-glazed road. The crew were well into their early morning banter, voices puffing clouds into the chilled air as they worked.

This was the quiet side of *Abergwaun*, as the local Welsh speakers called Fishguard. The side with the picturesque harbour and wooded slopes, nestled neatly around the corner from the busy ferry port at Goodwick, linking the United Kingdom with Ireland and Europe.

'Oi, Kes,' called out Jimbo, a burly figure in a yellow high-vis jacket above orange trousers. He was emptying a green food bin onto the food section maw on the lorry. 'Bet you a tenner Alan's heater's on full blast up there. No way that baldy's feelin' this cold.'

From the cab, Alan's reply came muffled but audible through the window, open a good three inches despite the frosty air. 'Bald heads retain heat better than your mop, Jimbo. Scientific fact, mate.'

Kerry Mitchell chuckled, tugging his gloves tighter as he grabbed another food bin. 'You been reading those books upside down again? If it's so scientific, why's your head lookin' like a frosted turnip, Al? Got icicles forming up there.'

'Jealousy is ugly, boys,' Alan retorted with mock dignity. He revved the engine. The green lorry lumbered forward.

Jimbo grinned, his teeth gleaming in the dim light. 'You know what's ugly? This bloody cold. What is it, minus five? My fingers 'ave gone stiff already. Should have brought one of them hand warmers. You got any, Kes?'

'Nah.' Kes dragged a blue bag into position, ready to empty. 'Stick your hands down your pants, mate. That's what to do. And good for the testicles, icy fingers.'

'Is that what you're doin'?' Jimbo shook his head. 'You'll get arrested one day. S'probably on all the doorcams, you with both hands in your pants like a perv. Besides, how the hell do you know that about testicles?'

'Saw it on Netflix, man. Some people that want kids have to keep their jewels cold all the time. Ice 'em an' that. Good for your swimmers, apparently. Mind you, with Abby up the spout again, yours must be bloody Olympic class, boy.'

'Don't bloody joke, mate. Abby's on about the snip for me all the time—'

'And who can blame her, Jimbo? Leave the poor girl alone, for God's sake. She might as well open a puppy farm.'

A ripple of raucous laughter filled the street.

The truck growled onward, stopping a few yards short of the entrance to Chapel Lane. The road was narrow here, the terraced houses pastel shades of blue and yellow and variants of cream in daylight. It was a no-through road and sometimes Bald Alan never got the wagon that far along, knowing he'd have to reverse out. Kes pressed ahead, his eyes adjusting to the dim light as he hauled a stubborn food bin over the rough road.

'I'll grab the top of the lane,' Kes called out and waved a gloved hand.

Jimbo waved back. His breath fogged the air as he replied. 'Good man. Careful how you go. I'm not coming to visit you when you break a hip. How is your arse, by the way?'

A loud guffaw reached Kes from Alan through the cab window. He'd taken a tumble on the second street they'd hit, not seeing the spill of ice from a leaky overflow and doing a mad dance as his feet went from under him, much to the delight of his crewmates. A delight that left them breathless and aching with mirth for a good five minutes, and which led to several choice quips.

'Strictly are looking for some new pros,' Alan had said, or rather wheezed out in between peals of laughter.

'Christ, Kes, I thought you were sending semaphore to the bloody ferry,' Jimbo, hands on his knees, had managed to say.

All Kes could do was massage his left arse cheek and hip and take his lumps.

'Wish I'd had a camera,' Alan said, through tears of laughter.

'It was the shout as you hit the ground that got me,' Jimbo said. 'I mean, what the hell is a fugbaster?'

Kes had no idea. It was simply what had erupted from his shocked mouth. Probably a combination of two oaths that had got mangled through surprise and pain.

He went up the narrow lane, his hip twinging as he muttered to himself about three-week bag limits and scanning the area for stray rubbish. This was a dead end leading to the backs of houses. He stopped short when his headlight fell on a crumpled shape near the base of the steps leading to a pathway that wound up towards the hill. At first, he thought it was another overfilled black bag.

'Bloody hell.' He shone his light on it more closely. 'There's a bag limit, people.'

But something was off. The bag hadn't split, and it wasn't lying quite right. He moved closer, the beam of light flickering as he shivered in the cold. That's when he saw it. A pale face emerging from the shadows of a black puffer jacket. He'd not twigged it as a person because the legs were hidden behind two sacks.

Kes halted. For a moment, his mind refused to process what he was seeing. Frost had turned the cheeks alabaster white, the lips blue-tinged and still. A shock of dark hair clung to the frozen ground beneath the head. For three seconds, it was as though time itself had paused; the world narrowing to that lifeless face and the stillness of death that surrounded it, nothing but the rumble of bald Alan's wagon and the blink of its orange light behind him. The torchlight caught on a glint of frost clinging to the boy's eyelashes, a detail so small and intimate it made Kes's stomach churn.

'Jesus,' he whispered.

He stepped back instinctively, nearly slipping again on the icy ground. A frozen puddle cracked beneath him. The noise seemed to shatter the spell, and he turned, running back to the street, waving his arms frantically toward the truck.

'Jimbo! Alan!' he yelled, his voice cracking. 'Get up here! Now!'

Jimbo appeared first, jogging up the lane. Alan followed shortly after, leaving the truck idling in the middle of the road. They both stopped short when they saw Kes's face, pale and stricken in the weak light.

'What?' Jimbo asked. Kes pointed wordlessly to the crumpled figure.

'Bloody hell,' Jimbo muttered, his usual bravado wafting away in the exhalation of breath that accompanied the oath. Alan stood silent, his mouth slightly open as he stared.

'Call it in,' Kes croaked out the words. 'We need the bloody police. Now. And an ambulance.'

Jimbo fumbled for his phone. Kes turned back to his workmate, younger by only a couple of years. The image of his white face, with all the ribaldry of the morning washed from it, seared into his mind. The frost was relentless, but somehow, it felt colder now than ever before as he shivered. But it was the older man, Alan, who walked over and knelt by the body. Several seconds passed as Jimbo explained the situation to the dispatcher. Then he ended the call, and into the silence, Alan spoke. 'I don't think an ambulance is going to do any good, Kes.'

'Shit,' Kes muttered in a tremulous whisper.

But Alan was right.

# AUTHOR'S NOTE

Thank you for joining me once more on this journey into the misty hills of Wales, where ancient folklore rubs shoulders with very modern darkness.

This story brings together several threads: the cold case of a missing boy, Freddie Sillitoe; the suspicious deaths of the Mount sisters; and the everyday battles of those who seek the truth. At the heart of it all are the people—DCI Evan Warlow, whose fight is not only with crime but with his own frailties, and Jess Allanby, resilient as ever, balancing loyalty, love, and an unflinching pursuit of justice.

These books are never simply about procedures or puzzles. They are about the human response to crisis. The way grief, guilt, and horror shape lives. That's why, at times, you'll find elements that are invented for the story's sake. Sugawara's congenital muscular dystrophy does not exist, though there are other diseases like it, or worse than it. The point is that recessive diseases such as these can lurk unseen sometimes. And my intention is never to patronise or cause distress, but simply to remind us how fragile and unpredictable our biology can be. Fiction allows a little bending of reality, not to deceive, but to dig deeper into how people stumble, adapt, and sometimes discover unexpected strength.

I hope you find yourself drawn into the world of these

characters, their struggles and small triumphs, their humour in the face of despair, their courage when shadows threaten to overwhelm.

If the story has entertained you, unsettled you, or left you asking what you might do in their place, then it has done its job.

And while Warlow and his team may be fictional, the truths they encounter are anything but.

All the best,

Rhys

P.S. For those interested, there is a glossary on the website to help with any tricky pronunciations.

## CAN YOU HELP?

With that in mind, and if you enjoyed it, I do have a favour to ask. Could you spare a moment to **leave a review or a rating**? A few words will do, but it's really the only way to help others like you discover the books. Probably the best way to help authors you like. Just visit my page on Amazon and leave a few words.

# FREE BOOK FOR YOU

Visit my website and join up to the Rhys Dylan VIP Reader's Club and get a FREE novella, *The Wolf Hunts Alone*, by visiting the website at: **www.rhysdylan.com**

**The Wolf Hunts Alone.**

**One man and his dog... will track you down.**

DCI Evan Warlow is at a crossroads in his life. Living alone, contending with the bad hand fate has dealt him, he finds solace in simple things like walking his neighbour's dog.

But even that is not as safe as it was. Dogs are going missing from a country park. And not only one, now three have disappeared. When he takes it upon himself to root out the cause of the lost animals, Warlow faces ridicule and a thuggish enemy.

But are these simply dog thefts? Or is there a more sinister malevolence at work? One with its sights on bigger, two legged prey.

Only one thing is for certain; Warlow will not rest until he finds out.

**Please note, this is a FREE eBOOK available in digital format only.**

# ACKNOWLEDGEMENTS

As with all writing endeavours, the existence of this novel depends upon me, the author, and a small army of 'others' who turn an idea into a reality. My wife, Eleri, who gives me the space to indulge my imagination and picks out my stupid mistakes. Tim Barber designs the covers, Sian Phillips edits, and other proofers and ARC readers sort out the gaffes. Thank you all for your help. Special mention goes to Ela the dog who drags me away from the writing cave and the computer for walks, rain or shine. Actually, she's a bit of a princess so the rain is a no-no. Good dog!

But my biggest thanks goes to you, lovely reader, for being there and actually reading this. It's great to have you along and I do appreciate you spending your time in joining me on this roller-coster ride with Evan and the rest of the team.

Printed in Dunstable, United Kingdom

71140640R00184